Dazzling

Dumpster Fire

The Trailer Park Princess Cozy Mystery

Book Five

Kim Hunt Harris

Kim Hunt Harris Books, LLC
Lubbock, TX

Kim Hunt Harris Books, LLC
3410 98th St Ste. 4-157
Lubbock, TX 79423
www.kimhuntharris.com

Publisher's Note: This is a work of fiction. Names, characters, places, and incidents are a product of the author's imagination. Locales and public names are sometimes used for atmospheric purposes. Any resemblance to actual people, living or dead, or to businesses, companies, events, institutions, or locales is completely coincidental.

Book Layout ©2013 BookDesignTemplates.com

Ordering Information:
Quantity sales. Special discounts are available on quantity purchases by corporations, associations, and others. For details, contact the "Special Sales Department" at the address above.

Dazzling Dumpster Fire/Kim Hunt Harris -- 1st ed.
ISBN 978-1-7368343-1-2

DEDICATION

This book is for Christa, with gratitude for your immense generosity and unfailing encouragement. Love you, Cousin.

ACKNOWLEDGMENTS

I turned to several people to help me get this book right. If I have failed in any way, that's on me and not them, because I swear they really tried.

Matt Sherley seems to never tire of my endless questions about law enforcement procedure, and he manages to make me believe I have not asked a single stupid question. Thank you, Matt.

Ray Morris helped me with questions related to trucks and gave me some fantastic ideas for my plot. Thank you, Ray.

The folks at the Cops and Writers Facebook group – what an amazing group! Patrick O'Donnell has built a community of knowledgeable and supportive law enforcement professionals, and there are always fascinating conversations going on to eavesdrop on, even if you don't have a question of your own. But if you *do* have a question, they'll answer it most generously. I highly recommend checking out this group if you want to make sure you don't write the kind of crime stories that make cops groan.

A NOTE FROM THE AUTHOR

This book contains references to childhood sexual trauma and human trafficking. Although not graphic, these scenes could be disturbing for some readers.

Table of Contents

Chapter One 1

Chapter Two 37

Chapter Three 77

Chapter Four 115

Chapter Five 159

Chapter Six 197

Chapter Seven 249

Chapter Eight 297

Chapter Nine 331

Chapter Ten 363

Chapter Eleven 401

Chapter Twelve 441

Chapter Thirteen 487

Chapter One

New people who walk into Flo's Bow Wow Barbers must wonder, for a second, which decade they've stepped into. There's Flo, the owner, who still wears a beehive hairstyle. Then there's Tammy, the dog bather. She's had the same Big 80s hair that she had in high school. You have to admire that kind of commitment, right?

The shareholders of Aqua Net probably send them fancy gift baskets from Omaha Steaks every Christmas.

Then there's me. My style is however-the-girl-at-ProCuts-translated-what-I-just-asked-for. That stuff is timeless.

I love these women, though, and I love my job at Flo's. I get to work with dogs, who I usually find more pleasant to be around than people; it's steady; there's not a lot of drama except for your occasional biter or the sometimes ninja-like reflexes one must develop to protect a freshly bathed and blow-dried dog from stepping into a mess said dog had, from anxiety-induced gastrointestinal distress or merely revenge, just deposited on one's grooming table.

You know how people say, "Oh, I just hate drama!" That's not me. I like drama, as long as it doesn't involve me. And Tammy doesn't need much to get her own drama going. Usually, it's a harmless drama that only she gets caught up in, but it's interesting for the rest of us to watch. For instance, the time she thought the car dealership had put a tracking device on her car when she went in for a safety recall on her seatbelts. "Think about it," she'd said. "Why would they just call all these random people in like that?" She knows who really shot JFK. She knows that's not really Paul McCartney. Tupac isn't really dead, he's running a barbecue joint in Mississippi. Every politician that comes on television is a puppet for some rich puppet master somewhere. Once, a road trip took Tammy near Roswell, New Mexico and now every time she forgets something or loses something, she blames it on a likely abduction by a secret government agency when she got too close to finding their top-secret hiding place. They messed with her memory and she's still feeling the effects today. She doesn't remember being abducted or even finding something that looked like it might be a top-secret hiding place, because duh—she wouldn't, would she?

One of Tammy's conspiracy theories that had been a through-line since before I'd started work at Flo's was that Charlie Polk, the owner of one of our favorite Keeshonds, Hieronymus Bosch Polk, was an east coast mobster like in the movies. As far as I could tell, this was based on the fact that he was a successful real estate developer, and he had a thin mustache. Plus, "he just looks it," according to Tammy.

And maybe Charlie Polk didn't look like your typical West Texas cowboy. He was thin and on the short side, with coal black hair courtesy of

Just For Men. Texas men didn't usually dye their hair, not that I'd noticed. That was a pretty big leap to east coast mobster, though.

Still, every time we saw Hieronymus (whom we all called Hero) on the appointment book, Tammy would start up her mobster theories. He'd come down to Texas to infiltrate and before we knew it, the place was going to be overrun with men wearing pinkie rings, putting out contracts on who knew who. "I mean, who names their dog hire-on-a-bus or whatever? Weirdo. Guy's probably whacked so many people it isn't even funny. Probably pets Hero and feeds him Jerky Treats while he watches his henchmen break people's kneecaps."

So anyway, Tammy wasn't allowed to talk to Mr. Polk, so she hung at the doorway of the next room, half-hidden by the door jamb, and glared at him as Flo or I checked Hero in and out, then talked for the rest of the day about weird new theories.

When Charlie Polk asked me to step outside for a chat when he picked up Hero one day, Tammy just about swallowed her gum. She popped her head around the corner, her eyes bugged. She darted a look between me and Flo and back. She looked at the phone, then back at Flo, as if it to telepathically scream, "911!"

"Sure," I said as I opened the swinging half-door and led Hero through it. "Let's just go out here."

In the reflection of the front windows, I could see Tammy rush up to the counter and stare at us in disbelief, as if I had just casually agreed to Mr. Polk's suggestion that I step outside so he could bust a cap in me. I picked up the pace, anxious to get outside before she did something like scream, "Salem, no!"

3

I had no idea what the man wanted to talk about, but figured it was likely a dog-sitting job, or else he had a concern about Hero that for some reason he wanted to discuss outside of the hearing of the strange woman with the 80s hair who always glared at him from the kennel room.

"Listen, I see on the news that you work for a private investigator," he said as Hero nosed around the front sidewalk.

I had not expected that. "Nope," I said, shaking my head. "I do not."

He frowned. "But...I saw on the news about you finding that scammer with that painting and solving that murder."

"I'm sorry," I said. "Yes, we have solved a few murders, and we did find that scammer with all the art. But those were accidents. We're not private investigators."

Here's the thing. For a while, my friend Viv and I did go around telling people we were private detectives. Well, mostly Viv did that. I tagged after her because, like I said, I like drama I can watch—and we did help a few people. But I'd found out a few months ago that it is illegal to call yourself a private investigator if you didn't have a license—like, it's an actual felony. So, I'm now very careful to make things clear, because I cannot afford the ten-grand fine, and I certainly never want to go back to jail. Things in my life are finally going pretty well. I don't want to mess up my trajectory now.

Polk just looked confused. "I could swear I saw you on the news and that woman you were with—your grandmother? I thought maybe it was a family business."

"Viv is just a friend," I said. "We just happened to be in the right place at the right time to give the police a little help." Should I tell him about the podcast? When Viv found out about the whole accidental-felony thing, she'd invented a story that we were investigative journalists with a podcast. That way we could continue nosing around in other people's business and not get arrested for it.

Something caught my eye and I looked into the shop to see Tammy's head emerge from behind a shelf of shampoos and flea treatments. Obviously, I didn't want Mr. Polk to see her acting like such a whacko, but I also—and I know this is mean—enjoyed the thought of Tammy inside the shop, panicking that a black limo with blacked-out windows was about to slide up and I was going to get inside.

I reached out for Hero's leash. "Let's go around the corner so Hero can find some grass to pee on."

When we reached the strip of grass between our parking lot and the street, I asked him, "What did you need a PI for? I could probably recommend someone."

He sighed. "It's a sad story, really. I'm doing this big downtown redevelopment project. You might have read about it."

"Oh yeah," I said. "A little bit."

To say the redevelopment project had been controversial was an understatement. It was going to revitalize downtown, but it was also wiping out an entire neighborhood of small, low-budget houses where families had lived for generations. The owners had been compensated, but there was a lot of talk about how the prices they were getting wouldn't be enough to get another house in town. The buyouts had forced many who'd once had the benefits of stable homeownership into renting, and scattered neighbors who'd been friends for years to different parts of town. Most of this had taken place when I was still deep in my drinking days, and I hadn't been particularly interested in the happenings around Lubbock unless it involved drink specials.

After I got sober, got this job, and started hearing Tammy's crazy theories about Charlie Polk, I went back and studied up a little bit on the redevelopment. There was many a contentious town hall meeting about how the project would be good for the people who already had things pretty good—business owners, banks, big corporations with chain hotels and restaurants, and it was great for the university—but was devastating to low-income families who just wanted to stay in the neighborhood they were familiar with. Their houses might be small and not worth much, but they were their homes.

You might guess how much good that did. The last time I'd driven through that part of town, I saw lots and lots of cleared dirt lots ready for some new hotel or apartment building.

"Those Yankees don't care about family," Tammy had declared when I brought up the subject at work. "Unless, of course, it's *the* Family." Then she winked.

But I'd seen plenty of West Texas good ol' boys in those town halls, using phrases like, "trickle down" and "a rising tide lifts all boats."

"We're making good progress," Mr. Polk said, bringing me back to the present. "But I have one holdout that I simply cannot convince to sell."

"One of the homeowners?"

"Yeah. The only house left on that block, and he's holding out. I've offered the guy four times what the other residents got, and he's not budging."

"Some people can't be bought," I said, and instantly regretted it. Charlie Polk wasn't a great tipper, but I did like Hero and, on the off-chance Tammy was right on this one, I wanted to stay on Polk's good side.

"It's a sad story, really. The homeowner's daughter ran away last year, and he's afraid if he sells, she won't know where to find him when she comes back. He says he's staying, no matter what, until she comes back."

"Wow. That is sad." I was confused, though. If the owner didn't go for four times the going rate, what did Polk think Viv and I were going to do? For half a second, Tammy's lunacy got to me, and I wondered if he was going to ask us to head over there and break the guy's kneecaps.

"So, I told him I would find her. And that's when I thought of you and your grandmother."

I pictured the poor father, sitting in a cracked leather recliner in his little wooden house, a plastic flower pinwheel that was once his daughter's stuck into the ground near the front porch. All around his tiny house, bull dozers cleared away his neighbors' homes, men in hard hats ate lunches out of metal lunchboxes, three-story apartments rose and threw his tiny little house into the shade. And all the while he sat and waited, the plastic pinwheel fading and cracking.

It was enough to make me almost consider committing another felony.

But, no. There were others much more qualified than we were. And this wasn't the kind of story for Viv's true crime podcast. I would feel sleazy, capitalizing on such a sad story just so Viv could have something interesting to do—and let's face it, that was exactly the purpose of the podcast. Viv had more money and energy than sense, and she liked to get into people's business. I liked going along for the ride, because she had a nice car and would sometimes buy lunch. I had no money, and since I'd quit drinking, I was kind of bored, too. That's why we'd continued our private investigator act after we accidentally solved our first murder.

But there wasn't really a crime to solve here, and anyway, we weren't qualified to address it if there was.

I heard metal scraping against metal, and I looked at the back door to Bow Wow Barbers. The dumpster blocked most of the view, but I saw the door open softly, then close again. Above the dumpster, white frizzy bangs made their way along the edge and then disappeared behind.

If it's possible to mentally roll your eyes, that's what I did. I shifted so that Polk's back would be to the dumpster, then leaned close and said in a low voice, "That is very sad, and I understand the position you're in. But we really can't help you. There are other people in town, though, who probably could."

"Oh, they charge an arm and a leg," he said with a dismissive wave. "I was hoping that because we already had this relationship built, you and I could work out a deal."

You cheap son of a monkey, I thought. So that's what this is about.

At the words 'relationship' and 'work out a deal,' Tammy's face appeared above the dumpster, her eyes bugged.

Okay, enough was enough.

I straightened and said loudly. "Listen, just hold tight. I know a guy. Don't do anything until you hear from me." I shifted like I was moving away, but then said, "And it's probably better if you and I don't meet here anymore. This place isn't safe for these kinds of discussions, if you know what I mean."

From the look on his face, he clearly didn't know what I meant, but I repeated, "I know a guy. He'll be able to get this worked out to your satisfaction."

I walked away, knowing I'd left a confusing impression, but if he wanted clarity, he'd have to pay for it. Sheesh.

Like most people in AA, I have a few different meetings that I attend on a regular basis, but only one meeting that I consider home. My friend and mentor Les told me I had to attend 90 meetings in my first 90 days of sobriety, so out of necessity I'd learned where all the meetings in town were. But the Tuesday morning meeting in the basement of the First United Methodist Church was my AA home.

And like home, I considered it that because of the people there. Viv went there, Les went there, several other familiar and friendly faces were always around. And like home, there were also a few obnoxious faces I'd prefer to avoid if I could but would tolerate if I must.

Todd was one of those I could tolerate, but only from across the room and only for minutes at a time. He was just a straight up know-it-all, and he liked to overshare what he knew. He criticized everything with a condescending 'don't drink the Kool-Aid' attitude. At the moment, the Kool-Aid he was complaining about was actual Kool-Aid. Kool-Aid and soda and chocolate cake, because we had a sober anniversary to celebrate at the end of the meeting.

We met in a small room that could be made into a slightly bigger room by folding back a plastic accordion divider. There was a kitchen at one end, and as soon as I came into the room that morning, I got excited because two things had lined up simultaneously to my advantage: I had weighed yesterday at my Fat Fighters meeting, and there was chocolate cake to celebrate Irene Drummond's fifteenth Sober Anniversary.

Since I had just weighed yesterday, I didn't have to worry about weighing again for a week. Plenty of time to eat that scrumptious chocolate cake without guilt or fear of it showing up on the scale—I would walk some extra laps around Trailertopia or something. If I hadn't just weighed the day before, I would still eat that cake. But I would feel guilty about it and then have dreams that I woke up and couldn't fit through my bedroom door.

I settled into my chair, ready to get the meeting started so we could get to the very good part after. Freaking Todd sat down behind me. "Here we go again," he muttered to no one in particular. "Ego cake time."

"You can skip it if you don't want any," Viv said.

"It's not the cake I have a problem with," he said. "It's the entire concept of celebrating a number. It's--it's asinine."

"It's not at all," Viv said. "It's encouraging to new members. We get a chance to show them that sobriety—long term sobriety, at that—is possible."

"Don't encourage him," I muttered out the side of my mouth.

"Our lives should show them that's possible. We don't need a contrived benchmark for that."

"Irene has actually been sober for 15 years. That's literally the definition of not-contrived."

"Celebrating it is. Treating that time like some kind of—some kind of social currency is. It's contrived to make it a status symbol or to—to set some kind of hierarchy within the group." He sneered. "How many people do you know who have a fifteen-year pin or a twenty-year pin and they're the driest drunks around? They're white knuckling through every day just because they don't want to lose their precious number of days? And they strut around the meetings like they're the cock of the walk, not because they're healthy, or whole, but because they've turned counting sober days into their new addiction."

Viv turned to me and said loudly, "Salem. I am going to strut my sober self up to the coffee maker and get a cup. Would you like me to get one for you?"

"Yes, please," I said. "With two cocks of the walk, please."

Todd muttered, but he got up and moved to another chair, so it all worked out.

Les came over then and sat beside me. "What was that about?"

"Just obnoxious Todd, waxing philosophical about the silliness of celebrating sober anniversaries." I rolled my eyes.

Les sighed. "Yes, well..." He shifted in his seat. "He has a point. It's good to celebrate our achievements, but we don't want to forget that sobriety is about a lot more than just adding up the days." He nodded toward some friends coming in. "My thinking is, it depends on the person with the anniversary. If they want to celebrate, we celebrate. If they want a quiet acknowledgment, we do that."

"Yes, well, as you might remember—" He would remember because I'd brought it up at least four times over the past few months— "My two-year anniversary is coming up in ten days. And I want cake, and ice cream, and donuts, and good coffee. Not that stuff." I nodded in the direction where Viv stood by the industrial size coffee urn, having forgotten about my coffee while she chatted with someone.... "I will take my pin and my accolades, and I will add a tiara and a feather boa, too, just because I know it will upset Todd."

"As long as you're learning humility," Les said, but he smiled.

I sighed dramatically. I was not a fan of humility, or of Les's reminders that it was supposed to remain important to me. Not that I didn't understand the purpose of humility, or recognize how damaging an inflated ego could be. It was just that, good grief, how much more humble could I get? I lived in a run-down trailer park—okay, it wasn't the worst in town, but it wasn't the best, either—and I drove a 1970s model Monte Carlo. And not because I was trying to be retro, either—I'd found a deal because I needed a deal. I was a dog groomer. I mean, I loved my job, but it wasn't like people went out of their way to impress me because of my social influence.

Honestly, if you had seen me two years ago, seen my DUIs and evictions and unpaid bills and ruined friendships and then saw me now, you'd be impressed by the new me. I didn't understand why I couldn't also be a little proud of myself.

But remaining humble was a thing with Les, and rather than argue with him, I jumped a little like my phone buzzed, then pulled it out like I had an important message.

I moved out to the stairwell so I could pass the few minutes until the meeting began with my new guilty pleasure: a Reddit thread called Am I The Jerk?

Here's the story about Am I The Jerk (or AITJ). People write in and describe arguments or situations they're in with friends, family members, co-workers, etc, they tell what they did and why, and then ask the thread, Am I The Jerk in this situation? People from all over the world write in. Like, one woman wrote that she was working double shifts while her husband sat at home playing video games, and their dog ran away. She came home, exhausted, and he wouldn't help her look for the dog, so she threw his expensive gaming system away. Am I The Jerk for that (I voted NTJ on that one—not the jerk). Another woman wrote that she refused to name her baby after her husband's family tradition, because it was a really weird name that would definitely get the kid bullied (again, I voted NTJ, but with a little less conviction. Sorry, grandma).

Normally, I try not to be judgmental about other people's personal decisions. Live and let live, right? Keep your own side of the street clean. In AA, they call judging other people 'taking their inventory.' Step 4 of the 12 steps is to make a searching and fearless inventory of ourselves, and Step 10 is to continue to take a personal inventory and admit when we're wrong. The point is, I have enough stuff of my own to deal with, I don't need to worry about anybody else's stuff.

But, I mean...in AITJ, they're asking you to judge them. They posted a whole story just so you could judge them. Some of them don't like the feedback they get (it can get brutal), and they argue with people in the comments section, but sometimes they get a new perspective and realize their mistake, and they fix things if they're able to. Often, they get support and encouragement from the responses when they're so clearly NTJ, and some actual jerk is trying to convince them that they are (I'm looking at you, Mr. I-laughed-really-hard-when-my-family-made-fun-of-my-girlfriend's-facial-scar-and-now-she's-overreacting-by-breaking-up-with-me).

Reading other people's problems is just straight up fascinating. I don't know why it's so encouraging to realize how many screwed up people and screwed up families there are in the world. But it is.

It was so enormously satisfying—judging other people's problems from a safe distance, objectively, with none of your own emotions involved. I wondered if this was what counselors felt like. I doubted it, though. As much as I loved AITJ, I recognized on some level that it was a teensy bit unhealthy. Like, the dopamine rush when I saw there was a new post—the crazier the situation was, the more thrilling it was. It was like watching a car crash. And the thrill when your own judgment lines up with the general consensus? When I entered a comment that got a bunch of upvotes, the sense of affirmation was heady.

Maybe a little too heady. The urge to pile on the original poster once they'd been deemed TJ was very strong. That's why I didn't tell Les about it.

Above me, someone started clumping down the stairs. I scrambled to get out of the way.

"Don't mind me, I'll bet I can clear you."

I looked up to see one of the new members about three steps above me, grinning and poised like she was about to leap over me to the landing below.

She probably could clear me. She was about five foot eleven or maybe even six feet, very fit, and a former Marine. Ash was her name, I remembered. If she didn't clear me, she'd probably still just roll to her feet and be fine, whereas my head would sustain permanent damage from one of those big combat boots she wore.

"Maybe next time," I said as I edged out of the way. I didn't know her well enough to know if she was joking or not, but based on some of the stories she told about her drinking days, I didn't want to chance it.

"Get in here." Viv poked her head out the door and beckoned to me. "Todd's in here drinking up all the Kool-Aid."

After the meeting, I stood with Les and Viv, enjoying the cake—triple-chocolate, bless you Irene—while Viv went on and on about the new podcasting equipment she'd just bought.

"You wouldn't believe it. I took my recorder down to the pool and interviewed Harv Barnaby during the women's water aerobics class, then took it back up to the computer and I was able to isolate our voices like the Monday Morning Maidens weren't even in the room! No splashing, no echo, nothing!"

"Wow, that is amazing," Les said. I don't think he was honestly amazed, but Les loves hearing what other people get jazzed about.

"And what kind of interesting intel did you get from Harv Barnaby?"

"Oh, the man's a total snoozefest. Just droned on and on about the stock market. The point is, I can get quality sound with this thing." She pulled a handheld recorder out of her jacket. "See?"

She hit a button. "The man's a total snoozefest," her voice repeated back to her.

"Oops," she said. "I didn't realize I was recording." She hit a few more buttons.

I looked at Les, who was looking at Viv with wide eyes. "How long have you been recording?"

"How long have you been recording inside an AA meeting?" The unspoken question roared between us.

Viv looked uncharacteristically guilty. "No clue," she said.

Les pointed at the framed sign by the door that said, "Who you see here, what you hear her, when you leave here, let it stay here."

"I'll delete it as soon as I get home," Viv promised.

Les nodded, "Let's do it now." He took the recorder from her and scrolled through the tiny screen, tilting his head back to see through his trifocals.

Viv and I concentrated on our cake while he deleted the file. Viv definitely needed a safer outlet for all her energy, I thought. She was going to get herself into trouble.

"Maybe you should start a podcast on Belle Court," I suggested. "Interview all the residents. I'll bet there are some good stories there."

"Are you kidding? Salem, when I say snoozefest, I mean it. What I need is a new case. Some crime. There are plenty of missing persons cases around here, and a few unsolved murders. Or we can go up to Amarillo. They've got them up there, too."

"I'm sure they do."

"Or, we could do a falsely convicted story, like In The Dark. Find some innocent person in prison and work to free them? We could do that."

"Sure, we could," I said, not bothering with the very obvious question of 'how would we go about that?' "I did talk to a guy yesterday who needs someone to find a missing person. Well, a runaway girl, actually," I said, before I remembered that I was not going to share this information with Viv.

"Oooh, we could do that. We'd be great at that. Who is it?"

I shook my head. "Really, I don't think it's for us. I don't know why I mentioned it."

"Oh, I see how you are. You want it for yourself."

I laughed. "No, I just think we should steer clear. It's a sad story."

"What's a sad story?" Les asked as he returned the recorder to Viv.

"That Salem wants to hog all the action for herself."

"Viv, you know that's not it. I'd be completely helpless at finding anything without you."

"Exactly. That's why you need to tell me who it is we're looking for."

"We're not looking for anyone. It's just..." I sighed. There wasn't any point in not telling, at this stage. "You know that big redevelopment project downtown? One of my grooming customers is heavily involved in that. He's handling all the acquisitions for it, and there's one holdout. A man whose daughter ran away last year, and he won't sell because he doesn't want her to come home and not find him waiting for her."

"We could find her."

"We could, but we probably wouldn't, and don't take this the wrong way, but sometimes you can be a bit..."

"What?" Viv lifted her chin.

"A bit insensitive, that's all. I know it's just because you're focused on the objective, but sometimes you get blinders on and plow straight through without thinking about the feelings of the people around you." Sometimes was actually all the time. "I don't think this is a good case for the podcast. I think we should let the professionals handle this."

Viv crossed her arms and sneered, "Let the professionals...after everything we've done together?"

I nodded. "Yep." Yes, we had solved some crimes. We'd also had guns pointed at us, been kidnapped, accidentally set a few fires, and wrecked my car.

I was glad we'd done all those things—I didn't regret one minute, even the fires. But lately I'd begun to feel like it was about time my life was headed in a slightly different direction. I had almost two years sobriety. My husband, Tony, and I were getting along well. Well, we were getting along well when we saw each other. He was working long hours lately, and I hadn't seen him much. When I had seen him, he was preoccupied with work. But he would get that sorted out and everything would get back to normal. Tony begrudgingly supported my adventures with Viv because he knew I enjoyed it, and I'd needed something in my life to help me feel like I was capable of being a productive member of society. I'd met Viv at a time when I really needed to do some good.

But I'd done good, and I was doing well. I'd held my job for almost two years. I'd gotten my life back on track. It was time to move forward.

I'd said as much to Tony just the other night. After a decade of a most untraditional marriage, maybe it was time for us to think about moving in together. Starting our family. The idea of becoming a mother freaked me completely out, but then again, I never thought I'd have two years sober, either, and here I was, on the cusp of achieving exactly that. Plus, I'd have Tony by my side, and he would be the world's best father. My alcoholism had already stolen ten years from us. We couldn't afford to lose any more time.

Tony had seemed less enthusiastic about all of this than I'd expected him to be, and that had bothered me at first. I realized, though, that he was just distracted from work, plus he's naturally a closed book. Doesn't get too excited about anything. I knew he wanted a family, though. He needed a wife. Not a true crime podcaster, chasing missing girls and getting shot at.

Plus, I hated talking into Viv's recorder. Blech.

"What's this guy's name?"

"What guy?" I pretended not to know what she was talking about.

"The one with the runaway daughter."

"I don't know his name." I hoped she'd leave it at that, but no such luck.

"What about the real estate guy? What's his name?"

"Viv, I'm not going to tell you," I said. "You should call Bobby and ask him about some unsolved murders here in town. I'm sure he'd love your help with that." Bobby Sloan was a detective with the Lubbock PD, and my schoolgirl crush from fourth through seventh grades. He would not love Viv's help with any such thing, but he was still a safer direction for Viv to go than the runaway girl's family.

I looked at the clock on the wall. "Oh, shoot! It's time for me to get to work! I'll text Bobby and give him the heads up that you're going to call him."

"Come over tomorrow and listen to some music files I bought, for intro and outro tracks."

"I can't," I said as I grabbed my purse. "I have work, and then I'm making dinner at Tony's house. It's the first date night we've had in three weeks."

Viv frowned at me, so I grabbed her for a quick hug. "Love you, friend!"

She batted me away. "If I find out you're looking for that girl behind my back, I will mow you down with my Cadillac."

The next afternoon I was finishing up my last dog of the day when my phone rang. It was Viv.

"You know that real estate development guy? Turns out his mother lives over in the east wing. The old wing," she clarified. Viv is very proud to be living in the newest and most expensive part of Belle Court Retirement Home. "So, I had a little chat with him and got the information on that runaway girl."

"Oh?" I said idly as I bent and studied the Lhasa Apso's ears I was trimming. Were they even? Or was the dog's head crooked? Was I crooked? "How'd you find him?"

"I called Tammy," she said. "She told me the guy's name and I found the rest on my own because I'm an investigator, Salem."

I scowled in Tammy's general direction. "An investigative reporter," I corrected.

"Gia Perez," Viv said, ignoring me. "That's the runaway. We have an appointment at the Perez family home in 45 minutes. Better not bring Stump, not to this first visit. We don't know how tolerant they are."

I straightened and frowned. "I was pretty clear yesterday that I thought this was a bad idea." But who was I kidding? Viv and I both knew she wasn't going to consider my reservations for one second.

She was going to do what she wanted to do. The question was—did I want to join her?

I had to admit, it was tempting. But...no, I did not. The story was heartbreaking, and it would be great to be able to help them. But what did we know about finding runaways? The police were already involved. What did we have to offer them?

Besides, I really wanted to focus on my marriage. I did have a marriage, after all—even if it did feel like Tony and I had just been going steady for over a decade.

"Did you tell them that you're not really a private investigator?"

"Sure, of course. You'd be impressed with how I spun it. Well, it's not spin, I guess. Think about it, Salem. As freelance podcasters, we basically have no regulations. Unlike licensed PIs, who have all kinds of regulations. It's like the wild west out here for podcasters. We have the freedom to pursue angles that the regular PIs don't have."

I combed the Lhasa's ears again and crouched, stroking her chin to raise it a bit. "Hey, remember back when we didn't realize we were committing a felony by telling people we were PIs but we didn't have a license?"

"Umm, yeah. I remember that."

"We pretty much thought it was the wild west then, too. Turns out we were just ignorant."

"And your point is?"

"My point is, maybe you're breaking all kinds of laws that you don't know about."

"Yes, well, you know what they say: ignorance is no excuse. So, are you going to meet me in 45 minutes, or not?"

I stood, deciding both to accept the Lhasa's ears as they were and to not pursue Viv's nonsensical thoughts about ignorance. "Sorry, I'm going over to Tony's after work. You can handle it without me, though."

"Sure, I'll be fine. I'll debrief you later."

She ended the call before I told her I thought I would be the one debriefing her. It didn't matter. Viv was going to go off on whatever she was going to go off on, and it would either peter out and amount to nothing, or I would get looped back in at some point. Until such time as that became clear, she would be fine without me.

I was more interested in seeing my husband. Tony and I didn't live together because our relationship was the poster child of "It's complicated." We'd been married for over ten years, but for most of that time we'd been separated. I thought we were divorced. I signed divorce papers and sent them to Tony, then promptly disappeared into a bottle and didn't emerge again until I sat in a jail cell years later, having just been arrested for my third DUI. Unbeknownst to me, Tony never signed those papers. Once I was ready to be a productive member of society, God threw us back together, and we've been what I call "somewhat-married" ever since. He has his nice house in a nice neighborhood. I have my mediocre trailer in Trailertopia. We see each other three or four times a week—well, less than that, lately. I stayed over at his house some nights. He has never stayed over at my place. It is working for us.

I am ready to be more than somewhat-married, though. I am ready to be normal.

I had texted him five times since last night and had only gotten a couple of three- or four-word responses. Tony isn't much of a texter, but he's usually more generous with his words than that. It was making me kind of nervous. Well, not nervous, exactly. But it made me want to see him in person just to reassure myself that everything was okay.

So, I finished up my dogs, completed my paperwork, took the high-pressure dryer out and blew the dog hair off my clothes, and my dog, Stump, and I headed to Tony's. I called his office on the way there, because I was pretty sure he would be working late again, but hopefully not too late. He didn't talk a lot about his work, but apparently someone wasn't pulling their weight because he had been putting in more hours. Tony owns a building services company, and he told me once he has two main tasks: finding new businesses to service and replacing employees. He's a good boss and he has some loyal employees, but there aren't a whole lot of people whose ambition is to stay in a job that entails emptying trash cans and sanitizing toilets. It's noble work and nothing to be ashamed of, but most people do consider it a stepping stone.

He wasn't in the office when I called, but Greta, his secretary, said he was out on a sales call. Good. Then I would have time to thaw something for dinner and surprise him. My man deserved some pampering.

Except my man was already home. I pulled to the curb in front of his house, because the driveway was filled with his work truck, a Solis Building Services van, and a black SUV.

As Stump and I climbed out of my 1974 Monte Carlo, Tony's front door opened and a beautiful young woman came out. She was looking back over her shoulder and laughing at something, so I got a nice long look at her dark chocolate hair, her tan lean legs, the long column of throat as she threw her head back in the laugh.

I stood on the grass and blinked. I wished I had gone home and showered before I came over. Put on fresh clothes, fresh makeup. Did my hair. Lost 25 pounds.

Tony emerged from the house behind the supermodel, also laughing.

A sales call, huh? Just who was selling what?

Tony's eyes widened when he saw me, but he smiled. He didn't duck back into the house. He didn't try to hide this beautiful person on his front porch.

"Surprise," I said, and tried to sound breezy.

"A very pleasant one." He reached out to me and turned to the supermodel. "Joanna, this is my wife, Salem."

Joanna smiled a wide, perfect-teethed smile and held out a hand with perfectly manicured nails. Who cleans for a living and has perfect nails?

"Joanna is helping me out with a situation at work," he said.

Did they exchange a loaded look?

They exchanged a loaded look. They totally exchanged a loaded look.

"Is that right?" I asked. I might have sounded a little less breezy. "Greta said you were on a sales call."

"I was on a sales call," Tony said. "But we have this situation that I needed to discuss away from the office." He nodded toward Joanna. "We'll talk tomorrow, okay?"

She gave him a mock salute. "Sure thing. It was nice to meet you, Mrs. Solis."

"My pleasure, Joanna," I said brightly. I barely tripped up on the Mrs. Solis thing. The truth is, I don't get called that a lot, because I don't go by that name. I didn't mind her thinking of me as Tony's wife, though.

Unless she was one of those women who see a married man as a challenge.

I followed Tony inside. "How was your day?" he asked.

"Fine," I said. My mind swirled with uncomfortable questions, but they mostly all sounded like, 'Why are you meeting with a beautiful young woman about a work situation at your home when you have an office?'

But this was Tony. Tony was a rock. If you wanted to create a statue to the ideals of faithfulness and integrity, it would look just like Tony.

So... there was no reason to be jealous except for the situation. And he could probably explain the situation.

I waited for him to do just that.

But instead of explaining, he went back to his home office.

I sat at the kitchen table and considered that for a few minutes. I mean, the workday was still underway, and Tony worked long hours—that was why he had a home office, so he could address some issues from home if he needed to. Plus, there was, apparently, this Very Special Work Situation that needed to be handled. And I wasn't, like, a guest in his house. Yes, I lived elsewhere, but I had spent enough time here that it was perfectly reasonable for him to assume I would make myself at home while he retreated to his home office.

I sighed and decided to do just that. It would be stupid to let my own insecurities set the tone for this evening. So what if I felt like an old and ugly step-sister next to the beautiful Joanna and her long legs that probably didn't have a single bump of cellulite? That meant nothing. What Tony and I had was strong, it was real, it had withstood challenges that few marriages could withstand.

I had come here to find something in the freezer to thaw for dinner, so I would do just that.

I went out to the garage to check out the upright freezer there. Tony's mother and sisters were always making extra food and freezing it for him, so he had dozens of packages of tamales, some brisket, some sausage, and a bunch of smaller bags of frozen side dishes, complete with dates of freezing and directions for preparing. It was kind of sweet, but also kind of silly, because Tony was an excellent cook in his own right. He was more of the cook-on-the-grill type, but he could still whip up chicken enchiladas that would make you weep tears of joy.

I decided I was in the mood for chalupas, though, if he had all the fresh ingredients. If he didn't, I would make a quick run to the store.

I grabbed a package of taco meat out of the freezer and moved back inside to check out the contents of the pantry. Tostadas. I needed tostadas.

I opened the door and scanned the shelves, but all I could see was those long legs. That wide, white smile. That long, thick dark hair.

Perfect skin. I mean, like, gag me, perfect. I was pretty sure she didn't even have pores.

What kind of situation would Tony be dealing with that would require him to lie to Greta? What kind of work situation would they need to talk about at his house?

Was I being a complete fool for falling for that line? I imagined if someone had come to me with this story. "I came home early to find my husband at home with a beautiful young girl, and he said it was a special work meeting." I know exactly what I would think. "He's cheating on you, girlfriend, don't be stupid."

But...this was Tony. When I was mad at him, I called him St. Anthony, because he was honestly the best person I knew—an actual living saint. When I said that we'd been separated for all those years? He knew we were still married, and he acted like it. A young, hot-blooded male who honored his marriage vows even though he didn't really have a marriage.

At least...that's what he'd told me. And even though I acknowledged that it was unbelievable that he would honor his vows of faithfulness...I'd still believed it.

I spun and sat back down at the table with a thud. Was I just too stupid to live?

But...this was Tony. I kept coming back to that. Tony had always been honest with me. No matter what. His integrity mattered to him. He had a deep desire to be an honorable man.

But...why hadn't he told me what this special 'work situation' was? He told me stuff about his business all the time. Simple stuff, and I never could keep people's names straight, but still, it wasn't like I couldn't be trusted with information.

I sat at the table and stared down the hallway. He was quiet in there. What was he doing?

I tiptoed down the hallway. I could hear him clicking computer keys, then rummaging through the drawers and mumbling to himself.

I watched him in silence for a moment, then said, "So what's going on at work?"

He threw me a distracted look, but then found what he was looking for—a pen that worked. He clicked it a few times and then scribbled on a notepad. "I'm not even sure yet, so...I don't know. I don't want to..." He trailed off before he finished. He looked at something on his computer screen, scribbled something else, then flipped to another screen.

I realized after a few minutes that he'd forgotten I was there.
Well.

I went back to the kitchen. I was mad, but I wasn't sure I had a right to be mad. Tony hadn't done anything. And as a business owner with many people counting on him, he was often distracted with work. There was no reason to be insulted by that.

And as I said, he told me he'd been faithful to our marriage during those years we were apart. We both knew that I had not been. I thought we were divorced, of course, but I would imagine that was pretty cold comfort to the man who had cut off his entire sex life for almost a decade.

And that was the thing. I had so much guilt over that, even though Tony insisted he forgave me. I had a very hard time forgiving myself. So, this voice in my head wondered: even if Tony had brought the lovely Joanna to his home because he was cheating on me, even if he was having a fling with someone at work...did I have any right to be jealous?

Did I not deserve that?

I stood. I wanted to run down the hall and scream at Tony, insist he tell me what was going on, insist he banish Joanna and every other beautiful woman from his life from this day forward. I wanted to be unreasonable and shrieky. I wanted to pitch a fit.

But Tony was so calm and preoccupied, I knew how it would go. He would be patient. He would be longsuffering. He would get that faintly condescending air that always made me feel stupid and belligerent.

I sighed, then picked up my purse. "Hey Tony," I called. "I need to run out and talk to Viv for a little bit. Do you mind if I leave Stump here?"

After a few seconds, he called back, "Sure, no problem. I'm not going anywhere."

"Stay here," I whispered to Stump. "I'll be back soon."

She lifted an eyebrow but otherwise didn't move. Tony and my next-door neighbor Frank were the only two people I could leave Stump with, in total confidence that she would not pitch a loud screamy fit. In fact, Stump might like Tony better than me. Something else I was foolishly jealous of, if I was honest.

I'll admit, I did think of doing a half-hearted pursuit of The Lovely Joanna when I left Tony's, but I'd been too distracted to see what kind of car she drove, other than it was large and black—and black SUVs and crossovers are thick on the ground in West Texas. Even Tammy drove a black SUV, and I certainly didn't want to run one down now and accidentally find her. Besides, it had been too long since she left. She could be all the way across town by now.

I drove aimlessly for a few minutes, debating whether I should go back to Tony's and have a discussion, or do what I said I was going to do—meet Viv.

I checked the time. Viv's meeting at the Perez house had started about ten minutes ago, so I was going to be walking into the middle of things. And I might not even be able to find their house—I hadn't gotten an address.

But I needed something to occupy my brain, so I didn't work myself up into a hysterical fit and go back to start a fight with Tony. If nothing else, I could try to minimize any damage Viv might be doing in her insensitive zeal.

The house turned out to be very easy to find. There was nothing but dirt for three blocks, filled with heavy equipment and vague (to me) construction stuff: PVC pipes running along the ground, metal boxes that suggested electricity connection, a concrete mixer.

At the edge of the last block stood one lone white frame house with a shaded front porch. Two blue metal chairs sat on the porch. Viv's Cadillac was parked on the street out front.

Viewed from a certain angle, the scene looked like something from a dystopian movie. I imagined the people inside felt they were living in post-apocalyptic times, too.

Before I had a chance to talk myself out of it, I parked and knocked on the front door. Through the screen, I could see Viv, standing with her back to me and talking to someone in the next room.

"Oh, that's Salem, my assistant!" Viv hurried to let me in. "Good, you were able to make it after all!"

"Your assistant, huh?" I whispered as she opened the door for me.

Viv introduced me to Sid and Helena Perez, Gia Perez's father and her older sister. I must have had "where's the mother" written on my face, because Sid Perez said, "My wife passed on about fourteen years ago."

Mr. Perez appeared to be in his mid- to late-fifties, with black hair shot through with grey. His cheeks and around his eyes had the dark brown patches that I thought was an indication of diabetes.

Helena Perez was about my age, so I realized she must have been Gia's much older sister—older by at least ten years. And her mother had died when Gia was only a baby. So, effectively, we could be talking to the two people who had raised Gia.

They both looked vaguely familiar, but it wasn't until I spotted the school picture of the teenage girl in the frame on the shelf that everything fell into to place.

I'd seen that girl. I'd seen her family. They were on the news occasionally, asking for help finding their daughter and sister, and complaining that the police weren't doing enough to find her.

"Everyone else gets big searches and crime tip lines. My sister gets nothing! She gets discarded like she's nothing!"

Helena had stood in front of their house, holding that same picture. Then a woman detective had been interviewed, who had assured the public that they were doing everything they could to find Gia, and they would continue to pursue every lead until she was found.

"What do you say to the criticism that the police department isn't doing enough to find her?"

"I say I understand their concern—they want their loved one home. We do, too. And I'm glad Gia's family is keeping this in front of the public eye, because we need the public to help find her. The way we operate is to investigate leads. Some of you watching this program may have seen something that you do not even realize may be important. It could be an unusual vehicle that was in the neighborhood—even if it was a few days prior to the date Gia went missing." She gave the number for the tip line.

I remembered because I'd talked about it at work the next day. I'd wondered, too, why I had seen so little about it. A fifteen-year-old girl going missing? Why weren't there Amber alerts and big search parties scouring the area?

"I heard she's a runaway. It's not like she was kidnapped off the street or something," Flo had said.

"Yeah, the family doesn't want to talk about that part," Tammy said.

And at the time, that explanation had made sense to me. Yes, the girl was too young to be on her own, but also old enough to get pretty far away, if she wanted to. It was probably hard to find someone who didn't want to be found.

But she'd been gone a year now. And she was still only sixteen. Even if she had left of her own volition, it had to be torture to not know if she was okay.

Viv had already made significant progress with Sid—when I arrived on the scene, I'd interrupted him bringing out boxes of photographs from a cabinet in their small dining room.

Helena was a different story. "Like I said, how can we know you're going to find Gia? How do I know you're not just looking for something sensational to sell your show?"

I prepared myself for "spin" from Viv, but to my surprise, she was completely honest. "You don't know. I mean, you don't know that we'll find her, because we don't know that we'll find her. How could we know that?"

Helena looked at me. I shrugged. It was true.

"What I can say is that we haven't failed yet to solve a case. And you'll never meet anyone more stubborn that I am."

Sid looked at Helena, who had her arms crossed over her chest, her mouth set. "Well, I guess we'll see about that," was all he said.

He hefted one box onto the dining room table with a groan and opened it. He pulled out a brown envelope. "These are the flyers we placed when she first went missing. And these are some more that we did later."

He laid everything out on the table while Viv chattered on about interviewing Gia's friends, taking notes about who had seen her last and what they'd done to locate her so far.

I tried to listen to the conversation and take mental notes, I really did. But the image of Tony smiling at The Lovely Joanna was front and center in my mind. I made a conscious effort to point my face in the general direction of whoever was speaking at the moment, and nod slightly as if I were taking it all in, but my head was not in the game.

"We'll need to speak to all of these people, and they'll need to sign waivers if they want to be on the podcast."

"We're not signing anything," Helena said. "How much is he paying you? Polk?"

"That tightwad isn't paying us a dime," Viv said. "We don't sell advertising, either. We don't charge to pursue a case. We are privately funded by a foundation whose only objective is truth and justice."

"Yeah, right," Helena said. "I'll be doing a background check on you."

Viv shrugged as if she had no skeletons in her closet, but I figured this meant the end of our search for Gia Perez. The "foundation" was just Viv and the buckets of money she'd inherited from the final two of her five deceased husbands.

In an attempt to redirect the conversation, I reached for a stack of photographs that Sid had placed on the table beside the brown envelopes. "Is this Gia?" I asked. I hadn't even really looked at the picture, but Mr. Perez was beginning to look pained, and I wanted to steer the conversation in a more productive direction.

"No, that's Helena and Janet, her cousin," Sid said, coming around to look over my shoulder.

"Oh," I said, then smiled at Helena. "Very pretty."

Helena wasn't having my empty flattery. "Those are old pictures."

"This is Gia," Sid said.

"Dad, that's old. She's, what, nine there? We need up-to-date pictures."

"I know. I was just going through, looking for good ones. That's her." He pointed as I sifted through the photos.

I pulled out the picture and flipped it around so Viv could see. "Look at this cutie," I said, hoping to remind her that there was a young girl here who was the point of this whole situation.

"Adorable," Viv said. "I'll send the waivers to your lawyer to review, if that'll make you feel better."

I sighed and sat beside Sid Perez, and together we flipped through the photos while he pointed out cousins, aunts, friends, telling whose house they were at, what occasion it had been, while Viv and Helena entered into an unspoken contest to see who could be the most determined and impossible to please.

In many of the pictures, I recognized the house where we sat, with the tableau of family and friends during happier times. Helena, frosting a birthday cake. Gia with her hair in enormous rollers and a ridiculous amount of lipstick for a child. Sid in the living room recliner, feet away from where we now sat, listening as a cousin or uncle stood before him and told an apparently fascinating story, judging by the rapt attention of everyone else in the room.

"You have a big family," I noted.

"Eight siblings on my side, ten on my wife's. And they all live within fifty miles of here, for the most part.

That was a lot of aunts, uncles, and cousins. "I'll bet they're all anxious to find Gia," I said.

He nodded and swallowed. "Yes. Everyone wants her home, safe."

Again, I wondered what Viv and I could do. There must be 50 or 60 grown people in these pictures. Most of them had probably been looking for Gia. If they couldn't find her in a year, how could we?

Mr. Perez seemed to have lapsed into a trance, looking through the pictures and telling me the names of everyone there, how they were related, if they had any secondary relationship to Gia. "She's the same age as Gia, but she went to a different school." Or, "They did first communion together."

There was no way I would remember it all, but I nodded and commented appropriately anyway. He slid one picture by me, and I almost let it pass by, until a familiar face caught my eye.

Everything in me froze.

Heart hammering, I watched as if from a distance as my hand picked up the picture. "Who is this? I mean, when was this?"

"That's Gia's ninth birthday party. Here at the house."

I nodded and smiled. Too much, a voice in my head said. You're nodding too much. Smiling too much.

It took everything in me not to stare. The focus of the picture was Gia, grinning ear to ear with one of her birthday presents, but my focus was on one of the many faces around the room, watching her.

I knew that face.

"Oh, here's a better one. This was when she turned fifteen. We didn't have – " Sid cleared his throat. "Of course, we didn't get to celebrate her sixteenth birthday with her."

I pretended to study the more recent picture, but my head spun.

It wasn't him. Surely it wasn't him. It *looked* like him, but of course it wasn't him.

It was him.

I hadn't seen him in over 20 years, not except in the occasional picture when Susan, his mother, visited her best friend—my mother.

Shawn. The man who had abused me as a child.

Chapter Two

I nodded and made all the right noises as Sid continued to sift through the pictures.

Viv and Helena continued their negotiations for how the podcast would be handled. Then, mid-sentence, Helena turned to Sid and barked, "Did you take your medicine?"

Sid blanched, then nodded. "Yes, yes, of course." He frowned.

Helena frowned back and sighed, shifting to move toward the kitchen.

Sid stood with a groan. "I'll get it. You two just get the details worked out so we can move forward."

I sat and stared silently at the pile of photos on the table. My heart pounded and my mouth was dry. I had to look at it again. I had to be sure.

Instead of reaching directly for that picture, though, I feigned interest in the entire pile, going back over the ones Sid had already shown me, pretending to take mental notes. I felt like I was reaching into a snake den. I pretended to study one picture of a backyard party, two other houses visible in the background behind the Perez's alley, but already the birthday party picture was visible from the corner of my eye. My mind approached it like I was approaching the door to an abyss, irresistibly drawn even though I knew it was the door to my own destruction.

I looked up and nodded at whatever Viv and Helena were discussing, then flipped back through the pictures. I picked up that one as if it were any other inanimate object, marveling at my body's ability to function. A question, I thought. I need to ask a question but not that question.

"Is this a birthday?" I asked, lifting the picture and turning it around to Helena as if it weren't a grenade in my hand.

Helena leaned forward and peered at the picture. "Didn't Dad just tell you that was her ninth birthday?"

I blinked. "Oh, yeah. Sorry."

Crud. How was I going to ask questions now?

But Helena leaned over and frowned. "I know, she's too old for that unicorn. Dad bought it for her. I said it was too young for her, and she wouldn't like it, but she loved everything unicorns. When she ran with it, it played this little tinkly sound." She shook her head as if remembering. "Like, bells tinkling, you know? And not just when she ran with it, actually. That silly thing would go off at all hours of the day or night. Freaked me out a couple of times, going off in the middle of the night."

I smiled again. Good job, something inside myself said. She can't tell. "And who are all these people? Your cousins, or..."

"Let's see. He's my cousin Ramon." She pointed to the man on the sofa. "That's his wife Cynthia. That's a guy I was dating at the time." She tapped the face. "Shawn. The creep. And of course, that's Dad in the recliner behind her."

In the photo, Sid sat forward on the edge of his recliner, the same recliner he spent his days in now. Gia posed for the camera, straddling the unicorn's stick, holding the reins with one hand and the other lifted in triumph. Her weight was cocked on one hip, jaunty. Her father behind her grinned, delighted at the girl, at the gift, at the joy of the occasion.

Before, I thought. This was his before face. Seven years had passed, but Sid looked twenty years older than that man in the recliner.

I was drawn back to Shawn's face. He leaned against the door jamb, fingers curled around a beer bottle, his other hand tucked into his jeans pocket. He looked at Gia, a smirk on his face.

Would anyone else be chilled by that smirk? Would they even see it as a smirk and not a genuine smile? If they didn't know him, if they didn't know what he was capable of, if they hadn't seen that same face as it smiled and promised that this was okay, that nobody would know, he wouldn't tell her mom, she wouldn't get in trouble—if they hadn't also seen him in that moment, would they be chilled by his face in this moment? If they hadn't seen that same smiling mouth as it charmed her, manipulated her as if they were deciding to do this naughty thing together...would that smile fill them with the same dread and fear for that unsuspecting little girl who was, in fact, not too old for a unicorn that made tinkling sounds? Who was unbearably young, after all?

I honestly didn't know. It was a thing I could not unsee, so...I didn't know.

"And do they all live here in town?" I motioned to the picture as if I was interested in all of them. "Can we talk to them?"

"Ramon and Cynthia live here. I don't know about Shawn, of course. We broke up not too long after that picture was taken." She frowned at me. "This was years before she ran away, though—even the first time she ran away."

I nodded. "Of course. I'm just trying to get an idea of all the people in her life." I slid the picture back into the stack. There was no graceful way to ask why she and Shawn had broken up, or if it had anything to do with Gia. If she knew that Shawn was a pedophile, that would have been a part of this conversation, maybe. I would have to think of a way to get the information without—

"Why did you two break up?" Viv asked.

Well, alrighty then.

"He was a thief," Helena said. "He stole a bunch of stuff from my uncle. Just...." She shook her head. "So obvious about it, too."

"What did he steal?" I asked.

"Some tools. Expensive tools. Took them right out of my uncle's truck while we were all having a barbecue over here."

"That was dumb," Viv said.

Helena huffed in agreement. "Idiotic. He was lucky he got out of here with all his extremities intact." She scowled, then turned away with a flat-lipped look. "But like I said, this was way before Gia ran away."

"Of course," I said. "We need to focus more on the people who were in her life at the time she ran away."

"A list of her friends," Viv said. "Where did she go to school? Did she have a job? What kind of hobbies or interests did she have?"

Viv and Helena kept talking and I nodded along as if I were considering every word. In the pit of my stomach, a rock was forming, growing bigger and heavier until it felt like it was pressing up against my lungs, and I couldn't get enough air. I told myself to take deeper breaths, but I couldn't make it work—my body was working independently from my mind.

I have to get out of here, I thought. And immediately stood up.

Viv broke off whatever she was saying and looked at me, brows drawn.

"I'm sorry," I said to Helena. "Can I use your bathroom?"

"Sure." She pointed around the wide dining room doorway and into the hall. "The door on the left, in the middle of the hallway. The door sticks, so don't close it all the way or we'll have to get a crowbar to get you out."

I nodded and made a beeline for the bathroom. I very carefully pushed the door to the point that I felt it begin to wedge into the jamb, and then stopped. There. My brain was functioning. I was focused—hyper-focused—on the next thing I needed to do.

I leaned against the wall. What now?

I had to keep it together until I could get home. I had to. How? How could I possibly?

Luckily, I knew that Viv had a phobia about barf. If I made her think I might have a stomach bug or food poisoning or something, she'd be more than happy to kick me out of there.

I took two deepish breaths, the best I could managed, then flushed a commode that didn't need flushing, washed my hands, took two more deep breaths, and tugged the door open.

Back in the dining room, someone else had come in—a handsome man around Helena's age.

"This is Mateo," Helena said.

"Helena's boyfriend," Viv clarified.

I nodded but cut right to the chase—I didn't have it in me to make small talk with another stranger. "Pleasure to meet you, and I'm sorry to be rude, but I think I need to go home. I'm feeling a bit nauseous."

Viv shot up. "Oh no."

"Do you feel okay?" I asked her and put a hand on my belly with a frown.

Viv put her hands to her face. "Oh no, no, no. I don't know."

"I'm sorry?" Mateo said, looking confusedly from me to Viv and back again.

"Did you come into my house feeling sick? Or did it just start?" Helena asked. She darted a glance in the direction of the bathroom, and I could see her wondering if I'd left nasty stomach bug germs in my wake.

"I'm sure it's nothing," I said. "I didn't puke or anything, I just feel a little iffy and thought it might be a good idea to—"

"I have to go." Viv snatched up her purse.

"I came in my own car," I reminded her.

"Good, hope you feel better soon," she called over her shoulder. "Helena, I'll call you tomorrow!" She was peeling out before I even made it off the front porch. She was going to outrun stomach bug germs.

Back at Trailertopia, I killed the Monster Carlo's engine and I practically ran into my trailer. I slammed the door behind me, my heart hammering.

It was him. It was definitely him.

I put my hands over my ears and paced my small trailer. What the heck what the heck what the heck? What was happening?

I stopped in mid-stride and scrubbed my face in my hands. I had to get a grip. What was I freaking out about? Nothing was happening. I was just freaking out for no good reason. Yes, it was him. What did I think, that he would be gone from the face of the earth?

I thought about that leer on his face and my blood turned cold.

I groaned and began to pace again, then let out a yelp when someone knocked on my door.

I checked the window. It was Frank. Why was Frank knocking on my door? He always just walked right in.

I grasped the knob, but it didn't turn, and I realized I'd locked it behind me when I came in. I hardly ever locked my door. I took comfort, in that regard, in knowing I didn't have anything worth stealing. But my first instinct today had been to lock it.

Get a grip, I told myself again. You're getting yourself worked up over nothing.

"What's up?" Frank asked as he came inside and fell into the recliner. He was already reaching for the remote.

"Nothing," I said. I didn't even come close to pulling it off, though.

He froze before he hit the power button. "Where's Stump?"

I looked around, then gasped as I realized I'd left Stump at Tony's house. I'd forgotten all about her! My own baby!

What kind of horrible person was I, forgetting her own child? I groaned as I realized I would have to go back over to Tony's to get her.

What if he asked me to spend the night? What if he wanted to talk about the 'work situation' with Joanna? What if that turned out to be awful, too?

I dropped to the sofa and looked at Frank. "Frank, would you mind doing me a huge, huge favor?"

"Sure," he said. Frank was the most uncomplicated guy I knew. Feed him, let him watch your cable TV, and he would do pretty much anything.

"Will you go over to Tony's and get Stump for me?"

He studied me then. "What's going on?"

"Nothing. It's nothing, I just...I left her over there while Viv and I were meeting with a potential client—" I wasn't really going to do this job with Viv, was I? How could I possibly? "Anyway, I left Stump there, and I forgot to pick her up, but I don't think I can go back over there right now." Why? Would he ask why? What would I tell him?

Frank didn't ask why, though. He just studied me. Then he sniffed.

He was smelling for alcohol, I realized. Frank was well aware of my history. Not long after he moved into the trailer beside mine, I'd come home drunk one night and made it only as far as my front deck. I threw up over the railing, then sat down to wait, in case I wasn't done yet, and passed out. He called 911 when he came out the next morning and saw what he thought was a dead next-door neighbor on her front deck.

Waking to ambulance sirens had not convinced me to stop drinking. It had taken getting my third DUI, and Les showing up to preach to me in the jail, to do that. Frank had decided we were friends that first day, though, after he found out I wasn't dead, and I invited him to come inside for coffee. He'd been there when I first got sober, been there when I found Stump on the side of the road and brought her home, and been there all through almost two years of sobriety.

I guess you never get over that initial impression, though, because his first thought when I acted weird was that I must be drinking.

Here's what my own brain said as I watched Frank's wheels turn: why didn't I think of that? I could be drinking right now! This whole situation could be wrestled down to a manageable size once I had the perspective of a glass or two of wine. Or a bottle. I could get completely plastered, so blitzed that I didn't know my own name, much less a runaway teenager's name, or the name of the pedophile at her ninth birthday party.

It had been a long time since the craving had hit me so hard.

"I'm not drinking," I said to Frank, but I was also kind of saying it to me. The voice in my head said, *You could be. When it comes right down to it, there's nothing to stop you.*

While Frank was getting Stump, I could run down to the convenience store on the corner and grab a six pack. I would be back before he knew it. I could hide the beer in my bedroom and drink it—he would never know. No one would ever know.

Frank was still looking at me suspiciously. I have been told that my face can't keep a secret.

"I'm not drinking," I said again. I sounded defensive.

"How about we go together, and you wait in the car while I go in and get her."

I shook my head. "Tony might come out and want to talk to me."

"Y'all had a fight?"

"No. I just..."

"I can call Les," he said.

I didn't want to see Les. Les would ask questions. I had no answers—I only had more questions. Everything felt so huge and dark, and I had no idea how to put it into words. I didn't know what I thought, I didn't know what I felt aside from abject terror. And I didn't understand why I felt that.

But Frank wasn't going to let this go, and I needed Stump. I sighed and slumped against the back of the sofa. "I'll text him," I said.

Frank waited until I pulled out my phone.

I'm having a moment, I texted to Les. *I don't want to talk about it, but Frank won't leave until someone else is here with me.*

Three dancing dots...

We'll be over in fifteen minutes.

I showed the screen to Frank. He nodded.

We'll be over in fifteen minutes meant Les's wife Bonnie was coming, too. Ordinarily that wouldn't bother me. I liked Bonnie, and she'd certainly been generous enough to not complain all the times Les answered my calls or sat with me on the hard nights.

But right now, the thought of more people around me made me want to scream. I needed to be alone. I would have preferred to be alone with Stump, but I would have taken fifteen minutes of just being alone. Alone to gather my thoughts, to release some of the tears that kept threatening to spill out, to just breathe without being watched.

"You don't need to wait for them," I said. "I'll be okay for fifteen minutes."

Frank blinked but didn't move. Was he also calculating how long it would take for me to run down to the convenience store?

"I'll wait until he gets here," he said.

I launched myself off the sofa, too antsy and irritable to sit still. I went into my bedroom and stood there staring at the wall and wishing I could just run away.

I had to get out of there. I stalked back to the living room and pointed a finger at Frank. "I'm just going to walk around Trailertopia until Les gets here!"

He looked at me, wide-eyed, but let me go without an argument.

I slammed out the front door. Good grief. I hated being watched! I hated being treated like I was a bomb about to go off. What made it worse was that I *felt* very much like a bomb about to go off.

"You're making too big a deal of this," I muttered under my breath. I wasn't sure if I was talking about me or Frank, but I figured it applied to us both.

But Frank was taking his cues from me, I realized. I had to get my head on straight, or I was going to drag him down with me.

"God," I whispered as I stomped down the winding streets of Trailertopia. "What? I need...something. Peace. Comfort."

It suddenly hit me that an omnipotent God would know I was going to see that picture today.

"You could have given me a little heads up," I muttered. I felt blindsided, and that made me angry.

Maybe God had tried to prepare me, though. I tried to recall my Bible verse from that morning. We were doing a church study of the Psalms, and so far, it seemed that it was mostly David swinging wildly back and forth between, "I will sing the praises of God, the powerful who vanquishes my enemies!" and "God, why won't you vanquish my enemies?" Apparently, David had a lot of enemies.

I'd read Psalm 9 that morning, and the main thing I remembered was that it was, once again, David talking about the blood of his enemies and nations falling into pits. There was something in there about how the Lord is the refuge of the oppressed.

I wasn't oppressed, though. I was freaking completely out and acting irrationally, and I really wanted a drink. Did that still count?

"Anyway, I think I need some refuge," I muttered.

"But God will never forget the needy!" I cried out loud as I remembered one particular verse. It had caught my eye that morning because I'd spent so much of my life feeling both needy and forgotten, and I was feeling particularly thankful because I had a stable life and people who cared about me now.

The Lovely Joanna's face popped back into my head. Tony's smile. Shawn's leering grin. Things suddenly felt much less stable.

"...huh?"

I looked up to see Naomi, who lived in the trailer at the end of my row, giving me a confused look as I marched past her house.

"Psalm 9," I explained. "God will never forget the needy."

"Oh, yeah, right." She wheezed out a laugh. "Well...have a good day!"

By the time I made the circuit of the park and reached my trailer again, Les and Bonnie were making their way up my front deck, Frank was pulling out of his driveway to go get Stump, and the howler monkeys had stopped screeching in my brain.

Yes, that had been Shawn in the house with a girl who had later run away and hadn't been seen in a year.

Yes, Tony had a beautiful woman in his home, and it didn't make sense to me.

These were facts. They weren't good facts. Actually, they were very bad facts—I didn't like any of them. I would need to face them both, and decide what, if anything, I was going to do about those facts. Just acknowledging that had me feeling a heavy rock in the pit of my stomach.

But in my head, the crisis had shifted from there's-a-fire-tornado-with-me-inside-my-trailer-right-now to there's-a-Category-5-hurricane-two-days-offshore-and-we-have-to-react-or-we're-all-going-to-die. Both situations were very bad. But one allowed me a moment to think about how I was going to deal.

"What's going on?" Les asked.

I shook my head. "Nothing. Well, something. I just...I saw someone that I knew a long time ago, and...I wasn't expecting it. That's all. It freaked me out. I got freaked out." I wasn't going to even bring up The Lovely Joanna. That felt like a betrayal of Tony.

"Who was it?"

"I don't want to talk about it," I said. "I mean, I *will* talk about it. But not right now."

Les studied me for a long moment. I knew his philosophy. Get it out, fast. Don't sit on things, because they fester.

But finally, he nodded and said, "Okay, then. Do you want us to stick around?"

Now that I was calmed down a bit, I took a deep breath. My throat closed and I had to swallow before I could say, "Yes. If you don't mind."

"We don't mind," Bonnie said.

"I'll order dinner," I said. So what if I was one day closer to weigh-in day? I was having a major crisis. "Cluckers? Do you like Cluckers?" Crises called for fried chicken strips and extra Cluckers sauce.

"Of course," Les said. "Nobody doesn't like Cluckers."

Les and Bonnie made themselves comfortable, Les turned on the television, and I ordered Cluckers' family-size dinner with extra sauce and four fried apple pies to be delivered.

Frank and Stump made it back just after the Cluckers van pulled away, and Stump followed her sniffing nose up the front steps.

"Where've you been?" Les asked Stump.

Stump didn't answer, of course. The question was meant for me.

I ignored it. I didn't want to talk about why I was uncomfortable going over to Tony's. I crouched to greet Stump. I tried to cuddle her, but she was way more interested in the chicken strips, so I decided to give her some room. I didn't like it when people got between me and my dinner, either.

"Did Tony say anything about me not picking her up?"

Frank shook his head. "Nah. No big deal, man."

I'd reassured Tony often enough that Frank was nothing to worry about. Frank wasn't interested in me, and I wasn't interested in him, not romantically. It was good, I reminded myself, that Tony wasn't the jealous type, because I relied on Frank a lot to help me with Stump. So, it was a good thing that sending Frank to pick up my dog instead of coming myself didn't raise any red flags.

A good thing.

Was he alone? I wanted to ask Frank, but didn't. If the answer was no, what would I do?

I cut the breading off a strip and chopped up the chicken part for Stump. I had no idea if this was any healthier for her than just giving her a whole chicken strip, but I was in a place where I needed to give her a treat and that eased my guilt a little bit.

"Frank, let's watch one of your telenovelas," I suggested gaily. We watched those dramas together sometimes, and Frank always had to explain what was going on because it was all in Spanish, but that was even better. I could focus on what he was saying and forget, for a few minutes, about the hurricane bearing down on me.

I grabbed plates and plunked them on the coffee table, made sure everyone had a drink, napkins, salt, sauce, and settled in. I was acting a bit manic, and I could feel it—could feel the other three going along with it. On one hand, I hated it and wanted to tell them to get over it. On the other, I really kind of appreciated it. I was only feeling a bit less like a bomb about to go off. I could still get knocked over and explode.

I munched my chicken strips without tasting them and nodded along as Frank explained the drama playing out on my television. But corralling my mind wasn't going as well as I'd hoped.

That *was* him. Really him. He was back in my life, somehow. No matter how much I'd grown, how much I'd worked to convince myself all of that business was in the past and I was no longer that same person...here we both were.

It was bizarre, thinking about that time again. I'd confronted my mom about that night, months ago, so it had been months instead of years that I'd thought of him. Thought about that night.

He'd groomed me, I realized as I pretended to listen to Frank's translation. *And of course, I'd been easy prey. Mom dragged me around when she went to her friends' houses because she had to. I was still too young to be left alone, even by her lax parenting standards. She didn't like me getting a lot of attention or being 'all up in her business,' so I was usually parked in the corner with something to 'keep me out of her hair.' At least this time there was TV. It was the middle of the day, so The Price is Right was on. I liked that show, because I liked pretending what would happen if I won the prizes. Obviously, the best prizes were the cars or the trips, but I even got excited thinking about winning the boring ones like a washer and dryer. No more laundromat.*

Some of the games I didn't understand—they required being good at math and at seven, I wasn't there yet. My favorite was Plinko, because it looked like there wasn't much involved besides luck. The players stood on a platform at the top of a giant pegboard the size of a wall. They dropped big chips, about the size of paper plates, into the top of the peg board and the chip fell, bouncing off pegs on its way down. When the chip landed in a slot at the bottom marked with a prize, the player won that prize. When it landed in a slot marked with nothing, the player won nothing.

Shawn came in while I was watching Plinko and mentally willing the woman playing the game where to put her chip.

"Hey, Plinko," he said. "My favorite." He dropped onto the sofa beside me. "Where's she going to put it?"

The woman was moving the chip back and forth between a few of the slots, listening to the crowd shout instructions at her.

"Not there," Shawn sneered to the woman on TV. "You're going home with nothing."

I giggled, excited that someone was taking the time to sit with me, to include me in something.

"You're going home with a big fat zero," I said to the woman on the TV.

The woman let her chip fall and it bounced, bounced, bounced its way down the board, landing in a slot marked with a zero.

"Told ya," Shawn said.

"We told ya!" I echoed.

"Which one should she try next?" he asked me.

I grinned and jumped up, pointing to a slot on the board.

"Good choice. She could win either the $5000 or the $1000 on that."

I felt very smart.

I remembered a lot of details about that day. I remembered feeling special, feeling happy that I was getting the attention of a grownup. I realized now that he wasn't a grownup yet. He was probably 17 or 18. But to a seven-year-old, he was an adult, and he wanted to hang out *with me. He took me to get dinner at Dairy Queen, and I remember looking out the passenger side window and wondering what the kids at school would think if they could see me now. I was obviously very cool if I was hanging out with adults who weren't my parents. I was practically an adult.*

He didn't treat me like a kid. He treated me, I thought, like he would treat someone his own age. Like we were the same.

"Hey, wasn't she dying last time I was here?" Les asked Frank, pointing to a woman dressed in a handkerchief hem dress and chunky heels.

I blinked and tried to focus on the television.

"No, she—oh wait. Yeah. She *was* dying, but then the new doctor came to town, and she got a shot. So now she's entered this salsa dancing contest."

Les looked at me with a 'how do you like that?' face. "Must have been some shot."

I tried to smile. I turned back to the television as if I couldn't wait to see what happened next. I could see from the corner of my eye that Les was still watching me. I widened my eyes and whispered, "Whoa!" He went back to watching the TV.

Mom and Susan were happy to have me out of their hair. They left for a while and then came back, drunk and giggling, but we were fine because Shawn and I had our Dairy Queen tacos and were watching Liar Liar, that movie with Jim Carrey where he had lost the ability to lie. I laughed so hard I gave myself the hiccups, then Shawn laughed

57

at my hiccups, which made me both laugh harder and get more hiccups.

It had probably been the best day of my life, up until that point. Which was what we call irony, I supposed.

The thing about grooming dogs is, it gives your hands something to do, but your mind is often free to wander down all sorts of rabbit holes. I could be perfectly productive and still swirl down a cycle of bad memories and anxious thoughts. Seeing Shawn's picture the day before had stirred up so many memories, and I couldn't seem to cram them all back into their box.

And then, of course, there was Tony. Tony and The Lovely Joanna. Tony and The Special Work Situation *with* The Lovely Joanna.

The more I thought about Tony, the more I decided that I was kind of mad – and justifiably so. I mean, he knew how that had to look yesterday. He knew more information – more assurances – were called for. But he didn't do any of that. Instead, he just let me twist in my insecurities.

I had to talk to him. I had to tell him that, yes, of course, I trusted him, but I also needed a little more than just "it's a work situation" when I found him at his house in the middle of the day with a beautiful woman.

As I combed, I argued with myself. "Just what are you accusing me of, Salem?" my mental-Tony asked, defensively.

"I'm not accusing you of anything, I'm just saying that you could give me some assurance, some more information, so I can know that you're not – " Even mental-me couldn't bring herself to speak the words.

"You mean cheat? Like you did to me?" Mental-Tony said.

And that is the point where real-me sighed and went back to wondering about Shawn.

"You combing that dog for future reference, too?"

I blinked and dragged myself back to the present. I realized Flo and Tammy were both looking at me weird.

I looked down at Caspar, the poor little Maltese who had been quite patient as I combed him for five times as long as necessary.

"Just making sure he doesn't have any little hidden knots," I said. I laid the comb down and patted my chest.

Caspar hopped up and put his paws on my chest, and I lifted him for a cuddle.

Flo nodded and picked up the phone. "I'll call his mom to pick him up."

I carried Caspar back to his crate, got him a clean towel to rest on and a fresh bowl of water. Tammy followed me into the kennel room and now stood, arms folded across her chest, her lips flattened into a grim line as she studied me.

"What?" I asked, and immediately regretted it. I did not want to know 'what'.

"How deep are you, child?"

Oh, good lord. What fresh heck was this? "What do you mean?"

"You don't have to play innocent with me, Salem. I warned you, remember? I was onto that mobster from the beginning."

I blinked. In all the shock of seeing Shawn's face again, I'd completely forgotten about Polk and Tammy's theory about his mobster connections.

Instantly, though, I decided to just go with it. Tammy's theory about what had me so preoccupied was much preferable to the truth.

I slipped Caspar into his crate and sighed. I shook my head and stared at the floor. "I really don't want to talk about it."

"Oh, hon." She crossed the room and hugged me.

I stood, limp, and let her.

"What's that monster got you doing?"

I shook my head and stepped back. I didn't know what Tammy suspected, but it really didn't matter—Tammy lived in a world of her own creation. "I mean it, Tammy. I don't want to talk about it."

"He has you doing the donkey for him, doesn't he?"

My head snapped up. I couldn't keep the horror from my face. "Doing the...*donkey?*"

"Yes. I saw it on 20/20. They use poor unsuspecting women to carry their drugs for them, so they don't get caught with them. The call it doing the donkey."

I gaped. "You mean *mule?*"

She thought. "Maybe. Maybe mule." She cocked her head and mouthed 'mule' again like she was trying the word out to see how it fit her mouth.

And here's where you should know something about me. Sometimes, to deal with stress or confusion or whatever, I just...burst into uncontrollable laughter. And man, was I stressed and confused. Then here comes Tammy with her 'doing the donkey' and ensuing bewilderment. It all came together like a mad scientist pouring unstable chemicals into a too-small beaker.

I stood there and *brayed* my laughter at Tammy. Like, wide-open mouthed, wheezing, spit-flying, tears-streaming laughter.

I didn't mean to do it. I swear I didn't. I thought Tammy was kind of weird, but I never wanted to be rude to her. I was just...balanced on a knife-edge, and if I fell one direction, I was going to melt down into a rage-filled crying jag where I lashed out at people. Luckily, the perplexed look on Tammy's face while she mouthed, "Mule?" sent me the other direction.

Or maybe 'luckily' isn't the right word, because Tammy was looking none too pleased at my reaction. And that just sent me further down. I couldn't breathe. I clung to the edge of the metal cages and cackled.

Tammy frowned and flounced out of the room.

Once I'd managed to compose myself, I wiped the tears from my eyes and took a few deep breaths. I picked up my next dog, a black Schnauzer named Trixie, and went back to the main room to apologize to Tammy. "It's not you, I promise," I said, and meant it. "I'm just a little sleep-deprived and my nerves are all on edge. I'm half-hysterical. I'm really sorry I laughed like that."

She gave a grudging nod, but a few minutes later I caught her whispering to Flo. Flo shot the occasional worried glance my way. I started to just let it go, but after the worried looks turned to suspicious looks, I couldn't take it anymore.

"I'm not a mule," I announced to them both.

Tammy gave Flo a flat-lipped look, then scraped a stool across the floor and planted it beside Flo. She sat on it and crossed her arms over her chest, hooking her heels on the bottom rung.

"Look, Salem. Everyone knows the mob is into three main areas." She counted on her fingers. "One, drugs. Two, prostitution. And three, gambling."

"Wow," I said. "I'm also not a prostitute or running a blackjack table out of my trailer."

Tammy pointed at me. "You make jokes, but these guys are smart, Salem. They're manipulative. And they have access to drugs you don't even know about. Like, he could have slipped you something that completely erases your memory. You might be don—I mean, you might be doing that mule thing every night. You don't know."

"I think I'd know," I said.

"You'd be able to sense something," Flo said.

"Stump would be tearing the place down if I was leaving her alone every night."

That, actually, seemed to sink in with Tammy. Stump's separation anxiety was well documented.

My phone beeped.

Thank you, I prayed silently. Tammy was probably 30 seconds away from calling in to some tip line and volunteering me for heinous crimes that *no one* had committed.

"Excuse me," I said. I was taking the call and dragging it out as long as necessary, even if it was some spammer trying to sell me aluminum siding *and* encyclopedias.

It was Viv.

"Are you watching the news?"

"No, I'm grooming a schnauzer and getting interrogated. Why? What happened?"

"They found a body, south of town."

My stomach dropped. "Is it..." I couldn't bring myself to say her name.

"They're not saying, just that a body was found. No information on age or gender."

"Okay." I rubbed my eyes. *Had he killed her?*

But Helena said Shawn was years ago. He had nothing to do with Gia's running away.

Nothing. My stomach knotted.

"Call your boyfriend and see what he knows," Viv said.

Detective Bobby Sloan wasn't my boyfriend, and he wouldn't give me any information, of course. But calling him would give me something to do besides face more of Tammy's interrogation. I hung up with Viv and moved the schnauzer to the crate beside my table so I could step outside. I told Tammy and Flo, "They found a body out south of town."

They both gasped and reached for their phones to check out social media.

"I'm going to call Bobby Sloan and see if he knows anything."

"Do you think it's him?" Tammy asked. "Polk?"

Then, because I'm kind of mean and also pretty stupid, I looked her dead in the eye and said, "Oh my gosh. I hope I didn't kill him and forget about it."

Out on the sidewalk, I called Bobby. I honestly didn't expect him to answer. In fact, I remained surprised he had yet to block my number.

He answered, though. "Hi Salem I'm not going to tell you anything about the dead body we found bye." He hung up.

I called him back. It went straight to voice mail. After his greeting message, I said, "Selfish," and hung up.

I called Viv. "He confirmed they found a dead body, but that was all I could get."

"We're going to need to develop a better source at the police department," she said. "So, how's your stomach?"

"My stomach?" My brain flipped around, trying to work out a way my stomach could get us a better source at the police department.

"From yesterday. Your, you know..." She couldn't even bring herself to say the word nausea.

"Oh, that. All better today. Must have just been something I ate."

"Good. Let's go over to the Perez's house and see if they've heard anything from the police. Want me to swing by and pick you up, if you're sure you're not going to...you know?"

"I'm not going to *you know*, but no thanks. I have two more dogs to finish before I can leave for the day." What if he'd killed her? How could I face them, knowing what I knew?

I reminded myself that six years separated Gia's running away from Shawn watching her play with her birthday unicorn. He couldn't have reached across six years to snatch her and kill her. It didn't make sense.

Still, I had to prepare myself before I saw them. And as afraid as I was of what I might find out, I couldn't make myself stay away. I had to know if that was Gia.

As loathe as I was to part with my security blanket, I knew the Perez house was no place for Stump right then. I swung by the grocery store for some needed supplies, then headed to Trailertopia and to check if Frank's truck was parked on the slab beside his trailer. It was, so I went into my trailer and turned the TV to the Spanish station, made a BLT and pulled a bag of chips from the pantry. I put fresh food and water out for Stump. By the time Frank came over, I was all ready for him.

He dropped into his recliner, I handed him a plate with the sandwich and chips, and said, "There are ice cream cones in the freezer. I need to run with Viv to talk to some people. Do you mind staying with Stump while I'm gone?"

The request was merely a formality. Frank has been known to doze off in my recliner and spend half the night. I was perfectly fine with this arrangement. He rarely spoke, but if I spoke first, he would engage. He ate quite a lot for such a skinny guy (dang him!) but whatever I spent in food was a pittance to what I would spend on replacing all the stuff Stump tore up when I left her home alone. Stump was comfortable with Frank. I was comfortable with Frank. Frank was comfortable in my recliner, eating my food. Win win win.

I did a quick washcloth cleanup in the bathroom to get the scent of Furr-Ever Lovely dog cologne off me, scrubbed at my neck and cleavage to rid myself of any stray dog hairs that might have found their way in, changed my shirt, and headed out the door.

When the urge to drink hit, it always felt like a ball of tangled-up cords just inside my rib cage. Solar plexus. I was pretty sure that area was the solar plexus. It felt like a humming ball of what your junk drawer looks like – twisted and tangled charger cords, headphone cords, maybe a necklace or two thrown in there for who knows what reason. Jangling. Pulsing. Desperate for soothing, relaxing, untangling.

I felt that as I drove to the Perez home. It was just anxiety, I tried to tell myself. This was an anxious situation. A teenager had not been seen for a year. A body had been found. A family was beside themselves with worry. And the family now held an association for me, to the man who'd first molested me. Feeling anxious was perfectly normal—was appropriate, even—and not a sign that I needed to drink.

The knot in my solar plexus grew tighter as I entered the Perez's neighborhood. I tried to remind myself of how bad a hangover felt. How shameful failing felt. But that knot was louder than all of them.

"Too bad," I told it as I climbed out of the Monster Carlo. Viv stood in the yard, talking to some people I had not met before.

"There's my partner," Viv announced to them as I walked up. "These are some of Helena and Gia's cousins."

So, I'd had a promotion since yesterday, I thought. Was it the stomach bug?

"Aunt," said one woman. "I'm Janet."

She may have been Helena's aunt, but she couldn't be more than eight or nine years older than her. I supposed that was common in big families—the generations kind of blended together.

People kept showing up, parking on the street and in the dirt lots around the Perez home. Even from outside, I could hear Helena ranting.

"She's upset that she had to learn about this on the news," Janet explained.

"I don't blame her," I said. "That must have been a shock."

Janet sneered. "They don't care about the families. They never do."

I murmured something noncommittal. I wasn't sure who she meant by "they" – the police, or the news, but I had friends in both professions, and I knew for a fact that they cared. They cared a lot.

But I could also understand the family being frustrated with the way things were handled. It was a very frightening situation to be in and emotions were running high.

Janet and Viv headed into the house, but I decided to stay outside and see if I could work my way into a conversation with someone who might give me more information about Shawn, but wouldn't wonder why I was asking about someone from that long ago.

"Are you the podcaster?"

I looked around to see a boy about 13 or 14 holding a basketball.

I nodded and smiled; I started to turn away because he was too young for my purposes, but then I reconsidered. Being of Gia's generation, he might have information that grownups didn't know or had dismissed.

"I am," I said. "Do you listen to true crime podcasts?" I asked like it was a joke.

He laughed. "No, but I do listen to sports podcasts. I want to be a sportscaster when I grow up."

"Really? How cool. You know, one of my friends is an anchor at Channel 11. Maybe I could arrange an introduction to the sportscaster there."

He looked only mildly impressed, though. "Do you know Scottie Pippen?"

"Is he on Channel 11?"

"Umm, no. He was an NBA player and now does commentary on ESPN."

"Oh." Of course. *That* Scottie Pippen. "Well, no. I don't even really know the guy on Channel 11, just the anchor. But still..."

"I mean, you have to start somewhere, right?" He bounced the ball against the hard-packed dirt.

"Exactly."

"Is Channel 11 going to do a story on Gia? My mom says Helena ought to be at their front desk every day, asking when they're going to publicize her story."

"They might," I said. I hadn't thought of that, but I could ask my friend, Patrice, to do something on it. The thought put a hard rock back into the pit of my stomach. If the body they'd found turned out to be Gia's, I wouldn't need to ask.

I cleared my throat and remembered what I'd set out to do. I stuck out my hand. "I'm Salem."

"Joe," he answered, putting a warm and slightly dirty-feeling hand in mine.

"A pleasure to meet you, Joe. You look like you're about Gia's age. Were you close? Helena showed us some pictures of past birthdays and family vacations and stuff – I remember seeing you in some of them."

It wasn't true, strictly speaking. I remembered that there had been other people in the pictures, but I didn't recognize him, necessarily. Shawn had taken up much too much space in my brain to imprint anybody else.

He shrugged. "I mean, this whole family is close. If there's a birthday or holiday, you can guarantee there are pictures and we're all in them."

I smiled despite everything. "That sounds so nice," I said. "I have a very small family, and nobody likes to take pictures."

Just then, Helena's voice, loud and angry, came from the house. We couldn't make out the words, but the tone was very clear: she was not pleased.

He grimaced. "Maybe we could trade places sometime." Then he blanched. "Are you recording this?"

"Sure thing. Listen," I said. "In cases like these, it's necessary to ask a lot of questions, track down a lot of people, and unfortunately, the majority of it turns out to be unnecessary. Doesn't have anything to do with the issue at hand. But there's really no other way to know what's relevant and what's not. You have to look at everything. Sift through a lot of hay to get to the needle."

He looked confused, then said, "Oh, needle in the haystack. Yeah."

"Exactly. So, Helena let us go through a bunch of old photos and we were trying to get an idea of who all had been in the house where Gia lived, who all she might possibly have come in contact with. And I think it's probably mostly all family."

He nodded. "Yeah, like I said. They're all pretty tight."

They, he'd said. Not *we*. I wasn't sure what that meant, if anything. I made a mental note.

"Right. And obviously, none of Gia's family would have done anything to her." Of course, that wasn't so obvious, but this kid wasn't the one to be bringing that possibility up to. "I did notice a few people who didn't look like family, though. And like I said, they probably have nothing to do with Gia's disappearance. But it's good to know who all the people are, how they fit in. So we can eliminate them and move on."

I have to admit, even I was a little impressed by how I was selling this. Maybe some of Viv's delusion was rubbing off on me.

He nodded and waited for me to go on.

"There was one picture in particular that kind of..." I cast a glance toward the house, where Helena could still be heard. I definitely did not want to be on the receiving end of that rage. "Well, I guess it raised some red flags for me. The picture was of Gia's ninth birthday, Helena said. And there was a guy there that Helena used to date?"

"Mateo?"

"No, this was before Mateo."

"She's been with Mateo forever," he said. "For as long as I can remember."

My heart sunk a bit. If this kid didn't remember anything, that meant I was going to have to talk to someone older. I felt much less confident with that.

I gave it one more shot. "No, this was before Mateo. Like I said—five or six years ago."

He shrugged. "That's a long time. I don't really remember."

It's not *that* long, I wanted to say, but of course, I didn't. There are decades of time between 9 years old and 15 years old. Lifetimes.

"Yeah, it was a long time ago. Gia's ninth birthday, I think." I didn't think the big breakup happened on the same night as Gia's birthday party, but this would at least give him a frame of reference. "So that would have made you, what? Seven? A long time ago. I asked Helena about the guy, and she got kind of angry."

"Yeah," Joe said with a snort. "Imagine that."

"She said they only dated for a little while, but broke up when he stole some stuff from one of her uncles. Some tools or something."

He shrugged again, but then froze. I could see the wheels turning. "Wait...yeah, I think I *do* remember that." He frowned, then turned and looked behind where we stood. "Yeah, I do remember that. Those were my dad's tools. That *was* kind of a big deal."

I fought the urge to press him. I let him look around for a minute. He turned back, shaking his head. "Man, I'd forgotten about all that. This whole place used to be..." He spun a slow circle. "I kind of forgot how this place used to be. All the other houses. There was a big tree right there, and me and Gia climbed up it and saw that whole thing go down. I thought somebody was going to get shot that night." He cocked his head, as if collecting the memories. "If Helena had a gun, she probably would have shot him. Dad and Uncle Sid had to pull her back."

"Wow," I said.

But he was off, walking across the dirt to stand where he'd just pointed. "That tree was right here. It was one of those that wasn't that easy to climb. I remember because Gia was a little bit taller than me, and she had to help me up. I was so happy because Gia was older than I was, and I looked up to her. I thought she was super cool. She always had that attitude, you know?" He smiled at the memory. "I thought she was really cool. And she asked me to hang out with her."

I nodded and kept silent, working hard not to press him. *If Helena had a gun, she probably would have shot him.*

Did that sound like an overreaction to stolen tools? Had Shawn molested Gia, and Helena found out? And the tools were just the story they told everyone?

But Joe said his dad and uncle had pulled her back. If they had knowledge of Gia being molested and the guy was right there, they wouldn't have held back—they might have laid into him, too.

At least, I hoped they would have. It was comforting, picturing an entire family army coming to a young girl's defense.

I turned so I could gauge the mood around the front of the house. I could still hear Helena, angry, voice raised, but everyone else seemed to still be waiting, standing by. I figured if anything horrible had been confirmed, the whole atmosphere would change. So, I was pretty sure it was still just Helena, railing at the insult of not being notified first.

Maybe this *was* someone who would shoot someone over stolen tools, if she had a gun.

I was spinning through all this in my mind and nodding absently at Joe, when I realized he'd said something I had missed. "I'm sorry, what was that?"

He laughed. "I had to go really bad. Like, I was going to pee in my pants. But she insisted I stay up there with her. She said, 'climb up there and pee off the other side of the fence.' Which I thought was hilarious. So, I did it."

"Seriously?" I laughed. "Boys have all the fun."

"Oh man, I got in so much trouble. The neighbor called my mom and told her what I'd done. I had no video games for two weeks."

"For a seven-year-old, that's lifelong solitary confinement."

"Tell me about it. Gia snuck me an old Game Boy of hers, so I had something to occupy myself with. Since it was her fault."

I laughed. "Sounds like a resourceful kid."

He nodded, then swallowed. Uh-oh. I didn't want to get him crying or anything. "Why was she so insistent on you staying there with her?"

"I don't know. But she was." His brow furrowed and he remembered. "Like she was waiting for something. But then Ruben was walking by that guy's pickup—oh! Shawn. His name was Shawn, I remember because my mom kept calling him Shawn the Con.

Anyway, Uncle Ruben stopped and looked under this tarp, then he goes in and gets my dad, and my dad and he are looking under the tarp, then he goes inside and gets Uncle Sid, and they're all *three* looking under the tarp." He laughed and shook his head. "I didn't really get what was going on until Shawn is there, standing like—" Joe raised his hands and shrugged, shaking his head, indicating a man helplessly proclaiming innocence. "Then Helena comes out and loses it, yelling, he's a thief and a liar, she never wants to see him again. Stuff like that. And my dad pulls his tools out of the back of that guy's truck, and he leaves."

"Wow," I said. A thief and a liar. Not pervert. Not child molester.

I wanted to be relieved. I *tried* to be relieved. But I knew that it wasn't going to be that easy.

"And that was it?"

"Yeah. He just left." Then his brow furrowed again, just the tiniest bit for a fraction of a second. He said, "Yeah, everyone's cars and trucks were all kind of packed in, you know, so everyone had to come out and shuffle cars around to let him get his truck out. Majorly awkward. Helena's just standing there on the porch, like –" Again he mimicked, this time with his arms folded across his chest, jaw clenched, glaring daggers at something unseen.

"Did Gia say anything?"

He shook his head. "No, nothing. That was weird. She looked...I don't know. Happy?" He shook his head as if just remembering something. "Yeah, that was really weird. Because everyone just went quiet. Nobody was saying anything. Helena was on the porch, murder in her eyes. Everyone is moving their trucks around, the guy's sitting in his truck, waiting until he can get out, and he looks up at the tree. And Gia stands up, and she has this look on her face, like..." He drifted off. "I don't know. Happy isn't the right word. But satisfied, I guess. Triumphant, even."

"Triumphant?"

He nods. "Yeah. I mean, I was looking down at the guy, and he was just, like...murder in *his* eyes, but not back at Helena. He was looking at *Gia*. And she was standing in the tree, this nine-year-old girl, looking like—have you seen Game of Thrones? She was standing there like Khalesi watching the world burn." He held his arms out again, like Gia standing in the crook of the tree branches, holding on and looking down at the awkwardness with triumph.

"Wow," I said again. Murder in his eyes. My stomach clenched again. Murder in his eyes.

I watched as he remembered and processed everything from the perspective of six years out. "Man. I wonder..." He looked at me. "I wonder if she set him up?"

I drew my head back. "Really?"

He nodded. "Yeah. I mean, I remember I was confused because later, Gia and I were in her room, and she had this towel beside her bed and it was all covered with grease, and she shoved it under the bed. I remember being kind of freaked out for her, because Helena is really picky about keeping the house clean, and I was afraid for Gia that she'd get in trouble while Helena was already on the war path about her boyfriend. But later I wondered how she had gotten grease—like, you know, black grease like my dad had on his tools— how she had that on a towel, and why she would stuff it under the bed so I wouldn't see it. I was trying to tie it all together in my head. The boyfriend stole the tools and got a towel dirty, and hid it under Gia's bed? Like, was he trying to get her in trouble somehow? Because of the way he'd looked at her as he was leaving, you know..." He shook his head again, smiling, remembering. "Like, he'd tried to get her in trouble and it backfired. But, man. Maybe *she* stole the tools and planted them in that guy's truck to get rid of him."

"Wow," I said. "Do you think she could do something like that? Helena said they were expensive tools. Do you think she'd be able to do that? Break into your dad's toolbox and steal them, lug them around?"

"I mean, maybe. They were probably heavy, but I don't remember them pulling anything *really* heavy out from under that tarp. Not, like, an air compressor or anything like that. Some of those hand tools are really expensive *because* they're lighter."

I nodded. That made sense to me. Some of the most expensive grooming scissors were the lightest. Lightness was their selling point.

I imagined a nine-year-old girl, framing her sister's boyfriend for theft to get rid of him. That took...what? Courage. Resourcefulness. Cunning.

I didn't know if Joe was right in his new take on the situation, but I hoped he was. I wanted to believe Gia had all those attributes. Because wherever she was, she probably needed them.

The crowd gathered around the front of the house went silent. A white sedan was pulling up across the street—one of those standard issue cars that only grandmas or municipal government employees drove.

Chapter Three

A woman wearing charcoal grey slacks and a black button-down shirt got out of the car and went up to the front porch. She wore a silver badge on her chest.

Silently, the small knots of people stepped back to let her by. She nodded solemnly to a few as she passed, then raised her hand to knock on the front door.

Helena opened it before she could. "Better late than never, I suppose," she said as she let the detective in.

I searched for Viv, suddenly frantic to be away from here. Any second now, the detective could say something that would send this family into the throes of grief, and we did not belong here.

Viv was nowhere to be found, though. I scanned the street and saw her Caddy still parked where it had been.

I backed away, edging around to the side of the house, half looking for Viv, half looking for a way to exit gracefully. Then I spied her, inside.

The living room was packed with people, and Viv had made herself right at home. She sat beside Helena, her hand on Helena's knee. The detective was in the chair to Helena's right. She sat on the very edge of the chair, leaning forward, talking to Helena in low tones.

It was impossible to tell from the body language what was being said, but as the seconds ticked on, I felt the tension ease somewhat. Helena would ask a question, and the detective would shake her head. Helena jabbed an angry finger toward the television, and the detective nodded, said a few words. Viv patted Helena's knee.

Word was somehow traveling to the groups out on the lawn. I moved back in that direction. One of the uncles or cousins said, "They don't know anything. Nothing."

This wasn't surprising, of course. The body had only been found that day. If there was any decomposition at all, it would take more time than that to make a positive ID.

Helena's voice rose now, and I turned back to the window. She and the detective were both standing. "If I have to go down to the ME's office every day and camp out there, I will. Do you think I won't?"

The detective was still speaking low, but she wasn't backing down, either. She looked Helena in the eye as she spoke.

"You're not going to arrest me for trying to find out what happened to my sister!" Helena shouted.

The detective lifted her chin and said something else. Sid Perez stood. He put a hand on Helena's arm.

The detective said something else, and Helena frowned but didn't respond.

Viv sat on the sofa and watched it all like a tennis match.

The detective spoke to the father, then reached for his hand. She took it in both of hers, speaking low still, and I was reminded of Les and the way he would talk to me when he wanted to make extra sure I was hearing what he said. When he went into 'minister mode,' as I thought of it.

She spoke low, her eyes intent on his, and shook his hand as if to emphasize the words.

His face tightened, and he blinked hard, as if he was holding back tears, and he nodded.

The detective left, nodding again at the groups of people on her way out.

One of the aunts came onto the porch, and everyone gathered around to hear the updates. I hung back, but could still hear most of it.

"She said it was too soon to give an identification. They have no reason to believe it was Gia, but also no reason to rule her out."

"Did they say why we had to learn about it on the news?" someone asked.

The aunt shook her head. "Just that the reporters listen to the scanner, and they can't stop the stations from reporting what they hear."

"They could at least call the families," someone said.

The woman shrugged. "Yeah, Helena gave her hell about that. Believe me."

That drew a few awkward chuckles from the small crowd. "Not *Helena*," someone joked.

Someone else said, "That woman was still able to walk to her car. Helena must have been showing some restraint."

The release of tension was palpable. Everyone wanted to find Gia, and every day since her disappearance seemed to decrease the likelihood that she would be found alive—they had to know that. But in this moment, there was still hope. Heartbreak loomed on the horizon, but for the moment, there was still hope.

As if the tension had been the only thing holding me up, I felt the energy draining from my own body. I was exhausted, I realized. I needed to go home.

I looked for Viv to tell her I was leaving, but she was busy talking. She'd moved from Helena to another of the younger cousins, a girl presumably about Gia's age. Viv was so energetic, talking, listening, nodding, gesturing. Just looking at her made me more tired.

Viv lifted her head to look around, and I shrank back. I couldn't deal with talking to her right now. She'd want to hear all about what I'd learned from Joe, and she'd want to share what she had learned. I needed time to process, first. I moved back around to the side of the house, and when I saw Viv and the young woman going back inside to talk to Sid and Helena, I slipped out to my car and drove home.

It turned out that the young woman Viv was talking to wasn't a cousin, but Sierra, Gia's best friend and the last to see Gia before she ran away. Sierra had had to leave the Perez's not long after I did, and Viv didn't get a chance to interrogate Sierra to her satisfaction. She'd arranged to meet Sierra at her job the next day and had booked us a solid day of interviews and following leads. She let me know in a long-winded text message that I skimmed before I went to bed and skimmed again the next morning while I lay in bed and asked myself again if this was something I wanted to be involved with.

I checked my phone again to see if Tony had called or texted, but nothing. I groaned and dragged myself out of bed, and Stump stretched and followed suit, dropping to the floor with a thud.

I had the day off from Bow Wow Barbers, and Viv knew it. I'd already said I didn't have anything planned. For a moment, I considered making up another stomach bug.

But I kept thinking of a nine-year-old who was brave enough to frame her sister's pedophile boyfriend to get him out of her life. Yes, I was assuming a *lot* in that. Shawn may never have even looked at Gia in an inappropriate way. He may have been caught dead to rights on the theft of the tools. Joe had been only seven or eight years old himself, and a lot of time had passed since then. He could be completely wrong.

But he could be right. We both could be right.

I needed to be at least as brave as a nine-year-old had been. I was an adult, even if I felt like a cowering, terrified toddler at the moment. I needed to figure out if this was a God thing or not. If I had information that could help, I had to use it. That's what I wish someone had done for me.

Of course, in my case, it wasn't really lack of information that had been the problem—it was lack of will to do anything about it, in the people with the power to do so. Gia didn't have that problem. Gia had a whole tribe looking out for her.

I went to the second bedroom in my trailer. It's a tiny thing, barely big enough for a twin-size bed and a cheap dresser. I had neither in there. I had some floor pillows and some candles that I bought at Hobby Lobby. I have my Bibles in there, the daily devotional Les makes sure I pick up every quarter, and a couple of books that Les's wife, Bonnie, had given me over the years. Plus a stack of boxes of junk I didn't know what to do with. Important papers, unimportant papers, etc.

I had a headache from the fitful sleep, and I wasn't in the best mood. Normally, I would open the devotional, read the daily lesson and the scripture that went with it, and then pray about how it might fit into my life. It usually did, even if only in a general, "don't worry, pray" or "love your enemies" way. I never seemed to run out of things to worry about. Or enemies.

But this morning, I didn't even open the devotional. I collapsed onto the floor pillows, lit the candle, and then slid to a prone position. My head hurt and my mind spun.

I looked at the flame. Les had often talked about how fire could represent the Holy Trinity. The light, the heat, and the flame, all three representing the Father, the Son, and the Holy Spirit. He'd actually made connections that made sense at the time, but my sleepy, stressed out brain remembered only that Jesus was the light of the world, the Holy Spirit was the heat because we could feel it even when we couldn't see it, so I guessed God the Father was the actual fire.

I stared at the flame. Why was I here? Why was I in this position with Gia? *Did* I have pertinent information, or was I getting myself wound up by something that had no bearing on the situation? Would it make any difference in finding Gia?

"What do you want me to do?" I asked the flame.

It didn't answer. Which I supposed was a good thing.

I sighed and sat up. "I'm not in any way equipped to take this on," I said. Funny, two days ago I'd felt pretty dang strong. This morning I felt weak, afraid, vulnerable. Exposed.

I wanted to burrow under the floor pillows and hide.

In all honesty, it *wasn't* fair. I had done nothing wrong, and I had no reason to feel like I had to hide. I had no reason to feel shame at all.

But...ugh. I felt *so much* shame. The very idea of telling everyone—telling *anyone*—what Shawn had done to me made me want to crawl into a hole. Why didn't it matter that I'd just been a kid? Why didn't it matter that it had clearly not been my fault?

I didn't understand the shame, but it was there, so big and so powerful that I was terrified of the very thought of it being exposed.

I thought again of the tribe that had surrounded Gia. When bad stuff happens to kids, it's usually at the hands of family or friends. Any one of those uncles could have done something to her. Plus, the area was already a construction site. Some worker could have grabbed her. It didn't have to be related to Shawn at all.

Why was I so desperate for it not to be him? Was I protecting him? Or protecting myself, possibly at Gia's expense?

I collapsed on the pillow again. I stared at the flame and didn't know what to pray. "You could fix this," I finally said. "You created the frigging universe, you could just pluck Gia up from wherever she is and set her down at home right now if you wanted to."

I seemed to remember that happening somewhere in Acts, when that guy was talking to the Ethiopian eunuch and then popped up somewhere else. Of course, I had also experienced the joy of waking up and finding myself in places I had no memory of going to. In my case, heavy drink had always been involved. If that had been the case with the Ethiopian eunuch, Luke hadn't mentioned that part.

Thinking of the book of Acts reminded me of something. For the past few weeks, I had been working the ACTS method of prayer into my morning routine: adoration, confession, thanksgiving, and supplication. I find when I'm at a loss in my daily prayer, it helps to have a framework to follow—and I was at a loss. So, I started with adoration.

"God, you *are* the creator of the universe. You are all knowing. You know where Gia is and what she needs. You know what *I* need." I bit my lower lip. That all felt true, and I sensed the tension in my middle ease a bit.

Confession. I mentally ran a check from the day before and remembered my deliberate teasing of Tammy, so I confessed and repented of that. It was mean and didn't serve any purpose. I started to confess calling Bobby Sloan selfish, but decided I wasn't ready to make any changes in that direction, so I would just have to put a pin in that one.

What else was there?

Instead of confession of things I'd done, though, I chose a slightly different direction—things I felt. "God, I confess I'm afraid. I'm afraid of telling everyone—telling *anyone*—about Shawn. It feels different, having a specific face and name to the person who abused me instead of just a generic 'some guy abused me.' I don't want to tell anyone that."

I thought for a second. I had to bring up Tony. But in the light of morning, I found that my mood was once again swinging toward giving him the benefit of the doubt. Tony had forgiven me a mountain of transgressions. He'd stayed faithful to his marriage vows for ten years. Why would he cheat on me now, if he hadn't then — when it probably wouldn't even be considered cheating.

But I had to bring him up, so I said, "Also, I confess to being jealous about Tony and The Lovely Joanna." I knew that distrust and jealousy could be corrosive to a relationship, and Tony earned the right to be considered trustworthy. Even if I was still kind of mad at him for letting me be jealous.

"I confess to being jealous and insecure, so please help me be more trusting."

Okay, thanksgiving. I searched my mind—I had lots to be thankful for. Les, Viv, Tony, a steady job. But I said, "I'm thankful that there is something for me to do today. I can go with Viv and keep my mind busy and hopefully off of my own issues."

And finally, supplication. "Please, God, let Gia be alive and healthy. Safe, even. Let her be somewhere that we can find her. Let that not be her body they found. Let that not be her body they found."

I sighed again, then stood. From the other end of the trailer, I could hear my phone ding. Viv was already texting me.

After the restorative powers of a hot shower and two very large cups of coffee, I felt much better able to cope with the day. I might even tell Viv about Shawn, I thought as I dried my hair.

As soon as the thought popped up, though, I got butterflies. Okay, maybe I wouldn't. Not yet. Instead, I could gather all the information

Viv and I collected and add that to what I knew, see if there was any connection. Viv didn't have to know unless I had some way to be certain it was relevant.

I would tell, if it was relevant, I promised myself. If we found anything that led me to think Shawn was relevant to Gia's running away, I *would* tell. For sure.

Until then, I needed to focus on finding out as much as I could, and diverting my energy to freaking out *about* Shawn was just a distraction.

I heard a muffled honk outside my trailer. Viv was there.

I took a deep breath and pointed at my reflection in the mirror. "You *will* tell if it's relevant," I said. "You can definitely handle that."

And at the time, I honestly believed that.

While she drove, Viv filled me in on what she'd learned last night, while I hovered outside the Perez home.

"It was definitely the body of a female," Viv said. "But they wouldn't give an age – even approximately. The main takeaway was, it's too soon to tell, but they have reason to hope it wasn't Gia. The body they found was a full inch taller than Gia had been when she left."

Of course, a year had passed since Gia ran away. She'd been fifteen. She might have grown. Neither Viv nor I said that out loud, though.

Our first step was to interview Sierra, the friend who'd been with Gia the day she disappeared. As luck would have it, she worked at Barkademy, a pet store near the downtown redevelopment project. I would have to be very careful not to tell Flo and Tammy I had visited our competition. They would probably be less horrified if I told them I'd signed a contract to do the donkey for Charlie Polk full-time.

Viv took out her handheld recorder. "Good thing we're getting an early start," she said. "We have a lot of ground to cover today."

"Okay, but remember, I have Stump. I can't be going to any restaurants or stuff like that."

"We need to go to that game place where Gia and Sierra went the day she ran away, but we'll cross that bridge when we get to it. You'd be surprised what you can get away with, if you ask the right way." She patted the designer handbag that rested on the console between us.

I stroked Stump's head. "Viv is ready to bribe people for you. Do you realize how important that makes you? She probably wouldn't bribe anybody for me."

"Probably not," Viv agreed. "But I guess I would have to consider the circumstances."

"I'm truly flattered." I wish I was lying. Viv was notoriously stingy when it came to helping people with her money. Fortunately for me, she wasn't quite so stingy with herself, and I got to catch some scraps that fell from her table on a regular basis.

The pet store where Sierra worked was eight or ten blocks from the Perez family home, in a strip mall in a line of other strip malls. The neighborhood revitalization had benefited this area, for sure. The last time I'd been down this street, the parking lots had been a maze of potholes and most of the buildings were empty. Now there was a nicely landscaped strip that ran down the center of the street, and quaint black streetlamps had replaced the old industrial ones. A crisp navy blue and white striped awning hung over the Barkademy door, and some fancy white script over the wide windows proclaimed, "We love your pet like our own."

Viv took in the front of the building. "This is nice."

"I know." I felt bad, but...it looked *way* nicer than Flo's Bow Wow Barbers.

I lugged Stump up to cradle against my side and opened the front door. A little bell above it tinkled a pleasant sound.

I sniffed as I walked in. What was that scent? It wasn't Furr-Ever Lovely Canine Cologne, that was for sure. It smelled...nice. Like maybe how I'd want my living room to smell.

"Good morning." A cheerful woman wearing a smart navy and white striped apron came around the corner. Was it my imagination, or did she draw back just a bit when she saw Stump?

I narrowed my eyes. Love my pet like your own, do you?

"Well, you have what we call a spicey face," she said. She leaned toward Stump and stroked her ears. "We see sweet, we see noble, we see exuberant. And then we sometimes see dogs that seem to defy all other description. We call those the spicey ones."

Despite myself, I was impressed. I'd always considered Stump one of a kind, and I'd done my best to instill in her a sense of her own unique charm and beauty.

In answer to the woman's compliments, Stump sneezed, shaking her head hard and getting one snaggle tooth stuck in her lower lip.

"We're here to speak to Sierra, if that's not too much trouble," Viv said.

"Of course," the woman said. She stepped back and smiled as if she were greeting the most important customers in the history of her store. "Take a look around, make yourself comfortable. Sierra is in the back. I'll get her."

I strolled around the little shop, holding Stump close to me. Everything was so clean. At Flo's, no matter how often we swept, dusted, and cleaned displays, you could always find a few little clumps of dog hair built up somewhere.

I rounded a display and caught my breath. On the next aisle sat the most beautiful doggie bed I'd ever seen. It looked like a princess's bed. No, like the *queen herself's* bed. Rolled metal bars ran from each corner to the center, where they came together to form a crown. Not, like, a tiara. A *crown*. Like the queen would wear to her coronation ceremony and have a sore neck for days after. A dark, shiny, blue-green velvet pillow, trimmed in gold braid and finished off with tassels, filled the bottom.

I looked at Stump. She looked at me.

"You deserve that bed," I told her. I bent and looked at the price. *Yikes!* Almost four hundred dollars. *For a dog bed?* "Unfortunately, you are my baby, and I am poor." I scratched her head. "I'm so sorry."

She snorted at me.

Sierra came out then, wearing the same apron as the other woman, wiping her hands on a towel.

Those aprons looked really nice. Maybe I should suggest something like that to Flo. Get us some kind of standardized dress. And maybe a new sign. I think the one she had was put up when she bought the place over thirty years ago.

"Good morning," she said as she saw Viv. "Thanks for coming by. I think this will be easier, talking out of Helena's earshot."

Viv introduced me, and subconsciously, I tucked Stump close to me, and swiped at my clothes. Sierra struck me as the kind of girl who would have intimidated the heck out of me in high school. Smart, confident, eloquent. Her thick head of curly black hair was cut in a bob. Her makeup was understated but on point.

"Let's go to the breakroom." She led us around a corner and into a room filled with cute bistro tables, a coffee bar, and a full-size refrigerator and microwave. A coffee maker and revolving stand full of coffee pods stood beside a stack of lidded cups.

At Flo's, we cleared off the dog hair the best we could and ate around the front counter, or by the open back door, if the weather was nice. This place had weather proofing around every door. So that's how they kept the dog hair out of everything!

"Cup of coffee?" Sierra offered. She gestured toward the machine.

"Sure," I said. Definitely not telling Flo about this. I sat with Stump curled in my lap and made a mental note not to let her touch the floor.

"So, Helena said you were the last person to see Gia before she went missing." Viv held up her recorder. "Is it okay with you if I record this?"

Sierra studied the recorder and appeared to be considering it. "I think so. But listen...are you going to be sharing all of it with Helena? I mean..." She sighed, then shook her head. "I have no secrets. But she can be a bit..."

"Hot-headed?" Viv said. "Yeah, I noticed that."

Sierra nodded. "Exactly. But..." She waved a hand. "Whatever. If I say something she objects to, and she decides to get in a snit about it, I'll just deal with it. It's silly to be holding back anything at this point. We just need Gia to come home."

I swallowed. "Exactly," I said, a bit too emphatically.

Viv flicked on the machine. "Okay. Tell us everything you remember about that day."

"Well, I remember it clearly, of course, because of everything that happened after. It was the last day of school, a half day, and Gia and I went over to the Loose Caboose after class let out, to celebrate. A lot of kids did."

"That's kind of a tradition," I told Viv. "The Loose Caboose gives you a certain amount of game tokens for grades. You bring your report card in and you can play games."

"Yeah. And Gia was excited because she'd had a pretty good year. Helena had given her an extra $20 as a reward. We walked over with a bunch of other kids."

"Did you know all the other kids?"

Sierra shrugged. "Most of them, yeah. I mean, it's a big school, so you don't know everybody. But if I don't know everyone personally, I usually know who they are."

"And was Gia friendly with most of them?"

She shrugged again. "I guess so."

"Was she popular with the other kids?"

"I mean, I guess it depends on what you think of as popular. Did she have friends? Yes. A lot of people liked her. But was she, like, a cheerleader and class president and all that? No."

"But everyone liked her," Viv said.

"Not everyone. Gia had her share of enemies."

Viv perked up at this.

"I mean, it's high school. Everyone has enemies."

"Tell me about the enemies." Viv leaned forward.

Sierra frowned. "Look, it wasn't like there was someone who was mad enough to kill her and hide her body, if that's where you're going. There was a girl there that Gia had made fun of, way back in seventh grade. Called her Dog Face. They still didn't like each other. Just dumb stuff like that."

"Maybe you could just give us some names of other kids who were there, that might be willing to speak to us."

"Yeah, maybe," Sierra said. But she clearly wasn't going to do any such thing.

I figured Viv wasn't going to let this go, so I said, "So, you went to Loose Caboose to play video games?"

"Yeah. We were saving up our points to get a Nintendo Switch." She swallowed. "We were going to take turns using it. One week at her house, one week at mine."

"That's a handheld video game," I explained to Viv.

"I know that!" she snapped.

"I was just saying, for the benefit of the recording. There might be some listeners who don't know that."

"Oh, yeah. Good thinking."

"Anyway, we were having fun. We got some Cokes and fries and played air hockey and stuff. Just hanging out. She was having fun. There was this guy she liked, and he was there. She kept looking at him, he kept looking at her. That kind of thing."

"Did she talk to him?"

"I don't think so. She went to the bathroom, and when she came back, she was...weird."

Stump shifted, then stood on my lap and stretched. I don't know how she did it, but she managed to concentrate all her considerable weight into sharp little points that dug into my thighs when she did that. I wiggled a little and asked, "Weird how?"

"Like, she was mad about something. But she wouldn't say what it was."

"Mad, not scared?"

Sierra shook her head. "I don't think so. I mean, it was a year ago. But I remember at the time just thinking, 'great, she's mad at somebody. There's gonna be a fight.'"

"But there wasn't a fight?"

"No, she wouldn't even tell me what was bothering her."

"Would she normally say?"

Sierra nodded. "Oh yeah. She was never one to keep her feelings to herself."

"But she wouldn't say this time."

"Nope. She just said she was ready to go home. The place was stupid."

"So, you both left?"

"Yeah. We were under strict orders to stay together. I had to leave when she did. I wanted to stay a while. I still had about five dollars on my card, and I was on a roll on the skee ball. I hadn't even finished my fries."

"So, something must have happened while she was in the bathroom that upset her. Could she have..." Viv tilted her head. "You know..."

"Started her period?"

"Yes. Exactly."

Sierra shook her head. "No. I mean, she might have, but that wouldn't have been something she would have kept to herself. I mean, no offense, but my generation...we don't do that."

"You don't have periods?"

"No, I mean we don't act all ashamed about it. Like it's a big mortifying secret. It's just pointless to be embarrassed by something that happens as a matter of natural development to half the world's population. So, anyway..." She shook her head, her curls bouncing. "We just don't do that."

See? Empowered. Logical. I would have been so intimidated by Sierra in high school. I would have had to make fun of her to make myself feel better.

Now I wanted to be more like her. Empowered to speak up when speaking up was necessary.

I opened my mouth to bring up Shawn. Nothing came out.

"Maybe she got into a fight with someone in the bathroom," Viv suggested.

"That's what I thought at first, but I asked around a few days later, and no one even remembered her being in there. People talk about fights, you know? Plus, that's the kind of thing Gia definitely *would* have told me about."

"But no one even remembered her being in there?"

Sierra shook her head. "No, not that I could tell, anyway. After Helena started looking for her, I called around to everyone I knew who'd been there, and everyone I talked to said they'd seen her in the game rooms, but nobody remembered seeing her in the bathroom."

"She must have gone when no one else was in there," Viv said.

"A restaurant with an empty women's restroom?" I asked. "Does that happen, ever?"

"I take your point," Viv said.

I thought about women's bathrooms in general. There was never *not* a line. Plus, high school girls, fresh out of school, anticipating the summer, having fun in a place where there were boys? There would be endless makeup touchups, fixing hair. I made a mental note of this oddity.

Stump turned around on my lap and let out a little gas. I stifled a groan. "So, she came back from the restroom, upset or mad about something, and insisted it was time to go. What happened next?"

"We left." Sierra shrugged. "We walked home."

"Just the two of you?"

"Yeah."

"Did you go to her house, or she go to yours?"

"My house was first, because we lived on 12ᵗʰ Street then, before they bulldozed it."

"Did she go to your house with you?"

"No, by that point we weren't really talking. I just peeled off and she continued toward her place."

"You didn't see her get home?"

Sierra shook her head. "No. But it was just two blocks away, and there weren't a lot of other places for her to go."

I studied her for a minute. "How confident are you that, if she was lying about going home, you would have been able to tell?"

Her eyebrows rose. "Very. Because Gia never lied. I mean, she might tell you something was none of your business, or just shut you out. But if she said something, it was either the truth or she believed it was the truth. She could be painfully honest."

"What do you mean?"

She shrugged. "Just, you know...she could be brutal with her opinions."

"Such as..." Viv raised her eyebrow.

Sierra sighed. "Look, I told the police all about this. I felt really bad about it. But, on the way home that afternoon, I was mad at Gia for insisting we leave. I was kind of mad at myself for not fighting harder to stay, to be honest. So, I told her she was getting anger issues like Helena."

"Oooh," I said. "I would not have liked it if someone had told me I was acting like my mom."

Sierra nodded with a frown. "Yeah."

"Except Helena is not her mother," Viv reminded us.

"No, but I mean...everyone pretty much functions like she is."

"But, that's you being brutally honest with her," I pointed out.

"Yeah, and she came back with, 'Yeah, well, you have hips like your mom. That's probably why Nick doesn't want to go out with you.' Which was..." She blew out a breath. "I don't know if you'll ever meet my mom, but please don't say anything about this to her. I guess in the grand scheme of things, it's not that big of a deal, but...she's kind of self-conscious about her hips."

"I can relate," I said. "And who is Nick?"

"Just this guy I had a crush on, back then."

Her face colored a bit. Perhaps that crush wasn't as 'back then' as she wanted us to believe. Was that relevant at all?

"So, you had a crush on Nick, and she had a crush on...what was his name?"

"Jordan. Look, none of that is relevant, really. I just mention it because we had a fight, that's how we parted. What we fought about wasn't important."

"And that was the last time you saw her?"

"Yes," she whispered. "That night she, well, that's when she left."

"No phone calls or texts?"

"Yeah, we did text a few times. I thought Helena told you."

"She mentioned that Gia was supposed to go with some friends to Joyland the night she disappeared. Was that you?"

Sierra nodded. "After I got home, this girl from school, Brooklyn, texted me and said her mom was going to take her to Joyland, and she could take me, too. Her mom was just going to drop us off. That was kind of a big deal. I mean, I know we were fifteen and all, but my mom had just started letting me do stuff like go to the mall by myself, and it was a really big miracle for Helena to let Gia go. I felt bad about the fight with Gia already, and I guess I kind of knew something was bothering her and I was concerned about it. You know, she was having fun and then she was mad and shut down. *Something* had happened. So, I thought maybe if she went to Joyland with us, I could get her to open up. "

"You're a good friend," I said.

"Yeah, well, not that good. I was still mad about the comment about my hips, too. I texted her to see if she wanted to go. She didn't answer for a long time."

"How long?"

"Hour and a half, maybe. I know that doesn't sound like a long time, but it's long when you're talking about responding to a text. She said she would check with her *anger issues*." She made air quotes.

"She was still annoyed with you."

"Yep."

"But she did decide to go?"

"I guess. She didn't text me back, but Helena called my mom, got the number for Brooklyn's mom, you know, getting all the parents on the same page. Making sure we weren't colluding to do something nefarious."

I nodded as if I completely understood. My mother had not been anything close to that watchful over me. I could have lied to her eight days a week and she would not have double-checked.

"Anyway, my mom was used to Helena, she made all the reassurances that seatbelts would be worn, safety protocols at the park would be followed, we'd all stick together, home by eleven. The whole nine yards. I assumed from all that Gia was coming and I texted her back to be at my place by 5:30 if she wanted to go. She texted back 'K' and that was it."

"K. Like, okay?"

Sierra nodded.

"But she never showed?"

"She never showed. Brooklyn's mom was kind of antsy, you know. I found out later she didn't want Gia to go with us. Gia still had kind of a reputation from middle school. She'd worked hard all of ninth grade to get herself straightened out, you know. But you know parents." Sierra took a deep breath and rolled her lips, like she was remembering that day. "And Brooklyn's mom is kind of, you know...like a soccer mom? One of those perfect blonde women whose life looks perfect on the outside?"

I nodded. "Those women intimidate me," I said.

"Yeah, well, not me. Not anymore. I mean, congratulations on your Instagram life and all, but..." She looked over her shoulder to make sure her boss wasn't listening. "But I was intimidated by her that day, and I ended up making decisions I regretted because of it."

"Like what?" I asked.

Sierra disregarded the question, though. "Anyway, she was trying to hide it, but all her lectures while we were waiting for Gia to get there were focused on us not causing any trouble. Don't get flirty with the boys, make sure we were polite to everyone. Treat people with dignity. Don't steal anything. Like, she actually said *don't steal anything*. She acted like she was kidding, but I don't think she was really kidding. After she found out Gia wasn't going, it was all just 'have fun and watch out for each other.'"

"Did Gia tell you she wasn't coming, or did you just give up on her?"

"We basically gave up on her. Brooklyn's mom kept looking at the clock and looking for Gia, and she kept saying, 'Do you think she really wants to go?' I kept texting Gia, like, 'where are you, are you still going?' and she didn't answer. I felt bad because I was the one who invited her, and we were waiting for her, and Brooklyn's mom didn't want to drive through the neighborhood to Gia's house because of all the construction equipment, she was afraid she was going to get a nail in her tire or something. And Brooklyn's other friends were texting *her* saying, 'where are you, are you still coming, we're all here.' I finally just said, 'Oh, she texted me, she's not going to be able to go after all."

"She didn't really text you, though?"

Sierra shook her head. "I never got anything from her after the K." She swallowed. "Like, I really didn't want to lie, but at the time I was just in an awkward situation I didn't know how to get out of. I didn't want to come right out and say, 'We should just leave her, she's being rude and not answering,' because I *was* intimidated by

Brooklyn's mom, then. I was mad at Gia for ignoring me and keeping us waiting. So, I said that, and everyone seemed relieved, and we went to Joyland. And had a good time." She gave a flat smile.

Poor kid, I thought. "When did you find out she was missing?"

"After Brooklyn and her mom dropped me off. It was about 11:30, because we decided to go get ice cream after we left Joyland. I called my mom and asked if I could stay out a few minutes later, she said okay. By the time we got home, though, Helena was there, ready to tear into Gia for not calling and asking if she could stay out later, too. My mom had told her the plan, so she wasn't scared that she wasn't home yet, she was just mad that Gia hadn't cleared that extra half hour with her."

"Helena was at your house?"

"Yeah, she marched herself down there. She thought Gia had been with us the whole time. My mom did, too. Because we'd been waiting in the car out by the curb, then we left after I said Gia texted me that she'd changed her mind. Then it got really ugly because Helena was yelling at Brooklyn's mom for not being a responsible parent. Like I said, my mom is used to her, but even she was getting pretty annoyed with Helena."

"She's intense," Viv said.

Sierra nodded. "Yep. I was kind of freaked out, too, so when Brooklyn's mom said Gia had texted me that she wasn't going—and then she called Helena a lunatic and drove off—I didn't admit that I'd lied about Gia's last text."

"So, at that point everyone was under the assumption that Gia said she wasn't going."

"Right. Helena asked if she'd given a reason, I said, no, just that she had changed her mind." She groaned and put her head in her hands. "Of course, I regret that now. Looking back. I mean, we all thought she'd run away. She'd done it three times already. And she was upset when we parted that day. But later, when I started thinking about it...I don't know. It just didn't add up."

"Running away didn't add up?"

"No. This time wasn't like the other times, at all. All through middle school, she was constantly in trouble. She'd always been, like, confident. She wasn't afraid to speak her mind. But she went through this kind of shy period in sixth grade, which was weird but middle school is, well...it screws with your head, right? Right away, her grades started to really tank. She was in trouble a *lot* for her grades. And then she just seemed to rebel against *everything*. Helena, you know, was really strict, and that made Gia crazy. School made her crazy. She hated all the classes, she hated all the teachers, she hated most of the kids. Her shyness went away, and her confidence came back, but it came back...different. Like, she was mean. She said mean things. Suddenly, all she cared about was boys. Making flirty jokes—the kind of jokes Helena would have flipped out about. She flirted with all the boys, but in insulting ways, if that makes sense. Like, if she liked a boy, she'd insult someone he didn't like, to get his attention." She shook her head. "I don't know if I'm even explaining it right. It's just that, with those other times she ran away, her life was kind of a wreck, for weeks or months before that. This time, it was just like, everything's going great, oh, now I'm mad, and I'm going to split."

"Well, it could be that since she's already established this pattern, it was easier for her to go straight to it."

"I guess. That's what I thought at first. I don't know. Maybe she really did run away. It's just, she never ran that far, before. She always went somewhere she could be tracked down, within a day or so."

"Did she come to your house, those times she ran away?" I asked. They had been friends since Kindergarten, after all.

"No. We weren't really friends during all that. I was one of the people she hated. One of the people she insulted for attention."

"That must have been hard," Viv said.

"Yeah, well, middle school universally sucks, right?" She sighed and leaned back in her chair. "But the summer after middle school, right after school let out, she came over and apologized. She said she'd been going through some stuff, and knew she was being a really awful person to me, all through middle school. She was sorry."

"What did you think about that?"

"I mean, at first I told her to go take a hike, you know? But she really *was* so sorry. Like, sobbing. Remorseful. And I knew that she had to have been going through something, because she'd never been that mean before."

She'd never been that mean before. According to the timeline Helena had given us, the change in Gia would have coincided with Shawn's appearance in their lives.

"What do you mean, going through something? Going through what kind of something?"

Sierra sighed. "She never really said. She didn't want to talk about it. Just that she was screwed up in the head, and she'd tried to deal with it by acting like a jerk because she thought that gave her some kind of power, but all it did was make her more screwed up."

I felt the anxiety rise again in my stomach. Could this behavior be explained by Shawn abusing Gia? The first year after he and Helena dated and broke up, she was uncharacteristically shy. He'd taken her confidence, confused her. The second and third year her confidence was back, but she was mean. She'd processed the shock of the abuse, she looked around at her world with different eyes, with her and her peers beginning to experience puberty, the first flickers of real attraction to the opposite sex, and she already had knowledge of that world that her mind was trying to fit into the picture. She knew what girls were for. She knew where their place was in the relationship dynamic. People used and were used.

Inwardly, I sighed. Les had told me many times that I was an expert projector—whatever I was feeling, I assumed everyone else was, too. I needed to just ask if Gia had said anything to Sierra about Shawn. She might be afraid to bring it up to us—afraid to violate Gia's trust. But if I opened that door...

I opened my mouth to speak. Immediately, I clamped it shut. My heart thudded. I could barely breathe. My stomach lurched. Physically, I could not bring myself to ask the words.

Sierra was still talking, and I struggled to focus.

"Anyway, whatever it was, she'd realized over the past few months that wasn't the kind of person she wanted to be. She wanted to start fresh, with high school. She said she missed me. She wanted us to be friends again."

Her voice got tight and she sniffed. "After you go through something like that with another person, you get close, you know? Like, I felt like we were really going to be friends for the rest of our lives, after all that." She met my gaze and blinked. "I can't help but feel like I let her down. If I had waited longer, if I had insisted we drive over to her house to pick her up. Maybe if I'd told Helena that she wasn't going, or my mom...there are a thousand things I think I could have done differently. Wish I'd done differently. Then maybe things would be different now."

Viv squeezed her hand.

"Whatever happened to Gia, it was definitely not your fault."

Sierra reached behind her for a tissue and dabbed at her eyes. "I don't think it's my fault. That's not what I'm saying. I just wish I'd done something different."

I nodded, wondering why that attitude seemed so foreign.

Maybe because it was...healthy. Like, I recognize I could have done something different, and if I had it to do over again, I would. But I also recognize that I'm not to blame.

Wow. There were really people who could manage this kind of thing. There might be hope for the world yet.

"Gia never said what sent her off the rails back in middle school. Did she say what changed her attitude, made her want to get back on track?"

Sierra thought for a moment. "I honestly don't know if it was one thing or a combination of things. I don't know how it was back in your day," she said, looking from me to Viv and back. "But kids get a lot of lectures. Like, *the choices you make today are going to affect the rest of your life* kind of talks." She spoke in a heavy, pompous voice.

"Well, I'm sure Salem and I had our share of those kinds of lectures, back in our day."

Not one of us acted like it was preposterous to assume Viv and I were from the same *back-in-our-day*.

"You get a lot of them at the end of middle school. We got a lot. People go into that 'high school is the best time of your life' kind of thing. We were encouraged to start planning then for what we wanted to accomplish, what kind of experience we wanted to have. I think that was a lot of it. Gia saw what kind of experience she was on track to have in high school, and she didn't want it. Plus..." She stopped, looked a little embarrassed. "Okay, here's the thing. I pretty

110

much killed it during middle school. I was the yearbook editor, class president, president of the National Honor Society and the AV Club. I won the district spelling bee. So, during those last few weeks of eighth grade, I was getting a lot of positive attention. I mean, middle school had been hard, and I'd had some pretty nasty experience with some of the girls."

"Girls can be mean," I said.

"Vipers," Viv agreed.

Sierra chuckled. "But I'd just made myself determined that I was going to rise above it, do my best, show them all. And I did. And I think Gia saw that and...I don't know. Admired it? Wanted the same for herself, maybe."

"Do you know if she had someone she was talking to. A school counselor, maybe? Or some other trusted adult who was working with her?"

Sierra shook her head. "She never said anything to me about that. It's possible, I guess, but..." She wrinkled her nose. "Helena isn't the counseling type, you know? She's more the suck-it-up-buttercup type."

"What about their dad? He might have arranged it."

Again, Sierra shook her head. "Not without Helena's approval. She may be the daughter, but she's always been the boss."

After a few more minutes, Viv looked at her watch. "We need to go to the Loose Caboose and see what we can find. Why don't you text me the list of names you come up with?"

We walked back into the main area of the store, and I set Stump down to run around a little. I rubbed at the sore spots on my legs. I remembered Viv's offer to pay a bribe to let us into the restaurant, but I had my doubts that was really going to work.

I thought about options. Frank was at work and wouldn't be able to babysit. Tony could, maybe...if we drove out to his office and asked. Was I ready to do that?

Not especially, I thought. But I could, if Viv was with me. She would make sure the conversation stayed out of personal areas, and we'd be back on the road in no time.

Viv and Sierra were still discussing the possibility of getting names of other kids Gia's age, so I waited politely while they discussed.

Then I noticed that Stump was no longer sniffing around near my feet. I spun around. She was gone.

I felt a spurt of panic. Stump never ran away, though, unless there was food involved. People food, not dog food. And I hadn't heard the door ding, anyway.

I wandered the aisles, calling softly to her.

"Umm, she's up here."

That was the Barkademy owner's voice. And she didn't sound thrilled.

I headed back to the front of the store, ready to apologize and clean up a spill if I needed to.

Stump was curled up on the princess bed, looking from the store owner to me with her underbite stuck resentfully out.

"Aww, that's cute," Viv said. "Salem, you should buy that for her."

"It's too rich for my blood, I'm afraid," I said. I cringed at the barely concealed sneer on the shop owner's face at the sight of Stump on her expensive bed. But that's what she got for setting on the floor for Stump's little legs to get into.

"Not for mine. Listen, I'll make you a deal," Viv said as she plopped her designer bucket bag on the counter and dug through it for her wallet. "I'll buy the bed and pay you a boarding fee if you'll let Stump stay right there for a couple of hours while we interview people."

"Deal," the woman said.

Viv smiled triumphantly at me.

"Okay, no. This isn't going to work." Viv didn't know how much that bed cost, and the Barkademy lady didn't know how loud Stump could be in the throes of her separation anxiety.

"Hush," Viv said. "I have it under control." She handed her card to the woman without even asking how much it cost.

"But, Viv, you don't know—"

"I said hush. You know what your problem is? You're co-dependent on Stump. You need her separation anxiety to tell you how important you are. It's not healthy."

I raised an eyebrow. "Is that so?"

"Yes, it's so. You make this big deal about taking care of her and not letting her out of your sight if at all possible, but look at her. I'll bet we can leave her right here all day, and she'll be just fine." She turned to the owner. "Don't forget to add in the daycare fee."

"Oh, I won't," the owner assured her with a smile. "We close at 5 today." She ripped the credit card tape out of the machine and placed it for Viv to sign.

"No problem." Viv picked up the pen and pointed it in my direction. "Mark my words. Stump will be fine, right here, all day."

"Viv, you should know—" As obnoxious as she was being, I couldn't let Viv pay four hundred bucks for a dog bed.

"No, Salem. You should know." She pointed her pen at me. "You should know it's time to let go of this silliness."

I crossed my arms over my chest. "Fine." I squatted beside Stump and stroked her head. "You stay here and be a good girl. Mommy will be back in a little while."

Just wait until I got near the front door. Stump would be out of that bed and running after me so fast...

I waited for Viv to notice just how much she'd just agreed to pay, but she signed the receipt and slipped her wallet back into her purse without even looking. She hoisted her handbag back onto her shoulder and turned. "I'm glad to see you listening to reason finally, Salem. This has really gone on long enough."

I just nodded and stood, taking one of the Barkademy cards from the holder on the counter. I wrote my cell number on the back, then tucked another card into my back pocket. "Just call me if she gets too noisy," I said. It wouldn't come to that. We wouldn't even make it out of the parking lot.

"Okay, Stump, I'm leaving. I'll be back in a little while. You be good for Sierra," I called over my shoulder.

Behind me, I waited for the clicky sound of her nails against the tile floor.

I got closer to the door. "See you soon."

Silence behind me.

I crouched behind a shelf and waited.

Silence.

Stump was smart, though. She knew the door hadn't opened.

I reached out and pushed the door enough to activate the bell. "Be back soon," I said again before it closed.

I waited. And waited.

Finally, I peeked around the corner of the display. Stump was curled up in that stupid bed, nose on her paws, eyebrows lifted like she was just waiting with dread to be kicked out.

Viv patted me on the back. "See?"

I yanked away. "I see! I see just fine!" I gave one more wave to Stump. "See ya', Toots!"

I shoved through the front door and stomped to Viv's car.

Chapter Four

Viv didn't speak a word as we pulled away from Barkademy and headed down the road. She didn't need to. I could feel her gloating from the other side of the car.

What the heck? Seriously, Stump acted like a complete loon when I left her alone. She had destroyed two sofa cushions, three handbags, some potholders, *every single one* of my plants, and a couple pairs of tennis shoes before I accepted the fact that I had to either take her to work with me or find a babysitter. The only people I could leave her with were Frank and Tony. She was either with me, Frank, or Tony—or she was losing her little mind. That's the way it had been for almost two years.

And now she was done with me? She'd found her princess bed and she didn't need me anymore? What kind of nonsense was this?

As Viv drove down the street, I stared at my phone, waiting for it to ring. I was starting to feel really bad about the "see ya toots" remark. That had been petty of me. I hoped she didn't hold it against me.

The phone didn't ring. I checked to make sure it had service. Finally, I turned to Viv and said, "Give me your phone for a sec."

She slid it over to me, and I called myself. My phone rang, and for half a crazy second, I thought it was Sierra, begging me to come back and get my hysterical dog who couldn't live without me.

I ended the call and sat back in my seat. Jeez-o-Peet. I was walking a very thin, very unstable line, I realized.

Finally, I turned to Viv and said, "You have to admit, this is unusual."

Viv nodded. She'd experienced Stump's dramatics before. She'd been there once when someone in Trailertopia called the police because they thought an old lady was being tortured. That's what Stump sounded like in the throes of her separation anxiety hysterics.

Viv reached out and patted my knee. "Your little girl is growing up."

I threw her hand off my knee. "Stop it."

"It just means you've done a good job of making her feel safe and secure. That's what a good parent is supposed to do."

I sank in my seat, still kind of pouting. "I guess..."

"Do you want to call and check on her?"

"No." I crossed my arms over my chest and slumped in my seat. Although I really kinda did.

Once we arrived at Loose Caboose, though, I said, "I guess I *should* go ahead and check, though. Let them know I'll be interviewing and have my phone off. I'll be out of reach for a while."

Viv nodded with sympathy. "You do that, sweetie."

I rolled my eyes at the 'sweetie' comment and called Barkademy.

"She hasn't budged!" the shop owner said. "She's happy as a clam. I knew that bed would be comfortable."

It should be, for four hundred dollars. "Well, that's great," I said. "Let me know if you need me. I can be back within ten minutes."

"Sure thing, sweetie."

I jabbed at the *end call* button and shoved my phone into my back pocket. What was up with everyone calling me sweetie today?

I was somewhat familiar with the Loose Caboose. One side was a restaurant serving the typical American fare of burgers, onion rings, and various items fried and dipped in ranch dressing. The other side was a big arcade, with video games, foozball, skeeball, a few air hockey tables. Back when I was a kid, you collected tickets and redeemed them for prizes. I had been aware that the Caboose offered a reward program for good grades, but to my knowledge I'd never qualified for anything. Now they were fancy and kids got a card, like a debit card, and the playing tokens and reward points for prizes were all loaded onto the card.

Between the arcade and the restaurant was a bar, with stained glass hanging light fixtures, TVs showing various sports, three-top round bar-height tables. I was a bit more familiar with the bar than I'd been with the arcade.

Viv and I entered, and I wondered if she would offer to buy lunch. I could have gone for some fried mozzarella to soothe my frayed nerves and feelings of abandonment (Tony *and* Stump? *Really?*), even though I was now only four days from my Fat Fighters weigh-in and I had been eating junk for three days. Or one of those amazing fried chicken sandwiches. The Loose Caboose was kind of famous for their fried chicken sandwiches. I mean, they were probably really, really bad for me, but if Viv offered, it would be rude to turn her down.

It would also be a bit of a miracle. I wasn't sure what kept Viv going, sometimes. Not a decent night's sleep. Not a lot of food. As far as I could tell, she was mostly motivated by defying her age and buying new shoes.

Viv led the way, going through our game plan. I, as was customary, rushed to open doors and hulk nearby like I was her bodyguard. "We'll talk to the hostess first. Show Gia's picture. I don't expect them to remember much, but—" She stopped with a gasp. "Oh, my gosh! I forgot that our new cards came in!" She stopped in the vestibule and dug through her handbag.

She hadn't told me she was ordering new business cards, but I was AOK with that. Back when we told people we were private investigators, Viv had had the most cringe-worthy business cards made, with *Discreet Investigations* written in a red lipstick font, and a pair of handcuffs dangling along the edge. Every time Viv handed one of those ghastly things over to someone, they'd look uneasily from her (who did look younger than her 80-something years but not *that* much younger) to me (who was only late 20s but who was still a good 25 pounds overweight and often smelled of wet dogs and Furr-Ever Lovely Dog Cologne), it was met with an air of dread and horrified curiosity.

A podcast, of course, would not lend itself to any such kinky imagery, even accidentally. Podcasting was all technical gadgets and cords. The worst that card could do was a silhouette of a woman talking into a microphone, maybe.

"Here, look!" Viv handed me one. "Aren't they beautiful?"

The card was purple at the top, fading ombre style to pink at the bottom. In the center was a set of headphones, and in the center of the headphones was a shiny red lipsticked mouth, lower lip caught provocatively between bright white teeth. No face, just the headphones and the mouth. Chains shot out from the headphones to the four corners of the card. *Chains.*

Why were there chains?

Discreet True Crime Podcasts, it read across the bottom in the same lipstick font as she'd used on the first awful card. On the back was our website, an Instagram account, and a Twitter handle. I didn't even know we had a Twitter handle.

I sighed. "I just...is this really the image we want to present?"

Viv's brows went up. "What do you mean? It's all there, in one beautiful image. We're women, we're true crime podcasters. We're discreet."

Skipping over the obvious "I don't think that word means what you think it means" issue, I said, "But why does it have to be so...sexy?"

She rolled her eyes. "Salem, the number one rule in marketing? Sex sells?" She made a *pffft* sound and took the card back.

"I mean, I know it's *a* rule," I said as she strolled into the restaurant and looked imperiously around for a hostess. "But I don't think it's the number *one* rule."

It was no use, though, I realized with a sinking feeling. Viv and I could open an oil changing place, an accounting firm, or a dog walking business, and she would somehow make business cards for it that screamed "kinky sex."

We waited for the hostess, but when one didn't show, Viv decided to go looking for one.

"We can just wait here," I called after her.

She was already marching herself through the restaurant, though, head high, no time to waste on trifles like people who have jobs to do. "Can I see a manager, please?"

"Viv! They're going to think you're here to complain about something." I scurried to catch up.

"Yep. Everyone will get all freaked out and ready for a fight, and then they'll be relieved when they find out I just want some information. Throw them off their game, and then move in for the kill. Works every time."

A harried-looking woman with black trousers and a white shirt came out of the kitchen. I smiled as apologetically as I could.

Viv handed her a card. "We're with Discreet Investigative Podcasts, and we're investigating the disappearance of Gia Perez."

The woman stared at the card, then looked at Viv, then at me, then back at the card. Her eyes bugged a bit, but she tried to hide it. "I'm sorry, investigative *what?*"

"Discreet Investigative Podcasts. We are freelance journalists using our platform to solve cases the police—for whatever reason, we're not saying they're incompetent, not at all—haven't been able to solve. We have a 100 percent success rate, and we fully intend to locate the whereabouts of one Gia Perez, who was last seen at this establishment almost a year ago."

"You...what?"

I felt bad for the woman. Viv was shoving information at her so fast, and she was trying to make all the information line up with what she saw on the card, but it just wasn't fitting together.

Viv brought out her recorder. "Is this on the record?"

"On what record?"

Viv tapped the card. "Podcast. The *podcast* record. We're the new breed of journalists. Don't you listen to podcasts?"

"I..."

I took pity on the poor woman. "We're looking for a girl named Gia Perez. She's been missing for almost a year, since the last day of

school last year. She and her friend came here after school that day —
"

"Oh, *that* girl!" the manager said. "Yeah, yeah, I remember her. I mean, I remember about her going missing." She gave another suspicious glance at the card. "Is she, like, doing porn now or something?"

"Porn?" Viv said. "She's sixteen years old!"

"Well, I just..." She looked at the card. "I guess I misunderstood."

"It's the card," I said. "It throws people off. The thing is, no one knows where Gia is or what she's doing. She hasn't been seen by anyone in the family since before she came here that day. She and her friend left earlier than they'd planned because Gia was upset about something. They walked home. Her friend last saw her a few blocks from her house, headed in the direction of her home."

"What was she upset about?"

"Nobody knows that, either."

The manager sighed. "Well, I'm probably not going to be much help. I transferred here from the other location about four months ago. I remember seeing about her on the news, and I've seen flyers around town and stuff, but I don't know anything about that day."

"Is there anyone working here now who was here a year ago?"

She looked around the room, then said, "Hang on. I might be able to find someone who can talk to you, although we are pretty busy getting ready for the lunch rush."

Viv and I scanned the restaurant and bar area. Three women sat at a pub table at the bar. The bartender set three glasses of white wine on the bar, and one of the women hopped off her stool, grabbed them up, and set them down in front of her friends, doing a little hip wiggle of happiness. They all giggled, then clinked glasses.

"They're getting an early start," Viv muttered.

"Yeah." I tried to make it sound judgmental. But honestly, they looked so...happy. Carefree. Living in the moment.

Oh, I knew that appearances could be very deceiving—I'd probably danced and giggled just like that when I had a drink in my hand, was also unemployed and in debt, couch-surfing off the few friends I had managed not to alienate. Just because they looked carefree didn't mean they actually *were*.

Still...it would be nice to be able to forget about problems for a while. And wine did that. Not for long. But for a little while.

At the moment, feeling abandoned by both my husband *and* my dog, and with my stomach in knots, and the thought of Shawn having done something to Gia...it just looked so nice.

"This is Becky," the manager said when she came back. "And I'm Wanda." She handed Viv a card of her own. A perfectly respectable cream-colored card with black lettering, the Loose Caboose logo – a cute little train engine with a lopsided caboose – trailing smoke that spelled out "For Your Next Good Time" along the top.

See? And they probably could have done something risqué with the Loose Caboose name, but they wanted to keep it family-friendly, too. Maybe I could point this out to Viv.

Becky had worked at restaurant for over four years. "Oh yeah, I remember her," she said when Viv showed her Gia's picture. "Of course."

"You remember her?" Viv asked. She flicked on the recorder. "On the record?"

"I mean, I remember her disappearance. The cops were here that next week. They wanted to look at surveillance tape, but I don't think it led to anything. They never came back with more questions, so..." She shrugged.

"But you don't remember Gia being here that day?"

Becky shook her head. "No, sorry. I mean, the last day of school? That whole week before and week after are crazy. But that *day*, with high school half day? I don't even remember my own name by the end of those days."

"What kind of questions did the police ask you?"

"Just what you would expect. Did I see her? Was there any commotion, like a fight or anything like that? Anything out of the ordinary?"

"And? Was there?" Viv shoved the recorder closer to the poor woman's face.

"No. Like I told the police, it was a normal crazy busy day. A couple of small fights, nothing more than some shouting. Somebody tried to flush a whole roll of toilet paper and the bathroom flooded. A couple of kids walked their check. But basically, just the normal craziness and, as far as we could tell, unrelated to this girl." She nodded toward Gia's picture.

While Viv pressed for more information on the fights, I debated asking about Shawn. How could I do that, though, without bringing up his name? Even if I mentioned him by name, it would be a longshot at best that she knew him. I didn't have a picture of him. And even if, by some major coincidence, she *did* know who I was talking about—how would I explain asking about him?

At the bar, the women giggled and one pretended to fall off her stool. "No way, no way," she laughed. "You are not telling me you did that!"

"Oh yes, I did," the woman across from her said with a defiant tilt of her wineglass. "And I'd do it again in a heartbeat."

She caught me watching them and raised an eyebrow at me. I smiled to indicate I wasn't judging. I didn't need a mirror to know it was a pitiful, sad smile.

Becky was becoming annoyed with Viv's questions. She kept looking past us toward the door, and was visibly relieved when customers came in. She backed a couple of steps away from us, turning toward the table being seated.

"Wait!" I said. Too urgently. "I mean...what about other customers? Like..." My mind went blank. What were they called? "Like, regulars? Do you have regulars?"

Viv cocked her head at me. Becky frowned. "Regulars?"

"Like, regular customers? People who kind of, hang out here? Grownup people."

"....yeah?" Becky said. "We have regulars."

"I just—" I shook my head. "I guess I was just wondering, with the influx of noisy teenagers, how the regular customers reacted?"

Becky took a deep breath and sighed. "Well, most of our adult regulars come in the evening. The people who normally come during the lunch hour tend to steer clear on those early release days from school. It's too noisy, and the servers can never keep up, no matter how hard we try."

I nodded. I had no idea where I was going with my question anyway.

Becky made her apologies and left to serve her customers.

Viv looked around the place, then shrugged and said, "Well, let's make some notes on the layout of the building while we're here."

She muttered into her phone as she strolled through, scanning the place. Wanda came back out from the kitchen and frowned as Viv walked around the arcade, deserted now with the exception of a mom holding up a kid of about four years old as he wacked at moles with the big padded hammer and giggled.

Viv walked around the games, studying their artwork, the power cords that snaked along the walls, even looked under and behind machines as if Gia might be playing the world's longest game of hide-and-seek. She kept flicking her recorder off and on, making notes of everything.

"The room is eerily silent now, without the cacophony of bells and sirens and teenagers laughing and shouting at each other. It's as if

128

the joy went with Gia when she left."

"That's pouring it on a bit thick," I said.

"Listeners, that's my assistant, Salem Grimes, who asks the tough, probing questions, like, 'do you, uh, have, uh, like, *regulars*?'"

I couldn't help it, that made me laugh.

"Hush," I said. "You have to edit that part out of the podcast before you publish it."

"Oh, don't worry," Viv assured me. "I've already made a mental note to do that." She nodded toward the *Restrooms* sign at the other the end of the room. "Let's check that out before we leave."

The restrooms were at the end of a long, narrow hallway off the arcade, with the men's room on the right and the women's room off the left. Inside the women's room were three stalls, three sinks, two hand dryers, and one wastebasket.

Viv and I stood there, looking around. Neither of us had an idea what we were looking for, but finally Viv said, "Might as well empty my bladder while we're here."

I waited for her out on the sidewalk, checking my phone. Nothing from Barkademy. It has been almost forty-five minutes!

Viv came out a few minutes later and said, "Let's go scout out the Perez neighborhood and drive around." She nodded toward the phone in my hand and said, "Did you check on Stump?"

"No," I said, shaking my head like it was a dumb question. "It's only been about forty-five minutes." As I got into the passenger seat, I wondered if Stump having the bed meant I could leave her home alone like a normal dog, now? I had to admit, I had mixed emotions about that possibility. Was I ready for her not to be so needy anymore?

"Since we're just going to drive around, we should probably go pick her up."

"Not yet," Viv said. "We might need to do some more interviews. This gives us some freedom."

"Oh, please," I snapped. "You have a *ridiculous* amount of freedom! Stump, of all people, is not holding you back."

Viv, whose hand had been on the way to putting the key in the ignition, froze. She turned her head and looked at me."

I sighed. "Sorry. I don't know what that was about."

"Well, don't look at *me*. I have no idea what that was about, either."

"Look. I just..." What?

Now would be a good time to tell her what I was so preoccupied with. Not that she'd noticed I was preoccupied in the first place. But I could tell her about Shawn, get her take on what we should do.

"You just what?" She inserted the key in the ignition.

"I have some stuff on my mind."

"Like what?"

I opened my mouth. I closed it again.

Viv lifted her hands. "What? Out with it."

"It's Tony," I said. "He's been very busy with work."

Viv blinked. She waited.

"He's...distant."

"Good grief." Viv turned back to the wheel and put the Caddy in gear. "You're so spoiled."

I considered telling Viv about The Lovely Joanna, but I couldn't bring myself to say that, either. In my heart, I was *almost* positive Tony wasn't cheating on me. I was sure that, as worrisome as this situation felt, we would work it out and everything would go back to normal. But when we did, Viv would still think of Tony as a maybe-cheater.

"Yeah," I finally agreed with her. "I'm just spoiled."

"And you know Stump is not a person, right?"

"Yes," I said. I crossed my arms over my chest and looked out the window. What a dumb thing to say.

We drove around the redevelopment project, Viv muttering into the recorder from time to time, describing the scene in overwrought terms like, "wasteland" and "like a Star Wars film set exploded."

I took in all the concrete pads, mounds of dirt here and there, along with the newly finished and in-progress apartment complexes meant to house the college students who would take advantage of the proximity to the university.

One fifteen-year-old's body could be so easily hidden under one of those hundreds of concrete pads. One of those many digger-looking machines could have been used in the dead of night to bury her body, the ground smoothed over before morning. There were no neighbors around to hear anything going on.

"We need to find out what the progress on the construction was, the week Gia disappeared," I said. "Find out if they ran checks on the contractors who were working in the neighborhood those days."

"See, now you're thinking."

"Thanks. Can we go get Stump now?"

"Not yet. I want to go out to where they found that body. See what we can see."

A cold ball of dread formed in my gut at the thought of going there.

"Are we allowed to do that?" I asked.

"The police will have things cordoned off if there's somewhere we're not supposed to be." She pointed the Caddy toward 19th Street, and we headed east.

We got turned around and ended up at Buffalo Springs Lake. The sun glinted on the water and I remembered previous trips out here in my drinking days. Some days, it was easy to remember how bad a hangover felt. The nausea, the rawness in my head, the aching body. But there were times when it was easier to remember the lighthearted fun of drinking. That feeling that you were seizing the day, that all was right with the world. That feeling right at the beginning—maybe when you have the drink in your hand, and you haven't even taken the first drink yet, but you know. Everything in you relaxes and you know that for the next few minutes, it's just going to be a life being enjoyed.

And besides, my stomach hurt now, and I hadn't had a drink in almost two years. So...

Viv pulled over onto a narrow road behind the dam and pulled out her phone to get a better look at her online map. I rolled down my window and watched the warm wind flow through the tall grass. The world seemed so impossibly big. Gia could be lying in that grass right now and no one would know it.

"Okay, I see. I should have gone left back there instead of right."

She laid her phone on the seat and pulled back onto the gravel road. I rolled up my window and hit the AC up button. I found I could not bring myself to look away from the empty fields and ditches along the way. She could be out there.

Over and over it hit me, though, that perhaps she already was. Or had been.

They said they had reason to hope it wasn't her—the body they found was a full inch taller than Gia had been when she left.

"There it is!" Viv cried as we got close enough to spot a small wooden cross and a wreath with flowers that had yet to fade with the sun. "That has to be it."

"Wow," I said, looking around. We weren't even that far from the main road. I mean, the main road was a farm-to-market two-lane through a series of flat, tiny towns, but still...I'd imagine we'd have to get far into the brush to find the spot.

Viv pulled onto the shoulder and we hopped out. The sun was hot and the light wind did nothing to ease it. The white caliche crunched under our shoes as we walked up to the cordoned off area.

There was no one around.

The grass, about 18 inches high in the rest of the area, was flattened in where it had been trampled. Not a very big spot. A heartbreakingly small spot, actually.

That's how much space a life takes up, I thought. If I squinted, I could extend my thumb and forefinger to span that entire flattened down spot in the grass.

I shook off that thought and moved around. I considered briefly that I needed to watch out for snakes, but dismissed this as no more than a minor concern. I kicked at the grass as I circled that spot, studying the ground, looking back over the direction we'd come, to the bend in the road.

"I wonder who left the flowers," I said idly. "If the police didn't even know who it was..."

"On a barren stretch of deserted back road, under a blazing Texas sun," Viv was saying into her recorder.

Had she seen this same view, the girl whose body had been left here? Or had she been dead when she was left here? Had it been day, or night? Had she been afraid? Surprised? Unconscious? I really hoped she'd at least been unconscious.

"I'm going to wait in the car," I announced, surprising myself.

"Sure," Viv said. She brought her recorder out and said into it, "The scene was desolate when we arrived, nothing but a simple wooden cross and a pitiful bunch of plastic flowers to mark the spot."

I closed the door. The hot interior of the car immediately made me uncomfortable, but I didn't think I could hear any more of Viv waxing poetic into her little recorder without screaming and throwing something. I really was on the edge now, I thought. At any moment, I could just snap and say something I regretted.

It had been a mistake to come with Viv, I realized. I was too shaken by seeing Shawn again and having all those old memories come up, and I was too preoccupied with Tony's "work issue." My reserves were depleted, and I wasn't handling this well.

I reminded myself that saying no can be self-care.

Too bad Gia didn't have a chance to say no, a snide voice in my head said. *I'll bet Sid Perez would love the option to say no to having his daughter disappear.*

As soon as she got back into the car (appearing energized by our little field trip) I said, "I want to go get Stump now."

"Sure, okay. But I think..." She checked her text messages. "Yeah. Helena is off work now. I asked if we could stop back by there and follow up after the visit from the detective last night."

"But you were practically in Helena's lap the whole time the detective was there," I snapped. "What could you possibly have missed?"

Viv swung the car back toward town, then gave me a pointed look. "Call him," she said.

"Call who?"

"Your husband. Call him, ask him how his day is going. Ask him what he wants for dinner. Ask him if there's anything you can do to ease his burden."

"Ease his burden?" I made a goofy face. "No, thank you."

"See, you say he's preoccupied with work. Maybe he's waiting for you to ask about it."

"But I have asked about it. You know Tony. He's not exactly a chatterbox." I *had* asked about it, hadn't I? Yes, I definitely had. Once. He'd said he needed to think about it, he might be overreacting. And I hadn't asked again.

Should I have? Maybe Tony did want me to do more than meet him halfway, in situations like this. Maybe he was waiting for me to draw him out.

It couldn't hurt to call him. I pulled my phone from my back pocket and hit his number. He wasn't in his office, so I called his cell phone. It went to voicemail. "Hey, it's me," I said, doing my best to sound bright and cheery. The type of person to ease your burden. "Just wanted to check in and see how your day was going. See if you want me to bring something over for dinner tonight. And just—sorry, by the way, for sending Frank over the other night to pick up Stump. I wasn't feeling well so I wanted to stay close to home, you know."

He hadn't minded that Frank came over to get Stump. Hadn't even, I realized, called later that night or the next day to check on me.

"Anyway," I said, because I realized I'd just been sitting there in silence. "Call me when you get a chance."

I ended the call and checked the messages and missed calls. Nothing from Barkademy.

Viv was silent for a moment. "Well, he'll probably see that you called, and he'll call you back soon."

"Probably," I said. But I doubted it.

Ugh. I was suddenly exhausted. Too exhausted to remember that I didn't really want to go to the Perez house until we were entering their block. There was a new car at their little white house, one I hadn't seen before.

"That's Janet," Viv said. "Helena's aunt."

"You've just bonded with the whole family, huh?" I asked as I hauled myself out of the car. Jeez-o-Peet, what was wrong with me? I was too tired and cranky to be around humans. I needed to go home and lie on the sofa and watch telenovelas with Frank for a while. For about a month.

Helena's aunt Janet was, at most, five years older than Helena. She let us into the house, and Helena sat in the chair near Sid's recliner with her feet curled under her, a remote control in her hand.

"We're just watching this pig get what's coming to him," Helena said. She turned the volume on the TV back up. "Have you been keeping up with this?"

"Oh, that guy!" Viv said. She dropped her purse to the floor beside the sofa and sat beside Janet, rapt attention on the TV. "They finally arrested him?"

"Finally," Janet said.

I took a seat on the other side of Viv and pretended to be interested in the overweight Hollywood producer who was being walked, handcuffed, from his black SUV into a police precinct office. The entire block was a mob of reporters and cameras.

I had to admit, it was kind of shocking to see one of these guys getting arrested. You usually just hear stories of how they got away with it for years and years and then, at worst, took their gazillions of dollars and moved to a sun-washed villa in some European seaside village to live out the rest of their lives in simple luxury.

The four of us sat in silence while the scene replayed itself three times, then finally cut to a newscaster interviewing a leading actress. Behind them in the smaller picture-in-picture, the big shot Hollywood producer made the walk through the crowd again.

"See, those are the ones who make me sick." Helena pointed at the television with disgust. "Look at her. Those are the real bad guys—the ones who let him get away with it for years. Did you hear what she said? An open secret, they call it. They *knew* what a pervert he was, knew what would happen to girls when they met with him. The whole lot of them are worthless. Sell their souls to be rich and famous."

"Exactly," Janet said. "Women who care only about protecting themselves make me sick! It's their fault guys like that keep doing what they do. They're as much to blame as he is."

"Yeah," I said. But it bugged me. "But, I mean...what can they do? If all they have are rumors?"

"They can tell what they've heard. Warn people, for crying out loud," Janet said.

"Besides, if you've been assaulted by the guy, it's not a rumor," Helena said. "You have a duty to go to the police. Report the piece of trash."

I nodded. "True. That's so hard, though. Can you imagine, being an actress and saying a powerful Hollywood producer assaulted you? You know immediately it's going to be wall-to-wall news coverage. Everyone on the planet is going to be talking about the very worst moment of your life. And most of them will accuse you of making it up. Trying to make a buck."

"So what? So, you don't report, and just let the guy keep doing it? That's just..." Helena shook her head. "Disgusting. Just disgusting."

Janet sneered. "Miss Academy-award-winning actress. No way I'd let some pig like that do that to me and get away with it." She glared at me like *I* was the actress who'd fed a stream of innocent girls to powerful abusive moguls. "He'd regret every knowing me. And if he didn't? So what? Get another career. Save your soul. It's not worth it."

Beside me, Viv watched the actress being grilled about her experience with the creepy mogul. "I don't like her hair like that," Viv said. "Makes her face look too round."

I stood. "I'm going to go outside and call Stump," I said. "I need to go get her soon." I nodded toward Janet and Helena, who were too busy watching the TV to pay me any more attention.

I know it's ridiculous, but I was so happy to see Stump I almost cried. Maybe I needed more sleep, I thought. I felt exhausted and wired at the same time. I lugged her and her bed—that thing was heavy! -- out to Viv's car and slid it into the back seat. Stump hopped into the bed and rode back there like a queen on one of those sedan chairs, being carried through her realm on the backs of serfs. I kept turning around to smile at her.

Viv wasn't happy with me for forcing an exit at the Perez home sooner than she wanted, but had adopted a philosophical attitude anyway. "They were too focused on the director guy to answer any of my questions," she said. "I'll have to catch Helena alone tomorrow."

"What are you going to ask her?"

"I want to go back over her story of the night Gia went missing and compare it to Sierra's account."

"Do you think one of them is lying?"

"No, but if I can spot a difference in their testimonies, it will give me a place to look closer."

"Can it be called testimony, if it's just an interview with a nosy old podcaster?"

Viv ignored me. She was in too good a mood to be bothered by my peskiness. "If I've learned anything from watching detective shows, it's that one little clue—one *tiny*, odd thing—can blow a case wide open. Something nobody else noticed. That's what I always look for, Salem. The one thing." She tilted her head and pursed her lips. "Maybe that's what I should call the podcast. The One Thing." She spread her hand in the air. "The One Thing," she said again.

I reached over and took the wheel because between the head tilt and the hand spread, we were about to go off the overpass. "That's a good idea." The one thing nobody else knew. There would never be a better opening to tell her about Shawn.

I took a deep breath. I could do this. Just spit it out.

"Listen, Viv, I need to tell you something."

She looked at me, eyebrows raised. She was smiling. Energized by what we'd done today. My sweet, crazy friend.

Something about it all stepped so hard on my heart. I was sitting, what, 18 inches from her? But I felt miles away. On another planet.

"I've been trying to find a way to say this all day," I said.

"Say what?"

Just say it, I told myself. *Just say it.* But the words were stuck in my throat.

Viv gave a short laugh. "Is it about Tony? Because he's going to call you, Salem. It's going to be fine."

I shook my head. "No, it's not Tony. I..."

"...you what?"

I took another deep breath.

"Listen," I said.

"I'm listening."

You can do it, I thought.

But I couldn't. I couldn't do it.

"That bed you bought for Stump cost $400."

She gaped at me. "What?"

"I know," I said. I turned to face front, miserable. How could I feel such immense relief and immense disappointment in myself, all at the same time?

"Four hundred dollars for a *dog bed*? Why?"

"In all fairness, I did try to tell you."

She blinked and faced front, too. Then she sighed. "Well, it's a lot of money, but Stump is worth it." She whistled. "I knew that shop was cute, but I didn't realize we were going into the Cartier of pet stores."

"I can pay you back," I said. "If you don't mind installments." Of $25 a month for sixteen months, I didn't say.

"No, no, there's no need for that." She took another deep breath and squared her shoulders. "In fact, I am glad to have done it. I'm glad you didn't tell me how much it was, because I might have changed my mind. And Stump deserves a princess bed."

"I tried to tell you how much," I pointed out. "You shushed me."

"Salem, you do not have to feel bad for not telling me. It's fine. I'm not angry."

I had been feeling a bit guilty for not trying harder, but her attitude was helping ease that. "Okay," I said.

"I mean, I can understand why you *would* feel guilty for taking advantage like that."

"I did not take advantage. I tried to tell you and you shushed me."

"Because we both know that there was no way Stump was ever going to have a bed like that without my help."

I narrowed my eyes at her. "I tried to tell you," I said through gritted teeth. "You shushed me."

"Salem, it's fine. Stop apologizing."

"Stop—I'm not—ugh!" I couldn't believe just thirty seconds ago I was thinking how much I adored this woman.

We rode in silence for about ten minutes. As we were drawing close to Trailertopia, she said, "And you're absolutely sure it wasn't forty dollars?"

Back at Trailertopia, I lugged Stump's new princess bed into my trailer. I positioned it between the sofa and the television. It was easily the most expensive piece of furniture in the whole place. The sofa and recliner had been in there when I moved in. I bought the dinette at Goodwill for thirty-five dollars, and Les and Bonnie had given me one of their son's old beds.

Stump lapped up a bit of water then trotted back to her bed. I lay across the sofa and reached out my hand to stroke her ears. She liked that.

I'd wanted to be home, but once I got there, I didn't know what to do with myself. I turned on the television, but I couldn't get my mind to focus. I checked my phone. Nothing from Tony.

I paced around my trailer for the second time that week, Janet and Helena's words running through my head.

"They're as guilty as he is."

Of course, they weren't talking about me. They didn't know about me.

They didn't know about me, and that was the *only* reason they weren't talking about me. If they knew what I knew...

"They're as guilty as he is."

I swiveled with mind-bending speed between guilt, shame, resentment, anger, sadness, back to resentment, back to guilt, back to shame. Back to anger.

After all, what did *I* have to be ashamed of? I hadn't done anything! I was a victim, too!

Stump lay on her princess bed and watched me, eyebrows drawn in concern.

Women who care only about protecting themselves make me sick! It's their fault guys like that keep doing what they do. They're as much to blame as he is.

Didn't I have a right to protect myself? Was I *really* obligated to share my trauma with the world?

I needed to talk to someone. I picked up my phone and opened the contacts. I slid past the list of names that I would never feel comfortable talking to about this.

Mom? No. G-Ma? No. Flo? Good grief. If my mind hadn't been such a raging trash fire, I might have laughed at the awkward looks that would commence if I tried to talk to Flo about my problems. Flo is a great, "Hey, can I have Tuesday morning off for a dentist appointment" kind of boss. She's not the "Hey I'm suffering from an existential crisis, can you help me figure out how I'm supposed to feel?" kind of boss.

Viv? I'd been with Viv all day, and I hadn't been able to bring myself to say anything. Viv was a very good friend, but she was strong on action and significantly less strong on thinking. And right now, I needed to just slow everything down and figure it out.

What did I need to feel about this situation? What did I need to do?

Les? Yes, Les was definitely the one I should call. Nothing I could say would offend or confuse Les. He would remain steady. He would make sense. He would untangle the tangle of thoughts in my head.

But then he would *know*. I mean, he knew in general that I'd been abused as a kid. But knowing that in general wasn't the same as saying, "*this* guy did *this* thing to me."

Still, I had to call him. Les was my ad hoc sponsor. I needed to work it through. There was so much more at stake here than just what had happened to me. The guilt was making me crazy. The *resentment* about the guilt was making me crazy.

My thumb hovered over Les's name in my contact list.

And hovered...

And hovered.

Finally, I groaned and threw the phone onto the sofa.

I looked at Stump. "Stump, tell me what to do."

She raised her eyebrows but didn't say anything. She communicated a lot of sympathy in those raised eyebrows, though.

I fell onto the sofa and pulled the phone out from under me. I needed a distraction, so I pulled up Reddit and the Am I The Jerk thread.

And then it occurred to me—I could post this on AITJ and get some feedback! These were completely unbiased strangers. I could spell out the situation and see how people reacted.

I sat up, encouraged with this idea. Of course, it would take some thinking through, because my thoughts were all over the place.

I jumped up and grabbed a notepad I'd gotten free last time I went to pay my cable bill and dug through the junk drawer until I found a pen that worked.

I sat back on the sofa and jotted down my thoughts.

Am I The Jerk for not reporting a sexual abuser from when I was a kid?

I sat back and frowned. That made it all about me, and really this was about Gia. But it was harder to figure out how to post the question.

I finally settled on a lesser-used subheading of the AITJ thread—WIBTJ. Would I Be the Jerk—it's for people who are thinking about saying or doing something regarding a situation, and they want to know what the consensus is before they do it.

Would I Be the Jerk If I Didn't Report the Man Who Molested Me and Might Have Molested A Young Runaway?

Oy. I read through that. Pithy it was not, and if I read that headline alone, I would stop right there – I would so clearly be The Jerk. I could already tell this was going to start with the dreaded, "now, hear me out." Ugh. Maybe this wasn't the brilliant idea I thought it was.

I tried several different iterations. Would I Be the Jerk If I Told My Friend Her Ex-Boyfriend Had Molested Me, and He Might Be Behind Her Sister's Disappearance.

Am I The Jerk Because I Didn't Tell My Friend Her Ex-Boyfriend Molested Me, and Now Her Sister Has Run Away, and I'm Afraid He Had Something to Do With It.

I sighed and looked at Stump. I wasn't going to be able to put a neat clean headline on this. It would just have to stay messy, and I hoped people would read through the explanation and give me a clear, precise answer that told me how I needed to move forward.

I logged in and started the thread. I typed and deleted, typed and deleted. It was exhausting. But also, very clarifying.

It didn't really matter if it was my fault, when it came down to it. What mattered was what I did next. I mean, I didn't know Gia, I hadn't seen Shawn in years, and I had no responsibility for whatever had happened to Gia. I was feeling guilty after what Helena and her cousin had said, but there was no way they would *really* blame me, if they knew. I was a kid. Seven years old. How could I be responsible in any way?

I reread through what I had written one last time:

Hear me out. I (29F) recently became aware of a sixteen-year-old girl who ran away last year. I am helping her family look for her, and in that effort, I found some old pictures with the girl's family and

147

friends at her ninth birthday party. In the picture was a guy I knew from my past. The girl's older sister was dating him at the time the picture was taken, but they broke up soon after. This guy molested me when I was seven, so it was a shock, to say the least. There's no reason to believe he has anything to do with the girl's disappearance, since it had been almost five years between her sister's breakup and her running away, and apparently no one in the family has seen this guy since then. But I keep feeling like I should tell them about the guy anyway, in case he has something to do with it and I have relevant information that no one else knows about. But, like I said, he might not have anything to do with it, and I could just be muddying the waters. WIBTJ if I kept this information to myself?

This was as good as it was going to get, I thought as I laid the phone down. I had typed and deleted a few sentences about how afraid I was that Helena would lose her mind and scream at me if I told, because I just had to get past that, even if it was true.

I sighed and stood, feeling more relieved than I had expected to. Writing all that out had been clarifying, and it put things into perspective. Over the past couple of days, I increasingly had come to feel that Gia's disappearance *was* my responsibility—was, in fact, my *fault.* But what I had written was correct—there was no reason to believe Shawn had anything to do with it. That he had molested her, and that he had put her life onto a different trajectory was one possible explanation, but only one.

I looked at Stump. "Ready for dinner?"

Frank came in and plopped into the recliner. He had already turned the television on when he shifted his gaze to the left a fraction and noticed Stump's new bed.

"Whoa," he said.

"I know, right?" I dropped to the sofa and stroked Stump's ears again, then rubbed the velvet of the pillow. I felt the tension inside me easing a bit. Writing all that out had definitely been the right choice. "Viv bought it for her."

"Probably Queen Elizabeth's Corgis have beds just like that."

"Probably," I agreed. "Hey, you know what? Viv bought it for her because we were interviewing witnesses at the pet store, and Stump crawled in that bed, and she was happy there. So, we decided to see if she would stay there while we did some interviews. And she did!"

"And she did what?"

"She stayed there, at the pet store, while we left and conducted interviews."

"You left the store?"

I nodded. "Crazy, huh?"

"Like, you walked *away* from the building, and she stayed *in the building?* Without you?"

I nodded, gratified by his shocked expression.

"You left and closed the door and she couldn't see you and she just...sat there? In the bed?"

I really didn't know what I could do except keep nodding and saying, "Yes, that's right," so I did that.

He collapsed his head back onto the back of the recliner. "Whoa," he said again. "Maybe that's a magic bed."

"Maybe."

"Whoa," he said for the third time. "Am I fired as babysitter?"

"I don't think so," I assured him. "We need to make sure it takes, long-term, before we make any big changes."

Visibly relieved, he turned on the television.

"Anway, Sloppy Joes for dinner," I said as I rose from the sofa and pulled a pound of ground beef from the fridge. "And fries." I felt a moment of panic at the looming weekly weigh-in at Fat Fighters, but that eased when I remembered that Viv had not fed me all day. Besides, I had made it through the last few days without turning to booze, I thought with a tremendous feeling of relief. Even a tiny bit of triumph. I had not known how to handle this situation, but I was handling it. I had written the whole situation out and gotten a fresh perspective on it. I was doing okay.

Frank nodded and studied me silently. I smiled and nodded back. *See how fine I am?* I conveyed with my eyes. I am a grownup now, dealing with grownup things in a healthy and fully functional way.

I had set my notifications to ping when I got a response on my post, and I heard the first ping as I was breaking the ground beef up in the skillet. My heart raced, and I decided to just wait a few minutes before I looked. I was doing okay. I was feeling good about what I had written. I was open and ready for whatever came next—or I could be ready, at any rate.

I set the oven to preheat for the fries, took the bag out of the freezer, and ripped it open.

Ping. Ping. Ping.

I dumped them out on the baking sheet and shook it to spread them out.

Ping ping ping. They were coming faster now.

My stomach lurched.

They're probably all very supportive, I told myself. *I'm sorry that happened to you. You have a right to disclose what you feel comfortable with, and nothing more. You're not the bad guy here. NTJ, and here's a picture of a kitten to make you feel better.*

I took a bottle of vegetable oil from the pantry and carefully measured out a tablespoon. Even if I was treating myself to a comfort meal, I was a healthy grownup and cared about my cholesterol or whatever.

Pingpingpingpingpingping.

I glugged the oil out straight onto the pan. These fries needed to be extra crispy.

"Your phone is blowing up," Frank said. Just, matter-of-factly. No big deal.

I laughed. It might have sounded forced. "It's Viv. We're working on that story about that runaway girl." I shook my head and made another attempt at a laugh and shook my head. "When that woman gets an idea in her head…"

I slid the fries into the oven and stirred the ground beef, getting

151

nicely brown now.

Pingpingpingpingpingpingpingpingpingpingpingpingpingpi ngpingpingping.

"Good grief, woman!" I cried and forced another laugh. "Let me at least make dinner!" I stepped around to the sofa and snatched up my phone.

I had to turn off the notifications, I thought, my brain going into survivor mode. First, I just had to turn off the notifications.

My hands shook as I stabbed at the icons, accidentally hitting the Fat Fighters tracker instead of the settings. I closed that, then went to settings and silenced that horrible noise. It was pinging even as I slid the notifications to "off."

I took a deep breath. I could do this. Hadn't I, just minutes ago, been feeling encouraged? I had taken an objective stock of the situation and been encouraged. I had done that. I could face whatever was in those comments. I didn't know any of these people. They could think I was a monster or they could think I was a hero—it was nothing to me. I just had to get an idea for what I needed to do next.

I hovered over the Reddit app the same way I'd hovered over Les's number. I thought I was going to throw up.

"She okay?" Frank asked.

I lifted my head and stared blankly at him. "Huh?"

"Viv. She's not in trouble, is she?"

"Oh, that. No. No, she's fine, just kind of..."

I looked down at my phone and drew in a breath as I realized that

I'd accidentally hit the Reddit app while I was looking at him.

My stomach lurched again, even as my head thought, *I'm going in.*

At first, it was not that bad. *"I'm sorry that happened to you. You have to tell, though. It will be tough, but you have to tell."*

That seemed fair. And kind. Emboldened, I scrolled. *"Why bring this up now? It probably has nothing to do with her running away and will only confuse things."*

"Thank you," I whispered. Because I wanted nothing more than to get a shovel and bury this whole memory back where it belonged.

"Way to make it all about you," one commenter said.

"Kiss my butt," I whispered to *that* horrible person. Doing so made me feel even bolder. See, I could handle negative feedback just fine.

"I get that you were a kid, but you're obviously an adult now, if you're posting here. As an adult, you have a responsibility to keep vulnerable people safe. I can't imagine why you would even need to ask this. Of course, you would be the jerk."

I sneered a little. *Easy for you to say,* I thought.

"If I could lock up every person who doesn't report their abuser, I absolutely would," said another. *"Imagine knowing that a guy is a child predator and not saying a word. Just letting them roam free, able to hurt someone else. YTJ!"*

"You're 29? And still afraid to report? That's just ridiculous! Grow the freak up and take some responsibility!"

"Why would you wait so long to report this? What state do you

live in? The statute of limitations could still be open if you're only 29."

I gasped. Could it? I had assumed that the time had long since passed to report Shawn.

I had assumed I was, therefore, off the hook, I realized with a sinking sense of dread.

"How do you sit across from this woman while she's looking for her sister and not tell her this? What is wrong with you?"

I was relieved to see that someone had responded to that one in my defense. *"What's wrong with her is that she's been traumatized by childhood abuse. It has a way of messing with your mind, if you didn't know. A little kindness would help."*

"That girl is probably dead or being trafficked right now, and you could of done something to prevent it. Hope your happy with yourself. YTJ."

Ugh.

I heard something, and realized that Frank was staring at me and sniffing. Sniffing again. What?

Then *I* sniffed and realized that something was burning. I stirred frantically at the ground beef, which was, in fact, getting a bit pebbly and dark on the bottom. I put the phone down and opened the can of Sloppy Joe mix.

You could have done something to prevent it.

The statute of limitations is probably still open.

What is wrong with you?

I dumped the sauce into the ground beef and opened the oven to turn the fries. They, too, were a bit dark on the bottom.

"She stopped pinging," Frank said.

I looked up and nodded. "Yeah, she's..."

I didn't finish. I dove back into the fray, unable to stop myself.

"And while you're writing this, that pervert is out there, happy and looking for his next victim. Get the freak off of Reddit and do something about it."

I froze, put the phone down. How had it not even occurred to me that he was still out there, right now—like, he could possibly be *at this very moment*, grooming another kid. Right now. While I was burning French fries, he could be ruining another little girl's life.

I gagged. What *was* wrong with me?

I needed to talk to someone who might tell me there was nothing wrong with me. I needed to talk to Tony.

I checked my text messages. I checked my voice mails. Nothing from Tony. Did I call him again? Leave him yet another message?

I didn't trust myself to speak, so I texted him.

Hey, how's everything going? Do you maybe want to come over later?

I waited a few seconds for him to respond, then opened Facebook and searched on Shawn's name. If he was married or dating a woman with children, I was going to...I didn't know what I was going to do.

There were four men and one woman with his name. Shawna, I realized numbly.

The top one was him, though. We had no mutual friends, I was relieved to see.

His profile pic made me gag again. Wide, white smile. He was handsome in a devilish, bad-boy way.

"Sun's out, guns out," he had posted. He held his hand up in the signature Texas Tech Red Raiders hand/gun signal. Apparently, this had been taken on the day of the first Red Raiders football game last year.

Tailgating with my homies! he had written with the post of him standing at the back gate of a white pickup truck. *"Lucky for these guys I agreed to use the new pickup."*

I flipped idly through his pictures. Grinning from the prow of a fishing boat, a rod and reel and cans of beer in the background.

A beautiful sunset. *"Check out this sky in Wyoming! Worth the drive up here just for this."*

Another shot of a traffic jam, from a high vantage point. *"They'll finally get I-35 finished after I'm retired."*

I flipped back to his profile page. "Long haul trucker for Elite Moving," was listed under Worked At. "AAA Driving School" under Studied At.

Under Family and Relationships, there was only his mother, Susan. I stared at her ugly face for a while, feeling all the revulsion and rage that those commentors on Reddit were probably feeling for me. Susan was the one who'd thought it was a fine idea to put my seven-year-old self into bed with her eighteen-year-old son.

I tapped her profile and looked and...yep, there she was. My own dear mother. Was mom even friends with *me* on Facebook? I couldn't remember. I thought she was and I'd just stopped following her one day when I was especially bitter that she had, finally and to everyone's great surprise, married a guy who was not only *not* a bum, but could provide her a seemingly endless supply of luxuries to humble-brag about on social media. I knew I hadn't seen much from her lately, but as I checked and, oh good! She had posted fresh pictures from their long weekend trip to South Padre Island. "So glad we could get down here before all the Memorial Day craziness starts!" she wrote.

"Yeah, well, my dog has a four-hundred-dollar bed," I muttered.

I sighed. I was getting myself into a spiral. I needed to make sure Shawn didn't have a girlfriend or someone who had kids he could access. I searched through his posts, then did a search on posts with his name on them, and didn't find anything that raised any alarm bells. That didn't guarantee anything, of course, but still, I breathed a sigh of relief.

I went back to his pictures. He looked so happy. I knew that social media wasn't the best indication of how happy or unhappy a person's life was, but...ugh. That he had spent even five minutes actually feeling as happy as he looked...it made me furious.

He was a truck driver. Alone on the open road. Access to who knew how many little girls.

I turned back to Reddit to read through the rest of my replies.

It had turned even uglier. The general consensus seemed to be that, although it was reasonable that I hadn't reported when the abuse happened because I'd been so young, there was no excuse for not reporting the moment I became an adult. Of course, the moment I *had* become an adult, I was already on a path of destruction borne out of that buried memory of Shawn, followed by more memories of more men. Although I hadn't known it at the time, I was already pregnant with Tony's baby when I turned 18. That destructive path just got worse after I lost the baby and left Tony.

I considered posting a response to explain this, but realized with this crowd, the "I'm sorry, I'd made an even bigger mess of my life by that point" excuse wouldn't carry a lot of weight.

"Get off your butt and put this guy away," one commentor said. *"Save that girl if it's not too late."*

"You're not only the jerk, you should also be charged as an accessory to whatever crimes he committed. Women like you disgust me."

"There is no excuse not to report this. You have no excuse."

"At the end of the day, you could have done something to prevent this girl's life being ruined and you chose not to. There is no excuse for allowing it to happen again."

I flipped back to look at Shawn's pictures. That grin.

I checked my texts. Nothing from Tony.

I set the phone down and rubbed my eyes. All I could see was that smarmy grin.

Shawn was grinning, while I felt like digging a hole and burying myself alive. That's where we were.

That was my life at the moment. He was happy, while I was being blamed for ruining the life of a girl I'd never met.

God, I prayed. *This is so wrong. This is so, so wrong.*

I picked up my phone and said a little prayer that Tony would reply, that I could go lie on his sofa, my head in the crook of his arm, and watch some boring World War II documentary or something, like he always wanted to do.

I checked my phone again. Tony had replied.

Not tonight, I'm beat. Work.

That was it. No, *How about you come over here?* Or *Maybe tomorrow night?*

In the living room, Frank sniffed again.

I looked at him. I had to get out of there.

Calmly, and with a sense of duplicity I had not practiced in almost two years, I smiled at him. It was weird, once I no longer cared for whether it was right or wrong, how effortlessly I slipped back into bald-faced lying.

"I'm sorry, but I have to go talk Viv out of doing something crazy and destructive. Dinner is ready." I pulled hamburger buns from the pantry and laid them on the table, turned the burner down low under the Sloppy Joes, and slid the fries from the oven onto the trivet on the counter. "Do you mind staying with Stump until I get back?"

"Sure," he said. He groaned and stood, letting Stump flop down onto the chair by herself. "We'll be fine. You don't want to eat before you go?"

"I'll get something while I'm out," I said calmly. I picked up my purse and grabbed the keys off the hook by the door. I was going to get one of those humongous fried chicken sandwiches at the Loose Caboose. And one of those glasses of wine I'd watched the women drink earlier. At least one. Probably five.

Chapter Five

Someone had hit me over the head with a sledgehammer. I did not know who or when, but that was the only explanation for why my head felt like it did when I woke the next morning.

I opened my eyes.

Oh, good *grief.* That *hurt.* That was awful.

I shut my eyes in the desperate hope that I could fall back to sleep. Of course, desperation is not an emotion that lends itself to sleep. I lay with my eyes closed, full of dread.

What was that smell? It smelled like vomit.

I didn't move. I didn't want to see where the vomit smell was coming from. Did I throw up in the bed? Was I lying in it right now? Could I please please please fall back to sleep?

Out of habit, I started to pray.

Immediately, I stopped. Nope. Forbidden territory. Not going there.

I lay still. Maybe I could just...refuse to function. Refuse to move. Refuse to think. Refuse to exist. I could just lie here, still, until my body quit functioning and I quit existing.

My mouth was dry. The inside of my body felt raw, scraped. My stomach was poised to take flight at any moment.

I would lie perfectly still until I died. I would not move. I wouldn't even open my eyes. I would just lie here, and eventually I would fall back to sleep, and if I woke up again I would just keep still until I went back to sleep.

My bladder was full. My stomach was jittery. It would all go away as soon as I went back to sleep.

Beside me, Stump snorted.

And I knew in that moment that I could not cease to exist. I had Stump.

I contemplated sighing, but I knew that would hurt, too. Even *contemplating* hurt. My entire body felt like I'd been unzipped from my skin, my insides rubbed hard against rough asphalt all over, then zipped back in.

I forced myself to sit, and immediately regretted it. The hammer hit the side of my head again, my stomach lurched, and I saw where the vomit smell was coming from—a wastebasket at the side of my bed. I'd been somewhat functional when I came home last night, then. Enough to prepare for the inevitable.

I stumbled to the bathroom but left the light out. There was nothing going on in here that I needed to see. All I wanted was to crawl back into bed as soon as possible.

I was home. I wasn't in jail. I'd gone out drinking, and somehow, I'd gotten from the bar to my trailer, which mean I had driven drunk, but I hadn't been arrested. That was one small mercy, maybe. It didn't rule out the possibility that I'd done some damage along the way.

Everything hurt, of course. My head, my stomach, every nerve. I needed to brush my teeth, but I wasn't sure I could stand at the sink long enough to accomplish that. Later. I would lie back down for a while and brush them later.

I flushed and lurched back toward the bed, stopping long enough to slide the wastebasket into the hallway. There was nothing left in my stomach to empty.

Hobbled over, I crawled back into bed and reached for the covers to pull over me. Stump waited patiently for me to cuddle up to her.

In the kitchen, I heard a noise. The fridge door?

"Who's here?" I whispered to Stump.

She didn't answer, of course, but she didn't look alarmed, either. So that meant it was Frank.

Oh no. Had Frank been here when I got home last night? Oh *no.*

I dropped into a deep ocean of shame. Over my head in it, going down down down.

Footsteps marched down the hallway toward me, and I panicked. I fell into the bed and hid under the covers.

"Drink this," said a voice that was definitely *not* Frank's.

I flipped back the covers to see a tall woman with a mohawk place a glass full of green-tinted water on my nightstand.

I looked at her and blinked. My mind wasn't working very fast, but it *was* working. I wasn't alarmed, just *very* confused. It was that Marine woman from AA. The one who'd said she would jump over me on the stairs the other day.

Were they...were they making *house calls* now?

I lay frozen with the covers drawn up to my chin.

She nodded toward the glass. "Go on."

I would not have been more confused if Tom Cruise had stood there, insisting I air up his bicycle tire. It was just...nothing made any sense.

"...what?" I finally said. My voice came out a croak.

"It's pickle juice. Prevents hangovers."

"Too late for that. What are you doing here?"

Instead of answering, she picked up the glass and held it out to me. "Your body needs the electrolytes. Trust me. It'll help get rid of that headache."

"Thank you, but I'm fine. How did you—"

"Drink!" She barked it so loud and hard that the pickle juice shivered in the glass.

I jerked upright and took the glass with hands that trembled. I drank a bit, then retched. Then drank a bit more.

She grinned a crooked grin, gave me a thumbs-up, then headed back to the living room.

I sat up in bed, my mind a whirl of confusion.

"What is she doing here?" I whispered to Stump. Then, "Is anyone else here?" I listened hard for the sound of Les, or Viv, or Frank. Absently, I raised the glass of pickle juice to my mouth and took another swallow. It actually wasn't that bad, after that first shock wore off.

Maybe she'll go away, I thought. If I just stay in here, stay quiet, maybe even go back to sleep. Maybe she'll go away.

That was so dumb, though. What kind of person hunkered under their covers while a strange Marine hung out in their living room?

Easy, I thought. *The kind of person who'd purposely driven their life off the rails. Again.*

"Dang," she called from the living room. "Four hundred dollars for a dog bed? How drunk were you when you bought that?"

I frowned at Stump and swung my legs over the side of the bed. *That* was a horrible experience, but I just kept going. I tried to make my steps sound forceful as I moved down the hallway.

"Look, I'm not sure how you came to be here or how you know how much my stuff costs—"

She leaned and lifted the price tag hanging off the corner of Stump's new bed.

"Well, that answers the second question. Not the first."

"I'm here to help you."

"I don't need help, thank you."

She cocked her head. "You're welcome. I know you saw the puke bucket beside your bed."

My insides shrank a little bit at that. "Okay, I probably did need help last night. But I'm fine now. You can leave."

"Sure, I'll leave. We need to get a game plan first, though."

Game plan for what? I thought, then decided it didn't matter. I just had to get her out of here. "Okay yeah, game plan. We'll do that, for sure. But right now, I really don't feel well, and I need to take a shower. So, we're going to need to do it later. Tomorrow. Maybe the day after."

She cocked her head again and grinned at me. Then she nodded. "Nice to see you so agreeable. You have to know that a six-foot tall woman with a mohawk is used to people saying *whatever* just to get rid of her."

As if to demonstrate how futile that hope was, she dropped to my recliner, elbows on knees, and nodded toward the sofa. "Cop a squat."

I looked out the window toward Frank's trailer. Maybe he would come over and help me get rid of her, somehow.

I knew that was a futile hope, though. Frank would either be more terrified of her than I was, or he'd be enamored with her.

Frank. Frank had been here when I left last night. He probably wouldn't have left Stump alone, even after my story about the magic bed.

Had he been here when I came home?

I crawled onto the sofa and wrapped the afghan around me. Stump butted up so I could pick her up. I cradled her to me. At that moment, her choosing to be held by me over lying in her majestic magic bed seemed like the purest declaration of love I'd ever had.

Mohawk Girl pulled her phone from her back pocket. "I've been reading through this site you told me about. Man. People are whacko, aren't they?" She looked at me and laughed. "I mean, this guy with the peanut butter? Insane." She shook her head and laughed.

My head hurt. The pickle juice wasn't working, and I had Amazon Warrior Woman on my recliner. I kind of wanted to cry, but I was too dehydrated.

I felt disoriented, too. Like I'd just woken up from a very vivid dream, except the dream had been the last two years of my life. And reality was here. That I was sitting on my sofa, hungover. Again.

I drank. I did it. I screwed it up. Everything. I'd ruined everything.

I *drank*.

I failed.

I was a failure.

I was still deep in that ocean of shame, the pressure so high it was crushing me, making it impossible to breathe, to hear, to think about anything else.

Fatalistic. That's how I felt. Nothing mattered. Why worry about an ex-Marine on my recliner? Why bother with anything?

"There should be an entire category just about weddings," she laughed as she scrolled. "I'm so glad I never got married. No way now, that's for dang sure." She read for a second, then scrolled some more and mumbled. "Not now that I know it makes you this crazy."

A flash of memory came back to me then, and a piece of the bizarre puzzle slid into place. "You drove me home?"

She lifted her head and met my eyes, her mouth open in a slight grin. "Girl. I knew you were out of it, but I didn't realize you were blackout drunk. Yeah, I drove you home."

"Did...did someone send you?" Had someone seen me? Called Tony, or Les, or Viv? I crashed again to the bottom of the shame ocean, waiting for the pressure to make my head explode and scatter with the undercurrent.

She nodded once. "Uh, yeah. Uber. Uber sent me."

I went weak with relief. I'd called Uber! I'd been too drunk to drive, so I called Uber.

And Uber sent this woman, who knew me from AA. Because *of course* they did.

I narrowed my eyes and thought, *I see what you did there, God.*

Still, this new information was making me feel somewhat better. "So, nobody...knows?"

She studied me for a moment. "You're not going to try that, are you? The whole 'nobody knows so it didn't happen' thing?"

"No," I said irritably. "And anyway, it's, what..." I turned and looked at the clock on the coffee maker. "It's almost eleven o'clock. You don't need to be here."

Suddenly, it hit me, and I jumped up. "It's almost eleven o'clock!" I shouted. "On a Friday! I'm supposed to be at work!"

"You called in sick."

"I did?" I sat heavily. "When?"

"You texted in sick. I texted for you."

"You *what*? You had no right to do that!"

"Well, your phone was on the bar and your boss texted, asking if you were okay. Well, here." She handed me my phone.

She handed me my own danged phone.

UOK? was the text from Flo at 8:15 that morning.

"Hey, this is Salem's friend. I had to give her a ride last night, she was really sick. She's in no shape to work today, IMO, but I can wake her if you need her there."

A full twelve minutes later, Flo had texted back. "No, if she's sick, let her sleep. Tell her to check in when she gets up, though."

"Oh no," I thought. I imagined the freak-out that Tammy and Flo had gone through in that twelve minutes. Tammy had probably called the police and reported me kidnapped by Bugsy Malone.

I called Flo. "I'm so sorry," I said as soon as she picked up.

"You're sick?"

"Yes." That was true. I was sick.

"We were worried. Well, you know. *I* was worried. Tammy's called all the hospitals, and now she's trying to find out how much it would cost to drag the lake. She's a couple clicks past worried."

I covered my face with my hands. "Nothing as dramatic as all that," I said. "Just, you know...stomach stuff."

"Well, I heard that was going around." No matter what ailment you had, Flo would say she'd heard it was going around.

"I'm sure I'll be in tomorrow," I said. "I'm feeling a bit better already, after sleeping in," I lied.

"Don't worry about it. Barbara has been asking if she could come back a couple days a week to make some extra money. I called her in, and she's here now."

Barbara had worked for Flo before I started at Bow Wow Barbers, but she'd quit when her daughter started having babies, because she wanted to keep the grandkids. I guessed that wasn't working out like she'd thought it would.

Well, too bad, Barbara, I thought. You're not getting my job. "I'm sure I'll be better by tomorrow," I repeated.

"No problem, we don't want your stomach bug up here. Stay home and get to feeling better."

"I will. And thank you."

"Pssh," she said. "Have you even taken a sick day the whole time you've worked here?"

"No, this is the first," I whispered. I'd ruined my perfect streak in that, too.

I hung up.

Mohawk Marine said, "See? It's all okay."

"No, it isn't. You had no right to do that. You can't just..." I gestured at the phone.

"I know, but it seemed like you weren't in any shape to go to work."

That she was right in no way made it okay. I moved to shut off my phone when I caught another glimpse of the texts.

Frank: your boss called me to see if you're okay. Are you okay?

Me: Ash here. She's still asleep. I just checked on her and she's breathing fine. Snoring.

Frank: Yeah, she snores.

I frowned. "You know Frank?"

Ash—because as soon as I'd read that, I'd remembered that yes, her name was Ash—said, "Well, after last night, yeah."

So he *had* been here. "And he just...left you here with me?"

Ash shrugged. "He was tired."

Good grief.

Okay, I'd had enough. I stood and said again, "Okay, well, it appears that everything is in order, so you really don't need to be here. Thanks for everything, but..." *Leave*, I didn't say, but hoped she heard anyway.

"Of course, I don't *need* to be here. But I'm here." She flipped her phone around showed me the screen, and again the shame sucked me under as I recognized the Reddit screen. "And I can see why you'd want to escape from this." She shook her head. "What a... *Dude*. This is just a nightmare all the way around."

I'd told her about the AITJ thing? Oh, good Lord. I'd told her about the AITJ thing. I was half still drowning in shame, but the other half grasped for the sympathy life preserver she was throwing me. *I was justified in wanting to escape from that.* Of course, I was.

She clapped a hand to her knee. "So anyway, now that your detour is out of the way, we can get moving."

I blinked. "Moving?"

She nodded. "Yep. On taking care of it. As far as you know, *your* girl is still alive. So, there's still time."

"*My* girl?"

She pointed to the phone. "Dude. Do you remember anything about last night?"

I shook my head, but as soon as I did, a few things began to filter back in. Leaning over the edge of the seat, laughing while I told her about the whole AITJ thing and how the entire Reddit world had come down on my head. Except when I told it, it sounded a lot funnier—like a comedy about a loveable loser who does, eventually, win the day.

She'd pulled over so I could get in the front seat, then pulled over again so she could read through a few of the comments. It has taken us a while to get back to Trailertopia.

Oh no. At some point, I remembered, I'd gotten mad.

I was not, generally speaking, an angry drunk. I had my moments, but usually when I got mad drunk, I just got belligerently goofy. Repeating myself, mercilessly teasing, annoying everyone around me.

"I'm the jerk!" I'd sang last night at the top of my lungs. Throwing up my arms, accidentally knocking against Ash as she drove, shouting, "Huzzah! All hail the Queen Jerk of Jerkdom!" I'd rolled down the window and screamed it at the passing streetlights. "All hail the seven-year-old jerk, betrayer of her own kind!"

I remembered sliding down in my seat, the wind cool on my face. I rested my head into the notch between the seatback and the door, mesmerized as each streetlight approached, growing brighter, brighter, then bam, full on dazzle in my eyes, then passing again. That was the last thing I remembered.

"See, the way I see things, this is a mission. Like—" Ash put her hand to her chest. "I was put here, you were put here, to fix this. To step in. Find this kid and bring her home."

"I wasn't put here to do that." I shook my head.

"We're both here," she repeated, oblivious. "I'm not even from here, but now I'm here. Randomly. In this place. In this moment. We both have knowledge and skills that can make a difference. It would be wrong not to do what we can to find her."

"I'm fine with finding her. I mean, I *want* to find her," I said. "I went over to their house and spent the day with Viv, interviewing people and scoping out locations, just so I could see what I could do to find her. But..." I sagged into the sofa. My head hurt and I was swimming in the ocean of shame again. Who was I kidding? I wasn't equipped to deal with anything like this. "I can't. Also, you might have knowledge and skills, but I only have knowledge. I have no skills."

"You can't. But we can. You, me, Viv. We can."

Viv. I flipped the afghan over my head and slid down until my head rested on the sofa seat. Stump grumbled and shifted her position.

I could never see Viv again. Or Les, or Frank, or Tony.

Tony would not *want* to see me again. So, I supposed that should be some kind of relief.

Ash was silent for a few minutes, then said, "Okay, well. I'll give you until one o'clock. Then you're getting up, taking a shower, and we're going to get the game plan going. The first step of which will be, of course, to tell Les and Viv what happened last night."

Over the course of the day, I learned that Ash genuinely believed we had a divine appointment. She paced around my kitchen as she made toast, gesturing as she talked. "See, here's the thing. I had this—this *issue*. This problem." She cocked her head and narrowed her eyes at me. "You don't remember *anything* from our talk last night?"

I rubbed my forehead and tried to think. She had said something. That she was running from something.

"Big mistake," she had said. "Like, nuclear holocaust level mistake." At least, that's what I thought she'd said.

174

You're so self-involved, the voice in my head sneered.

"I only remember that you had a big mistake you were concerned with."

"But you don't remember what the mistake was?"

"You're not going to try that, are you? The whole, 'nobody knows so it didn't happen' thing."

She laughed and pointed a long, thin finger at me. "Aha! Yeah, you got me. Okay, yes. I have a thing. You have a thing. And I was just praying for help with *my* thing, and right then!" She snapped her fingers. "Right then, your ride popped up on my screen. I grabbed the ride, and then when I saw it was you, who I'd just seen a few days ago—you remember that, right?"

I nodded. "Yes, on the stairs."

"Right! On the stairs. Anyway." She opened my fridge door and stood back, perusing. She turned to me. "Butter?"

"In that bowl."

"Oh," she said. "No real butter?"

"I'm trying to lose weight," I said.

She sighed and pulled the bowl of fake butter out and popped it onto the counter beside the toaster.

"Anyway?" I prompted.

"Oh yeah. Anyway, it's definitely a sign. Right? I pray, then immediately I get a ride and it's you, who I know, and you're –" She gestured wildly. "I mean, you're in the throes of a full-on meltdown crisis. Like, you *needed* someone like me. Not someone *like* me—you needed me. And I was there."

"I needed an Uber driver. And you're an Uber driver."

"An Uber driver who just happens to know that you're twelve days away from your two-year chip. An Uber driver who knows this is no ordinary bad night. This is a bad night that needs. My. Help." She finished scraping butter onto the toast and slid the plate over to me.

I eyed it warily. The ridiculousness of this situation occurred to me again. I did not know Ash, no matter how she acted like we were brought together by divine intervention. She could be just toying with me before she poisoned me and stole my stuff. She'd already identified the most expensive thing in my house.

My stomach still felt unpredictable, but I was pretty sure the pickle juice had actually done some good. So maybe this would bring an improvement, too.

I took a tentative nibble and swallowed. Nothing horrible happened, so I took another one.

I had to admit, I thought Ash was full of nonsense, but her theory held a certain appeal. I mean, if the last few days had all been a part of a plan to get me and her together so we could join forces and find Gia...that kind of let me off the hook, right? I was just part of God's plan?

But even as my mind began to entertain this notion, I knew it wouldn't wash. God might have led me into this situation to help Gia, but I couldn't believe me going to Loose Caboose and drinking countless drinks was part of the overall plan.

And if it *had* been...well, that was one messed up plan. To get me so low that I turned, desperately, to drinking after almost two years of sobriety...

I slid down and laid my head on the bar. I stared at the toast plate, at eye level.

"You going to hurl again?" Ash asked, reaching for the waste basket beside the fridge.

"No," I said. I reached for the toast and took another nibble, my head still on the bar. "I'm just going to lie here and think about having zero days of sobriety."

Ash wouldn't leave until Frank came home from work. I thought several times about trying to make her leave, but the truth was, she hadn't poisoned me, and she was upbeat (if odd) and nonjudgmental. Besides, I wasn't prepared to be alone just yet.

Also, there was no point. She would leave when she was ready to leave, and not one moment before.

She'd made initial contact with Les for me, letting him know that I needed to talk to him. He would be selling ice cream out of his truck at the First Friday Art Trail that night but said he could get away for a few minutes if we met him up there.

"You didn't tell him?" I asked her.

"Of course not. That's your job."

Ugh. I didn't want her to tell him, but I didn't want to do it myself, either.

I had to, though. I'd probably be a lot better off if I'd just told him everything two nights ago, the first time I'd seen Shawn's picture. Hindsight was not only 20/20, it was *really* obnoxious.

I texted Viv. "I'm going to First Friday Art Trail tonight to talk to Les. Can you meet me there? I have some stuff to discuss."

I got the three dancing dots immediately. "Yep! I have some stuff to go over, too."

Once Frank got home and came over to check on me and Stump, Ash left. "I'm gonna shower and change, and I'll be back in about an hour. Be ready to jet then."

Frank and I sat in uncomfortable silence after she left.

Finally, I said, "So. You were here when I got home last night."

He nodded.

"I was drunk."

"Oh yeah. Way. Way drunk."

"That's the first time," I said. I don't know why I felt the need to defend myself to Frank. He wasn't a fellow AA member. He wasn't a family member. He wasn't an accountability partner.

But he was a friend. And he cared about my sobriety—I knew that.

I suddenly remembered that he *was* a friend who'd left me with a complete stranger while I was incapacitated, though.

"You just left me with her!" I said. "I didn't even know her."

"No? She said you were in the same AA meeting."

"Well, we have gone to the same meeting a couple of times, but I don't know her well enough to—to pass out drunk with her in my living room."

"Umm, well...you had already done that when I left, so..."

I sighed. I had to concede that point.

"I wondered if it was a good idea to leave," he confessed. "But to be honest, she kind of scared me."

I frowned. I was kind of scared of her, too.

"Do you think she's seeing anybody?" Frank asked.

"You *promise* you haven't told Les?" I asked.

Ash cocked her head at me. "How are we not past the point of lying about anything, here?" She waved a hand around the trailer. "I mean, come on. All the secrets are spilled. Everywhere."

"Not all of them." I folded my arms across my chest. "You've told me that you have a big secret, but not what it is."

"Okay, A, I did tell you, you were just too drunk to remember. And B, I'll tell you again, but that will keep. One major malfunction at a time." She twisted her mouth. "Look, yours wasn't a major malfunction. Mine definitely was. But I still think we need to deal with one big ugly hairy deal at a time, and my whole situation is a big ugly hairy deal."

I frowned. "I actually kind of want you to tell Les," I confessed. "Let the cat out of the bag."

She shook her head. "Sorry, this cat is your responsibility. I'm only going to be there to make sure you follow through. No way to get better until you get this part taken care of."

"And what are you going to do if I don't?"

She took a deep breath, drew herself up to her full height, hardened her jaw, and glared at me.

I felt myself shrinking in reaction. "Jeez-o-Peet, okay, yes, I'll tell him." My heart was actually thudding, even though I was pretty sure she was just bluffing.

She deflated with a laugh. "That was fun. I love doing that."

We got into her car to head to the arts district. My stomach was in knots. "Oh, another thing I should warn you about," I said as I buckled myself in. "It's possible Viv will get jealous of you. We're pretty good friends, and I wouldn't be surprised if she's upset that you knew I drank before she knew. I hope she won't make too much of a stink, but I never really know with her."

"Oh, I get that," Ash said as she drove, one lanky wrist resting on the steering wheel. "But like I said, I think it was a God thing. She can't argue with God's timing."

"You don't know Viv very well at all."

It was early in the evening, but the weather was so picture perfect that the crowds were already filling the streets. We parked in the library parking lot and joined the group of pedestrians walking over. The monthly Art Trail drew a diverse crowd—high school kids with friends or dates, young families with kids, young couples, old couples, groups of girls, groups of guys. They all mixed and mingled together, and they all looked so happy. Relaxed.

It made me furious.

I wanted to be relaxed and happy. I wanted to be looking forward to a leisurely stroll looking at beautiful paintings and weird paintings and inexplicable collections of what looked very much like trash stapled to canvases and painted over with whitewash and pretend that I could appreciate what the artist was saying about the nature of man or something pretentious like that. I wanted to be focused on how good the soft evening breeze felt as the sun dipped toward the western horizon, how good the street tacos and fajita trucks smelled.

I didn't want to be defensive, already preparing for the look of disappointment on Les's face, the look of betrayal on Viv's, I didn't want to be running through the arguments in my head, defending myself by ranting about how upset and stressed I'd been, how confused and awful I'd felt.

It hit me suddenly that Shawn could be here. He could be one of these grinning faces, walking around with a woman on his arm. A young, divorced mom who thinks he's the answer to all her problems.

He would be smiling that charming smile, buying her kid an ice cream, treating her like she was the light of his life. Of course, he would.

That thought made me even angrier. Why should he be here having fun while I had to play the penitent for being a normal human being who sometimes needed help to handle the unfair traumas of my life?

"Holy smokes, what's got you so bent out of shape?" Viv stopped dead in the middle of the sidewalk in front of us. "You look ready to murder someone."

Viv wore ripped boyfriend jeans with a breezy white linen blouse with a French tuck. Her skinny tanned feet sported a high gloss maroon pedicure and gold sandals, and a turquoise anklet circled one ankle. She wore large Audrey Hepburn sunglasses and a small lime green crossbody bag rested against her hip. Stacks of thin gold and silver bracelets hung on each wrist.

She could have been one of the artists. She looked fashionable and just a touch eccentric with her white hair and age-defying wardrobe. One would think that a late-20s woman would not feel like a frump next to her octogenarian friend, but then, one would not know Viv. Or me.

The Lovely Joanna popped back into my head. Joanna would probably be like Viv when she got older, too. Still managing to hold onto her figure, still managing to walk around looking like a supermodel no matter what she was wearing.

"I'm fine," I said, in a very pouty way. And then, because I was kind of jealous of Viv and wanted her to be jealous of me, I turned to Ash. "This is Ash. Sorry I haven't talked to you much today. Ash and I have been hanging out."

Ash stuck out her hand. "I've actually met you before."

Viv had her mouth open as she took in Ash's combat boots, tank top and cargo shorts. "Oh, I think I would have remembered you." She looked at Ash's toned arms and I could see the wheels in her head turning to "how do I get arms like that?" Viv held out her hand. "What a pleasure to meet you!"

We found an empty picnic table in the center of all the food trucks. I waved at Les in his ice cream truck. He waved back, and then turned to Bonnie and said something. She looked over and saw us and smiled, and waved, then shooed him on his way.

He climbed down from his truck a bit stiffly, and it hit me suddenly that he was older, too. I mean, I knew that, obviously. He had grown sons, and Bonnie was his third wife, after the first one divorced him when he went to prison for robbing a bank, and the second wife married him in prison, then divorced him when he got out.

I wouldn't say I thought of Les as a father, but definitely like a favorite uncle. I thought he saw me as family, too. You get invested in the lives of your AA friends. You get invested in their success.

You get a little sad when they fall. I mean, you jump in to do and say whatever you can to build them back up. But it's sad, knowing they were in that dark place. You imagine them in that moment, when they felt lost or desperate or resentful or...whatever, whatever emotion that sent them over the edge. You can relate, because you've been there – there, or a place very much like it. And it's just sad, knowing they were alone and so low in that moment.

I was about to make Les sad, and that made me sad.

Behind me, the happy crowd in line at the wine truck laughed and chatted and just sounded obnoxiously cheerful in general.

For a second, I considered excusing myself to run to the bathroom, then sneaking around to the wine bar at the front of the building and chugging a cup. Just one. Just one of those clear plastic cups of wine would make this so much easier. I mean, it would have been completely hypocritical, but I would have felt better. Bolder. Less like screaming and ripping apart my own body at the throat so I could flee the scene.

My knees bounced as I tried to return Les's smile. Les nodded toward us. "Miz Kennedy, Ash, Salem. How are you all doing this fine evening?" He slid into the seat beside Viv with a groan.

"This is Ash," Viv announced. "She was a Marine and now she's an Uber driver. And she has a mohawk!"

Les nodded as if he hadn't already greeted Ash by name and couldn't see Ash, and her Mohawk, sitting right in front of him. "Very cool," he said.

"Very cool," Viv echoed.

I had honestly not anticipated that Viv would get a woman-crush on Ash. I guessed this was better than her being jealous, though.

I cleared my throat. "Ash was my Uber driver last night," I said. Might as well get it out there.

"Is that right?" Les said. His voice was calm, careful. Waiting.

"What a lucky break," Viv said. "Hey, why did you need an Uber? Did your car break down?" She looked shocked. We'd all come to the conclusion that my 1974 Monte Carlo was immortal.

"No, I was..." My throat closed, though, and I couldn't finish.

Les nodded, expectant. It dawned on me then that he already knew. I believed Ash when she said she hadn't told him. But he could see it on my face, hear it in my voice, in the way I was avoiding words.

"So," I said. Then swallowed again. "She picked me up from a bar, where I'd gone to get drunk. I got drunk last night. I drank."

He just kept nodding. Honestly, I had not known what to expect, but there was absolutely no reaction. Nothing. For a moment, I wondered if he'd heard me. If I'd really even said it.

But Ash patted my back, Viv blinked and drew her head back. They had a reaction. But Les didn't. And the enormity of this hit me. For Les, there *was* no change. My drinking changed nothing for him. He didn't see me as one bit different than he had yesterday. He wasn't disappointed. He wasn't angry. He wasn't sad. He was exactly the same as he was when I saw him at the meeting on Tuesday.

My failure had changed nothing in his eyes.

I burst into tears.

Viv had been about to say something, but she stopped when I began to sob. She looked awkwardly from me to Les, then narrowed her eyes at Ash. "Did you---did you have something to do with this?"

185

"I was just the Uber driver home," Ash said. "A divine appointment, I think."

Les let me cry. Viv watched in uncomfortable silence, then, apparently compelled to do something, she patted my hand.

That made me snuffle a soggy laugh. I knew Viv loved me, but she was the most undemonstrative person I knew.

Les reached into his pocket and pulled out a cotton handkerchief. "It's clean, I promise," he said as he slid it across the table at me.

"Not for long." I took it and wiped at my eyes and nose. I kind of wanted to look around and see if anyone was staring at the sobbing woman at the picnic table, but I decided I was better off pretending we were in an invisibility bubble. It was too late to save face now.

I cried myself out, which took a while. Every time I thought I had it under control, I looked at Les and lost it again. I think it was just what I needed, though, because by the time I'd folded the handkerchief three times, I was thinking that maybe this whole situation was less cataclysmic than I'd taken it to be. I knew there were uncomfortable—maybe even painful—conversations ahead. But I'd lived through this one. I could face the others.

Once I appeared able to hold a conversation, Les said, "Tell me what happened in the days and hours leading up to it."

I took another deep breath and let it out with a sigh. "That's the thing. I feel like—I feel like I'm in a bit of a mess here." I turned to Viv. "It's this Gia Perez thing."

"Is it Helena? I mean, the woman is scary. She kind of made me want to drink the other day, too."

"It's not Helena. Well, it's kind of Helena." I looked at Ash for encouragement.

She nodded. "You're doing great," she said. "Get it all out there."

Viv looked at Ash with naked idol worship. "You are so smart and encouraging!" She whipped her gaze back to me. "She's right. You're doing great. Be brave. Get it all out there."

So, I got it all out there. I told them about looking through the pictures and recognizing Shawn -- "I knew there was something off with you that day!" Viv said—and about my hesitation to tell them. *Why* I didn't want to tell anyone.

That got me another pat on the back—kind of a rough one, to be honest—from Ash, and another hand pat from Viv. Les whispered, "Lord, in your mercy."

"So, anyway," I said. "I was already agitated over whether I should tell what I knew about Shawn, and trying to figure out the best way to handle it, and then yesterday afternoon when Helena and her cousin had been watching the news about that Hollywood producer getting arrested... the way they bashed the women who knew how dangerous that guy was and didn't warn everyone. They said those women were as guilty as he was." I shrugged. "And, like, I know that there is no way to tell if Gia's disappearance has anything to do with Shawn. I have no way of knowing if he ever even touched her. It was over five years before she left, and by all indications, she had been doing better the last year before she disappeared. No one seems to know why she did it. But—"

"But you still feel responsible in some way?"

I nodded. "And...well, last night when I went back to the Loose Caboose—"

"You went back *there*?" Viv looked perplexed. "That wasn't even a very nice place. Way too noisy."

"Well, I told myself that I went back there because I wanted to talk to the bartender and show her Shawn's picture. And I did do that," I said, in my own defense. "She said he did come in from time to time.

"Oh, so he's like, a *regular*?" She crossed her eyes and spoke in a derpy voice.

Despite everything, I had to smile. I nodded. "Yes, he's a regular. There's every possibility that he could have been there when Gia and Sierra were there the last day of school. We don't know that, of course. But it could have happened that way. Maybe Shawn was there that day. Maybe she saw him, and it scared her. Maybe she was acting mad, but really she was scared."

Les tapped my hand. "Let's put that aside for a moment, okay? You need to help yourself before you can help Gia. Understand?"

I nodded. "You're right."

Les shifted in his seat, then put his elbow on the table, his hand over his mouth, and studied me for a moment. "So, you went home and thought about what Gia's sister and aunt said, and that bothered you so much, you decided to go drink?"

"Well..." I didn't really want to get into the AITJ thing, because then I'd have to explain *that*, and that whole part suddenly seemed silly and pointless. That wasn't the reason I drank. Not really.

I could feel Ash beside me, though, waiting for me to bring it up.

I sighed, and did my best to describe, succinctly, how I had made a post about my darkest secret and asked total strangers to judge me.

"I was just very confused," I said helplessly. "Trying to figure out what to do next."

Les nodded. "Well, that's one way to handle it, I guess."

Viv looked at Ash. "Maybe we should go get some tacos and let these two talk it out."

As they walked away, I called to Viv, "Bring me back something, please."

Explaining 'Am I The Jerk' to Les was painful. He grasped the main concept—people post their conundrums or conflicts, and the public weighs in. What he couldn't seem to get through his head was...why?

"Are there points involved?" he asked. "Does anybody...win?"

"Well, no. You could get advice that you can use. Or you could get confirmation that you'd done the right thing. Or, you could get clarity on what you've done wrong. People rarely do get clarity, though. They argue their point and flounce out in a huff, more often."

"Flounce out in a huff." He cocked his head. "Salem -- "

"It's just a figure of speech." I wasn't doing such a great job of explaining it.

Viv and Ash came back with street tacos wrapped in foil. I grabbed one and dug into it. Ash stepped over the bench seat and sat with a satisfied sigh. "Want any of this?" She held out a little plastic cup full of hot sauce. The one that had the orange and red paper dots glued to it. That indicated the highest possible heat level.

I gave her the side eye. "You remember how empty my stomach is. If I swallowed that now, it would eat a hole right through my gut."

She nodded. "Good point."

"I'll have some," Viv said.

"It's super hot," Ash warned.

"I know that. Slide it over here." She took a plastic spoon and dug into the sauce.

"That's a lot," Les said as he watched Viv smeared a thick strip of sauce onto her taco. "A little bit of that goes a long way. Think in terms of drops, not dribbles."

"Would you all please stop treating me like an infant? I know what I'm doing." She wrapped the doused taco in a napkin and bit off a big chunk.

I had to hand it to Viv. She did everything in her power to maintain the appearance that she wasn't a flaming mass from the inside out. Her eyes watered, her skin turned red, and I could see the vein at her neck begin to throb.

Oblivious, Ash enjoyed her taco, taking in the crowds around us as she chewed. Finally, she swallowed and took a deep breath. "Whew! That'll get the blood pumping." She shook her head and drank some of her iced tea.

Viv lurched for her own cup and gulped down half of it. "Whew," she croaked. Tears leaked from the corner of her eyes. She eyed the rest of her taco with horror. "Yummy."

Les and I covered our amusement as we watched them eat, and I felt myself begin to relax a little. The cat was completely out of the bag. Now we could move forward.

But Les was still scrolling through the Reddit screen. Finally, he sighed and handed the phone back to me. "Okay. So, you had a difficult day, and you turned to this—" He pointed to my phone. "You turned to this to help you make sense of it. Do I have that right?"

I shrank a little and nodded. Upon reflection, it did seem like maybe not *quite* the brilliant idea 'yesterday-me' thought it was.

Les smiled at me, and that softened the blow a bit. But only a bit. "Salem. Tell me what we say at the beginning of every meeting?"

I cleared my throat. "Rarely have we seen a person fail who has thoroughly followed our path. Those who do not recover are people who cannot or will not give themselves to this simple program, usually men and women who are constitutionally incapable of being honest with themselves."

He nodded but didn't speak. Instead, he studied me for a long time. Then he said, "How often do these people tell the poster unanimously that they're not the jerk?"

I thought. "Never, actually." I couldn't remember ever seeing one that was 100 percent NTJ.

"There's always at least someone telling them they've handled things wrong."

I nodded. "Pretty much, yeah."

"So, you knew there was a very high chance that, on top of Gia's sister's and aunt's words, and on top of the anxiety you already felt, you would subject yourself to more judgement, more shame."

I cocked my head. *Had* I known that? Of course, I'd known that, on some level. I had to. I'd spent weeks reading the flaming comments on this dumb website.

"Throw this whole man away."

"Can you imagine having to live with this woman?"

"Launch this person straight into the sun."

And yet, I'd dragged my barely-clinging-to-sobriety self right into this lion's den and bared my most vulnerable self to them.

Les waited. I knew what he was waiting for. What's my part in this?

Finally, he said, "And what were you hoping to gain from that?"

I shook my head. "I don't know, Les."

"Have I ever told you that in all my years with AA, you might be the most honest-with-herself person I've had the pleasure to walk alongside?"

I wanted to be flattered, but I also knew what he meant: he didn't think I was being honest with myself right then. "I mean, I honestly didn't go in there looking to feel *worse*, Les. It was shockingly awful with all of them raining fire down on me."

"Doesn't mean you didn't walk right into it. You knew it could be awful—that it probably *would* be awful. You knew you could end up feeling worse than you did before. But you chose that route anyway. Why?"

I thought again about Helena and Janet, their sneering contempt for that actress.

"She's as much to blame as he is."

But that wasn't true. Could not be true.

Was it true? "Do you think I was looking for someone to *blame me* for Gia's disappearance?"

Les shrugged. "I don't know, Salem. Were you?"

I could feel fresh tears welling. "I don't know." Was I?

The emotions I'd experienced reading all those comments rose to the surface again. It *had* been awful. And yet...I hadn't been able to look away. I'd sat at the bar and drank my wine and read those comments again and again. I had some of the most hurtful phrases memorized. It was like a sore tooth that I couldn't stop poking with my tongue. Just...much worse. So much worse.

"Salem. Why would you seek out the opinions of people who don't care about you? People who you knew would be unkind, would be cruel, instead of coming to the people who know you and care about you?" Les gestured to himself, Viv, and Ash.

"I felt like...I just wanted an objective opinion on the situation."

"And we can't be objective?"

"Well, no," I admitted. "I'm sorry, but I don't think you can. You'd be more concerned about, you know, being *kind* to me. You would avoid saying anything that would cause me more shame."

He leaned his arms on the table and met my gaze. "And do you not deserve that, Salem? You don't honestly, objectively deserve kindness? You don't honestly, objectively deserve to avoid further shame?"

A few seconds later, Viv said, "There she goes again. Good grief. How can she still have any tears left in there?"

Ash got up and grabbed a handful of coarse paper napkins from the condiment table and brought the crumpled bunch back to me.

As I sobbed anew, Viv grasped this handy excuse and folded up the remains of her molten lava taco and said, "Who can eat with all this drama going on?"

Les covered my hand with his. "There's a meeting at the hospital in half an hour. Go to that. Go to another one tomorrow. Thirty meetings, thirty days."

"I know," I said weakly.

I'd often considered what would happen if I drank and had to start over with day one again. On that side of sobriety, with over 700 days and counting, the idea had felt awful.

But I was struck by how reassuring this felt. Thirty meetings, thirty days. I knew where thirty meetings could be found. And I knew what I would find in those meetings. Instead of defeat and shame, this felt like safety. Security. The last couple of days had felt like I was on a storm-tossed dingy in an angry sea. Now I was back on shore. Clothes still dripping, exhausted from navigating massive waves, making my way back inland.

Les stood and hugged me, echoing what was going on in my head. "God will never let us fall so far, Salem, that He isn't there to be the rock we land on at the bottom."

Les rejoined Bonnie in the ice cream truck. Ash and Viv went with me to the meeting. I said my piece. I took in the acceptance and comfort of my community. Drank it in.

Then I went home and collected Stump—and her bed, because I couldn't handle the thought of her choosing to stay with the bed instead of going with me—and piled it and a bag of clothes into my Monster Carlo. "I'm going to stay with Tony for a few days. I know he's been talking about how exhausted he is from work, but we have to do this together."

"Tony will be fine," Viv said. "You know Tony. He's a rock, and he'll be glad you came to him." She gave me an awkward hug.

"Steady as a rock," I agreed. It was going to be hard to tell him, but after telling everyone else, I had to do it. Get it behind me, so I could continue my journey inland.

I felt so sure, in fact, that I wasn't even surprised that he was home alone, with no sign of The Lovely Joanna. There would not be. Tony was telling me the truth. She was just an employee, and my wild suspicions were nothing more than a sign that I needed to get my head on straight. I could see that now. I'd gotten off kilter. Allowed myself to become too isolated, too resentful, too proud, maybe, to speak up and ask for Tony's reassurance.

That was behind me. I may be flat on my back at rock bottom, but I could see clearly from here. Stump and I arrived on Tony's porch, and before I even got all of our stuff out of the car, I told him I needed to talk to him.

It was a good thing, as it turned out, that I hadn't taken our stuff into Tony's house.

Because half an hour later, I left again.

Shocked, devastated, numb.

I hadn't even gotten to the part where I asked for his reassurance regarding Joanna. I hadn't made it past, "I drank."

I hadn't even gotten to the part of *why* I drank.

"Salem, what is wrong with you? You're just – you're just too much."

I drove the dark streets of Lubbock for two hours. When my phone pinged with messages from Viv and Les asking me how it had gone with Tony, I lied: You know Tony. He's great. He's sad, but he understands, setbacks happen."

I can't do this anymore, Salem. I can't keep living like this, with this looming threat that you're going to go off the rails again hanging over my head.

Chapter Six

My G-Ma owned a motel on Clovis Highway that one might pass and think, "I'll bet that was a nice place, back in its day," but it had never been nice. It had probably been clean and reasonably priced. I'd spent half my childhood there, during periods when either my mom was dating a new guy and they 'needed time to get to know each other,' and having a kid got in the way of that, or they *had* gotten to know each other, and I'd gotten to know him, too, and to know he was a jerk that couldn't keep his hands to himself (most of them had that problem), or Mom was just finding life in general and child-rearing in particular too much to manage at the moment. G-Ma never seemed keen to have me around, but I was free labor, and I didn't talk too much. I cleaned the rooms, carried out the trash, and I was happy to run down to the dark little grocery store on the corner and get her Mountain Dews and Pringles when she wanted them. I slept in a back room that was supposed to be a storeroom and watched her 'stories' with her.

After the Interstate and the Loop were built, though, the neighborhood started to slide. It wasn't bad, it just wasn't good, and there were lots of nicer places to stay in town. G-Ma kept the place going, though; I guess she hoped by some miracle the neighborhood would once again be a hub of profitable activity, business would pick up, and she'd be sitting on a pretty investment. She rented out the attached diner to Mario, who made the best tamales you've ever had, and kept the whole placed patched together with wire ties and crossed fingers.

Then, a miracle happened. The city passed that revitalization bond package and offered a bunch of small business grants and subsidized small business and career training. G-Ma converted the skeezy motel to a quaint and quirky shopping center, each of the rooms going to its own separate small business. Some of her previous customers who had rented the rooms by the hour for businesses of their own (of the oldest profession variety) took advantage of the training and the grants and now ran perfectly legitimate businesses out of those same rooms, updated with pretty colors.

When I reached G-Ma's motel, I lied to her with a perfectly straight face. "My water heater busted and my trailer is flooded. The water is turned off for a few days, until I can get it fixed. I hate to do this, but Stump and I need to stay here."

I'd lost count how many times I'd carried hastily packed bags of my stuff into this once-seedy little motel. The tradition began with my mom, of course, but I made the trek a few times in adulthood, too -- after I'd been evicted for non-payment of rent or I'd gotten into fights with roommates. One time, the house I was renting was foreclosed on, and I came home to find all my stuff in the front yard.

G-Ma was accommodating up to a point. She said over and over again that she was done raising kids and wasn't going to raise anymore, and when I stayed there, she reminded Mom and then me every hour on the hour that this was only temporary. But, when push came to shove, she would open her door a tiny crack.

G-Ma had always been my reluctant, short-term port in all storms.

As I lugged our stuff inside one of the vacant rooms in G-Ma's motel that hadn't yet been rented out to a small business, I lied by omission and complained that the metal frame was what made the princess bed so heavy, neglecting to mention the three bottles of wine and corkscrew I'd hidden under the mattress.

I drafted a text of another lie of omission to Flo: s*o sorry, I'm still not holding anything down. Can you manage without me for one more day?* All I would have to do in the morning was hit send. If I hadn't drank all the wine by then, I could maybe even a have a couple of sips to fortify myself for that.

I might be constitutionally quite capable of being honest with myself, but I also had no problem lying to everyone else, I thought as I chugged wine from the bottle and inflated the air mattress G-Ma had dug out for me. Besides mine and Stump's beds, the room held only some half empty paint cans, a thin roll of leftover carpet from somewhere, boxes of toilet paper and paper napkins, and the old headboard that was still attached to the wall.

No television, but that was fine with me. What did I need to be distracted from?

"You want to be the rock I land on at the bottom?" I prayed with contempt in my heart. I lay on my air mattress, my legs stretched out in front of me, my head uncomfortably resting against the bottom of that old wooden headboard and stared out the dirty motel room windows to the night sky. "Fine. Here we are. Let's see how much lower we can go, shall we?"

I wasn't sure when G-Ma caught on to what I was doing, but I was certain it wasn't Sunday at 2 PM, which was when she finally kicked me out. She might have been onto me from the moment I showed up with that lame story about the water heater. It might have been Saturday around 11 AM, when she knocked on my door and told me I had to pick up Stump's poo from the sidewalk.

"This is a respectable business now, Salem," she said. "Women are going in and out of the coffee shop for their lattes and the bakery for their keto muffins, and they don't want to be stepping over dog poo to get there."

"Sorry," I said. I stood in the doorway to block her view of the room. I was pretty sure I'd put the empty bottles out of sight, but I wasn't firing on all cylinders, and I could have missed one. "I told her to go on the grass."

G-Ma put her hands on her hips and frowned at me. "Why aren't you at work, anyway? Saturdays are your busy days." She would know; I'd told her that plenty of times when she wanted me to move something or paint something or get something for her on a Saturday.

I put my hand on my stomach. "I'm sick. Some kind of stomach bug. Maybe you should back away a little bit—you don't want whatever it is that I've got." I didn't want her to smell the wine on me. I'd brushed my teeth—gagging the entire time—and did a sink wash the best I could with the paper towels. But I still might smell.

G-Ma did not share Viv's vomit phobia. She backed away, but I was pretty sure she knew what was up. She'd seen me in this state before.

She didn't call my bluff, though. She just said, "Well, whatever you've got, get it under control or take it to your husband's house. We have customers to think about." She nodded back down the sidewalk to the dog poo that, to be honest, I wasn't completely sure *was* Stump's. There could be a stray dog around.

Still, I nodded. I took a handful of paper napkins, picked up the poo, and managed to keep from gagging until I dropped it into the dumpster behind the motel. I would like to think that G-Ma would have offered to clean it up for me if she really believed I had a stomach bug, but the truth was, that would have likely played out the same way, regardless. G-Ma had sympathy, just not very much.

I sat on the air mattress, feeling nauseas and wretched, until I saw

G-Ma leave a few hours later. Then I ran down to the small grocery store on the corner and got one of those boxes of cheap wine, two boxes of crackers, a bag of chips, a couple of cans of Vienna sausages, three cheap gossip magazines, and a small bag of dog food for Stump. By the time I made it back to the room ten minutes later, a small crowd had gathered around the door.

Stump was howling. "Oh, I'm so sorry," I announced. Another lie. I was kind of glad to hear that Stump had missed me, even if the volume and intensity were down from a normal Stump meltdown.

Take that, princess bed, I thought as I edged through the knot of people at the door. "I didn't realize she would become so loud while I was gone." I had to let Stump out to run around and show everyone that she was okay, so I hid my bag behind the door and together, Stump and I walked slowly around the parking lot. The sun felt good on my head, and I felt the fog begin to lift a little.

With it, of course, the stark reality of what I was facing came into focus. If I kept on this track, I was going to lose my job. It *was* kind of a big deal to miss a Saturday at work. Flo was understanding and probably didn't suspect anything, but eventually, she would. G-Ma had seen me in this state before, and so had I. This was the point where I started promising myself that I would definitely do better tomorrow.

This was the point where I started breaking those promises to myself. Over and over and over.

Over the past months that Tony and I had been reunited, I'd told myself that I didn't want to rely on his success and stability to provide a net for me. I was proud that I'd dug myself out of my hole, and that, shabby as my little trailer was, I was self-sufficient.

Now that we were maybe (*maybe?* Had there been in ambiguity in what he'd said?) breaking up, I realized how much I had thought of him as my safety net. A net I hadn't used, yet. But a net I'd known was there, if I truly needed it.

That was gone now.

I stood with the sun on my back long enough for Stump to get tired of sniffing around the motel and come over to me to be picked up.

I checked the time on my phone. It was now mid-afternoon, in my time zone. I could drink again. Shove all these pesky fears back down where they belonged.

I'll do better tomorrow, I lied to myself. I'll take stock and figure out what I need to do.

I was not a fan of room temperature wine, but one does what one has to do. I'd nosed through some of G-Ma's stuff and found a box of those old paper mouthwash cups and told myself it was funny that I was getting drunk three ounces at a time. I flipped through the gossip magazines and read about celebrities I didn't recognize. I went back on Reddit and read more AITJ threads. I started to read the relationship thread, but that got to be too much, what with my own relationship probably (*probably?* Had Tony not been clear that he could *not* do this anymore?) ending.

Anyway, I relearned that one can, if need be, lock themselves away in a room and drink for hours, doing nothing productive, until one falls asleep, then wake up and drink some more, provided one has enough wine, become somewhat sober and achy so that the thought of drinking again sounds awful, and yet do it anyway. That is a thing that can and did happen.

When Les called me asking what meeting I was going to that day, I let the call go to voicemail, then texted a lie: "Sorry! I already went early this morning before work. I meant to tell you, but I was running late! Tony wanted to go with me, so we went to that open meeting over at St. Matt's."

When he called again Sunday morning to see if I was going to church, I texted, "Sorry! I'm with Tony! Can't talk now. I'll text when the service is over."

Viv did not text me, and I admit I got a bit hurt over that, but then Ash did text me to say Viv was "surprisingly intense for a woman her age."

I just replied that she wouldn't mention Viv's age if she knew what was good for her, and threw the phone to the end of the bed. I refilled my paper cup—this was my sixth cup because they grew a bit soggy and precarious after four or five rounds—and toasted the brilliant concept of reaping and sowing. I'd wanted Viv to be jealous of my new friendship with Ash and here I was, jealous of Viv's new friendship with Ash.

"Awesome job, God," I said as I raised the cup to the popcorn ceiling. "Do not allow me to learn any lesson the easy way, whatever you do."

Anyway, as I said, by 2 PM on Sunday, G-Ma had had enough. She didn't knock. She used her key and entered the room. She took in my bleary eyes, the paper bag of empty wine bottles near the bathroom sink and the empty junk food containers. She sniffed.

"Okay, you have to go," she said. "Are you drunk right now?"

I shook my head. I didn't think so. It was hard to say, though. The wine box was empty, but I couldn't remember how long it had been since my last drink. I felt a bit wobbly, but that could be from dehydration.

"Good. Get your stuff together and go home. Take care of whatever you need to take care of. Serena is saying there's a black cloud over in this part of the motel and it's harshing everyone's mellow."

Serena ran the new age shop down the row that sold crystals and whale music CDs. She read people's auras and was annoyingly cheerful about it. "Did she really say that?"

G-Ma waved an irritated hand. "I don't know, something like that. I only catch about ten percent of what she says."

Serena probably *had* something along those lines, but I was still a bit cheered to see G-Ma's dismissiveness. Serena had read my aura a few months back and, long story short, my choice to take her advice had led to me almost being shot by police while I was trying to avoid being shot by a bad guy. She could say whatever she wanted about my

207

black cloud and repressed aura, as long as she kept it over there with her wind chimes and rain sticks. I didn't need anyone making me feel insecure about something I wasn't even convinced existed.

"Does Tony know you're here?"

I shook my head again.

She studied me and sighed. I could see her weighing all the possible courses for her here. She could lend a sympathetic ear. She could offer to let me stay in the empty room. She could call Viv or Tony or—heaven forbid—my mom. Set up some kind of intervention.

But those were all messy options, and at her age, she was tired of all my messy options. She wanted no fuss. So, she just said, "Well, you should go see him."

I nodded as if I were considering that. As if it has slipped my mind that I had a husband I should check in with at some point. "Good idea," I said.

I gathered my things and lugged them all back to the Monster Carlo. At that point, I was wined out. I would get the craving later, I knew. But at the moment I just wanted to be back in my own home.

Sunday evening, I had a stern talk with myself. Frank sometimes had Sunday dinner with his family and stayed late there (I was convinced between me and Frank's mom, he never had to cover a meal for himself), and I figured that's where he was, because he didn't show up at my trailer. I wasn't going to drink, but then caved at around 6:30 because I sensed the "Monday's coming, better get a few in before the window closes" feeling. I drove down to the convenience store and bought two 16-ounce beer cans. At first, I had three, but I put one back and considered that a step in the right direction. I went home, popped the top on the first can, and thought things through in the peace and quiet of my empty house.

With the beer in my system, I began to think that I was, perhaps, making too big a deal of things. Yes, I had drank, but it was also true that relapses were common. Didn't mean I couldn't bring it back around.

Yes, Tony had been furious with me Friday night. And that had been a shock—Tony was so rarely furious; I hadn't known how to deal with it. He had forgiven me for so much more than just drinking, though. Once he calmed down, he would realize that this little setback was nothing. No reason to throw away what we'd built.

I was so sure that we could work things out, in fact, that I decided to text him. I stared at my phone for a long time, typing then erasing words, bits of phrases. Finally, I settled on, "Hey, just checking in. Wanted to make sure you were okay."

I waited for him to answer, then finally pulled up Reddit to pass the time. I comforted myself with all the AITJ stories that were clearly more YTJ than mine was: the guy who threw away his girlfriend's doll that her late father gave her because he thought she should be more mature if they were ever going to have kids. The mother of the groom who smashed the wedding cake because the bride's father had made a snide comment about her dress. The guy who insisted his girlfriend wear "more professional" dresses instead of the colorful, fun dresses she sewed to wear to her work as a Kindergarten teacher.

Yes, the stakes on these were a lot lower. But those people clearly had worse intentions than I did. They were trying to control and belittle the lives of people they professed to care about. I had just been trying to survive. All in all, I had managed to encourage myself until my phone dinged and I checked the texts. Hoping desperately for something along the lines of, "I'm so sorry I lost my temper the other night. Let's meet tomorrow and talk," I held the phone tightly to my chest and said a quick prayer.

I checked the screen.

A thumbs up emoji. Not even a word. Just a thumbs up emoji.

I stared at that for a long time. Then I opened the second beer.

When I feel asleep on the sofa Sunday night, I fully intended to be a responsible, fully-functioning adult Monday morning. It wasn't that late. I hadn't drunk that much. I could do this. Life officially back on track.

But 2 AM insomnia hit and derailed everything. Whereas the night before, I had been sure that I could resurrect something of my life, 2 AM me knew it was all already gone. I'd lost Tony, I'd lost my job, I'd lost my sobriety, I'd lost my trailer when I couldn't pay the rent, I'd lost my car when I couldn't make the very tiny monthly payment (and what 29-year-old loser drives—*is still making payments on!*--a car that's almost two decades *older* than she is, anyway? Pathetic.) True, only a few of those things had manifested themselves in reality yet, but the others were waiting in the wings— no, not even waiting in the wings, they were already on stage, milling about as background characters, just waiting for the cue to speak their line.

I don't think I've ever had a positive thought or emotion in the middle of the night. It's always doom and gloom. On sober days, though, I could comfort and encourage myself by pointing to the victories. I didn't drink today. The electricity didn't get cut off because of nonpayment. I wasn't hiding from someone I owed money to. Or from someone I'd insulted in a "don't-take-this-the-wrong-way-but-you're-kinda" drunken ramble.

But I *had* drunk. And I'd reached out to Tony and he'd sent back an emoji.

He could not handle me anymore. I was too much.

If the Prince of Patience, Saint Anthony himself could not handle me, then...

There really was no hope.

I knew I should pray. Pray for peace, for a quiet spirit, for rest.

Every time I tried, though...I just kept thinking that God let me walk into the Perez house and be blindsided by Shawn's picture. If Les was right, and God *was* wherever we were, then He knew what Shawn had done to me that night after we ate stale Dairy Queen tacos

211

and watched *Liar, Liar.* And still, he let me walk in there and experience that shock with no warning whatsoever. At a time when I was already feeling bruised and uncertain after encountering The Lovely Joanna and my uncharacteristically distant husband.

So...no. Seeking peace in that direction didn't feel like a thing I wanted to do.

Of course, there was no peace anywhere else, either. There was just me, lying in bed staring at the ceiling, going over and over and over every mistake I'd ever made, every wrong ever done to me, every disappointment.

Hard to fall back asleep like that.

By 5 AM, I was nodding back off, but I'd already decided that I wasn't going to work again. Mondays were much slower than Saturdays, so although I was pushing my luck to take a third day off, it was pushing less than I already had. And part of me had already accepted that I was going to lose this job, anyway.

I texted Flo my apologies again. I didn't expect to get a reply for a few hours, but she replied almost immediately.

"Well, drink some Sprite and eat some saltines. We can hold down the fort. Feel better."

That was easy. Flo was probably already planning to ask Barbara to come back and replace me permanently. Barbara didn't tease Tammy. She showed up for work.

I rolled over and hugged Stump to me. She grumbled in her sleep, then stretched, her little toes shivering at the end of the stretch.

Then she snored.

Right before I fell back to sleep, I checked my messages. Maybe Tony had texted me. Maybe he wanted...

Still just the emoji.

I dropped the phone again and pulled the covers over my head. Maybe I could just sleep for years and years and when I woke up, I could be someone else. I didn't want to be me anymore.

I slept for hours, not years. Long enough for the sun to come up and Stump to start whining to go outside.

Did I not do enough for you, Salem? Did I not forgive you enough? Was I not patient enough? How many years and years and years do you need?

Tony's rage-filled face appeared in my mind, and I groaned and rolled over. "God," I whispered.

But that was as far as I got. Morning had not brought any fresh faith in that direction.

Stump whined again, and I dragged myself to the front door to let her out. Then I crawled back in bed and thought about Sid and Helena Perez, about all the aunts and uncles gathered around. How many prayers had they prayed over the last year? How many candles lit? How many sleepless, desperate nights had Sid lain awake, wondering where his daughter was? How many hours had he driven backroads and dark streets, looking for her, praying the entire time?

And God tossed me into this mixture and said, "Here. Here's

someone who might help. She *won't* help. She never does. But let's just get some popcorn and watch this whole thing catch fire. Should be fun."

If I had set out to make the biggest, most painful, most hurtful mess I possibly could, I could not have done better than the mess I was living in at that moment. What kind of God did this?

Honestly? It felt abusive.

I thought about that for a second, a bit shocked at myself. But yeah. It felt abusive.

I threw back the covers and stomped to the front door to let Stump back in, then to the bathroom. I'd emptied my bladder, brushed my teeth and even washed my face before it dawned on me that rage had motivated me to do what self-care had not.

Now that I was in that mode, though, I thought, *why not?* I ran hot water and splashed my face and hair, scrubbing furiously with a washcloth as I built up a head of steam.

My head still hurt, and my stomach still churned, but I was too mad now to concentrate on that. I stomped to the other end of my trailer, breathing heavy, ready to let loose. Stump watched me go from her princess bed.

I snatched up the lighter and lit the three wicks, muttering through clenched teeth. Once they were all lit, I stood and faced the candle, hands on my hips, breathing hard.

"You know what?" I said to the candle. "Would you like to know *what?*" I jabbed a finger at the flame. "I'll tell you what! This is—" I

214

held my hands out and spun around, gesturing at the world at large. "This is a mess! This whole thing is a flaming, awful mess! That's what!"

I remembered my last prayer time, when I'd decided to use the Psalm of Praise. "Oh yeah!" I rummaged through my books and found my Bible, knocking over stuff and almost ripping a page as I slapped my way through the thin pages. "Okay, here! How about this?"

I turned to the flame and said, quite loudly, "Why, O Lord, do you stand far away? Why do you hide yourself in times of trouble?"

I used my fingers to hold my place and closed my Bible. "Well?" I shouted at the candle "Why?" I shook my Bible. "What are you doing? People down here want to know!" I remembered something from this particular Psalm and ran my finger down the page until I got to that part. "Yes! He sits in ambush in the villages; in hiding places he murders the innocent!"

I slapped the Bible closed again. "He *murders*! The *innocent*! And you're just up there—just up there letting it happen! How is anyone down here supposed to trust you when you just let stuff like that happen? Huh!? And I know what you're going to do—you're going to trot Les over here to share some kind of lesson about Free Will, blah blah blah. Well, you know what I think? I think this *free will* idea of yours is a complete and total loss. If you'd been paying any attention to the people without power for the last, what—thousands of years? If you'd been paying *any attention at all*, you would have noticed that free will means that people *with* power hurt people *without* power! Have you noticed that?" I was shouting now, and it made my headache worse, but I didn't care. "Have you even *noticed* that grown men are hurting little kids down here? Like, totally destroying their lives? Why is that okay with you? You've got--" I waved wildly about. "You've got pestilence and floods! You've got disease." I jabbed a finger at the flame. "You've got lightning, for Pete's sake! Why are you not sending a bolt of lightning down to freaking *destroy* every piece of crap pedophile who ever walked on this earth? Why are you not protecting every single little kid? How many kids have prayed to be saved from some monster, and you just sit up there on your ass and do *nothing*?"

I was screaming now, and crying. I stood over the candle and wanted to just slap the whole burning thing into the wall. I wanted to splash hot wax everywhere. I wanted to catch the place on fire. I wanted to burn the entire world down.

"Have you even noticed that the whole world has gone to hell down here? That innocent people are being abused and *dumped*? On the side of the *road*? Like *trash*?" I remembered that little patch of trampled grass and imagined the lifeless, decaying body on the side of that road. That body had belonged to a person. Someone's daughter. That body had once gone to the first day of Kindergarten, wearing new shoes and carrying a brand new backpack. That girl had been nervous about making new friends, been worried about getting lost on the way to the school cafeteria. That girl had probably had a crush on a teacher, had made a painting her mother put on the refrigerator, had seen something in the mall she really, really wanted to buy. That girl had a favorite song she sang along to at the top of her lungs, a song that made her feel like the world was a beautiful place of infinite opportunity, a place she could walk freely, a place she could fall in love, have an adventure. A song that made her feel as if the world was a good and safe place.

"It's all a lie, and you don't care enough to fix it!" I screamed. "We're all just collateral damage to you in your precious creation! You created us to have feelings and think it's no big deal if we're utterly destroyed! Acceptable if we're beaten down and tortured and left for dead. No big deal if our hearts are broken, are minds are completely screwed up, our relationships are ruined! You won't do a thing about it! Because you're--"

Someone pounded on my door.

I froze. My words stopped so fast they choked in my throat. Tears covered my entire face, dripped onto my pajama top.

The pounding came again. "Salem!"

Who was that? I tiptoed to the window and looked out.

Oh no. Tammy.

What was *Tammy* doing here? How did she even know where I lived?

"Salem, let me in!"

She sounded panicked, and that panicked me. Had something happened? Was Flo okay?

I snatched a few tissues out of the box and swiped at my face as I hurried to the door.

"What is—" I stopped as Tammy shoved past me. She held a gun.

"Where is he?" She darted glances around the living room and kitchen.

"Tammy, what's going on?"

She stepped past me again, then swung around to face back into the direction of the small bedroom. "Is he back there?" She shouted down the short hallway, "He's back there, isn't he?"

"Who? What are you—put that gun away!"

"That's right, I have a gun!" she shouted. "And I know how to use it! I'd loooove to use it!" She waved it wildly, and I believed her.

"Tammy, stop! There's no one here. Please—put the gun away."

"I will not!" She leaned close and whispered, "Is he hiding in the closet? He's hiding in the closet, isn't he?"

"Who," I whispered back, then realized there was no reason to be whispering. "Who? There's no one here except me and Stump."

"Good job," Tammy whispered, then winked at me.

"Tammy, there's really no on here."

"I know Polk is here," she hissed.

"Polk is not here," I said. This was making my headache start back up.

"One of his goons, then?" She raised an eyebrow. "Did he send goons?"

"There are no goons," I said.

"Salem, I heard you," she hissed again. "I could hear you

screaming at someone. Don't tell me—"

Oh, good grief. "That was just the TV. One of those morning talk shows. People arguing about politics or something."

Tammy looked pointedly at the TV, which was most decidedly off.

"I turned it off when I heard you knocking," I said. "Why are you here? Is Flo okay?"

"Flo is fine," she whispered. She didn't believe me. She brought the gun up, clasped in two hands, and I realized that she was mimicking those old cop shows. She had the stance. She had the attitude. She had the big hair. She plastered herself against the wall and slid toward the back bedroom. She looked at me and put a finger over her lips to keep me quiet.

I crossed my arms over my chest and rolled my eyes. Flo was fine? Then what the heck was Tammy doing in my trailer? With a *gun*?

I could hear her sneaking around the room, looking for goons. Everything went quiet, then she suddenly let out a banshee scream. The closet door slammed open and hit the wall.

I jumped.

"Oh," Tammy muttered as she realized I had not, in fact, been covering for goons hiding in my second bedroom.

I covered my face with my hands. Please make it stop, I prayed to the God I'd just been screaming rage at.

From her place in her princess bed, Stump raised her eyebrows at me, then climbed out with a groan and headed for the door. For a second, I couldn't remember if I'd let her out already, but I had.

219

Probably she just wanted to get away from the drama. Between me and Tammy, she'd had enough.

"Oooh, this is pretty," Tammy said from the other room. She came back down the hallway carrying one of the journals I'd bought to journal my spiritual growth into. "Where'd you get this?"

"Hobby Lobby." I took it from her and stepped back to let Stump out again.

"Hi, Stump," Tammy crooned, and bent to pet her. Tammy rose and looked around my trailer, moving to tuck the gun into the back of her waistband. "Well, we thought—" She halted as she realized there was another part of the trailer she had not cleared yet. She stood on tiptoe to peer past the kitchen, toward my bedroom and bathroom. Then she turned back to me with wide eyes.

"Go on," I said with a sigh.

I stood in the open doorway and watched Stump idly. I still had no idea why Tammy was there, but I decided I would care later. Flo was okay. If Crazy Tammy could be believed.

Viv pulled up at the low curb in front of my trailer. She and Ash hopped out of the Caddy.

"Tammy, what is going on?" I shouted.

"We were concerned about you," she said from right behind me, making me jump.

"Who is we?"

"Me and Flo. So, Flo called Viv. Who's that guy?"

"That guy is a woman, and her name is Ash."

"No! Seriously?" She stepped close to me and watched Ash mounting the deck behind Viv.

"Be nice," I said. The thing about Tammy, though, was that she had no idea how to be subtle. She wouldn't intentionally be rude. She was just stare and then ask awkward questions. She wouldn't be able to stop herself.

"What happened?" Viv asked. "You okay?"

"I'm fine. I'm not the one who went to someone else's house packing a—oh, for crying out loud!" I just realized then that Viv was carrying, too – she had what she called her 'cute gun' held down at her side.

"We were concerned!" Tammy protested. "You called in sick!"

"Exactly!" I shouted, and immediately regretted it. I wanted to go back to bed. My head hurt and I was exhausted after my emotional outburst. "I called in sick."

"But you never call in sick," Tammy said. "But you've called in sick three days in a row. *And* you've been mixed up with that mobster."

"Three days in a row?" Viv asked at the same time Ash said, "Mobster? You never said anything about a mobster."

"Because there *is* no mobster," I said.

"Salem is naïve," Tammy said to Ash. She cocked her head. "Have you always been a woman?"

See? "Tammy thinks Charles Polk is mixed up with the mob and is using me as a donkey."

"Mule," Tammy corrected.

"Right, mule," I said. "But I'm not, he's not, and I'm really sick, so I called in sick, and now I have people in my house!" I might have shouted that last bit. I might have burst into tears, just a little.

The three women stood and stared at me, shocked.

"Three days," Viv said again. The look on her face said she was doing calendar math in her head. "Oh no. Did he—did you two..." She trailed off, unable to say the words.

I nodded and collapsed onto the sofa, sobbing now.

They all stared at me. Only Viv really understood what I was saying, and she's constitutionally incapable of offering sympathy.

"What happened?" Ash asked.

"He didn't break up with you, though," Viv said.

"Yes, he did," I said miserably. "He can't do this anymore, he said. I'm too much."

Stump scratched at the door.

"But not really," Viv said.

"But *really*," I said. If there was one thing I was perfectly clear on this morning, it was the fact that Tony was done with me. Done with us.

"But he'll change his mind," Viv said.

I thought about shrugging but didn't have the strength. The room grew silent as my friends stood over me and surveyed the ashen heap of my destroyed life.

"Is it because of the donkey thing?" Tammy whispered.

I fell sideways onto the sofa, curled my legs up beside me, pulled the crocheted afghan over me, and said, "Somebody let Stump in."

I lay in the dappled dark, deciding that I would, in fact, stay there forever. I could hear the whispered voices of the three women who'd come to my rescue. Tammy finally left, although I'm not sure if she ever fully understood that my issue had nothing to do with mob ties.

Stump slurped water then joined me at the sofa. She backed up to me so I could lift her up, and I curled my arm around her belly and hoisted her up to lie beside me. She turned around on the sofa, treading on my belly a couple of times while she found the most comfortable spot, then dropped beside me with a sigh.

Conversation over the next few hours was quite tedious. Viv simply could not believe that Tony had broken up with me.

She dropped onto the stool in front of me. "But what did he say, exactly?"

From under the afghan, I mumbled, "I can't do this anymore." I wasn't going to share the rest.

"But that doesn't mean permanently, Salem. That just means he needs a break."

I thought about that, and about the thumbs up emoji. And about the other words he'd shouted at me Friday night. Selfish. Self-involved. Short-sighted.

Disastrous. Hurtful.

Oblivious.

Viv was wrong, but I didn't have the energy to describe all the evidence I had for her being wrong.

She called Les, and they discussed – as if I weren't sitting right there – the fact that I had lied, had been lying all weekend, had cut myself off from my support system. Viv handed me the phone and I grunted agreement with everything he said, taking in only scraps. The main idea was, I had to get myself to a meeting that day. And someone had to confirm that I'd gone. No more lying.

"No more lying," I mumbled.

"You're lying right now," he said.

"I'm not planning to lie," I said.

"I know, but you're also not making any real commitment to tell the truth," he said.

"My head is messed up," I said.

"I know. Drinking isn't going to help that."

"I know." *But nothing else is, either,* I thought.

"Viv and Ash are going to stick with you. If you wanted alone time, you should have been honest."

"I don't care," I said.

"I know. I love you, girl. I have to go. I'll check on you later."

I hung up, and Viv took her phone back. She and Ash discussed plans for monitoring me like I was a nuclear power plant and we were in a disaster movie with an earthquake on one side of us and a typhoon on the other side. I lay curled up on the sofa and let them talk. I drifted into a doze until Ash made a sudden strangled sound.

I started awake.

Ash scrubbed at her hair, then shot to her feet and said, "Arrggh! I hate this."

"What?"

"This hair growing out. My clipper guy closed and moved to California. I have to find another one."

"Salem could probably cut it," Viv said. "She has clippers."

From my prone position on the sofa, I mumbled, "I'm not cutting Ash's hair." First of all, I didn't want to, and secondly, my hands were shaking. She'd end up bald.

"Please?" Ash pleaded. "Look at it." She lifted the long part to show half an inch growth on what had been shaved head underneath. "It's grossing me out."

"No," I said. "There are other clipper guys in town. Or you could go see Helena."

Ash shook her head. "She scares me."

"Have you even met her?" I asked.

She nodded. "Yeah, Viv and I went there yesterday. She's...intense." She turned to Viv. "I thought you were intense. She had me ready to apologize for whatever she put in front of me."

"Yeah, me too," Viv said.

I remembered Monica, at G-Ma's motel-turned-boutique-shopping. "My G-Ma can hook you up."

"Okay, great. Let's go."

Viv stood and reached for her purse. They both moved to the door, then stopped to look back at me.

"Let's go," Viv said. "Put your shoes on."

"I'm not going anywhere," I said.

"You are." Ash drew herself up and glared at me as she'd done Friday evening.

Unlike then, though, the stance was not particularly effective. Friday, I had cared a lot about how things turned out. Since I did not, in the moment, have any strong feelings about anything, I viewed this situation objectively, as if a spectator.

I was not going to move. Of that, I was sure. And yet somehow, I was pretty sure Ash *was* going get me G-Ma's place today. Would she throw me over her shoulder and carry me like a fireman? Dump me into a wheelbarrow? Who knew? Who cared?

I remembered again our late-night Uber ride, after I'd told her about my Am I The Jerk post, and everything leading up to it.

Your girl is still alive, she'd said Friday. And another memory surfaced, of Thursday night, when we'd driven around: her saying, *I have to make it right? Right? I have to. But how? Without going to jail, I mean.*

And yet in that moment, I wasn't afraid of her. Maybe I was just numb to everything. Maybe I didn't care if Ash *was* a dangerous person, and I would be safer giving her a wide berth. I remained silent and still on the sofa. I admit, I was kind of curious what was going to happen next.

Ash cocked an eyebrow. "Are you going to get up, or am I going to have to hurt you? Your call."

Viv looked at Ash, opened her mouth to say something, then shut it again. She cast a worried glance from Ash to me. "Maybe you'd better get up, Salem."

I rolled over and tucked the afghan around my shoulders.

Ash sighed. "Okay, suit yourself." She shuffled a bit, took a deep breath, then opened her mouth and bellowed.

"You can tell the world! you never was my girl!

You can burn my clothes up when I'm gone!"

I mean, this chick was *loud*. The windows rattled. Stump lifted her head.

"You can tell your friends! just what a fool I've been!

And laugh and joke about me on the phone!"

"Is that..." Viv whispered.

"You can tell my arms! go back to the farm!

You can tell my feet to hit the floor!"

Stump struggled to stand and nosed at the afghan until she poked her head out.

"Or you can tell my lips! to tell my fingertips!

They won't be reaching out for you no more!"

"It *is*!" Viv screamed. "Oh noooo!"

"But don't tell my heart!

My achy breaky heart!

I just don't think he'd understand!"

Stump growled. The walls vibrated. Outside, a car alarm went off.

"And if you tell my heart!

My achy breaky heart!

He might blow up and kill this man!"

"Salem, get up!" Viv screamed. She scurried around behind the sofa, her hands over her ears.

Stump lifted her head and howled.

Ash sang on. It was kind of amazing, really, that a human could get that loud. Because of Stump's separation anxiety, my neighbors were used to loud and unpleasant noises coming from my trailer, but I was still pretty sure someone was going to call the police about this. Because it was, objectively, awful. Ash's ability to carry a tune was inversely proportional to her volume.

Ash stomped over to stand above me.

"You can tell your mom! I moved to Arkansas!

"You can tell your dog to bite my leg!"

"Salem, please." Viv crouched over the back of the sofa, hands pressed against her ears. "Make it stop!"

I pulled the afghan tighter around me, but it was an empty gesture. I could feel Ash's voice vibrating up through the floor, through the sofa, into my bones. My fillings were coming loose.

"Or tell your brother Cliff! whose fist can tell my lip!

He never really liked me anyway!"

Ash stopped for one brief, glorious moment. Viv's face brightened. Stump stopped howling.

Ash filled her lungs.

"Or tell your Aunt Louise! tell anything you please!

Myself already knows I'm not OK!

Or you can tell my heart!

My achy breaky heart!"

I heaved a sigh of my own, flipped back the afghan, and stood.

Silence. Blessed, heavenly silence filled the world. My ears rang. I had to grip the arm of the sofa to keep from keeling over.

Stump whined. She looked at me, confused.

"Stump's going with us," I mumbled.

"No problem," Ash said.

"Let me get dressed."

I passed Viv, who was staring at Ash with the wide-eyed wonder you might give to a magician who's just stunned you with their tricks. "That was a nightmare," she whispered in awe.

"Why, thank you," Ash said humbly. "It's very effective."

I found jeans and a t-shirt wadded in the corner of my bedroom and pulled them on. I went to the bathroom and tugged a brush through my hair. My eyes were bloodshot and puffy, my skin blotchy. Everything about me sagged. My hands shook so bad I couldn't tie my shoes, so I ripped them off and slid my feet into raggedy old slides.

I shuffled back to the living room. "Let's go."

Stump beat us to the door.

Monica, one of the working girls from the motel's old incarnation, ran a beauty shop, and she was about to expand into a second unit to add a couple of mani/pedi stations and an esthetician, which, it turns out, is completely different from an anesthesiologist. Just FYI. They kind of sound the same so I could understand if you got those two confused and freaked out a little when you heard that.

Monica had been Felicia in her working girl days, and quite scary, to be honest. She was okay, though. She was happy with her new business, and she knew how to handle G-Ma.

"You look awful," Monica said as I trudged in behind Viv and Ash.

"Thanks." I collapsed into the black and chrome chair by the window. Stump sniffed a little under the chair Monica was sweeping around, then came and backed up to me so I could hold her.

The place was the perfect blend of kitchy and cool. There were black and white zebra print accents, silver hand mirrors collected in a pattern over the shampoo sink, a purple chandelier hanging from the ceiling, and a mural of a watered-down Audrey Hepburn lounging against the back wall, complete with dark glasses and big floppy hat. The place smelled like permanent wave and candles.

Monica was almost as tall as Ash. She had dark brown hair with blonde streaks and purple streaks that fell in long ringlets past her shoulders. She wore a wide-legged pants in a bright yellow and brown pattern and a cropped top to match. Heels. Monica always wore heels, even though she stood all day. I slumped in my chair and wondered why and how she did it, then decided I didn't care.

"Can you clean this up?" Ash pointed at the sides of her head.

"Sure, girl. 'Tis the work of but a minute!" Monica gestured to the open seat.

"Can you do mine, too?" Viv asked. "Like hers?"

"Whew, Gigi," Monica hooted. "You want to shave that head of yours?"

"Yes, but cool like that. Can you make me cool like that?"

"I don't need to make you cool like that, you're already the coolest chick I know," Monica said.

"But I want my hair—"

"I have something else in mind for you. Like this, but fancier."

Viv looked intrigued.

Monica pulled her tray of weapons to her and sang softly to herself while she perused her choices. "How 'bout you, sweet girl? You want a new 'do today?" She looked over at me.

"Yes, she does," Viv answered for me.

"No, I don't. I'm fine." I was not fine. My hair was not fine. There were mirrors everywhere, and I could see how awful I looked. Even if I wasn't ready to dig a hole and climb in it, it was clear I needed at least a trim. But I didn't have the energy to put myself into that chair.

"You sure? A fresh haircut can do wonders for a girl's outlook."

I didn't answer. I just turned and looked out the window. An RV pulled into the parking lot and circled around the back. Sometimes long-term RVers would stop at the motel for a place to take a real bath, hang out in one place that wasn't their RV for a while. They were going to be bummed to learn they now had to go to a nicer (i.e., more expensive) motel now.

Viv, Monica and Ash chattered on and I sat staring out the

window. Cars came and went. Serena at the new age shop came out and hung up a new round metal thing in front of her store, and it spun in the wind. Candace at the bakery brought out a chalk board with the day's specials and hung it on a plant hook outside her door. Stump and I just stared.

My brain was a fog, and I decided I was okay with that. One thing I had forgotten about drinking was that, when you stopped, depression set in. Sure, there was the come-down when the buzz wore off. But there was also the days-long general depression after that. I was there.

And you know what? I could just stay right there. If necessary, I could go the rest of my life in this fog. Just floating, doing whatever was necessary, but disengaged.

Monica finished Ash's hair, and they were both thrilled with it. "Now that's precision!" Ash said as she admired the clean line of her mohawk. Monica had added another razor cut to make a line that swooped along her temple, dipped to a V at the back of her skull, and then back around the other side.

"That's perfect," Viv announced. "Do mine like that."

"I told you, Gigi, I have something else in mind for you. Do you trust me?"

"Do you promise it will be cool?" Viv said. "Like, tough girl cool?"

"Could I even *do* something that would make you not cool? I'm not a magician, Gigi."

"Well, that's true enough," Viv allowed. "But I want something, you know." She flexed her bicep. "Tough. Strong. Cool."

"You okay with a bit of color, too?"

Viv giggled. "I'm always okay with a bit of color." She dropped into the chair and wiggled.

Monica hummed as she combed through Viv's silver locks. "You want a bottle of water or cup of coffee?" she asked me.

I shook my head. Either one would mean getting up in a while to go to the bathroom, and I preferred not moving, ever.

She smiled and nodded, pulled out her phone and tapped for a few seconds, then turned back to the chair. She faced Viv in the mirror and held her head from the back. "How do you feel about a surprise makeover? The whole works? Cut, color, makeup, all of it?"

"Ooh, yeah," Ash said. "Do that. That'll be fun."

"That'll take all day, and we have interviews to conduct," Viv said.

"No, RayAnn will be here in about ten minutes. She'll do your makeup, I'll do your hair, and together we can have you out the door in about an hour and a half, tops. What do you think?"

Viv was a sucker for this kind of thing, so she giggled again and nodded. "Okay. But I mean it. Tough. No girlie stuff."

"You will be the baddest Gigi in the land," Monica promised as she spun the chair around. "Okay, no peeking." She turned back to me. "How about you, sad thing? RayAnn got some new color pallets she's dying to try out."

"I'm fine," I said again. I looked out the window.

G-Ma was headed our way. *Ugh*, I thought. But I let that go

233

immediately, because irritation opened the door to feeling other things, and I was not here for that. So, I let it go with an internal 'whatever.'

There was another woman with her, and that was good news. If G-Ma had a friend with her, she was far less likely to pay any mind to me. I realized as they drew closer that this was her friend Yvette. The RV made sense now. Yvette had been driving around the country in an RV for as long as I could remember, and occasionally she and her husband would stop by the motel and visit with G-Ma. The two women would stay up late into the night, giggling and telling stories of their teenage years. G-Ma and Yvette had been best friends ever since they fought over a guy in junior high, until both realized they liked each other more than they liked that guy.

This was very good, I decided as I sank back into the fog. If Yvette was around, G-Ma would definitely not bother with me.

"Oh my gosh, you *do* look awful," G-Ma said as she swept into the beauty shop and stopped in front of me. "Even worse than yesterday."

"Now, Virgie," Monica scolded. "I did not say she looked awful. I said she looked like she needed help."

I sighed. Monica had texted G-Ma to come down and criticize me. "I do not need help. I need to be left alone," I said.

"You look like you've *been* left alone. On the side of the road. For days." G-Ma put her hands on her hips. "Did you talk to your husband like I told you?"

I nodded. The silence in the room spoke volumes.

"Oh," G-Ma said.

She gave me a look that said she was disappointed but not surprised. Long-lasting marriages were something of a rarity in our family.

Still, she was family, and she could feel everyone looking to her to do something about me. "Maybe you should talk to your mom. Have you spoken with your mom?"

"I'm fine. I haven't spoken to Mom in weeks."

G-Ma pursed her lips. "That would usually put you in a good mood."

"I am in a good mood." I turned back to the parking lot. "Hi Yvette," I mumbled.

"She needs a makeover," Viv announced. "Something to bring her out of her slump."

"Slump?" I blurted before I could stop myself. Stump misunderstood and raised her head to look at me.

"It's fine," I said and stroked her back. "I'm fine."

Monica tssked as she gathered Viv's hair into sections on the top of her head. "The pedicure chairs don't get installed until early next month, or else we'd do a head-to-toe makeover. But a cut and color can really lift a girl's spirits."

The notion that a change in hairstyle was going to fix my dumpster fire of a life was so ludicrous, I almost laughed. I thought about laughing. I imagined laughing hysterically while I stared blankly outside.

"So, what happened?" G-Ma put her hands on her hips. "Is this just about your marriage, or did something else happen?"

"I'm fine," I said again. "Nothing happened."

"I think I will call your mom," G-Ma announced. "She's got that rich husband now. She'd want to know what's going on."

"I'll get the cut and color." I stood, hoisting Stump with me. I had to just make everything just stop. "Something drastic and..." I waved a hand vaguely. "And just drastic, I guess."

"There you go," Monica said. "Good choice. You're going to be thrilled, I guarantee. Let me finish with Gigi's foils and I'll get started on a fun 'do for you." Her words were encouraging, but her look was gauging. She studied me while she began to wrap sections of Viv's hair in foil.

"You didn't answer my question," G-Ma said as she plopped into the chair beside me. "What's wrong with you? You don't go out of the house looking like that unless something is wrong."

"That's my fault, I'm afraid." Ash rose from her chair and came to stand beside me. "I told her a story that's got her kind of depressed. About my Marine days." She bowed slightly. "My apologies. I didn't realize it was going to bum you out so bad."

Yvette took in my wrinkled clothes. "That must have been some story," she said.

"It was bad," Viv said, catching on. She winced slightly as Monica tugged another hunk of hair into the foil wrapper and slathered it with something. "And then I gave her a stomach bug."

236

Yvette both drew back.

"She's over it now. Not contagious anymore. But she's, you know...wiped out."

"I'm wiped out," I said. It was so ridiculous, I once again imagined laughing hysterically. "But I'm all better now."

"You probably need some food," Yvette said. "I'll run over to the soup kitchen and see what they have ready."

"Sure," I said. "Thanks." It occurred to me that just saying yes to everything and allowing myself to be moved around like a Monopoly piece was an effective way to deal with things. Resistance just made people push harder. Just say yes. Just let them do whatever they want. Resistance took too much energy, made me have to think.

The bell over the door tinkled as RayAnn came in. "Look at us with all these customers! We're killing it in here!"

She edged past Yvette and Ash as she made her way to her own station.

"Gigi here is getting the full treatment," Monica told her. "I have about three more foils, then I'm going to hand her over to you so I can bring new life to girlfriend over there."

RayAnn turned and studied Viv's face. "Beautiful bones," she said.

"Why thank you."

"I have this amazing new cream with green tea, calendula, and – "

"Gigi wants to be fierce," Monica interrupted.

RayAnn nodded. "Well, of course she does. Highlight all those natural attributes."

"Exactly," Viv said. "Highlight my natural attributes to show my inner fierceness."

Monica folded the last foil and said, "Okay, she's all yours."

"All right, Gigi, let's get you over here." She patted the chair at her station.

"My names is Viv," she corrected. "Only Monica calls me Gigi, because I remind her of Gigi Hadid. That supermodel."

"Oh, no," Monica said. "I call you Gigi because you're too cool to be called Grandma."

Viv froze. She blinked slowly. "You. What?"

"I call you Gigi because you remind me of Gigi Hadid. You two are like twins," Monica said.

"That's what I thought," Viv said. She wiggled happily in RayAnn's chair. "Okay, work your magic!"

Monica led me back to the shampoo room, which was just a reconfiguration of the old bathroom. She hummed softly as she warmed the water, sweet-talked Stump curled up by my feet.

"How's that? Too warm? Too cool?" she asked as I leaned back and she sprayed the top of my head.

"It's good," I said.

"Are you up for a surprise makeover, like the Gigi?"

"Sure. Sounds good."

"How about after that we take you out and stand you buck naked in the middle of Clovis Highway?"

"Okay. Whatever you think best."

She was so good. Her hands were warm and strong, soothing as she massaged the shampoo into my scalp. She smiled down at me.

"You're going through some stuff," she said. It wasn't a question.

"Gone," I said. "It's all done."

She nodded, contemplating that. "I see."

It occurred to me that Monica was taking the same approach I'd decided on. Just say yes. Just go along. Except it was with me, and I had no agenda except to stay in my fog. She couldn't say yes to anything I didn't offer. So, I decided to just clam up. Sink back into the fog. If she offered any other conversation, I would just ignore it.

I prepared myself to ignore her until it became clear she was done, which was kind of annoying since I was so prepared. Then I remembered that annoyance was harmful to the fog, so I focused on how good her hands and the warm water felt as she massaged my scalp and neck. She hummed softly, that and the sound of the water the only noises in the room.

The bell over the door tinkled as Yvette returned with containers of soup and rolls from the bakery. "This place is so cute, Virgie! Now you'll never want to sell."

Monica, who'd been squeezing water from my hair, froze. "Sell?" She reached for a towel and tossed it in my direction, then returned to the main room.

"Sell? This place? Not now that it's a money-making enterprise, she better not. At least not until I save up the money to buy it from you. I don't want no other landlord."

I wrapped my own hair and followed Monica to the chair.

"You were going to sell the place?" Ash asked.

"Nah, not really," G-Ma said. "I mean, maybe at one point."

Yvette scoffed. "She left me high and dry. The original plan was for her to sell the place, and we were going to go on the road together. Two middle-age women, free as birds, touring the country and singing *On the Road Again* with Willie Nelson."

"Oh, hush," G-Ma said. "I was never serious about that."

"Well, I sure was," Yvette said with a laugh. "Obviously. I spent twenty years on the road and saw every state except Hawaii from my RV. Saw some of them a lot more than I wanted to." She leaned toward G-Ma. "We were supposed to go together, but I guess it's a good thing you changed your mind. If you'd been there when I landed in that RV park in Barstow, Ed wouldn't have looked twice at me. He would have swept you up and I would have been left at the side of the road with my suitcase."

"Hush now, I mean it," G-Ma said, but she didn't seem particularly bothered by this narrative.

And of course she wasn't, because Yvette's husband Ed was a total catch. Yvette had met him a couple years into her RV adventure when she parked her run-down Minnie Winnie beside his top-of-the-line diesel pusher, and they discovered a shared love of steaks on the grill and Grand Ol' Opry music. They had danced that first night under the stars to Ferlin Husky, and after that, Yvette's occasional visits to G-Ma had been in Ed's fancy RV with all the pull-outs and bells and whistles. Ed had made a fortune in some manufacturing business that he sold off while he was still young enough to enjoy his pile of loot.

"It's time, though, to hang up the keys," Yvette said. "We've seen everything we want to see, and Ed wants to buy a little place where we can grow our own tomatoes and have the grandkids come to us for a change."

"Are you buying here?" RayAnn asked. "They have some nice new condos they're building on the south side of town.

"Oh, good heavens, no," Yvette laughed. "Lubbock is great for visiting old friends, but we want to live somewhere pretty."

"Lubbock is pretty," Ash said. "The thing about Lubbock is, there's nothing to get in the way of the sky. The sky here is amazing."

"Yeah, when the dirt's not blowing," Monica said.

"But have you noticed, after the dirt blows, it's even *more* amazing? Like, crystal clear, and such a pure blue. It's like the air got dermabrasion or something."

"Dermabrasion is really good for your skin," RayAnn said. "But you have to be careful."

Everyone just nodded because what could you say to that, after all?

Monica ran the comb gently over my head, and I began to suspect she was taking much longer with my haircut than she needed to. I didn't care, though. It was nice.

She checked the clock on the wall. "You said you had interviews to conduct. What case are y'all working on now?"

"Looking for a runaway," Viv said. "At least, we think she's a runaway. She ran away before, but she always left a note before, and she never got very far before. This time she's been gone for almost a year."

"Is this that girl over by the university?" RayAnn asked. "I heard about her on the news."

"That's her," Viv said.

"That's Helena's daughter, right? You remember her, RayAnn? Works with Janet at Authenti-Cuts?"

"That one who's always mad?" RayAnn asked.

"That's her," Viv, Ash, Monica, and I all said at once.

"Except Helena is not Gia's mother, she's her older sister," I said. Then I frowned, because I was already becoming more engaged than I wanted to be.

"Well, I hope you find her," RayAnn said. "I hope she's not that girl they found out near the lake."

"We do, too," Viv said. "They're waiting for the medical examiner's report to identify that body."

"If she's gone that long and nobody's heard from her, she's either dead or being trafficked," Monica said. "Back in my day, they called it pimping. But now it's trafficking."

"Because they take them to other places," RayAnn explained.

Monica shook her head. "A person can be trafficked out of their own home. It just means you're a good or a service being sold to someone else, that's all."

"Well, she's not being trafficked out of her home, we know that for sure," Ash said.

"Hey, you probably hear talk," Viv said to Monica. "Having been in the business. Is there a place where girls are trafficked out of? Like, a seedy motel or a busy house or something?"

If Monica was offended by this, she covered it well. "Not that I know of, but I can ask around." She bent and looked at me. "You doing okay, there, sweet girl?"

"I'm fine." I didn't want to think about Gia being trafficked, though, so I stared out the window and searched my mind lazily for something else. I tried to remember if G-Ma had ever said anything to me about selling the motel and going on the road. It seemed like she had talked about selling, but it had been later— maybe around the time I was pregnant, and Tony and I were getting married.

At that time, though, the neighborhood was really rough, and she couldn't find a buyer. I didn't remember how much she was asking, but I did remember that at the time I thought it was unrealistic. I knew nothing about money, though—I thought Tony and I would be fine giving up our college plans (I, of course, had had no plans, but the hopes and dreams of the entire Solis family was that they would all get advanced degrees and make millions—Tony most especially) and make a decent living working blue collar jobs. Tony had overcome our bump in the road and built a thriving business. I was hanging on by my fingernails, grooming dogs. And I was maybe not hanging on very well to that.

Monica hummed as she tugged and snipped at my hair. I couldn't help but become curious about what she was doing, and I felt a little spark of hope that, whatever it was, Tony would like it.

Like it enough to forgive you for being selfish, disastrous, oblivious, and hurtful? A voice in my head sneered. *That's asking a lot of some highlights.*

I imagined stomping that spark of hope out like a small trash fire, and then turned my thoughts back to G-Ma selling the motel. At one time she'd had plans to go on the open road with Yvette, huh? That was interesting. I studied her as RayAnn touched up her mascara. G-Ma's eyes fluttered. To me, G-Ma had always been an old lady, of course, but I realized that when I moved in with her the first time, she must have been mid-fifties to early sixties—plenty young enough to have an adventure. She and Yvette were the same age, and Yvette had done it. Had driven that Minnie Winnie by herself, navigating with the old-timey folded maps and making reservations at RV parks through payphones at Waffle Houses along the way. She'd learned how to make minor repairs on the Winnie along the way, until she met Ed and his bucks made that kind of thing unnecessary.

"Okay, let's let that sit for a while and RayAnn will take over," Monica said.

RayAnn smiled at me and patted her stool.

Irritation threatened to rear its ugly head. I did not want to have fancy creams rubbed into my face. I did not want to look in the mirror and accidentally be happy with what I saw. I wanted to wallow, I realized, in self-loathing.

But self-loathing wasn't numbness. I needed numbness. I needed nothing. I needed not to care or feel or think. How did I turn my mind off?

While I was trying to figure it out, I allowed myself to be shuttled over to RayAnn's stool, where she complimented my dimples and my skin tone. "Ohh, and look at those eyes. Okay, girl, I know just what I'm going to do for you."

Ugh. This was why I needed to drink. It was possible to drink enough that thinking just didn't work anymore. That was possible.

True to her word, Monica and RayAnn were done with us within an hour and a half. Viv was thrilled. Monica had added purple streaks to her choppy pixie cut, and she'd cut the sides short enough that they *almost* looked shaved—close enough that Viv felt tough. RayAnn echoed the purple in Viv's eyeshadow and eyeliner.

Even G-Ma seemed impressed.

Then came my big unveiling. Monica rinsed and dried my hair, then took the curling iron to me and did a bunch of quick flippy things that I knew I'd never be able to replicate at home, even had I wanted to.

Then, with a big flourish, she spun me around in the chair and let me look in the mirror. Behind me, all six women gathered to take in my reaction. There was much oohing and ahhing. RayAnn even clapped.

They all looked so earnest and hopeful that I had to remind myself that *not* smiling would create more resistance than just going along with it.

"Wow," I forced myself to say. "That's amazing." And that, objectively, was true. The women had worked wonders. Monica had added a blond streak at the front of my hair, and it framed my face. She'd done something to the brown that made it shinier and healthier looking, and she'd used the curling iron to add waves that managed to look both glamorous and carefree. The makeup was perfect. There were highlights, my dimples were on full display, and my eyes were luminous.

If Tony hadn't broken up with me, I definitely would have been excited to run to his house so he could compliment me.

I took it all in, then reminded myself as I saw Viv's anxious face that I needed to smile to pull this off. So, I smiled. "That's amazing," I repeated. "Thank you, Monica."

"It *is* amazing," G-Ma agreed. "I can't believe you're the same sourpuss who sat there just hours ago."

"Like night and day," Yvette said.

I sat and waited for it to be over. Now that I'd done this, surely Viv and Ash would let me go home.

Monica took the cape off me and shook it out. "Come back here, girl, I need to wash some of that loose hair off the back of your neck."

She sat me back on the shampoo chair, but had me sit forward. She took a warm wet washrag and rubbed it against the back of my neck.

"Well," she murmured. "You are sure enough going through it. And I understand why you don't want to tell your G-Ma. I don't think even your friends get the extent of it."

"They're--"

"They're okay," she interrupted. "They understand the best they can, and they mean well." She dropped the washcloth into a wicker basket beside the sink. "They think you're gonna be sad for a few days and then you'll be back to your old self." She squatted in front of me. "But you don't believe that. Right now, you don't think your life will ever be the same again."

"My life is a dumpster fire," I said.

She nodded. "I get that. My life has been a dumpster fire before."

For some reason, this made me furious. She must have seen it in my eyes, because she held up a finger with a very long, very dark maroon fingernail. "I know. I don't know your trouble. You don't know my trouble. Let's just agree that we both have some hard stories to tell."

I had to allow that, given the fact that she had been a prostitute, had a criminal record, and had built this business after all that.

"My life has been a dumpster fire before, and my light has been snuffed out. Your light has been snuffed out, Salem. I can see that. You had a sparkle, girl. Even though you tried to play it cool, tried to play it like you were cautious. I see you. I see you playing the straight man off of your G-Ma, playing the straight man off of Gigi out there. You let them play the jokes, but I see your sparkle. And I see it out right now. And what I want *you* to know is, it'll come back."

I shook my head.

She put her hand on my chin. "It *will* come back," she insisted. "It will be different. And it might be a while. But it will come back. You might be a dumpster fire right now, and your life might always be a dumpster fire. But you are going to be a beautiful, strong, *dazzling* dumpster fire if you have to be. If that's what it takes, that's what you'll do. Do you hear me?"

I sighed.

"I said, do you hear me?"

I rolled my eyes. "I'm right here. I hear you."

"Good. Now get out of here and dazzle somebody. Put on some clothes that aren't wrinkled, and some close-toed shoes. Because we do not leave the house in sandals unless we have our toes done and our heel calluses scraped, okay? Do some justice to the work RayAnn and I just did. Good girl."

Chapter Seven

I nursed my foggy state for the rest of the day. Les came over and took me to a meeting Monday evening. I got yet another one day chip. Yay. I was markedly less comforted by this than I had been Friday night. But I continued in the theory that just saying yes and going along was the easiest thing to do.

I texted Flo and said, "I'm so sorry for all the recent trouble. You can count on me to be there tomorrow at the regular time." She knew I had my Tuesday morning AA meeting.

I slept like a log that night and woke feeling a little more balanced. I did not feel fantastic. I was exhausted by the enormity of the mess I had to clean up. And the fog was slipping away, leaving me feeling exposed and vulnerable.

I trudged to my second bedroom and sheepishly lit my candle. I sat before it for a while, trying to think what to say. I felt dumb for my outburst yesterday. But at the same time...I didn't feel *wrong*.

"I don't get it," I finally confessed. "I don't see what you're doing here. I don't understand why this is the way things need to happen." I sighed. "But I guess I'm still in."

After all, what choice was there? You either believed God was the creator of the universe or you didn't -- and I *did* believe. If I didn't care for the way he was operating, it wasn't as if I could go try another God. Christianity wasn't like keto. It wasn't something that, if it didn't work for me, I could choose something different and see how that worked. It was either the truth, or it wasn't. And I still believed it was the truth.

"I need help," I finally whispered. "Please send me some help."

I opened my reading for the day, and wouldn't you know it. Psalm 121.

"I lift my eyes to the mountains—where does my help come from? My help comes from the Lord, the maker of heaven and earth."

I squinted at the flame. "Okay, that was good. That was impressive."

I turned back to the page and read aloud.

> *I lift up my eyes to the mountains—where does my help come from? My help comes from the LORD, the Maker of heaven and earth.*
>
> *He will not let your foot slip— he who watches over you will not slumber; indeed, he who watches over Israel will neither slumber nor sleep.*

The LORD watches over you— the LORD is your shade at your right hand; the sun will not harm you by day, nor the moon by night.

The LORD will keep you from all harm—he will watch over your life; the LORD will watch over your coming and going both now and forevermore.

And despite everything—despite the breakup with Tony, the loss of my sobriety, the fact that we still didn't know where Gia was or even if she was alive...reading this brought me some comfort. I was still confused. But I could imagine that there were things I didn't understand.

Normally on Tuesday mornings, I just drug around the house, taking my time getting ready, and go to work after my 10 o'clock AA meeting. Today, though, I did my best to replicate Monica's waves in my hair, then Stump and I went into Flo's early.

Her lips flattened when she saw me, and I didn't care for that. I wondered if she had already made the offer to Barbara to return full-time, and she was hoping instead of firing me, she could count on me to go the rest of the way into the ditch and not show up.

"So," I said as I pushed opening the swinging half-door into the grooming area of the shop. "I just wanted to apologize again for my unpredictability over the last few days."

"Oh, that," Flo said. She waved it away. "Tammy said you were having some trouble."

Tammy came in then, and she smiled when she saw me. "You look so much better than you did yesterday! You looked awful yesterday. Man! Like, I've never seen anybody look *so bad.*"

"Yes, well...I was just apologizing to Flo for flaking out on you guys the last few days. As you can see, I'm getting my life back on track."

"Good for you," Flo said.

"Breakups are hard," Tammy said. "That's why I don't date anymore. Men are more trouble than they're worth."

I swallowed. Tony was most definitely *not* more trouble than he was worth, but I could see why he thought I would be.

"Plus, you need to concentrate right now on staying out of the clutches of that mobster. Oh!" Tammy cocked her head and took in my look again. "That's what you look like! A mobster's wife. From the 30s. Like, a girlfriend of Al Capon, maybe." She smiled and raised her eyebrows. I was pretty sure she expected me to be flattered by this.

"Anyway," I said, "I wanted to appear in the flesh this morning and show you that I am feeling back to normal, and I'll be back after my meeting, just like normal."

"Just like normal," Flo said. She gave me a thumbs up.

I held back another sigh and tried not to think about Tony's emoji and Barbara's years more experience than I had.

I lift my eyes up to the mountains, I prayed silently.

Except I was in West Texas, with nary a mountain in sight. Over the next few hours, I kept thinking of that verse, *where does my help come from?* Instead of thinking of God coming in from the mountains to help, though, the face of Bobby Sloan kept coming to my mind.

Bobby was not the detective working Gia's case. But I'd prayed for help that morning, and Bobby's face was the one that came continually to mind.

I had to tell Bobby what I knew. It was that or tell Helena and Sid Perez about Shawn. Carrying this information around with me was too much – I could see that now.

Neither idea held much appeal. But I kept thinking that, if nothing else, Bobby would know what to do next.

I thought about it all through my AA meeting, and as much as I dreaded the thought of telling Bobby everything, I knew it was the obvious next step.

Before I could stop myself, I told Viv and Ash after the meeting that I was going to the police station after work to tell Bobby about Shawn, that very afternoon. "He'll know what to do," I said. "Go with me?"

"Absolutely," Ash said.

"Absolutely," Viv echoed. Viv was high on the compliments she'd received for her purple hair. Today, I saw, she wore combat boots very similar to Ash's. I bet they cost at least three times as much, though.

"I'll pick you up after work," Viv said. "Then we can go to the police station together."

Les looked on. "Do you want me there?" he asked.

I shook my head. "That's not necessary. Viv and Ash will be there."

He nodded. "I'll come by your trailer this evening to check up on you."

My stomach was a ball of nerves for the rest of the day, but I was still sure I was doing the only thing I could do. Too bad I hadn't done it last week, I thought ruefully.

Frank agreed to stay with Stump, so I dropped my car off at home and waited for Viv to pick me up. She had changed from her combat boots to a black suit and aviator sunglasses. This suddenly felt like a bigger deal than I wanted it to. We pulled into the Lubbock Police Department and Viv turned to the backseat to look at me. "You ready?"

I was *not* ready. But I would never be ready, and I needed to get this done.

Ash turned around, too. "We're just going to go in there, get it over with, and then it will be done. Rip it off like a Band-Aid. Everything after that will be easier."

I nodded.

"And it feels like a big deal, but remember, he probably hears stories like this all day long," Viv said.

I tried to smile. I knew Viv was trying to be helpful, and I loved her for it.

Ash put in words what I was thinking, though. "Yes, well, those are other people's stories. That's, like...hypothetical stuff. There's a world of difference in talking about hypothetical stuff and talking about your own stuff."

"Yes," Viv said slowly. "Just so I'm clear, though, when you say stuff, you're referring to..."

"Yep," Ash confirmed. "Trauma.

"Well, I don't want to talk about anybody's stuff," I sighed. "But let's go."

I reached for the door handle, but Viv stopped me. "Hang on," she said.

She got out and scanned the parking lot through her aviators, then reached for my door. She was in Secret Service mode today, I realized, and I was her protectee. I told myself it was sweet and funny. I told myself that I was fortunate to have her and Ash on my team. I told myself I was grateful.

And as soon as I was able to feel anything other than exhaustion, fear, and shame, I definitely would.

The officer at the front desk recognized Viv and me. We'd been in to see Bobby on several occasions—sometimes under our own volition and sometimes not.

"Let me check if he's available," he said. He picked up the phone, talked low for a few seconds, then hung up. "You can go back," he said.

Viv strode with purpose before me, and Ash backed me up. Viv checked each door we passed like she was scanning for possible assassins. She reached Bobby's office and rapped twice on the open door.

"Wow," Bobby said, taking us all in. "Am I in an episode of Miss Marple Gets a Makeover?"

"Miss Marple is in the Secret Service now," I said. "Do you have a minute?"

"I have nothing but minutes for you," Bobby said and stood. He took Ash in. "Are you a new member of this detective agency?"

Ash stuck out her hand. "Ash. I'm a friend."

"She's a friend of ours," Viv echoed. "A colleague. And we're not a detective agency, we're an investigative podcast."

"Oh yeah, I forgot about that. I can get another chair," Bobby said, since there were only two.

"No need, I'll stand," Viv said. She took the stance of a guard, feet shoulder width apart, hands clasped before her.

Bobby nodded, then looked at me as if to say, "What the heck?" and nodded toward the chairs. "Well, okay. You two take a seat and tell me what's going on."

Ash and I sat, and I took a deep breath.

"We are in possession of information related to the Gia Perez case," Viv said.

"I'm not working that case," Bobby said. "I'll need to get Detective—"

"I know you're not working that case," I said. "But if it's okay, I want to talk to you first. Then we can bring her in if you think it's -- it's necessary." Oh no. My voice was already cracking a little. *Please don't let me cry please don't let me cry*, I prayed silently.

I took a deep breath.

Bobby studied me for a minute, then nodded. "Fair enough." He cast another glace at Viv and Ash, then back at me. "Go ahead."

One more deep breath. "At the Perez house, when we asked to see some photographs of Gia, Sid Perez let us go through some albums. Not just current pictures, but some from years past. One of the pictures was of Gia's ninth birthday. In that picture, I recognized someone that I knew from—from several years ago. Over twenty years ago."

Bobby nodded. "Okay." It was like I could see mentally calculating the age difference.

"Helena said he was an old boyfriend of hers. They'd broken up not long after the picture was taken. She's had no contact with him since. I knew him because my mother was best friends with his mother. I knew him because—I knew him because he molested me when I was a kid. When I was seven."

I would not cry. I would *not* cry. I blinked back the tears and took a deep breath.

I had to give Bobby credit. He just nodded. He didn't interrupt. He didn't look shocked. He just let me say the words and get them out.

"I haven't told any of the Perez family about this, or even that I knew him," I said in a rush. "She said they broke up because he stole some tools from her uncle or cousin or something, and she hasn't really had contact with him since then. We don't know that this is in any way related to Gia's disappearance. But..."

He nodded. "Well, it's definitely something to know." He tapped a pen against the desk. He looked at me, then at Viv and Ash. Ash shifted, her shoulders back.

"Of course, it's something to know! It's a lead to be pursued," Viv said with great indignation.

"It could be a lead to be pursued," Bobby allowed.

"Here's what else I know," I said. "He drives a truck. And he goes, sometimes, to the Loose Caboose. I asked the bartender there, and she said she recognized him as someone who goes there occasionally. It's possible he was there the same day Gia was. The day she ran away."

He nodded again. As if this was a minor fact to be considered.

"Look," I snapped, irritated. Irritation was so much more appealing than shame. "This could be relevant to Gia's case."

He raised his eyebrows. "Yes, it could be. I agree."

"Don't placate me, Bobby. It's condescending and insulting."

"I'm not placating you. I'm taking in the information you're giving me, and we will see if it's relevant to Gia's case. I promise."

Suddenly he reminded me of Tony, being patient with me as if I were someone who needed to be tiptoed around. Someone who couldn't be trusted with honesty.

"Bobby, look—I know it's probably not connected. But if someone in her past is—"

"Salem, I didn't say it wasn't connected. We will collect all the information, and we'll look into him. But..." He stopped and rolled his lips together. "You're positive it's the same guy?"

I gave a short, humorless laugh. "You never forget the face, Bobby."

"I know, but...twenty years is a long time. You were very young. Memories are unpredictable—"

"His mother was best friends with my mother. They hung out together all the time. It's the same name. He looks the same. I checked out his social media, and his mother is one of his contacts. *My* mother is one of *her* contacts. This wasn't some random guy who caught me in a back alley, Bobby. We knew them. I wasn't around him a lot, but I was around his mother. She doesn't have two sons with the same name. It's him."

He nodded. "I understand." He took a deep breath and then sat back in his chair. "I do think we need to get Detective Scott in on this. She'll be the one to decide how to use this information." He looked from me to Viv and Ash, then back at me. "We can do that now, or we can wait if you're not ready for that."

I realized then that he wasn't being careful with me because he thought I was unpredictable. He was being careful with me because he cared about me.

Don't cry don't cry don't cry. "No time like the present," I managed.

259

He nodded again and stood. "I'll see if she's available, and then we'll move into the other room. My office is too small for all of us."

We all moved to a small conference room down the hallway. I could feel Bobby behind me. I felt like I was made of the thinnest glass, like there was nothing in the world except this moment I had to get through, and then the next, and then the next.

The detective came in that I'd seen at the Perez house, and she recognized Viv. "Oh hey," she said with a smile. Then she turned to Bobby. "Wait. Is this that PI team you're always talking about?" She drew her head back and took us in like she couldn't quite believe it.

"We're freelance investigative podcasters," Viv said. She reached into her inside jacket pocket and pulled out one of those tacky business cards.

The detective took it and then gave Bobby a bit of a bug-eyed look. He wasn't playing back, though. He was all business now.

"In their interviews with the Perez family, they came upon some information that might be pertinent to the Gia Perez case." He looked at me.

This was about the fourth time I'd told this story, and to my relief, I found it was getting easier. Not easy. But easier. She nodded, asking questions, taking notes.

"And this guy is still in town?" she asked.

I pulled out my phone and pulled up his Facebook page. "This is him," I said. My stomach turned at that wide, bad-boy smile.

She took the phone and wrote down a bunch of things.

Finally, she laid her pen down and looked at Bobby. "Thank you for coming in. This might not have anything to do with Gia. But then again, it might just be the lead we're looking for."

"Are you going to tell the Perez family about this?"

Detective Scott looked at Bobby. "I think we should," she said. "There are a couple of things that need to happen first. But I think they have a right to know." She tapped her pen against her notepad. "They're getting ready for the vigil tonight. It'll be the one-year anniversary of her disappearance, and they're having a candlelight vigil at the park. If—"

But she stopped when Bobby clapped his hands on his knees. "Mrs. Kennedy, Ash, I'd like to speak to Salem alone."

Viv frowned. Ash crossed her arms over her chest.

"I mean alone with Detective Scott." He nodded toward the door. "Please wait out in the lobby, and we'll be through in a minute."

After they were gone, he turned to me, his elbows on his knees. "Salem, this is one hundred percent your choice, okay? But you need to know, we can't really go to the Perez family with this information unless you file an official report."

My stomach dropped. I had hoped I could just tell what I knew and then drop out of the picture.

"File a report? What does that—what would I have to do?"

He shook his head. "It doesn't mean anything except we have a paper trail. It doesn't mean you're pressing charges. It just means you came in here and told us this happened, and we have a record of the conversation."

I swallowed. "Will you tell *him*?" I blurted it out without thinking, and immediately felt so stupid and childish for even wondering that. What did *I* care if they told him? Did I want to protect him, for crying out loud? Of course, I didn't.

Then I wondered if that question made me sound like I was afraid for him to find out—like I had some reason to hide. Like I was making it up. Immediately I felt defensive.

Ugh. No wonder women didn't want to report stuff like this. It was awful.

But Bobby didn't seem fazed by the question. He just shook his head. "Not necessarily. Look, there are still a lot of options. You could fill out the report and that's the last we ever talk about it. We check him out and find out there isn't reason to think he has anything to do with Gia's running away, don't find anything connecting him to any other assaults, and that's basically the end of it, unless you decide you want to pursue things further in your own case. And you could do that. But that's up to you, Salem. It's all up to you. But basically, for our purposes, if it's not in writing, it didn't happen. If someone else comes in with a complaint on him, it'll be like it's the first time we've heard of him. And we couldn't go to the Perezes with any information unless we have something official."

I nodded, but I felt like I'd already done enough. I felt more exposed than I wanted to be.

"Do you want to call Tony? Would that be helpful?"

I swallowed and shook my head. "No, Tony and I are..." I couldn't finish.

I didn't have to. Bobby's eyes widened a bit, and then he frowned.

"My fault," I said. "This last week or so has been rough. You know, remembering all this and trying to figure out how to deal with it. I went back to some of my...previous coping mechanisms. Tony didn't...like that."

Bobby gnawed on his lower lip and nodded, contemplating this. "Well, I know he has a lot on his plate right now. But maybe you two can work it out."

I sighed. "Let's just get this over with."

I knew it was common for people to have sketchy memories from their childhood, and I certainly didn't remember every moment of that day. I did remember how much fun I had. I did remember how I felt special, that I was getting attention from someone older and cooler than I was. I remembered how I thought it was the best day of my life.

And I remembered the confusion when things started going bad. When he turned the conversation to 'what boyfriends and girlfriends do.' I remembered wondering if he understood that I was only seven. I did have a bit of an attitude, and I remembered thinking, at the time, if he thought I might be twelve. To me, twelve was practically a teenager, which was just a quick jump to adult. I was a bit flattered that he thought I was older than I was, but I also knew fundamentally that it wasn't right that he would think of me as a girlfriend. I didn't understand why, but I knew it was odd.

At the same time, I still believed he was a good guy. A fun guy. And grownups do things all the time that they *say* are good for you but that you, as a kid, don't like. Getting shots, taking disgusting medicine, going to school, wearing uncomfortable shoes. You have to take their word for it that this was a good thing. And that's the sense my mind was trying to make of what he was doing to me and telling me. He said this was a good thing, a fun thing, and he was older and smarter than I was. It didn't make sense to me, but I was only seven, and I didn't want him to think I was a baby, did I?

Recounting this, as an adult to other adults, out loud, getting it out of my head and into words, it was so clear to me just how I'd been groomed. Just how stereotypically I'd been manipulated, and how much of a child I had been. I had known this, of course, and yet as I remembered—my God! I'd been seven years old! -- just how little I'd understood and how little I had responsibility for. Why had I ever thought I had?

We filed out of the conference room and Bobby walked me to the door. "Thanks," I said as we approached the door, expecting him to turn back to his office.

He surprised me by nodding silently and then holding the door open for me and following me out onto the sidewalk.

He took a deep breath. "Look, Salem. I'm really sorry that happened."

I couldn't speak past the lump in my throat, so I just nodded.

"I mean it. It was wrong. He was wrong. It shouldn't have happened. You understand that, right?"

I nodded. "Of course." *I do now,* I didn't say. I thought of all the shame I'd carried since I'd been seven years old. Why had I ever thought that shame was mine to carry?

"Were you planning to go to the vigil tonight?"

I shrugged. "We talked about it." Although honestly, I couldn't imagine going anywhere except home.

"You need to know, if Shawn had anything to do with Gia's disappearance, he'll probably show up. They almost always show up. They have to get a look at what they did—see the effect they've had. He might stick around the periphery, but he could put himself right into the middle of things."

My heart thudded at the thought of seeing him. Being an old boyfriend of Helena's, he would have a good cover story to "put himself right into the middle of things."

"So, if you don't want to go...don't go." He lowered his chin and met my gaze. "Okay?"

"Okay," I whispered.

He studied me for a second. "In fact, even if you do want to go...don't go."

I attempted a smile. "Okay."

"I'm serious, Salem. You don't need to get mixed up in this any more than you already are. We can take it from here." He cupped a hand to my shoulder. "You take care of you."

Ash and Viv gathered around me on the sidewalk—well, as close to a 'gather 'round' that two people can.

"Are you okay?" Ask asked.

I nodded. Surprisingly, I felt okay. Like, hollowed out, relieved, a bit numb. No, more than a bit. A lot numb. I'd done it. It was done.

And so was I, I realized as we moved toward Viv's car. I was *so* done. Every step I took seemed to drain more energy from my depleted reserves. It was as if, now that everything I'd feared had been brought into the light, I realized it was the only thing in me. And now I was empty.

I fell into the back seat of Viv's Caddy and fought the urge to just lie prone on the seat. I buckled up and let Ash and Viv's chatter flow by me as we pulled out of the parking lot and onto the street.

I needed to sleep, I thought. Immediately.

"Okay, we were talking while you filed your report, and here's what we're thinking. We stake out this Shawn guy, follow him for a few days. See where he leads us. It's entirely possible that Gia could be right here—"

"If she's still alive," I mumbled.

"Right. If she's still alive, she could be right here in town, or being held somewhere in a nearby town. She could be right under our noses, but nobody knew because we didn't know how to track her. So, we'll go tonight to the vigil. If he had something to do it her disappearance, he's guaranteed to show up. They always come back to—"

"That's what Bobby said, too," I interrupted.

"Don't worry." Ash turned and looked at me over the back of her seat. "We'll stick with you the entire time. Even if he's there, he won't get within an inch of you without—"

"I'm not going."

Viv and Ash looked at each other. Then Ash frowned. "Well, okay. I can understand why you wouldn't want to go. Viv and I will take notes and report back to you tomorrow. You do look like you could use a night off."

"I'm not going to the vigil, and you're not going to report back to me."

As soon as I said it, I realized this was definitely the route I was going to take. Bobby was right. They could take it from here. I didn't owe the Perez family anything, I didn't owe Charles Polk anything, and as much as I loved Viv and had come to appreciate Ash, I didn't owe them this. It was time to think of what I needed. And I needed a break.

"This has nothing to do with me, really, and I've done what I need to do. My obligation is fulfilled. I'm done."

Viv looked at me in the rear-view mirror. "What does that even mean? I'm done? How are you done?"

"I mean, I'm done. I've done my duty. I told. I filed the report, and now the police will follow up on it. If there's anything more than needs to be done with it, they can do it. Or you two can. But I'm finished."

They looked at each other. Viv opened her mouth to say something, but Ash shook her head.

"What?" Viv mouthed.

"Just wait," Ash mouthed back.

"No, we're not going to wait," I said. "We're not going to talk about it later. You're not going to find a way to present things to me so that I'll be persuaded to change my mind. I didn't have any say when that pig touched me, and I didn't have much say in when or how—or *if,* even—I talked about it, but I have a say now. And I'm saying no. I'm finished."

"But you can't be finished. Gia is still out there, somewhere, and we could—"

"If she's still alive," I said again.

"If she's still alive!" Viv shouted and slapped her steering wheel.

"Listen, I know this has been very hard for you," Ash started.

She stopped abruptly, though, when I barked laughter at her.

"Very hard for me!" I cackled. It turned out there was something left in me, after all. Maniacal laughter. I laughed and laughed and fell over onto my side in the back seat and kept laughing. "It's been," I said between hoots. "Very hard! For me!" I tried to slap my thigh, but all I could manage was a pitiful swipe. I was weak.

"Just let her go," Viv advised as she drove.

That set me off again. It was as if I rose outside my body and watched it all from above. Ash and Viv in the front seat, silent and frustrated with me, and me in the back seat, unable to catch my breath because I was laughing so hard.

It all made me laugh harder.

Ash cast another glace over the back of the seat at me. She turned to Viv. "I don't think she's even breathing. She's just—" Then she opened her mouth wide at Viv, like a picture captured in the middle of a roar.

As you might imagine, that did me in. I curled up on the back seat, my head bent toward the floorboard, and laughed so hard I drooled. I actually drooled in Viv's backseat floorboard.

We pulled into Trailertopia and Viv parked at the curb behind my Monster Carlo. I sat up and looked at the twenty or so yards that separated me from my front door. I wasn't sure how I was going to make it.

Frank must have been watching out the door, though, because he opened the door, and he and Stump came out onto the deck. Stump bumped her fat little bottom down the steps and headed for the grass.

With a fierce intensity, suddenly all I wanted was to be back in the days when it was just me and Stump, before I met Viv, before Tony and I had reconciled, before any of this...this *whatever my life could be called now* happened. Just go to work, come home, have dinner, watch TV. Yes, I had been gaining weight at an alarming rate, but so what? I was gaining weight now, and I was a wreck on top of everything else.

"How'd it go?" Frank asked as I trudged up the steps, Viv and Ash behind me.

"It went," I said.

I opened the door and headed inside. Frank said, behind me, "She okay?"

"She's not okay, and she's just fine," I said loudly. "She's a wreck and a shell and a husk of her former self, but the general consensus is that she needs to *press on*! Because why not? Who wouldn't be chomping at the bit to *get back out there* and *see justice done*!" I jabbed my hand in the air like a coach giving a last-minute locker room pep talk before the big game.

Viv huffed. "Well, no one is saying that you have to get back out there *today*! You could take the evening off, recuperate a bit, before—"

"Why, thank you Vivian Walker Reed Carson Kennedy for your permission!"

"You don't have to get nasty with me. I just want to see justice done. I just want—"

Okay. I know what I'm about to say is going to be very bad. I understand that it might seem, well... Okay. Here's what I did. I picked up a box of dried pasta I'd left on the bar and threw it at Viv's head.

Ash, she of the very quick reflexes, stepped forward and batted it away. Which, honestly, I was kind of relieved to see. Because I wanted to hurt Viv, but I also *never* wanted to hurt Viv.

I screamed at her. "How dare you! How dare you imply that I have no interest in justice being served! How dare you take some kind of moral high ground when everyone knows that all you care about is having your nose in the middle of an interesting story!"

"Well!" Viv gasped and put a hand to her chest. "And for your information, it's Walker *Carson Reed* Kennedy!"

"I'm sorry I can't keep up with the sequence of your many, many ex-husbands!" I looked around for something else to throw at her, confident now that Ash would save me from my darker impulses.

Ash just rolled her eyes and moved toward me. "I will throw *you* down if I have to. You know I can."

I knew she could. I did not want her to throw me down.

But I did want to give her a piece of my mind. "And you!" I shouted, shoving a finger in her face. "You think this is all some kind of divine plan to right wrongs and settle debts. That's! *Insane!*"

She gently closed her hand around my finger and forced me to lower it. "Okay," she said evenly.

"Don't 'okay' me!" I shouted and snatched my hand back. "I'm not crazy. *You're* crazy! Why would God go through all the trouble of orchestrating this—this big, elaborate plan to heal wounds and right wrongs instead of just *preventing the wounds and the wrongs from happening in the first place?* Huh? Why?"

"We can talk it through tomorrow," Ash said. "Right now—"

271

"It's going to be every bit as stupid and delusional tomorrow as it is today!" I shouted. "We're so freaking desperate to believe we are loved by a benevolent, all-knowing God that we—we make these ridiculous, illogical *leaps* and—and these conspiracy-theory justifications to tell ourselves, 'Oh, *that's* why I had to be violated and abused as a child! So, I could then help this *other* girl who's also been abused as a child. God can be glorified, and my completely *devastating* pain can be put to good use for others!'" I raised my hands and shouted at the ceiling. In my trailer, that wasn't very far above me. "Hallelujah, my pain and trauma were for a reason. To help someone else! Never mind about me! Never mind that I had twenty years of shame over it! What does that matter that I was completely destroyed? God had a plan!" I turned and slammed my hands on the counter. "Who cares about that? Who cares about me? I'm all a part of The Plan. That's all that really matters!"

I was screaming, I realized. Viv, Ash and Frank all stared at me like they didn't know what to say. Probably because they *didn't* know what to say. I didn't know what to say. But that didn't stop me from talking.

I leaned close to Ash and said, "Tell me this. You think this is all part of God's Big Important Genius Plan, right? You lost your job, you got transferred here, how many thousands of miles away? Transferred here where you knew no one, and you just happened to be on the one who answered that Uber call that night because it was all part of God's BIG PLAN? God orchestrated all that so we could help each other?"

I waited, but she didn't respond.

"He made all that happen? He had his hand in all of it so it could all work out to his glory." I raised my hands like jazz hands to the sky. "His glory! If he can do all that, why wouldn't he just make sure the abuse didn't happen in the first place!" I slapped the counter again. "If he can move us around like pieces on a chess board, why not just protect! Little! Kids!" I slapped the counter with each word. "Why get so focused on cleaning up the messes instead of preventing the abuse to begin with? What kind of—of useless, clueless God is that?"

The trailer went silent, and that's when I heard Frank, speaking low. He stood by the door, his phone to his ear. He realized I'd stopped talking and he cast a wary glance my way. "Yeah." He nodded. "Okay." He thumbed off the phone.

Anyway. Les and Bonnie came not long after that. Even though it was early evening, I went to bed. I thought I was too enraged by then to sleep. But I slept.

I slept really hard, in fact. One of those times when I woke up but just lay there, staring ahead, unsure of where I was or what day it was. Was it still the same day? I had to think back to even remember *who* I was.

I shifted just enough to get my face out of my own drool. I felt Stump wiggle against me, then settle back into a soft snore. Wouldn't it be wonderful to just go back to sleep?

I heard the TV coming from the living room. Spanish. So that meant Frank was still there, probably watching his telenovelas.

"That's the one who tried to kill her," Frank said. "But she forgot about it."

"Who forgot about it? Her?" That was Les.

So, it was still the same day, probably.

I glanced up at my window. The light was fading. Ugh. I'd slept for what, two hours?

"Yeah," Frank answered. "She got all freaked out and, like, forgot everything. She thinks it's two years ago."

"Wow," Les said.

"It's pretty trippy. Oh! Here's the guy I was telling you about, who's hiding the stolen money."

I burrowed down in the bed, wishing I could fall back to sleep like Stump. I was awake, but I felt...safe, I guess. Knowing Les, Bonnie and Frank were just down the hall. Like they were guarding the entrance to my bedroom.

It reminded me of something, the echo of a long-ago memory. I let my mind drift, feeling the sense of being cocooned, of being on the periphery of activity, listening from the shadows. Soft voices, my presence forgotten to them.

It was G-Ma, I realized, and her friend Yvette. I remembered waking during one of her visits, the two of them in G-Ma's living room at the motel while I slept in my "bedroom," that was really a storage closet that G-Ma had wedged a twin bed and a box for my clothes into.

"But we could be having so much fun, Virgie," Yvette said.

"We're having fun right now," G-Ma replied.

"This isn't your job. You've done your time. You deserve to have a little adventure of your own."

"Look around you," G-Ma said, then laughed. "You're saying this place isn't an adventure?"

I remembered that conversation because just that day, we'd had to call 911 on a man who fell in the parking lot, and someone had called 911 on *us* because they said the maid had stolen their stuff. I remembered thinking that G-Ma's place was anything but boring. I had lain there, feeling safe and content, until I drifted back to sleep to the sound of G-Ma's and Yvette's voices, rising and falling as they laughed and reminisced into the night.

My phone dinged.

Tony?

My hand was already reaching for the phone to see if it was him, but I stopped.

It probably wasn't Tony. It almost certainly wasn't Tony. And if it wasn't Tony, did I really want to know who it was? Did it really matter?

My phone dinged again.

Tony, something wistful inside me whispered, hoping against hope.

I reached for the phone and saw the text was from Viv.

I was about to drop the phone when I saw the first line of the text.

It's not her.

Actually, that was the only line. *It's not her.*

The next text was a link, again from Viv. No words, just the link.

I looked down at Stump, who was curled up at my side, watching me. She looked at the phone, then again at me, brows raised as if to say, "you gonna open that?"

I thumbed the link open.

"The body found on County Road 3100 last week has been identified as Charlotte Franks, a 22-year-old woman from Kansas City, Missouri." There was a picture of a sweet looking girl with black hair and wide, laughing eyes.

There was more, but I thumbed my phone off and lay back down, closing my eyes.

It's not her.

It's not her.

It's not her.

Finally, I sighed and pushed myself to a sitting position on the edge of the bed. My head still felt fuzzy, and I thought maybe I could go back to sleep. But I wouldn't.

I sat for a long time, then made myself stand. I went to the bathroom, splashed my face with water, and brushed my teeth.

I stared at myself in the mirror.

"This isn't your job."

I had sheet creases on my face, and my wavy hairdo was smashed.

"You've done your time. You deserve an adventure."

I stood there and stared at myself long enough that my face did that thing that words sometimes do, when we say them over and over: my face became unfamiliar to me. It wasn't just the red lines from the sheets; I looked different. I looked like a different person.

This was the me everyone else saw, I realized. But it wasn't the me I saw when I usually looked in the mirror. This woman was an adult.

I scrubbed my hands hard through my hair, then wiped my face with the washcloth again. I supposed it was because I'd spent the last hours recalling a traumatic event from my childhood, followed by recalling a safe memory from that same time.

My equilibrium felt off.

Was that all of it? Is that why I didn't recognize that face in the mirror, even though I knew at the same time that was, in fact, *me* standing there?

I gave the back of my neck a good scrub with the washcloth and sighed. I would just have to be off, I supposed.

Out in the living room, Frank, Les and Bonnie watched me as I trudged to the sofa and sat.

"You okay?" Les asked.

I took a deep breath and let it out. "I think so."

Bonnie patted my knee.

I opened my phone and clicked on the link that Viv had sent, showing Les and Bonnie the story about the dead girl.

"It's not her," Bonnie said.

I nodded.

"Gia Perez might still be alive," Les said.

"Maybe."

"That's good."

"Maybe," I said again. My voice sounded resentful to my own ears. Did I care?

No, I thought. I had too much on my mind, processing a brand-new suspicion—no, more like a brand-new realization—to care if I sounded resentful to Les.

Frank eyed me warily.

Les was silent for a moment, then said, "Salem. I'm sorry for what you've been through. Both in the past, and today."

I cleared my throat. "Thanks."

"I want you to know that your pain is never what God wanted for you."

I shot a look at Frank.

"That soldier woman told him what you said," he said.

"It's fine," I said. I wasn't sure if Marines were called soldiers, but I decided to let that be. I knew who he meant.

"And it's fine that you said it," Les said. "I understand your frustration."

"Do you?"

"On a certain level, yes, I do. But I also want to make sure you understand that a loving God would not allow you to be hurt just so he can use your pain to help someone else. He doesn't work that way."

"Well, I don't see him doing a lot to stop it, either."

"No, and you wouldn't. You *wouldn't* see what he's done to protect you, because you're not God."

I was too tired to roll my eyes, but I supposed my irritation with that statement was clear on my face, because Les grinned.

"Salem. God uses *us* to take care of each other, to protect each other. It's the failure of man, not God, that leads to us being hurt."

"Oh yeah, that convenient evergreen 'free will of man' card." *What's even the point of praying,* I wondered?

Les shrugged. "It's true."

"Yeah, well...I guess I'm just not smart enough to understand the whole 'free will' and 'God's timing' stuff, because I think it's sad that here we are, thousands of years on and God hasn't caught on that this isn't exactly working out so well for some of us down here."

Frank threw another anxious look at Les.

Les's smile softened. "It's okay to be mad at God, Salem. It's okay to question."

"Well, it's a dang good thing," I said. "Because I have lots of questions." *And a lot of mad.*

"It is," he assured me. "That's where growth happens."

I started to make a crack about how all the stress was causing growth in my thighs. But I didn't; I was too tired, and I wasn't in the mood to make light of anything. So instead, I just shrugged.

"Growth can be painful."

"You're not trying to convince me that all this is about growth, are you?"

"Everything is about growth, if you want it to be. Do you want it to be?"

"No," I said shortly. I groaned and stood. "Growth is just about the last thing on my mind, at the moment. But I just realized, someone in my life made sacrifices to keep me safe. Someone *was* looking out for me when no one else was. And that mattered to me. I could have ended up like Gia, or – or like Charlotte Franks – if they hadn't. I've been so busy feeling sorry for myself for how my life went, I haven't taken the time to think of how much worse it could have been."

Bonnie started to say something, and I held up a finger. "No. I'm sorry, and I don't want to be rude, but please, Bonnie. Don't say something about silver linings or blessings in disguise or *anything* like that. I'm sorry I'm being rude, but I just...I can't handle it right now. No matter what else happens, I want it noted that this *sucks*. To have to tell yourself, well, at least I haven't been murdered and my body left at the side of the road. That's a ridiculously low bar to set. It's..." I could think of no other words. "It's stupid! This world is stupid and I'm not going to waste my time pretending like everything is beautiful and works out for the best and God has some big mysterious plan that I'm just not smart enough to discern. I'm not going to do it. It's disgusting."

I made myself stop before I got worked up again and needed another nap.

"But," I said, and took another deep breath. "But someone—a human, not a god—helped me. And I'm going to help Gia. It's something I *can* do. So, I'm going to. Not for God. For me. For Gia."

Les nodded. "Okay."

"I'm going to the vigil." I realized with a sense of grim satisfaction that I didn't care if Shawn was there or not. Let him come. I wasn't afraid of that toad anymore.

"I'll come with you."

"No, I'm fine. Viv and Ash will be there, and probably Bobby Sloan, too."

"Are you going to drink?"

"No."

"You're sure?"

"Quite sure. I'm too tired to even be tempted." At the look he gave me, I made him the promise I hadn't made in several months. "I promise, I will call you first, if I do."

I swung a couple miles out of my way to visit G-Ma's motel-slash-shopping center. Most of the shops were closed for the day. She was crossing the lot toward her apartment and office as Candace carried in her specials chalkboard and locked up the bakery.

G-Ma eyed me as Stump and I got out of the car. "I'm sober," I said. "Not looking for a place to stay."

Uncharacteristically, she patted me on the shoulder on her way past. "Good to see you back on track. Did you talk to your husband?"

I took a deep breath. "I have talked to him. We're still...well, we're working things out." What else could I say? I had no idea what was happening with Tony and me. *He gave me a thumbs-up emoji, so I'm sure we're fine* didn't feel like a thing I wanted to share.

I followed G-Ma into her front office and ignored her pointed look at Stump, who trotted in after us.

"It was nice to see Yvette," I said. "I had kind of forgotten about her."

"Yeah, it's good to see her," G-Ma said absently as she rummaged through her desk, putting things to rights.

"So they're selling the RV and staying in one place?"

"Mmm-hmmm."

I took a deep breath and then plunged in. "You had planned to go on the road with her." I didn't phrase it as a question, because the answer was already clear to me. I just needed confirmation.

"Oh, I was never really serious about that. That was just Yvette's big plans. I've always liked a little more stability."

Should I push it? The thing with G-Ma was, I never really knew what was going to make her furious. Being a grownup who could leave at any time, I shouldn't have been afraid of my grandmother's temper. But I still kind of was.

However, I was feeling fatalistic, and I needed to know. "I know that's not true. You may have changed your mind. But I know, at some point, you really wanted to join her on that adventure. You planned that."

"Well, it's a woman's prerogative to change her mind."

I nodded. "True. You changed your mind because of me."

"Oh, Salem, I did not."

"I know you did. *I* was the one who needed stability. *I* needed security. You changed your plans, because you knew you were the only one who was going to give that to me." I was surprised to find my throat closing again. Dang it. I kept thinking my emotions were numb, and they kept rearing their annoying heads.

G-Ma made a grumbly noise but didn't dispute that.

"Thank you," I managed to squeak out.

"Pfft," G-Ma said with a wave of her hand.

"That was...quite a sacrifice."

She shrugged. "We did okay here."

We both remembered the lean years, though, and the repeated attempts at injecting the motel with fresh energy, with shoddy paint jobs, questionable price promotions, one failed shot after another at keeping the restaurant up and running. Things were going well now, but she'd had a tough time of it for a long time.

"What about now?" I asked. "The place is a money-maker now. You could probably get a good price for it."

"Oh, I'm too old for all that, Salem."

"You're not," I said.

"I am. And it's fine. When I was fifteen, I wanted to be the lead majorette, and I didn't get that, either. I am fine. I have lost all desire to twirl a baton and march in calf boots and a funny hat. It was a passing thing, and it's passed now. I'm not going to look back."

The thing was, she *almost* sold this story. I almost believed she had no regrets. I think she almost believed it, too. Neither of us was 100 percent sure, but neither of us really knew what to do about it, either.

"Well...thank you," I said again. "I think we both know how much worse I could have turned out if you hadn't stepped in."

"Yes, well," she sighed again. "I figured if I'd done a better job being a mom, *your* mom would have been better at it, too. So..." She shrugged. "I had some stuff to make up for."

I considered that. My mom complained a lot about G-Ma, but then again, she had complained a lot about everything. In my typical self-involved fashion, I'd never thought much about G-Ma's motivation for taking me in—aside from the notion that she wanted a free housekeeper, which she got. I had no doubt she loved me and cared about my welfare, gruff and undemonstrative though she was. I had never considered that she was making up for some of her own failings.

The notion actually brought me some comfort. The idea that, even if we messed up, we could step in later and make a difference.

I checked her clock. If I didn't get a move on, I'd miss the vigil completely, and then Les, Viv, Ash and Frank would all be up in my business. Bless them.

I patted the counter, "Well, I'm sorry those were the circumstances, because we both know, if you'd been with Yvette when Ed pulled his big diesel pusher in next to you, you'd be the one with him now."

She cackled. "I know that's right. Don't tell Yvette I said that."

The vigil was being held at Mackenzie Park because that was one of Gia's favorite places. It was one of my favorite places, too. People have this image of Lubbock being perfectly flat, barren, dust in the air and tumbleweeds blowing by, and we have plenty of that. More than enough. But there's also Yellowhouse Canyon and Yellowhouse Draw, and Mackenzie Park is along that, with a rocky cliff on the west side and a beautiful green space with big trees along the east side, and the gently flowing river between. Sid Perez said he'd brought Gia here to fish often when she was younger.

The sun was low in the sky and the park already dark enough that the candles were visible by the time I parked the Monster Carlo and Stump and I got out. I let her walk a little way, but I didn't hesitate to pick her up when she quickly got bored with sniffing and trotted to me to be carried. She would become heavy soon, but I didn't care.

There was a sizable crowd, and I saw vehicles from all four local stations.

I looked for Shawn. Good grief. Half the cars in the parking lot were either white pickups or black SUVs. The other half was white SUVs and black pickups.

Shawn could be here. The odds were good that he was there, right now. Maybe even watching me lugging Stump across the grass.

The notion shot a thrill of something—something I didn't fully understand—through me. It was part dread, but a bigger part almost hoped he was there. I felt this kind of "bring it on" defiance. I remembered Bobby's words that afternoon. I imagined meeting his gaze, then sneering at him. Jerk. Why should I be afraid of him? He couldn't hurt me anymore.

Still, a part of me was also frightened, if I was being honest. I didn't like that part.

From the other side of the parking lot, I saw a woman walking toward the crowd. Sierra. What would Sierra say, I wondered, if one of her friends was afraid to see the man who had abused her when she was young? Sierra, who was no longer intimidated by the perfect soccer mom, who had chosen not to buy into the unfair shaming of girls and their natural cycles?

She would tell that friend to lift her chin, put her shoulders back, and go wherever the heck she wanted to go. She might use stronger language than that, actually. Probably *would* use stronger language than that.

Of course, if she knew I--a woman almost twelve years her senior--was using her as a mental life coach, she would think I was straight up coo-coo for Cocoa Puffs, too.

Still, I felt emboldened enough to approach the crowd gathered near a concrete picnic table. Janet, Helena's and Gia's cousin, jumped onto one of the benches and began motioning for everyone to quiet down. Through breaks in the crowd, I spotted Helena and Sid, and then saw Viv.

She stood near Helena like a bodyguard. She smiled and gave me the thumbs up when she saw me, and I felt unexpected relief. On the one hand, I knew my meltdown that afternoon was perfectly understandable. On the other hand – I had *chunked* something at Viv's head! Ugh. I felt like an idiot now. I was glad she didn't seem to harbor a grudge.

I spotted Ash talking to some of the Perez family, and Mateo, Helena's boyfriend, a few feet from the rest of the crowd. Stump and I joined them.

Janet whistled loudly from her perch on top of the picnic table.

"Helena and Sid want to thank everyone for coming tonight. The love and support from family and friends has meant so much to them through this awful, awful year. They asked me to tell you just how important it is to them that you keep praying for Gia's return, keep looking for her, keep asking questions."

"Keep harassing the police!" Helena shouted.

Janet nodded, but didn't echo her cousin. She said, "Someone, somewhere knows what happened to Gia. Someone, somewhere knows where she is. Someone, somewhere can bring this nightmare to an end and let this family have the healing they need and deserve."

The crowd was growing even since I'd arrived. I scanned it, almost willing Shawn to appear so I could prove to myself that I would not run scared. There were a lot of people, though, and I wasn't sure I'd spot him even if he *was* there.

After Janet finished, some of Gia's friends got up and spoke about her. They were nervous and a little awkward, but their feelings were also authentic. One girl said through tears, "Gia was a very good friend to me. I've missed her so much this year. School is not nearly as fun without her." Another said, "Gia always made me laugh. She had a wicked sense of humor. She made everyone laugh. Gia, wherever you are, I hope you're laughing."

After the girls, one of the teachers got up. "Gia was one of those students who sticks in your memory. She always kept me guessing. Some days she would be sweet and hardworking, and some days she just was not in the mood for school. I get that. Some days I'm not in the mood for school, either." The crowd laughed. "I never knew what kind of mood Gia would be in. But one thing I never doubted: Gia had a will of iron. That girl was strong. Mentally strong. She could take care of herself. I never saw her back down from a challenge. I'll tell you this, and I mean every word of it." She held up a finger to the crowd. "Of all the kids I ever had the privilege to have in my classroom, if *any* of them has the strength to go through a difficult ordeal and come out the other side of it stronger, it's Gia."

Gia's cousin Joe got up, the young one who'd told me the story about the stolen tools in Shawn's pickup. He started talking about how cool Gia was, but he was overcome with emotion and had to stop. His dad stepped up beside him and threw an arm around the boy's shoulders. A lump formed in my own throat. Joe finally said, "Gia, wherever you are, I can't wait to hang out with you again!" and jumped down from the table.

I was pretty much a wreck by this point. All the sadness and fear in the crowd were overwhelming. I hugged Stump to me.

Then I saw him.

I don't know why I had thought there was any possibility I wouldn't recognize him. Of *course*, I recognized him--especially after looking at his social media pictures. His smarmy weasel face was unmistakable.

Out of a reflex I didn't understand, I spun around and moved behind a tree. My heart thudded and my mouth went dry.

I had thought I was prepared. But look at me.

I held Stump close to me. What was wrong with me? I was in no danger *here*.

Still, I was terrified.

I peeked around the tree and saw Ash looking my direction, her head cocked. I tried to form my face into some semblance of calm and confidence, but honestly, I just felt miserable and small, and I'm sure it showed.

She was by my side in an instant. "He's here?"

I moved back behind the tree and leaned against it. "Yes. Blaargh," I said. "What is wrong with me? I thought I was prepared for this."

"There's nothing wrong with you. Your reaction to a dangerous situation is completely appropriate." She put her hand on my arm and scanned the crowd. "Where is he?"

"He's wearing a white ball cap and a light blue t-shirt. Jeans."

"Oh, yeah. I see him." She glared at him. "I'd really like to just walk over there and slug him."

"Me, too." Actually, all I really wanted to do was run. Run home, crawl under the covers. I felt furious, terrified, and helpless, all at once. I thought I had cried everything out earlier in the day, but tears threatened again.

"You're safe," Ash said, still keeping an eye on Shawn. "Oh, hey. It's that detective."

I breathed a sigh of relief. "Bobby?" I turned to look.

"No, the woman. Detective Scott?"

"Oh." I searched the crowd, disappointed not to see Bobby.

This wasn't his case, I reminded myself. If he wasn't working the case, he didn't have a reason to be here.

But then, he *was* there. He strolled up behind Detective Scott, and they exchanged a few words while both surveyed the crowd. I was so relieved my knees went a little weak.

At the table, Sierra was reciting a poem she'd written for Gia. How could a sixteen-year-old girl be so composed? I was almost twice her age, and I practically ran to Bobby for safety.

"He's here," I blurted.

Bobby nodded. "What's he wearing?"

I described Shawn's outfit and his general position in the crowd.

Bobby nodded again. He sidled over and he and Detective Scott had a whispered conversation out of the sides of their mouths. Then she nodded and moved off to circle around to the other side of the crowd. Bobby returned to stand near us.

I waited. "Is that it?"

"For now."

One of the other cousins came running over and gave us all candles, followed by another cousin with cardboard discs to slip over the bottom of the candles to protect our hands.

Viv joined us. "What's going on?"

"They're getting ready to take him down," Ash said.

My heart thudded.

"We're not taking anyone down," Bobby said. "Not tonight, anyway."

"But he's right there," I said. "Arrest him."

Bobby slipped his sunglasses off and looked directly at me. "Salem. Do you trust us to do our job?"

I took a deep breath. "Yes. Of course."

"Then let us do our jobs." He looked at Ash and Viv. "You two stay close with her, okay?"

He turned back to me. "I want your word that you'll steer clear of this guy."

One would think, based on my indignation at this proposal, that I *hadn't* just run and hid behind a tree when I spotted Shawn fifty yards away. "You will get no such thing."

"You can't tell her to do that," Viv said.

Bobby, to my astonishment, shot Viv such a look of fury that it made me draw in a sharp breath. He held a hand up to Viv. "You. Stop talking."

Hand still holding Viv back, he said, "Salem, you've been doing so great. You're off probation. You've been staying out of trouble. Don't blow all your progress now on this guy. *Trust us* to do our jobs."

Too late not to blow it all now, I thought. I didn't answer, though. How could I explain to Bobby why I was there, when I didn't understand it myself?

He frowned, his lips tight, then said, "Could there even *be* a bigger trigger for you than this guy?"

I swallowed. "I can't think of one."

He nodded, then took a step back, taking in Viv and Ash. "*Good* friends would keep that in mind before they drag you through stuff like this."

And with that, he stalked away.

Viv and Ash flanked me.

"Wow," Ash said.

"I know," I said. I felt like a kid who'd just been chewed out by the principal.

"Sanctimonious jerk," Viv muttered.

We were all three silent for a long moment. Then Viv said, "I'm a good friend to you. Right?"

I took too long to answer. "I mean...sure. Of course."

"He's right," Ash said with a sigh. "To Viv and me, this has still been mostly hypothetical stuff. We keep forgetting this is your real stuff." She turned to me and said again, "He's right. You probably should sit this one out."

292

I watched Bobby disappear into the crowd, watched the night begin to glow as the candles were lit, first one or two, then more and more as each candle touched off one more. The area around the tables glowed with the light.

There were enough lights, I realized. I didn't have to be one of them. There were enough people who loved Gia and wanted her safe at home. I didn't even know her. Everything I'd said that afternoon was still true. I'd done my part.

That afternoon, I'd been so sure that what I'd done was enough. More than enough. I hadn't asked for any of this. None of that had been my fault. I'd had it dumped in my lap, and I'd carried that burden for more than twenty years. And I'd carried it badly—I'd been overcome by it, undone by it. My life had gone on a completely different trajectory because of it. Had been made the worse for it.

This isn't your job.

You've done your time.

"We should all sit this one out," Viv announced. "He's a sanctimonious jerk, but he's right. This one is too personal."

One of Gia's former classmates ran up to us, shielding the flame of her candle with the palm of one hand. She lit Viv's candle and said, "Pass it on!" before running off to another group.

Viv tilted her candle toward me and Ash. Ash held hers out and lit the tip.

I held my candle at my side, unlit. Just...thinking. After waiting a moment, Viv withdrew hers. She stepped to my right side. Ash stepped to my left. I stood, a dim shadow between the light that they held.

You go before me and follow me. You place your hand of blessing on my head. Psalm 139:5

I hadn't realized I'd remembered them but, standing in the glow from other people's candles bringing light to my own space, the words from Psalm 139 floated to my mind.

I could ask the darkness to hide me and the light around me to become night, but even in darkness I cannot hide from you. To you the night shines as bright as day. Darkness and light are the same to you. Psalm 139:11-12

"No," I finally said. "Nobody is sitting this one out."

Viv and Ash looked at me.

I shook my head. "Bobby's right. It's too much for me. But it isn't just me."

I turned to face them both. "I didn't drink because I saw Shawn. I drank because I saw Shawn, and then I isolated myself. I cut myself off from—from the light around me. I just...have to make sure I don't do that again." I bit my lip. "Provided, of course, you still want to be around me after I lost my whole mind today and called your ideas stupid," I looked at Ash, then turned to Viv and said, "and threw macaroni at you. I'm so sorry. I really am a dumpster fire right now."

Ash clasped my shoulder, much as Bobby had done earlier that day.

Viv nodded. "Of course."

I blinked back tears and tried to pass off a laugh. "Well, I would call for a group hug, except I don't want you two catching my new hairdo on fire."

I thought about telling them the memory of G-Ma that had surfaced earlier, sharing with them what she'd sacrificed to keep me safe. But I needed to work that out in my head, first.

So, I just said, "We're not going to sit this one out. We're going to stay safe, and you two are going to stick close to me, and if I feel like it's too much, I'm going to say it's too much."

"Excellent plan," Viv said.

"We'll stay right beside you," Ash said. "Won't let you out of our sight."

"Good," I said. I held my candle up and they both lit it. It was like some kind of odd commitment ceremony.

"Okay, let's go, then. I have some things to say." Viv headed toward the crowd.

"Are you going to talk to Helena and Sid?"

"No, I'm going to tell that sanctimonious jerk that I bought your dog a $400 bed and you threw a box of macaroni at my head," she said as she stalked across the grass. "Tell *me* I'm not a good friend..."

Chapter Eight

My phone buzzed around noon the next day, and I checked the texts. It was Viv.

You done?

3 left, I answered.

Perfect. We'll be there when we get done with our reconnoitering.

Apparently their 'reconnoitering' was a bit more time consuming than she had expected, because I finished the schnauzer, cocker spaniel, and the poodle, swept up my station, cleaned my scissors and brushes, and let Stump run around on the grass behind the shop before the Caddy pulled up in front of Flo's Bow Wow Barbers.

Viv jumped out carrying a stack of papers. She wore tan cargo shorts, a black tank top, and had a camo green cadet cap. It was an exact replica, I realized, of the clothes Ash had been wearing when we met Viv at First Friday Art Trail. She'd just added the hat because Viv was nothing if not extra.

Flo sat on her stool and watched Viv coming up the sidewalk. "I don't know how she gets around on those little sticks she calls legs."

Viv *did* have skinny legs, and the shorts and the clunky army boots weren't doing them any favors. The woman moved like lightning, though, so I figured she was making it work for her.

She hurried up the sidewalk, Ash behind her, and burst through the door. "I had the best idea!" She slapped the papers on the counter. "I'll bet the police haven't even thought of this."

I picked up one of the papers. It was a flyer for a lawn service company.

I read it and nodded. "I'll bet the police *haven't* thought of this." I looked at Viv. "Because why would they?"

"It's not about lawn service, Salem." Viv tapped her temple. "It's about us getting something..." She paused and cupped her hands together, then lowered them dramatically in front of her as if she were gingerly placing a bomb. "...into his house."

I took in the stack of papers. "Okay. But...why?"

"Okay, look." Viv spread her hands, then picked up a flyer. "We put these all over the neighborhood, right? But his?" She picked one up and tapped it. "We mark his. Hidden somewhere on the sheet, very covert, we put a mark so we can recognize it."

I nodded. "Yes, I follow, but still...why?"

"So, when we dig through the trash, we know we have the trash *from his house.*"

"I feel like maybe you've skipped over an important step. We're going through his trash?"

Viv sighed. "Of course, we are. That's what investigators *do*. Imagine the treasure trove of information could get from it."

"His neighborhood uses dumpsters," Ash said. "Probably ten or twelve houses to one dumpster. We need a way to be sure we're digging through the right bags." She clapped Viv on the bony shoulder. "Viv came up with the perfect plan."

"But, wouldn't it be easier to just leave one, on only his door? So when we find that one, we know?"

Viv held up a finger. "It would be easier, but would it be *better*? I think not, Salem. Think about it. He's the only one who gets a flyer on his entire street. He starts to get suspicious. He asks his neighbors, hey, did you get that lawn service flyer? He starts looking over his shoulder. He doesn't throw the flyer away, he keeps it. Or he burns it."

"Plus, if we do the entire street, we have time to hang out there for a while."

"Stake it out."

"And we can interview a few of his neighbors, on the down low. Ask about his comings and goings. See if anyone has seen or heard anything."

That actually sounded like it could be worthwhile.

"You don't have to go if you don't want to," Ash said.

"Yes, Ash and I can handle the mission," Viv said.

I did a gut check, then shook my head. "No, I'm good."

"You tell us if that changes." Ash pointed at me. "Promise."

"I do solemnly swear." I held my palm up.

Shawn lived on the outskirts of town in a new subdivision of cookie cutter homes. His house was at the end of the street, and across from that was a cotton field with green plants half a foot high.

I smiled, thinking of the dust that probably got in his house when the wind blew. Ha ha.

Viv cruised past his street and parked a few blocks over. She turned in her seat and then nodded toward Ash.

"Viv, these have your real phone number on them." I held up one of the flyers.

"Oh, I know. That's what took us so long to pick you up. Harv made these and I didn't think to tell him not to put my real number on them." She made an exasperated sound. "I would have thought it was obvious I wasn't starting a real lawn service business."

"Yeah," Ash said. "Someone at your—"

"Obvious income level isn't going to be out mowing yards," I rushed to finish for her.

"Exactly," Viv said. "I wanted him to change it, but the printer was out of toner and he couldn't run another set. It's fine, though. How many people really call these things? Okay!" She clapped her hands once. "Let's divide and conquer this street! Salem, you take the south side of the street on that end, I'll take the north, and Ash can start at this end of the south side, and we'll meet in the middle so we can all be on hand for the jerk's house. That way it'll look like we're just naturally converging on his place all at once."

"Sounds like a plan to me," Ash said.

I was quite happy with my assignment, actually. There was a little park with a playa lake nearby, and ducks floated lazily around. Even though it was still hot, the occasional cloud passed over and provided some shade. The houses were small, but it appeared the owners took a great deal of pride in their yards. It felt good to be doing something to find Gia, even though I had my doubts it would lead to anything.

After a week of feeling physically awful, it was nice to get my body out in the sun and moving again. Stump was feeling it, too. She sniffed the grass along the edges of the sidewalk as she trotted along beside me, and I remembered that it had been at least week since I'd taken her for a walk around Trailertopia. I wasn't the only one who suffered when I wasn't taking care of myself. Stump did, too.

I left her sniffing intensely at a spot near the mailbox and turned down the sidewalk toward the first door. I rolled a flyer into a scroll so I could slip it into the front door handle.

I stopped a few feet from the front porch, though, when I spotted a *No Solicitors* sign. Surely, I would not be letting the team down to skip this house.

I turned to walk back down the sidewalk and on to the next house.

A very tall, quite angry goose blocked my way.

I yelped.

I love geese. I love their V formation. I love their honking sound as they fly over. I love seeing them in the playa lakes. But man, up close those suckers are aggressive.

The goose took a step toward me and spread its wings.

"Well, you've done it now," said a voice behind me.

I shifted on the sidewalk and tried to look at whoever said that while also keeping one eye on the goose. "...hi?" I said.

"She's very territorial," the woman said. "She's got a nest in that bunch of Pampas grass and you're too near it. I'm amazed she let you get this far." She nodded toward a decorative garden in the corner where her yard met the sidewalk.

"Umm," I said. I edged one foot toward the street.

The goose took another step and spread out her wings. The thing was like a freaking condor. A pterodactyl.

She shrieked at me.

I shrieked back, a little bit. Actually, it was more like a soft, quavery, "*Oooh nooo*" while I crouched, frozen. "What should I do?" I asked the woman behind me.

"You should stay off my sidewalk," she said. "We come through the back because we're smart enough not to mess with territorial geese."

I frowned and refrained from mentioning that I would have avoided the goose, too, if I'd known she was there.

I would have to cut through her yard, I realized. I took a step back, keeping my eye on the goose. I lifted my hands like I was backing away from someone with a gun.

"Don't you dare step on my grass!" the woman shouted.

I froze. "Well, what am I supposed to do?" I shouted back. Kind of whiny, to be honest. Getting pecked by that beak was going to be like being hit with a hammer, I just knew it.

"Don't whine at me! I didn't invite you here. I put up a No Soliciting sign *because* I don't want you people putting crap on my door anyway."

"I didn't put crap on your door! I turned around as soon as I saw the sign."

All our racket was drawing Viv's attention. She headed across the street to rescue me.

"Careful!" I shouted at her. "She's aggressive!"

"Oh, she's just a silly old goose. I can handle—"

The goose turned and shot toward Viv, wings flapping.

Viv screamed and her flyers went airborne.

I took advantage of the distraction and ran across the grass.

"You get off my grass!" the woman screamed. "I'm calling the police!"

"Call them!" Viv roared. With her purple streaks and combat boots, she looked like the tough-as-nails matriarch in a post-apocalyptic movie.

The goose flapped and honked toward Viv, then toward me. Papers churned.

Stump, normally satisfied to watch from the sidelines unless food was involved, joined in the melee. She barked furiously at the papers, then sat and smiled at me.

"You pick those papers up!" the woman screamed. "Look at this mess!"

"Call off your attack goose!" Viv screamed back. "I'm going to sue!"

Jeez-o-Pete.

The goose advanced on Viv, backing her across the street. I tiptoed back toward the pile of papers. Maybe I could grab them up while the goose was focused on Viv.

The thing saw me moving, though, and veered back in my direction. Then it stopped, triangulating between me and Viv, keeping a bead on both of us.

The three of us stood there like we were in a high noon shootout scene in a western movie. The goose's eyes narrowed at me. Deadly silence fell on the street.

"You're not leaving those papers on my sidewalk," the woman called from her front porch, like a very unhelpful saloon owner watching the gunfighters prepare to draw.

We accidentally found a solution when the goose lunged at Stump. With a banshee shriek, I threw myself after the goose. It turned on me, but not before I made a running dive and grabbed Stump. The goose stuck her neck out and grazed my arm with her rock-solid beak, but I moved fast.

She came after me, of course. I ran across the street and she chased me halfway. While she was distracted in the middle of the road, Viv dashed back and snatched up papers.

Out of the corner of her eye, the goose must have seen Viv's movement, because she turned around and flapped back toward the yard.

With three or four pages still on the ground, Viv called it good. She clutched the crumpled sheets to her skinny chest and trotted down the sidewalk.

"Hey! You're not done!" the homeowner called.

"Oh yes I am!" Viv singsonged as her run turned to a brisk sashay. "Keep us in mind for all your lawn care needs!"

Two houses down, across the street, Ash was collapsed against a brick mailbox, laughing so hard she couldn't breathe.

I stomped up to her. "Thanks for the help!" I snapped.

Ash hooted and wiped at her eyes. "Oh my gosh. That was one of the best things I've ever seen."

"Salem is helpless when animals attack," Viv said. "You should have seen the fit she threw when a possum hissed at her."

"Me? That was you!" I protested as we headed toward the next house. Viv and I had encountered a possum one night out in the country, and she ran so fast she almost abandoned me there in the middle of nowhere.

"I love possums!" Ash said. "They're so cute."

"Right?" Viv said. "I'd keep one for a pet if I could."

Since we were already together, we took the rest of the street as a group. Ash proved to be excellent at small talk.

"What a beautiful yard! You probably don't need help, but sometimes it's nice to get a break, spend the day lazing away in the hammock while someone else does all the sweating, am I right?"

"This neighborhood is so cute! Reminds me of the one I grew up in. All the kids playing together, neighborhood barbecues in the summer. Y'all do that here?"

I think maybe the difference between her appearance—tall, muscular, mohawk hair—and her personality—charming, easy-going—threw people off, and before they knew it, they were making small talk right back.

Unfortunately, it didn't appear that we were going to get any useful information except that they were planning a Fourth of July parade down the block, and three other homeowners had called animal control about that aggressive goose.

"Kids aren't safe out here," one lady said.

Ash and I listened with sympathy while Viv tuned out and headed to the next house. It was the last one before Shawn's, and the owner was already outside—a skinny older man with a belt holding up his jeans, no butt, wearing a button-down western shirt.

"Are y'all any good?" I heard the man ask Viv.

"We're the best!" Viv said. "You'll have the best yard on the block by the time we're through. Is there a neighborhood contest? Because if there is, get ready to win it."

He slapped his hands together. "Hot dog!" He trotted into the garage and after a moment, began to push out a lawnmower with one hand, while he carried an edger with the other hand. He placed them on the driveway and hurried back inside. For what, I couldn't imagine.

"Viv!" I protested under my breath. "We have no idea how to use any of this stuff."

Viv gasped and spun to face me. "Oh my gosh!" She clamped her hand over her mouth. "You're right!"

"What in the world are you doing?" Ash asked.

"I don't know, I just—I got carried away!"

The man came back out of the garage carrying a gas can and placed it beside the mower and edger. "This is great! You are saving my bacon."

"Well, like I said, you're going to be thrilled when you see what these women can do. They work magic.

Uh-oh. I looked at Ash to see if she'd noticed that we'd just been thrown under the bus.

Ash was unperturbed, though. "Ladies, we've got this. We can do this."

It didn't take her long to learn that she'd been unreasonably optimistic. Viv was, of course, completely helpless and didn't even try. She got relegated to Stump watch and small talk with Ken, the homeowner. Ash reminded her he was our best bet for finding out information about Shawn, since he lived next door.

As for me, well...the spirit was willing, but the flesh proved to be weak.

Viv and Ken stood on the front porch with Stump while Ash tried to show my awkward self how to edge without running the thing into the sidewalk. This shouldn't have been that difficult for me. I worked with my hands all day long. I could do a pretty impressive precision cut on a Bichon Frise. All I can say is, edgers are different from shears. If I had my good scissors with me, I thought, I could get down on my knees and cut a nice, neat line all the way across.

It got really awkward the third time I accidentally ground the edger blade loudly against the concrete, and I heard Viv say, "Let's go inside out of this heat. Do you have any iced tea?"

After that, Ash put me on the mowing, and she did the edging. All I had to do then was walk a straight line. That worked out better. It didn't make me any happier that I'd somehow been roped into doing yardwork after I'd already done a day's work, but at least I had the hope that Viv was inside, getting the scoop on Ken's next-door neighbor.

Ash and I were wiping sweat off our foreheads and emptying the mower bag when Viv came trotting back down Ken's front steps, carrying Stump and looking all excited.

"Oh, good," I said. "You got some good information on Shawn."

"What? Oh, that." She cringed a bit. "Sorry, no. I got a date!"

Ash and I looked at each other and sighed. "I'll go dump this," she said as she wheeled the trash can around towards the end of the street so she could access the alley.

Ken came out on the porch and admired our handiwork. "Now,

that is perfect. This will get my daughter to stop nagging me. She thinks I'm too old to be out here in the heat doing stuff like this. I don't want to agree with her because the moment I do, bam! I'm off to the old folks home."

"You?" Viv asked, as if that was the craziest thing she'd ever heard.

Ash came back around the corner, pulling the empty trash can, and decided to take matters into her own hands. "Hey, I think I know that guy," she said, hooking her thumb back in the direction of Shawn's house. "He's a truck driver, right?"

"Yeah, that's right," Ken said. "Owner operator, in fact."

"Well, la-de-freaking-da," I said before I could stop myself.

He gave me a funny look but didn't stop talking. "I look in on his place while he's on the road."

"Oh, that's nice of you," I said, to redeem myself. "Does he have pets? Plants to water?"

"Get this." He leaned forward and looked pointedly at me over his glasses. "He has a *snake*. A ball python named Lucifer."

"Oh, cool!" Ash said. "I had a friend once whose boyfriend had a ball python. So, I guess he's on the road now? Or does he keep his cab somewhere else?"

"Nah, he parks it right there when he's in town." He nodded toward the grassy strip beside the cotton field.

I cleared my throat. "So, is he gone a lot, then?" I wanted to ask if he had a girlfriend. I wanted to ask the man if he'd ever seen any young girls at Shawn's place. But I got out as much as I could manage.

The man nodded. "A fair bit. He works mostly for Elite Moving. Driving all over the country." He shook his head. "Man, wouldn't that be the life? Seeing the whole country from the cab of a truck? If my back wasn't so cranky, I'd try my hand at that. There are lots of places I never been, and I don't figure now I'll ever go."

"You should ask him to take you on some of his runs," I said.

"Then who would look after Lucifer?" he laughed.

Back in Viv's car, Ash and I continued to wipe sweat and fan ourselves, while Viv wondered out loud what she should wear for her date with Ken.

"I think I'll call him Kenneth," she announced to no one in particular as she steered the Caddy back onto the street. "And I'll wear my black wide-legged slacks with the cream satin blouse and my Saint Laurent sandal flats. He isn't very tall. He won't want me being taller than he is."

"Well, that endeavor yielded less than I wanted it to," Ash admitted.

"What? I got a date out of it," Viv pointed out.

"Yes, but we got very little information about Shawn."

"We put the flyer on his door. That was really the whole point of this—"

Suddenly she stopped, and we three exchanged a look. Wordlessly,

Viv turned the Caddy around and we drove back by Shawn's house. Ash drew a little smiley face on the back of a flyer, then rolled it up and trotted it to the front door.

"Okay," she said as she dropped into the passenger seat. "*Now* we put the flyer on his door. I'm thinking we need to talk to some of Gia's other friends. The ones she went to when she ran away before."

"Helena gave me a list," Viv said. "I have it here somewhere." The Caddy hit the ditch as she leaned over to dig through the glove compartment.

"Let me," Ash said. She dug while Viv steered us back onto the road. "There's nothing in here."

"Shoot," Viv said. "I must have left it at home."

I stifled a groan. Belle Court was all the way across town.

Viv's phone dinged, and Ash lunged for it. "Want me to read it for you, so you can focus on driving?"

Viv shrugged. "Who's it from? If it's a spicy text from Kenneth, then read it out loud for sure."

"It's Helena."

"Oh, well then, yes. Go ahead."

"It just says, *Can you come by here? I'm at the shop.* Where is the shop?"

"Authenti-Cuts," Viv said. "Not far from here. I can ask her for names of Gia's friends while we're there."

Authenti-Cuts was in a shopping center on the newer side of town. When we pulled up, I spotted a white sedan just down the row from us. Detective Scott sat in the driver's seat, tapping something into a tablet. As I watched, she stowed the stylus and slid the tablet into the area beside her seat, then put the car into gear and pulled out.

"Detective Scott has been here," I said. "She just left."

"Maybe she gave Helena some news," Ash said.

Viv and Ash both got out of the car, but I froze in the back seat with Stump. Ash noticed my hesitation and sat back down, facing me. "You okay?"

"I wonder if Detective Scott told her about my report on Shawn? What if she's called us up here to scream at me?"

Viv leaned in through the driver's side door. "Then we scream back. I'm not afraid of her."

"Do you want to wait out here, Salem?" Ash offered. "We can handle it. There's no need for you to be there if you don't feel prepared for it."

I did a gut check.

You go before me and you follow me.

Was I prepared for another meltdown?

Maybe not. But... I had to face her at some point. Would it really be better to hide from the inevitable?

Both options felt unpleasant. Fearful.

"How about this," I suggested. "I'm going to walk Stump around that side of the building, in the shade. You ask Helena if it's okay if I bring her inside. When you mention me, she'll definitely let you know how she's feeling about me. Based on that response, text me and let me know if it's safe for me to come in."

"Good thinkin', Lincoln," Ash said.

"Yeah, Lincoln," Viv echoed. "And don't worry—if she is mad at you, we'll defend you."

I was equal parts relieved and embarrassed. I was less embarrassed at the notion of hiding from Helena's wrath than I was at the memory of me scream-laughing in the backseat of Viv's Cadillac yesterday, though.

I need not have worried, though. Ash texted me within 60 seconds. "Come to the back door. She's fine with you and with Stump."

I let Stump sniff a bit more, then picked her up and lugged her to the back door, which Ash was holding open. Just inside was a space that appeared to double as a laundry room and staff breakroom. Helena was pulling towels from a dryer, snapping them and folding them with military precision into a growing stack on a breakroom table.

"Detective Scott just brought her some news," Viv explained. "They found something with Gia's DNA on it, out at the place where that girl's body was found."

"But..." I said. "They said they identified her as someone else. Do they think now..." It was too awful to even contemplate.

"No, they're still positive of that girl's identity. Charlotte Franks."

"Did Gia know her, then?"

Helena shook her head. "No idea. I have no idea."

I was kind of getting used to Helena. She seemed to react with fury at everything. Now she was folding those towels like she hated every thread in them—was it the uncertainty about what she'd just learned? Or was there something more?

"Was Gia there, then? At the scene?"

"Might have been." Helena shook her head, hard. "I don't know. Something of Gia's was found at the place where they found the body." She collapsed into a chair at the table.

Viv pulled up another chair and put a hand on Helena's arm. "Do you mind if I turn my recorder on?"

Helena hesitated for a second, then shook her head. "Go ahead."

Viv pulled her small recorder out of her purse and flicked it on.

"What did they find that had Gia's DNA on it?" Viv asked. "Did they say?"

"Yeah, one of those black rubber hairbands. Like, for ponytails."

I pulled up a chair. "Well, that's a lead, right?"

Helena shrugged. "I guess. They know Gia was either there, at the side of that road, or had come into contact with that girl, or someone who had come into contact with *that* girl had also come into contact with Gia."

That didn't seem to narrow it down much. "And they don't know anything more about the girl they found?"

Helena shook her head. "Not that they're sharing, anyway. Just that she was 22, and originally from Kansas City. Gia's never even been to Kansas City." She stared at the table. "A black ponytail holder. One of those rubber ones, you know?" she repeated.

We didn't know what to say to that. But she wasn't talking to us. She was just talking. Processing.

"She wore those stupid things all the time. We found them all over the house. Made me *crazy*." She shook her head and laughed ruefully. "I swept them up from the hall floor. I found them in the soap dish in the shower. I found one in the silverware drawer one time—can you imagine? Half my job is making sure everything in this shop is sanitized to health and safety code, and then I come home and there's a ponytail holder in the silverware drawer. With hair on it. Nasty." She sniffed. "I told her, 'Gia, I'm gonna chop your hair off if you don't keep those things picked up!' All over the house, I swear. She wore them like bracelets. Always had at least one with her. Usually three or four, she had 'em like a stack of bracelets on her arm. Always pulling her hair up, letting it down, pulling it up, letting it down. Like an obsession with her. She couldn't just leave it alone." She trailed off, then said softly. "That girl had so much hair."

Helena's phone dinged and she checked it absent-mindedly. As she did, Janet entered the room carrying a broom and dustpan full of hair. She dumped it in the large wastebasket as Helena said, "Mateo. Working late tonight."

"You should ask him to come get you," Janet said.

Helena shook her head. "I have two more cuts, plus Mrs. Nash's foils to wash out."

"We can cover it. They would understand."

"I said no," Helena said, her voice steely.

"Okay, but you should at least tell Mateo. He would want to know."

Helena made a scoffing sound, then rolled her eyes. "Yeah, he would want to know."

I cast a glance at Ash and saw that Helena's response had seemed odd to her, too.

"What does Mateo do?" I asked, hoping to prod gently at this line.

"He's a teacher. Art. At Evans Middle School."

"Oh," I said. Then thought, *Oh.* "That's where Gia went?"

"Yeah. That's how we met. He was Gia's art teacher in sixth and seventh grade."

"Not eighth?"

Helena shook her head. "No, she wanted to change to Digital Media for eighth grade."

"Why is he working late today?" Viv asked. "I thought yesterday was the last day of school."

"No, the last day is today," Helena said.

"But Gia went missing on the last day of school last year, and the one-year vigil was yesterday."

Helena stared at her, then blinked slowly.

"But..." Viv said slowly. "I guess the last day isn't on the same date every year."

"No," Helena said. "It's not."

Helena's disdain for Viv's questioning seemed to have thrown her a bit off balance, so we left not long after that. I checked the time. Just now about 5 o'clock. Still plenty of daylight left.

"Too bad we didn't think to ask her for any of Gia's friends' names while we were there," I said.

"Should we go back?" Ash asked.

"Nope," Viv said. "Not today. Give that woman time to process."

"That's a lot to process," I said, leaning over the back of the front seat. "I didn't want to bring it up back there, but if they found Gia's DNA at a murder site...I mean, it has to be obvious now that she's no longer a runaway, right?"

Ash blew out a gust. "I guess."

"Helena's been convinced all along that she hasn't been staying away of her own free will."

I leaned back into the seat, my mind spinning. "What could it mean? It could mean she's mixed in, somehow, with whoever killed that girl."

Ash turned in her seat. "See, that's the thing. We're just assuming murder, because she was found at the side of the road. We don't know how she died. She could have died by natural causes, an accident, anything. And her body left there."

"By Gia?" I frowned.

Ash shrugged. "That's the thing. We really don't know, do we?"

Viv made a face. "I don't like this. We get a break, a big lead, and instead of making things clearer, it makes them more confusing."

"Well, I keep thinking about the boyfriend, anyway," Ash said.

"We should look into him."

"Gia didn't have a boyfriend," I said.

"But Sierra did say there was a guy she liked. They saw him at the Loose Caboose."

"No, not Gia's boyfriend," Ash said. "I'm talking about Helena's boyfriend. Mateo."

"We could look into him," I said. I felt a guilty spark of hope at the notion that someone besides Shawn might be responsible.

"What makes you suspect him?" Viv asked.

Ash shrugged. "Well, his proximity to Gia, in the first place. It's almost always someone you know, right?"

"And Sierra did say Gia's first signs of being troubled were in middle school. That's when she first met him."

"Exactly. And, she had two years of being his student, but then switched in the last year of middle school."

"And it was also when she was leaving that school that she decided she wanted to get her life back on track," I said.

"That's true. Sierra put it down to Gia looking ahead to her future, hearing all the end-of-year speeches, but that could be just because that was what her *own* mind was on."

Viv nodded. "Exactly. We see what we're looking at, and if Sierra was looking at 'this is your future' type things, she would see it everywhere."

"But..." I frowned. "Mateo was still in her life. She was only getting away from him during the day. If he and Helena were planning to get married, he would still be a part of her life."

"It was weird, though, when Helena said, 'yeah, he would want to know.'"

"Right?" I said, leaning forward. "There was something odd there."

I thought back on the times I'd met Mateo. There was the night Viv and I had visited, while the whole family had been gathered to wait and hear from the detective about the body that had been found. That first day, when we met with Sid and Helena and went through the pictures. And the night at the vigil. He'd been kind, attentive. Watchful and caring toward Helena. The whole family seemed to like him – a few even revered him, for taking on the challenge of Helena.

"I keep thinking of what he said at the vigil," Ash said. She turned to me. "Remember that? How defeated he kept talking?"

Had he seemed defeated? The mood of the entire evening had been one of sadness and anger.

He'd stood at the periphery, I remembered. I'd been too focused on Shawn, on whether or not he would show up, and then on his presence, to pay much attention to Mateo.

In fact, he reminded me a little of Tony. I thought about what Viv had said. Mateo had reminded me of Tony right away – the way he carried himself, his calm demeanor. Maybe I had been mentally ruling Mateo out because I knew there was no way Tony would ever be a threat to anyone.

Briefly, I wondered if Tony's family also revered him for taking me on. But I didn't really need to wonder—they all thought he was crazy for not divorcing me years ago. Oh well. I guess they were probably all throwing a party now.

I drew my attention back to the topic at hand and shook my head. "I don't remember talking to him at the vigil." He had said something, though—not to me. To Joe, maybe, or Joe's dad? What had I heard? "I know he said something like, 'Gia disappeared and this whole world stopped.'"

"Yeah, he did say that," Ash said. "I heard that, too. Like, he was frustrated, I think."

Viv considered that. "That's odd. He's expecting the family to just move on? Get over it?"

"The impression I got—Salem, now that I think about it, this was before you came—but the impression I got was that he is quite sure Gia ran away, and that she probably doesn't want to be found, even now. Someone made a comment about his wedding to Helena being on hold until Gia can come back and be a bridesmaid."

"And how did he react to that?"

"Frustrated but resigned, I guess I'd call it. Like, he said, 'Yeah, if that ever happens.' But then he laughed like it was a joke."

Viv drove as we all considered that in silence.

"We should look into him," I stated, again feeling that little spurt of hope.

"Wouldn't hurt," Ash said.

"No time like the present," Viv said. "Helena said he was working late. Unless he's working from home, he should be easy to find."

"Wait," I said. "I have Stump. Let's swing by—" I stopped when I realized I was about to suggest Tony's house, since it was closest. I swallowed, then mumbled "Hang on," while I texted Frank to see if he was available to Stump-sit.

"My behind is in the recliner as I type this," came his reply. "Her throne awaits."

After we dropped Stump off to burrow into her princess bed, Viv headed the Caddy to Evans Middle School, and we drove slowly through the parking lot. I recognized the sports car I'd seen at the Perez home the day we'd met them. There were a few other cars, but not many.

It looked like it was move-out day. Two different people came out carrying plastic totes to their cars. We smiled and nodded. Ash might have turned some heads with her height and hairstyle, but Viv was the ringer who made us look benign – even with purple hair. Since classes were out and there were no students to protect, security was a good bit more lax than it would have been if we had been there a week earlier.

"Just act like we know where we're going," Viv said as we approached the black metal doors. One was held open with a brick and the other with a big rock, so we strolled in like we had any business being there.

Viv made an immediate turn to the left and we headed down a

hallway that looked like every school hallway you've ever seen. Lockers lined the right side of the wall, and above the lockers, posters proclaiming "Mustang Pride" and "Strive for Excellence" alternated between posters of middle schoolers in action shots--giggling over lunch, intense concentration over a chess board, high-fiving after a softball game.

Viv stopped briefly in front of an open classroom door and read the name above. "Mrs. Kapen," she muttered.

"Do you know her?" Ash asked.

"If anybody asks, I do."

We passed classrooms in various states of disarray and a man pushing a cleaning cart, but nothing that looked like an art room. As Viv advised, we just kept going like we knew what we were doing and rounded the corner to the wing that held the gym and cafeteria.

"Man," Ash said. "I love this. I wish I could go back to middle school."

"Really?" I asked. Middle school had been a nightmare for me.

"Absolutely. I was the king of the basketball court. And I killed in dodge ball."

Viv gave her a look. "Not literally though, right?"

"Not literally," Ash confirmed. "But a couple times it was close."

There was another corner coming up, and it began to dawn on me that perhaps we weren't doing the smartest thing here.

"So, what if Mateo sees us?"

Viv cocked her head and gave me a look. "We *want* him to see us."

"Won't that make surveillance harder?"

"This isn't the surveillance part, Salem. This is the intimidation part. We let him know we're onto him. Let him know he has something to fear from us. Then, we go underground and tail him, watch while he does something foolish in his panic."

"Ahh," Ash said. She tapped her forehead. "Playing the mind game. Smart."

"It's what we call three-dimensional chess," Viv said.

"This is the exact opposite of the approach you said we needed to take on Shawn," I pointed out.

Viv frowned. "Yes, well, you have to tailor the investigation to fit the suspect, Salem. That's investigating 101."

"Can I help you?" came a voice to our right.

We all three jumped.

A tall, thin woman with short white hair approached us. She wore jeans and a Mustang Pride shirt, but everything about her said, "In charge." This had to be the principal. I'd had plenty of experience with school principals. I could spot a principal at 50 paces.

I stepped behind Ash.

Viv smiled at the woman. "We're looking for Mrs. Kapen."

"You mean Mrs. *Ka*pen." She pronounced it differently – hard A.

"Uh," Viv said. "I mean, if that's how *you* pronounce it."

"That's how I pronounce it because that's how Mrs. Kapen pronounces it," the woman said.

It occurred to me with a jolt of dread that this woman had a lot of experience with lying middle school kids. My stomach lurched.

"What did you need with her?" the woman asked. "This is a school, you know. We don't just let people wander the hallways."

Viv blinked in indignation. "First of all, you might have heard that school let out already. And second of all, I'm sure Iris *Kapen--*" she emphasized the soft A as she leaned toward the woman--"wouldn't appreciate you asking nosy questions about her business. The woman has a right to privacy."

"*Iris?*" the woman said.

Oh no. Viv had totally overplayed her hand.

Ash stepped up and put a hand on Viv's elbow, but she faced the woman. "I'm so sorry. I was afraid of this." Then she turned on me with a frown. "See! I told you."

I blinked. I had no idea what was going on.

Ash turned back to the scary principal lady. "I'm afraid..." She flattened her lips and darted a pained look at Viv. "She gets...a little confused these days. She retired from teaching years ago, but..." She patted her chest. "It's still in here. You know? And she insisted her old teaching partner Iris needed her help and would *not* let it go until I brought her up here."

The principal frowned, but she looked a trifle sympathetic. "I see. Well, you can't just go wandering around school buildings."

"I know. I'm so sorry." She sighed and looked at me again. "To tell the truth, I really just did this to show my sister how..." She stopped and turned to Viv. She said loudly. "Mama, you wait here with Sissy while I talk to the lady, okay?" Then she took a couple steps away, motioning with her head for the principal to follow.

"Here's the thing," Ash said, her back to us, head bent toward the woman. "I've been trying to tell my sister for months that Mama's confusion was getting worse. She doesn't believe me. Because how can you see it if you're just – just talking on the phone with her once or twice a month. Right?"

The principal nodded.

"I mean, you're not there to see when she put the poor cat in the refrigerator. You're not there when the neighbors call to tell you your mama's wandering the neighborhood in her nightgown and an old miner's helmet. No, you're busy with your high-powered attorney job in the city. You don't have time to see the hard truth of what's going on back home."

The principal looked at me and I felt a complicated mixture of shame and pride.

"So," Ash said in low tones that were still plenty loud enough for us all to hear. "When we passed the school and Mama kept insisting we stop, I just..." She sighed and shrugged. "I figured it was time for my sister to see with her own eyes. I thought since classes had let out, it wouldn't be that big a deal. That was wrong, I see that now. I was just...a little desperate, I guess. The time is fast approaching when we need to make some decisions, and they need to be fully informed – " she emphasized the words with another glare in my direction – "fully informed decisions."

Viv stood there with her mouth agape.

The principal nodded and put a hand on Ash's elbow, guiding her toward the door. She was sympathetic and probably not going to call the police, but she was still getting us out that door.

That was fine by me. We could figure out another way to intimidate Mateo, if that was necessary.

The mood was somber as walked back out to the parking lot. Now there were only three cars in the lot – Viv's Caddy, the sports car, and another luxury sedan. Principaling must pay well, I thought.

Ash turned back and waved at the principal, who stood in the open doorway and watched us leave. "Viv, let me drive," Ash said, speaking low. "She's watching and it would be a bad idea to let her see us allow you to drive."

Her mouth grim, Viv slapped the keys into Ash's open palm.

"Good," Ash said. "Keep it in character."

Viv stomped to the passenger side, yanked open the door and slammed herself into the seat.

I made a show of checking her seatbelt, which earned me a glare of my own. I got into the back seat and fought back a smile.

Ash drove us to the nearest Sonic and ordered three large Oreo Blasts with extra whipped cream.

"Okay troops," she said. "Sorry, I slipped into Marine speak. That whole thing just put me in mind of the kind of mission we used to do. I hope you don't mind."

"No problem," I said.

Viv grunted.

"Anyway, we always met to debrief after a mission, go over what went right and what went wrong, see what we could learn from both. And I don't know about you two, but even though we didn't accomplish our ultimate goal of letting Mateo see us and become intimidated, I think there was plenty that went right on that mission."

"Oh, is that right?" Viv spit out. "And what exactly would that be?"

"An effective team has to learn how to work off each other. Use their strengths in tandem and know when to pivot to a new direction when the landscape changes. And man," she shook her head with a laugh. "That landscape changed quick, didn't it?"

The carhop appeared with our shakes. Ash paid and handed them to us. She took a bite of her shake, then pointed her spoon at Viv, who sat glaring at her own shake like it was a Styrofoam cup full of dog poo.

"You, my friend, were expert. Very intuitive. You could have played it subservient, but something in you knew that was a situation with more potential if you went on the offensive. Well done!"

Viv blinked, then spooned a bit of whipped cream into her mouth. "Yes, well..."

"And your—your *confidence*!" Ash took a bite of her ice cream. "Like, you knew it was BS, and she knew you were wrong, but you were so sure! That's the kind of thing that throws people off.

327

Confuses them."

I leaned forward and nodded at Viv. I was fairly confident that Ash was peddling a whole new basket of nonsense, but Viv was looking markedly less angry, so I wanted to get on board.

"Exactly," I said. "She wasn't prepared for *you*, Viv."

Ash nodded. "She was *not* prepared. And for someone like her, in charge of all those kids—that's someone who's used to being prepared. Prides herself on being prepared. So, finding herself in that situation -- it confused her. And her confusion allowed me to swoop in with a story that she could latch onto and feel like she was back in control."

"Yes, well," Viv said again, sneering as she stabbed her shake with her spoon. "You didn't have to come up with a story that made me sound like a dithering idiot."

"I know," Ash said. "But I had to think fast, and I'm not quite as fast on my feet as you are."

Viv sighed and spooned her shake. "That's true."

"And look, I get how ridiculous the 'she's confused' story is, when it comes to you. If she'd spent even half a second looking at you, she would see how ridiculous it is. That's why I had to throw in all the detail, with Salem being a high-powered lawyer, the wandering the neighborhood in your nightgown, to keep her mind confused so she wouldn't look too closely at *you* and see through it."

Viv nodded slowly.

"A fire hose of information," I said. "Keep her overwhelmed."

"But you were brilliant, Viv," Ash said. "Like I said, you know how to pivot. That could have been a difficult role for you to play. People think the hard part of battle is working up the courage to charge in. But it can take just as much courage to fall back, when falling back is what's called for." She lifted her cup in salute to Viv. "I know it must have been hard not to show her that you clearly had all your faculties intact, but you knew just when to drop back and let the story play out. Well done."

"Yes, well done," I said, but I was thinking more of Ash.

Viv stirred her shake. "Yes, well, like I said. Three-dimensional chess. You have to play the whole game, not just the next move."

"Exactly. And as we used to say, any battle you come back alive from is a successful battle."

Ash sighed and leaned back against the door. "That was fun, though."

"Yes," Viv said with a laugh. "Did you see the look on her face when I said *Iris?*" She shook her head. "She was so confused."

I felt a twinge of guilt that we were so obviously snowing Viv. Although, she *had* gotten us into that mess, and Ash had gotten us out. And I was pretty sure Ash wasn't doing it to be meanspirited— she was building Viv back up.

"You got her, that's for sure," I said. That wasn't exactly a lie—I did consider the Principal Lady to have been gotten.

By the time we'd finished our shakes, Viv was back to her old self.

"Okay, boss," Ash said. "Where to next?"

"Let's drive back by the school. If Mateo's car is still there, we'll go back to his house and maybe snoop around a bit. Find a good place to set up for a stakeout."

"Excellent idea. See, you're a natural tactician."

"Well, I've had a lot of practice," she said. "But I don't care if that busybody is watching or not, I am driving my own danged car."

Chapter Nine

When we got back to the school, though, Mateo's sports car was the only one left, and the front doors were now closed. Viv drove past, then rounded corner to leave when I looked back and saw Mateo entering a back door.

The door swung shut behind him. *Almost* shut.

"Hey," I said. "I think he's propping that door open."

Ash and Viv looked at each other. Viv slowed the car, then pulled to the curb.

We all looked back toward the school.

"See," I said. "He must be carrying stuff out, and he's propped the door open, so he won't have to keep locking and unlocking it."

"Want to give it another shot?" Ash asked.

Viv nodded, a satisfied smile playing on her lips. "Heck yeah. Let's do this."

We parked by the tennis courts and slipped around to the door. As I'd thought, a rubber doorstop was wedged between the door and the metal frame. Viv opened it and we all strolled through.

We'd gone a few yards when she stopped and motioned for us to huddle up.

"He thinks he's alone," she whispered. "Let's let him keep thinking that and see if he reveals anything."

She plastered herself against the wall and slid along it, although there was no one around.

Ash watched her for a second, then sighed and turned back to me with a fatalistic shrug. She motioned toward the wall. She and I plastered ourselves against it, too, and like fools we all three inched along as if we were hugging the ledge of a cliff.

The hallway we were on went to the front of the building, but another one bisected it halfway down. At the intersection, Viv stopped, darted her head around then snapped it back. She made frantic gestures, then disappeared around the corner.

Ash drew her head back, then looked at me with her head cocked.

I shrugged. We rounded the corner behind Viv. Again, there was nothing but a long stretch of closed doors on a long hallway. Viv was still doing the cliffside ledge creep. I heard Ash groan, but we stayed in character. It was becoming very hard for me not to collapse into a fit of giggles, but I knew I had to keep a lid on it. Viv had only recently come back from the brink and I didn't want to send her over again.

We were about halfway down that hallway when we heard the slam of a door.

We all three looked at each other. Footsteps echoed down the hall. Someone whistled happily as he walked.

It had to be Mateo. Whistling as he finished up his room and faced the summer before him?

The footsteps drew closer, and the whistling grew louder. My heart thudded in panic.

Viv checked the knob of the door closest to her. Locked. Ash darted across the hall and checked a knob on the other side. Locked.

I closed my eyes. That's what Stump did when she didn't want me to see her.

The footsteps approached our hallway. I tried to blend into the tiles. I opened my eyes into slits, my shoulders around my ears, and waited to be discovered.

Mateo strolled by, whistling, holding a cardboard box. Facing straight ahead.

The footsteps faded as he drew close to the back door. He stopped, and we heard *beep beep beep* sounds. Then the sound of the back door closing.

I let out a breath and collapsed to the floor. My hands shook and my heart thudded.

"Holy smokes!" Ash said. She laughed and ran a shaky hand through her mohawk. "That was *so* close!"

Viv stood frozen against the wall, eyes wide. "Shhh!" she hissed. "There could be someone else here."

"There's no one here," Ash said. "Come on! Let's go explore a little."

Once we knew we were alone, it *was* kind of fun. We wandered the hallways and peeked through windows. A couple of the classroom doors weren't locked, so we entered and snooped around. We found the art room – it was clear by the Mustang painting on the classroom door and the Art Saves Lives poster beside it. The door was locked, though, and a peek through the little window in the door revealed tables smeared with years of dried paint, several racks of drying paintings and a stack of easels, folded and leaned into the corner.

Viv took a look around, then clapped her hands together. "Well, I guess we need to go find our stakeout place by Mateo's house."

"Yeah, not much we can do here," Ash agreed.

The sun was on the other side of the building now, and while we could still see clearly enough to make our way to the back door, the shadows were growing. It was dark enough, in fact, that I began to notice thin red lights that I hadn't noticed before.

I suddenly remembered the *beep beep beep* when Mateo left the building.

Viv approached the back door just as I noticed one of those thin red lights was actually a thin red *beam* of light. A thin red beam that ran from the white disk near the top of the back door to the floor on the opposite side of the hallway. A thin red beam that Viv had just walked right through.

"Uh-oh," I said.

Outside, a siren sounded.

Viv's hand was already on the backdoor when Ash – having apparently just come to the same conclusion I had – shouted, "Wait!"

Viv froze.

"They're out there," Ash said. "The cops."

"We tripped an alarm," I said. We'd probably set it off immediately after Mateo left, as soon as we began to wander around the building like fools.

We gathered at the back door and looked through the window. I could see the red and blue swirl of cop lights as they flashed against the brick. Then a shadow as someone rounded the corner.

"Run!" Ash whispered.

Our footsteps slapped against the floor as we pounded down the hallway, slid into the turn at the corner and pounded down another one.

"Let's get out on the other side, then try and circle back to the car," Ash whisper-shouted.

That hallway opened into one of the ones we'd walked down earlier that afternoon – the one with the gym and cafeteria on it.

Ash tried the doors along that wall. One opened – the one to the gym, and I breathed a sigh of relief. We'd already set off the alarm, so we had nothing to lose by opening an outside door, and there should be one from here.

We jogged across the floor and toward the back of the gym. We passed a locker room and what looked to be an equipment room. An office sat to the left, and an outside door to the right.

Ash looked at me and Viv and said, "Ready?"

We nodded, and she pushed open the door.

I tiptoed out, hands on the back of my head, ready to be shot down in a hail of police gunfire. We just startled a few retirees walking on the track in the early evening glow, though. I waved at them. "Hi."

They gave confused waves back.

We hurried around the back of the building to where the tennis courts – and Viv's Caddy – sat.

The rotating of the cop's lights flashed against the side of the building and to Viv's car, but I didn't see any people. No cops with guns drawn. No furious principal.

Were we really going to get away? Ash and Viv were pounding the pavement toward the car, and I found myself crouched down as I ran after them, still anticipating a bullet in the back.

I looked back over my shoulder to see the people on the track, gathering in a small group now, watching us warily.

I forced myself to straighten. I was making us even more of a spectacle than we already were.

I cast one more look over my shoulder and saw that the group wasn't watching us anymore but had now turned attention to the direction we'd just come from--the door from the gym. Then three of them nodded in that direction and pointed in ours.

"Run!" I screamed.

We were already running, of course. I slammed into the Caddy and yanked open the passenger door. Viv and Ash jumped into the front seat, Viv started the car, and we barreled over the tennis court and out the other side. My head almost hit the ceiling as we bounced off the curb and onto the street.

I checked behind us as Viv barreled down the street. A cop came around the side of the building from the direction of the gym. Another patrol car was turning the corner onto the street we were currently hurtling down. It moved to pull into the parking lot but swerved at the last second to follow us.

"Oh crud!" I shouted. "That one's after us."

Viv slammed on the gas.

Ash grabbed at the roof. "Hold on!" she said. "Do we really want to run from the law? This could make everything way worse!"

"We're running!" Viv cried. "If he catches us, I have dementia and you two are going against your will!" She cackled. "He's not going to catch us, though!" She swung a wide right, then a left, then another right.

I kept looking back, and after that last corner, told Viv, "I think we lost him."

She slowed some, to Ash's and my enormous relief. We reached a major street and she entered, blending into traffic.

I sank back into my seat, exhausted.

Ash dropped her head back onto the headrest of her seat. "Holy!

Moly! That was bonkers!"

"I'm going to need a nap after that," I said. "If my heart ever stops pounding. Let's go back to my place. I need to check on Frank and Stump anyway."

Viv headed in that direction, going over and over the lunacy of what we'd just done.

"Did you see those people when we barreled through that tennis court?" Viv crowed. "It was like a movie!"

I rubbed my forehead and sank low in the seat, strangely simultaneously exhausted and jumpy with nerves. I remembered the way I'd been crouching as I ran across that parking lot and started to laugh.

I turned and stopped laughing. A patrol car was behind us. Not directly behind, but still close enough to be very uncomfortable.

"Guys," I said. "I think they're still following us."

Ash whipped her head around. "Okay, Viv," she said. "Let's play it cool. We're on major streets now, we don't want to cause an accident."

Viv frowned at her. She would have loved an excuse to go full throttle on her Caddy.

"Let's take a left at the next corner," Ash advised.

Viv maintained a reasonable speed but didn't signal until the last possible second. The patrol car passed us and continued straight while we turned.

I breathed a sigh of relief as we turned. But then I saw that the cop was moving to turn left at the next block.

Ash and I looked at each other.

"Keep it under the speed limit," Ash advise. "Just continue on as if everything is fine."

Viv did as she was told. The patrol car showed up behind us again. Still half a block back. No lights. Nothing aggressive. Just...there.

Viv made several corners, and at Ash's insistence, kept her speed reasonable. The patrol car matched us turn for turn.

"I could outrun him," Viv said.

Ash shook her head. "Not for long. He's been behind us plenty long enough to get your plate. They know who we are now."

"But what's he doing?" Viv whined. "Why isn't he pulling us over?"

A car approached from the other direction. It swerved toward us, then parked sideways before us, blocking the road.

Viv slammed on the brakes to keep from hitting it. The patrol car braked behind us, penning us in.

My heart slammed against my ribs. What was going on?

Then Bobby Sloan got out of the car blocking us from the front. I went weak with relief once again.

He walked toward our car and motioned for the patrol car behind us to stay put.

Viv rolled down her window. "What do you think you're doing!" she snapped. "I could have t-boned you!"

Bobby planted a hand on the roof of the car and leaned in the window. "What do I think I'm doing? *What do I think I'm doing*, crazy lady?"

Viv drew her head back. "Crazy lady?"

I figured it was time for me to step in. "Bobby, are we glad to see you! We thought the cops were after us!"

Bobby glared daggers at me. "I. *Am*. The. Cops."

"Well, I know that. But you're not...I mean, you *are* a real cop, of course. I just – "

He held up a finger to me, his mouth clenched. I shut my mouth.

Lips still clamped shut, he held his hand clenched so tight, it was vibrating. He glared from me, to Ash, to Viv, his jaw tight.

"Did you just break into that middle school?"

Viv shook her head. "Nope. The door was open. We broke into nothing."

A vein started to throb on Bobby's forehead. The car became deathly quiet.

"I could have you arrested right here," he said.

I was quiet for a long time, then said in a slightly squeaky voice, "But you're not going to, right?"

He looked at me for a long, long time. Then said, "What the heck are you doing at that school?"

Viv and Ash and I looked at each other. "Don't tell him," Viv mouthed.

"The art teacher there is dating Helena Perez. Gia Perez's older sister."

Viv grunted her frustration with me and whipped around in her seat.

Bobby nodded. Well, it was less than a nod and more like a...not a seizure, exactly. It was as if he had every nerve in his body under tight control, and then he let the nerves in his head loose enough to indicate agreement, so his eyes bugged a little and his head kind of shivered up and down like, "yes, of course, this is common knowledge, and also my head is about to explode."

"So, we thought we might just surveil him a little bit. Make sure he didn't have anything to do with Gia's disappearance."

"That doesn't explain how you tripped the alarm in the school."

"Well, he didn't realize we were in there, and he set the alarm when he left. He locked us in, actually. Are you going to give him a citation for that?"

"The principal said she'd already thrown you out. She watched you drive away. How did you get back in?"

I sank in my seat a bit. "You heard about that one, did you?"

"Yes, I heard about that one!" He pushed himself off the car and stepped back, running a frustrated hand through his hair.

And I know this was bad timing, considering how thin the ice was that I was already standing on, and plus my heart was completely broken over Tony, but...he was so cute when he was frustrated. Like, seriously adorable.

He made some motion to the patrol cop who stood beside the car behind us. Then he turned back to us. "Ladies, you do know that this town has a perfectly competent police department, right?"

"Of course," I said.

Viv said, "Well, I mean –" before Ash slapped her arm.

"We've looked at Mateo. We looked *very closely* at Mateo. He's not the guy. We're still at the point where we don't even know if there *is* a guy, but if there's a guy, it's not him."

"How do you even know that, though?" Viv asked.

"Because we interviewed him, and he has an alibi for the night Gia went missing."

"Well, alibis can be – "

"At least two dozen people saw him, fifty miles away!" Bobby roared. "He was at a graduation ceremony and a party afterwards! He spent the entire weekend there! There were pictures! There were videos!" He stuck his finger at Viv. "The man gave a speech, for crying out loud! He was nowhere near the area when Gia went missing! He's! Not! The! Guy!"

"....oh," Viv said.

Bobby took a deep breath and looked at the houses around us. A car blocked in by cops is a bit of an attention grabber and he didn't need to make an appearance on social media, screaming at an old lady.

"We're sorry," I said meekly from the back seat. "We just want to help Gia."

"I know," he said, his voice tired. "So do I. So does the entire department. And it doesn't help when we waste resources chasing after nonsense like this."

"We're really sorry," Ash said.

We both looked at Viv. Everyone waited. She just smiled at him.

He sighed again and shook his head. "Did you damage anything in that building?"

We all three swore we didn't.

"I mean it, Salem. If I find out there's so much as a chalkboard eraser out of place, I will make sure they bring charges."

"They use dry erase boards now," Ash said. Then, at the look from Bobby, said, "But okay. Yeah. We understand."

Bobby looked like he wanted to say something else – maybe a whole lot of something else – but he just slapped a hand on the roof of the car, stalked away, and motioned for the patrolman to let us go.

We pulled silently away. As Viv made the next corner and headed for Trailertopia, she looked at me in the rearview mirror and said, "I told you not to tell him anything."

"Yes, well, you put the cat in the refrigerator. I don't need to listen to you."

The next day, Viv called me at work to tell me she'd realized we had neglected an important source: my friend, Trisha. She and Ash would be by to pick me up as soon as I got off work.

"If Gia has some connection to that girl who was found, Charlotte Franks, then Trisha Watson might have some information on that girl that they didn't share with the public. They do that, you know.

Have inside scoops on stuff."

Trisha anchored the six and ten o'clock news on Channel 11, except on air, she was known as Patrice Watson.

"Okay," I said. "But let's not tell her about the ponytail holder thing. Unless you want to clear it with Helena, first."

"I do not want to clear it with Helena, first," Viv said. "So we'll keep that scoop to ourselves."

"This is really cool," Ash kept saying. "I can't believe she's your friend."

"More of a frenemy," Viv clarified.

"It's not *that* complicated," I said. "We were friends when we were kids, then she hated me, then she forgave me and now we're friends again." I was almost positive Trisha didn't hate me anymore. As long as I remembered to call her Patrice—which wasn't easy! I still slipped sometimes and called her Trisha.

"And why did she hate you?"

"I did some stuff while I was drinking," I said.

"Ahh." Ash nodded. "Say no more. She just had a baby, right?"

I nodded. "A little girl, Lola." Patrice brought her to our Fat Fighters meetings sometimes, and she credited Lola's breastfeeding with her rapid (rapider than mine, at any rate) weight loss.

The girl at the front desk at Channel 11 waved us back. Viv and I came to see Patrice from time to time, and we knew the best times to come in so we would have a decent chance of a ten- or fifteen-minute conversation—provided no one got shot or no cows got loose on the

Loop or anything.

I tapped on Patrice's door. It was open a little already, so I edged it open and peered in.

She sat at her desk, her phone to her ear. "Yes, it's fine to do it that way. One dose of acetaminophen, then one dose of ibuprofen.... That's what the pediatrician said. Oh, gosh, she does sound upset...I know. I know. But I promise, she's okay. It's totally normal. She's fine."

She reached for a tissue in the box on her desk and dabbed at her nose. "Well, just rock her and hug her. Or let her lay on the floor on her pallet. Or put her in the car and drive her around. I don't know, Scot. Just keep trying stuff until something makes her feel better. I know. It feels awful, but it's totally normal. You too, sweetie. Love you."

She hung up and snatched another tissue. "Oh my gosh," she wailed as she sank into her chair.

My heart thudded. "What's wrong?" She'd seemed so calm when she was on the phone but fell apart the moment she hung up.

She let out this little laugh-cry and blew her nose. "It's nothing. I mean, it's horrible, but it will be fine. Lola got her three-month immunizations today, and her poor little legs are swollen and she's cranky. She's got a little bit of fever." She sniffed again. "I could hear her when I was on the phone with Scot. Crying her poor little eyes out. This is so horrible."

"Well, you held it together while you were on the phone."

"I have to. Scot will fall apart if I start crying. Like, you know it's not that big a deal, she'll be fine. But it just hurts so much when they're hurting." She tossed the tissues in the trash and grabbed another one, dabbing it at the corner of her eyes. "Everyone tells you parenting is hard, so you're not surprised that it's hard. You're just surprised at the *way* it's hard, you know? Like, you think it's sleep deprivation and temper tantrums in the Target checkout line. But it's stuff like this—how truly *awful* it feels when they hurt, and you really can't do anything about it." She gave a half laugh. "I would gladly have cut off my own arm if that would make the pain she's in go away."

"Well, it's a good thing you can't do that, because that would be stupid," Viv said.

Fortunately, Patrice laughed. "Yes, it would." She took a deep breath. "I have to get it together before six o'clock. If I show up on set with red eyes, we'll be getting calls and emails before the first commercial break. What brings you here?"

I told her about Gia, and about how we'd thought Charlotte Franks was her, at first. "Do you know anything about her? The story just said was from Kansas City, but that doesn't explain how she ended up down here."

"Yeah, we do have a little bit more about her, but we decided it wasn't relative to the story. She was arrested for prostitution in Dallas, maybe a year or two ago. There are a few other minor offenses on her record."

346

I frowned, thinking about the reports I'd read. "That part wasn't in the news," I said. "Why didn't you report that?"

Patrice shrugged. "As far as we know, it has nothing to do with how she died or how she ended up here. I mean, it *could*. And if it turns out to have something to do with her death, we'll report it. But as of now..." She shrugged again. "The information is available to anyone who cares to look. But we decided not to bring that up in our story. It was...gratuitous."

She tapped at something on her desk, then heaved a great sigh. "She's fine. It's totally normal."

I felt so bad for her. I knew how bad I felt when Stump was sick, and it was probably much worse when it was your flesh and blood.

I had to admit, though, it couldn't be that much worse. Just then I was feeling very guilty at how much time I'd been leaving Stump home with Frank and her princess bed. On the one hand, I was glad her separation anxiety seemed to have improved some, but on the other hand...I still felt like a neglectful mother.

We left not long after because Patrice had to get ready for the newscast, and she had her plate full with that and trying not to cry for Lola.

Ash had thought ahead and found out that the trash in Shawn's neighborhood was scheduled to be pick up the next day. "We have to do a run tonight," she said. "It may be too soon to get anything, but then again, we have to make sure we don't miss it."

I hid a frown as I checked the time. This meant I'd probably be out until at least 11 o'clock. And Frank would need to stay with Stump again.

To make up for being gone all afternoon and then again at bedtime, I decided to make Stump and Frank a special dinner of street tacos. Okay, I *bought* a special dinner of street tacos. Viv and Ash joined us, and we spent hours combing through the Am I The Jerk posts, passing judgment on all and sundry.

Am I The Jerk Because I Didn't Give My Special Edition Pokemon To My Nephew?

Am I The Jerk For Feeding Earwax To My Cat?

Am I The Jerk For Getting Mad At My Mother-in-law For Breaking Into My House And Cooking A Meal?

Am I The Jerk For Applying To Be On The Bachelor? My Girlfriend Thinks So.

People are a mess, y'all. After a while, I remembered what it had felt like to be on the receiving end of one of those public beat-downs and suggested Frank moderate another episode of his favorite telenovela for us. This kept us occupied while we digested our tacos and waited for the sun to go down. Once it was fully past my normal bedtime and I was beginning to nod off, Viv slapped her knees and said, "Okay, it's time. Let's head out."

Ash looked at me. "You're sure you want to go? It's no big deal if you sit this one out."

"Nah, I'll go," I said, groaning as I dragged my body off the sofa. I'd already been in Shawn's neighborhood once, I figured I could do it again, now that I knew to avoid the goose.

Viv drove over to Shawn's neighborhood and Ash instructed her to turn in a few streets before Shawn's. We found a house that was in the final stages of construction, and Ash instructed her to park there. "Everybody has those doorbell cameras now, but this one won't."

Viv parked the Caddy behind a cement mixer on a trailer and killed the lights. She pulled her recorder out of her purse and slipped it into her shirt pocket. "I'm going to leave it on record and just capture whatever comes up."

With Ash walking confidently in the lead, we hit the sidewalk and rounded the corner. Then Ash sidestepped out of the streetlights, into the shadows close to the fence.

Viv followed, dropping into an elaborate stealth stance, arms out for balance, walking on tiptoe. Faintly, I could hear the sound of her whispering into the recorder in her shirt pocket. I brought up the rear, trying not to laugh.

A silver truck was parked across the street, in the grass beside the cotton field. Shawn was home.

I froze, terrified.

How did I not anticipate that he could be here? What was the point of us going through his trash if he hadn't been home to throw anything away?

What if he caught us? There was a light on in the front of his house.

I wanted to turn back. I didn't have a key to get into the car, though – Viv had them. And Viv...Viv and Ash had both reached the alley behind Shawn's house and were entering it now.

Leaving me to stand there by my lonesome. In the dark. Staring at Shawn's truck.

I sprinted for the alley. I entered it and immediately tripped over something. I planted into the dirt with a grunt.

"Oh no!" Ash shout-whispered. She came rushing back.

"I'm okay," I said, although my knee hurt. I rose to my knees and brushed dirt off my hands.

Ash reached me, grabbed me by the shoulders and yanked. "Get up!"

Jeez Louise. "I'm up," I said as I stumbled to my feet. "I'm fine."

"Are you sure?" She patted me down.

"I'm sure."

She took a deep breath and stepped back. She pointed a finger in my face. "You stay safe!"

I brushed myself off. "I'm fine."

The alley was so dark. A few houses had lights in the backyard, but illumination didn't extend into the alley. Viv and I got our phones out and turned on the flashlight app, keeping the thin beams pointed toward the ground. I sure didn't want to fall again—Ash might come completely unglued.

She seemed to have pulled herself together now, though. She reached the dumpster first and, after peering over the fences of the yards nearest, slowly lifted the lid.

Viv and I shined our phones inside. It was full to the rim.

"How do we know which ones to take?" I whispered.

"We'll have to take them all." Ash reached in and grabbed a plastic bag.

One by one, she lifted the bags out. I didn't know how we were going to get them all into Viv's trunk, and I cringed at the thought of sitting beside a stack of garbage bags in the back seat.

"Okay, I think we can leave the ones closest to the bottom," Ash said. "He's only been home for a day, so his would be in this top layer." She grabbed two bags in one hand, then two in the other.

I shut off my light, slid my phone into my back pocket, and did as Ash had done. The bags were heavy.

Viv tucked her phone into her waistband and gathered the tops of two bags in her right hand.

"You don't have to do that," Ash said. "We can make two trips."

It was too dark to see Viv's glare, but I could feel it. "Step. Back," she said.

Ash stepped back.

Viv gathered the two bags in her right hand, then bent to snatch up the remaining two in her left. She heaved them and stood.

Immediately, she began to list to the right.

"It's lighter if you hold them closer to your body," Ash said.

Viv did that, then said, "Eww. It stinks." She extended her arms back out.

Viv *was* uncommonly strong for a woman her age. She'd been taking all of Belle Court's fitness classes, and she swam regularly. But still, I thought it was shear stubbornness that was keeping her arms up.

"Viv, I'm serious. We can leave a couple and I can come back for them—"

"I am fine!" Viv snapped.

Uh-oh. We all froze. That was a bit loud.

A light over a back porch flipped on. A back door open.

We all three ducked.

"I don't know," a man's voice said from the back door. "But if it's that dadgummed peeping Tom again, he's fixin' to get a butt full of buckshot."

We scrambled for the street. The streetlight at the end made visibility a lot better going that direction.

Ash stayed low and close to the fence, running quickly toward the end of the alley. Viv ran down the center, arms spread wide, two bags held at the end of each arm, her skinny legs tiptoe-running down the grassy center.

The movement got the bags swinging. The bags swinging pulled her first one direction, then the other, like a pendulum. She tottered to the right, then to the left.

Her legs were so skinny, and dressed all in black, running against the streetlight, she looked like a cartoon.

I couldn't help myself. I giggled.

Viv tottered to one side of the alley. The bags swung and the weight pulled her to the other side.

"What are you doing?" Ash hissed.

"I'm – I'm running," Viv stammered. Then the momentum became too much, and she fell into a heap of skinny limbs and plastic trash bags.

"Oh no!" Ash said again. "Get up!"

The light in Shawn's backyard flipped on, too. I had been about to laugh over Viv falling (quietly, to myself, of course) but I gulped it back.

They say that stress gives you superhuman strength. I crammed all four of my bags in one hand, then gathered all I could of Viv's. Ash did the same. Then we sprinted for the car.

Viv popped the trunk as we approached, and we shoved all the bags in. That was the fastest I'd ever moved in my life. We slammed the lid down, threw ourselves into our seats, and then Viv was backing down the street as fast as she could.

"You're sure you're okay?" Ash asked for the fourth time as we drove through the night back to Trailertopia.

"Of course," Viv said.

Ash looked over the back of the seat at me. "And you? No permanent damage?"

"My knee kind of hurts," I said. "But no. Nothing permanent."

"Whew!" Ash leaned back in her seat and I thought that, whatever her secret story was, it had to involve someone falling.

Back at Trailertopia, we lugged the garbage bags onto my deck, and I turned on the porch light.

Frank stood in the doorway and watched us, growing more visibly unsettled by the moment. "What?" he finally asked, waving a hand to take in the stinky mess.

"This is a thing that private investigators do," Viv explained. "They go through suspects' trash to learn what they can about them."

"Oh," he said. "Gross."

Stump, however, was in heaven. I pointed my finger at her. "You will not be eating anything from any of these bags," I said. "That is an order."

She snorted and trotted over to a bag, sniffing like she could ingest it through her nose.

We pulled on latex gloves and opened the first bag. We'd decided on a method. Viv bought plastic tablecloths at the dollar store, and we dumped the first bag out onto it. It stunk. But honestly, it wasn't as bad as I feared. It also, I thought, wasn't Shawn's. This trash had all the earmarks of a family. There were empty, colorful yogurt cups, an empty bottle of children's pain killer, and a few coloring pages with scrawled green crayon all over them.

The next bag smelled *really* bad.

"Oh no," Viv said. She retched. "I think it's--yes, it's a litter box."

"Well, we know that's not his, then," Ash said. "He doesn't have a cat."

"How do we know that, though?" I asked.

"The neighbor said he came over to take care of his snake. If he'd been taking care of a cat *and* a snake, he would have mentioned that."

That stood to reason, so we gratefully bundled that tablecloth up and crammed it all back into the bag.

We pawed through bag after bag of crumpled Whataburger wrappers, empty hairspray cans and shampoo bottles, junk mail, and a broken dinner plate ("probably a fight," Frank said, characteristically unhelpful as he watched from the sidelines).

By the fifth bag, I was starting to grow irritated. Yes, we had twelve bags. But I did not want to go through all twelve to find something worth finding.

On the seventh bag, though, Ash said, "Oh! I think this might be something." She pawed through a clump of wood shavings. "Do they use wood shavings in snake habitats?"

I was on my knees at the opposite corner of this tablecloth. I shrugged. "Who knows. But probably." I spotted a piece of cardboard and dug it out. "Oh. Nope. No snake. Whoever this belongs to has mice, not snakes." I held the thin cardboard up for them to see. It was one of those plastic bags that hang from a hole in the cardboard strip at the top. It showed a little mouse sitting at a red-checkered tablecloth, holding an oversize knife and fork.

I was ready to gather up this bag as well when a thought occurred to me. "Unless..." I looked at Ash.

"Unless that's food for a mouse who is, in turn, food for the snake."

Viv shuddered. "Eww."

I knew that snakes ate rodents, but..."Don't they usually feed them rodents that are already dead?"

"Yeah, I think so." She thought for a second. "Yeah, they do. That friend I told you about, whose boyfriend had the ball python? She was freaked out because there were rats in her boyfriend's freezer. He thawed one out at feeding time. Heated water up in the microwave and soaked the poor thing until it thawed out. She was as upset about the frozen rats as she was about the snake."

I reached for the corner of the tablecloth to gather it up. "So, not this one, either –" I gasped and scrambled to my feet.

"What?" Viv jumped behind me and peered over my shoulder.

I pointed to the slithery thing that had caught my eye. "Is that –"

Ash leaned close and poked at the garbage in the direction I was pointing.

"Ooh!" she said. She gripped the thing between the tips of her fingers and gently tugged it loose. "It is!"

I backed up a step, pushing Viv with me.

The snakeskin hung loose from Ash's hand.

Frank popped back into the trailer and watched, horrified, from the other side of the glass.

Behind me, Viv shuddered. She pulled out her recorder. "To our astonish—put that thing away, Ash! – to our astonishment, there appears to be a live snake in the garbage."

"It's just the skin," Ash said.

Stump stepped close, neck stretched out, sniffing.

"Stump! Get back!"

"What?" Ash asked with a laugh. "*It's just the skin*. It can't bite her."

"I'm afraid she'll bite *it*," I said as I bent to pick her up. "If she eats that..." I shuddered, too. It would be hard to look at my precious baby in the same way, knowing she'd eaten a snakeskin.

"You two are silly." She looked at Frank and waved the snakeskin in his direction. "You *three*."

"Stop waving that thing around!" Viv snapped. "Good lord, how long is it?"

Ash popped up and held the skin beside her leg, letting it drape down to the deck. "Longer than 34 inches, anyway, because that's how long my inseam is."

"Well, anyway," I said. "We know we've found the right bag, I guess."

"You don't think..." And suddenly Viv was down on the steps of the deck, backing toward the car. "You don't think it..."

"What?" Ash asked.

"That it shed its skin in there, do you? And it's still in there?"

Somehow, I'll never really know how, I was suddenly *on* the railing of the deck. Weird guttural sounds were coming from my throat.

Ash – with nothing but latex gloves to protect her! -- sifted through the trash and assured us that it was reptile-free. I nodded and agreed. I didn't see anything slithering away. But still. The deck railing was a perfectly fine place to be, and where I intended to stay.

Ash picked through the remaining contents of that bag. A Whataburger bag, some junk mail, empty toilet paper rolls, an empty shaving cream can, various trash of unidentifiable origin.

"Look!" Ash cried as she unfolded a piece of paper. "Here it is!"

It was our landscaping flyer, complete with the smiley face on the front.

At this triumph, we beamed at each other. We'd done it!

Of course, this really didn't tell us much. We already knew Shawn had a snake. It was a given that he would eat Whataburger (hello? It's Texas) and use toilet paper (at least one would hope) so once that moment of triumph had passed, I was left with once again wondering how, exactly, we were helping anything. Plus, I had trash all over my deck.

"Is that it?" Viv asked. She was still staying a safe distance away at the bottom of the deck steps, ready to bolt for her car at the first sign of a reptile.

"He takes vitamins A, C, and B12," Ash said, holding up a bag. "Oh, wait. What is this?"

She unfolded a small wadded up piece of paper. On closer examination, it was thicker than paper--more like card stock. It was ripped at the top, probably where it had been ripped from whatever it had been attached to.

"A clothing tag?" I asked, dropping off the railing and peering close.

"Yeah, I think so," Ash said. "There's a part of a bar code, and the letters WMS. Then more letters. XS – extra small."

"What's WMS?" I wondered aloud.

"Womens?" Viv said. She flicked the recorder back on. "Lying beside the snakeskin was a women's clothing tag, extra small." She flicked it back off and said, "I'll add a pause for dramatic effect in editing."

I tried to think of anything Shawn could buy for himself that would be sized extra small but came up with nothing. He wasn't a huge guy, but he was at least average size.

"So, he bought this for someone else. Let's look for the receipt."

There was no receipt, though – at least not for that. And nothing else out of place for a single man.

Ash and I studied the pile of trash while Viv pretended to be involved. Frank had gone back to watching his telenovela.

I bent over the pile. "He could have more than one bag," I said, looking at the remaining unopened bags unhappily. "How would we know which ones were his now that we've found the flyer?" I picked the mouse food package up again and looked at it. This was a clue, of sorts. I had to imagine that whoever fed their snake live rodents had a masochistic streak.

Again, something I already knew.

I looked closer at the cardboard strip. It had a price sticker on it – one of those old-school ones that were put on with a sticker gun.

Wally's Exotic Pet World, it said. $3.49

"Is there a Wally's Exotic Pet World here?" I asked.

Viv and Ash both shook their heads. "Not that I'm aware of. But I haven't been in the market for exotic pets, either."

I was almost positive there wasn't. At Flo's Bow Wow Barbers, we knew about all the local grooming shops, but even if a pet store didn't have grooming, we still pretty much knew who they were.

I pulled my phone out of my back pocket and entered the name in the browser. The first entries were sponsored links to local pet shops, but the fourth entry was Wally's. I tapped the link.

The browser opened to a colorful but amateurish website extolling the joys of owning exotic animals. Birds, reptiles, small animals, arachnids, anything that was legal to own could be procured through Wally's. "If we don't have it, we can get it for you!"

I scrolled the page for more information. There was only one location.

"He got these in Dallas," I said to Viv and Ash, holding up the package.

"There's an Elite Moving hub there," Ash said. "I did a little research into the company. It stands to reason he would travel there a lot."

I nodded, thinking.

"Patrice Watson said Charlotte Franks had been arrested in Dallas," Viv said. "Remember that?"

Ash and I nodded.

"It's a very big place, though," Ash said. "The odds that this is just a coincidence are very high."

We considered that in silence for a moment.

"I guess you're right," I finally said, glumly. "Still, it's something to know."

I took the mouse food label and the clothing tag inside and set them on the bar. As far as leads to find 16-year-old girls went, those two little pieces of paper were tragically small.

Chapter Ten

I had been exhausted a few hours before, but after Viv and Ash left, and Stump and I went to bed, I lay on my back, staring at the ceiling of my bedroom. From under the covers, Stump's snores rattled softly.

I kept seeing that extra small clothes tag sitting on my bar. It felt simultaneously like a murder weapon and like a whisper thin piece of glass that would shatter at the slightest touch. I got up to look at it, make sure it hadn't...I don't know, blown on a phantom wind into the sink drain, to be lost forever.

I couldn't just leave it there, I realized. I needed to take it to show Bobby. He would say it wasn't evidence he could use, but still. He would know what to do about it. I had to believe he did, because I sure as heck didn't.

I trudged to the kitchen and stared at the tag. I took a sandwich bag out of the pantry and slipped it inside, along with the label from the mouse food. I zipped it up tight and stared at it. Then I found a butter bowl with a matching lid and put the baggy inside. I popped the lid on and stared at that.

It might be nothing. It could be anything. Shawn might have a niece, a cousin, a friend with a young daughter.

He might have access to any of them.

I groaned and carried the bowl back to my bedroom. Stump had stayed put and watched me warily as I set the bowl on the nightstand and then fell back into bed. She crawled over me to sniff at the bowl but, finding nothing that piqued her interest, gave a soft snort and burrowed back under the covers.

I stared at the bowl.

It was so little to go on. It was nothing. There was no law against him buying anything extra small.

I flopped onto my back. The bowl felt like a bomb beside my head.

Finally, I threw the covers back, slipped on my flip-flops, and carried the bowl out to my car. Trailertopia was silent in the dark night, and I moved quietly to not wake anyone. The Monte Carlo had a huge glove compartment, and I tucked the bowl inside. I slammed the door shut, locked the car door, then backed away from the car.

"What?" Frank said from behind me.

I jumped and spun. He wasn't there. I spun back toward the car. Not there either.

"What happened?" he asked.

"Where are you?"

He tapped at the screen of his bedroom window. "Here," he said.

"Oh." I looked up. His shadow was barely visible in his dark window. "Did I wake you? I'm sorry."

"Nah, man, no big deal." He stood there silently for a moment, then said, "What happened?"

I sighed. "One of the things we found in Shawn's trash – I couldn't stop thinking about it. I can't sleep because of it. I had to put it in my car so I could get it out of the house."

"I mean...I guess that's a good idea." He hesitated for a moment. "It's not like it's a *live* snake or anything."

"Oh," I said. "Not the snakeskin. It was just a clothing tag. A girl's clothing tag, extra small."

"Oh." Clearly he didn't understand why that would be more disturbing than a snakeskin.

"Hey, I was thinking," he said. "Remember when we wondered if a live snake was inside the bag? What if it *had* been in there but it was just hiding good?"

"We looked, though. It wasn't in there."

"Maybe it just moved really fast, though. Maybe it was under the trash and it slipped between the boards of the deck and is hiding under your trailer right now."

I hadn't thought of that. But I sure as heck was now.

"Geez, Frank!" I cried, stepping really, *really* high as I raced up the steps to the deck. "Why?"

"Sorry," he called after me.

I kicked my flip-flops into the corner of my bedroom and yanked back the covers to make sure there wasn't a snake hiding in the bed. I tossed the pillows and slapped them between my palms, fully prepared to shriek, throw them against the wall, grab Stump and flee the trailer if I felt anything slithery inside. That was, thankfully, unnecessary.

Finally, I crawled back into bed. Tomorrow, I would take the butter bowl to Bobby and tell him what we'd done. He wouldn't be happy, especially after that business at the middle school, but what could he do? And he might know a way this was all connected to Gia. It could be the clue that blew the whole thing wide open. How could I know, unless I told him? Everything had to be out in the open. Full transparency.

Everything.

I groaned, then I grabbed my phone off the nightstand. It was 2:47 AM. Maybe I shouldn't, but...

I texted Viv and Ash.

"I'm going to see Helena tomorrow. I have to tell her about Shawn. She's going to lose it. Go with me for protection and moral support?"

I took a deep breath and reached to set the phone down. I could sleep now.

It dinged twice before I could get it there. I looked at the screen.

Ash: We're with you, Sis.

Viv: I ain't scared of her. Let me know time.

I turned off the lamp and snuggled into my pillow. I could definitely sleep now.

Bobby stared at the butter bowl on his desk. Then he looked at me, Ash, and Viv.

"You went through his trash." It wasn't a question.

"That's what detectives do," Viv said.

"But we're not detectives," I pointed out. "We're podcasters."

"Oh, yes." Viv dug through her handbag and dug out her recorder. She flicked it on.

"Turn that off," Bobby said.

"So, this is off the record, then?" Viv asked.

Bobby closed his eyes for a long moment.

"It's just that," I said, leaning forward and opening the lid. "There's this tag. Women's clothing, extra small."

Bobby opened his eyes but didn't say anything.

"He's not a woman, and he's not extra small," I whispered. "He's a man."

Bobby blinked.

"I know it's not exactly a smoking gun, Bobby. But it is odd, right?"

He sat, impassive.

"And it could be a clue. The girl that was dumped outside of town – she might have been wearing something that would match this tag.

You – you could get surveillance footage from the store where it was sold and see when it was bought. That could be a connection."

More stone face.

"Aren't you going to say anything?"

He shook his head. "Nope."

"Aren't you even going to yell at me?"

Again, with the head shake.

"Well, good," I said. "Why not?"

"Because it doesn't do any good. I yelled at you yesterday and then you went and dug through his trash. You want to dig through trash, then dig through trash. It's not against the law."

"We know that," Viv said with a sneer.

"You want to break into school buildings – "

"We didn't break in," Ash reminded him. "The door was open. We got locked in."

Bobby stared at her for a moment. She shrank back into her chair.

He turned back to me. "Look, Salem. I understand why you're personally invested in this case. I do. But I really went out on a limb for you yesterday. By all rights, you all three should have been charged with trespassing." He looked at each of us in turn. "The only reason you weren't is that I called in some favors."

There wasn't a lot we could say to that. I shrank in my own seat a bit. "I'm sorry," I said.

"I don't have a lot of favors owed to me, Salem."

"I understand."

He studied me for a minute. Then he looked at Viv and Ash. "Did you see the news of that arrest last week? The arrest we made based on an investigation we did? The arrest we'll probably get a conviction on, because we followed good solid police work and did the job right?"

"What does this have to do with Gia?"

"It has to do with the fact that we have a good police department, and you could *trust* us to do our *jobs.*"

At our silence, he said, "But you're going to keep getting yourself into the middle of things, aren't you?"

I shrugged. "Not the very middle. Maybe just around the periphery. Until Gia comes home."

He sighed and shrugged, too. "Go right ahead. You might get caught somewhere you're not supposed to be, and I certainly won't run interference for you."

"Well, that's fine, Bobby, I don't expect you to run interference for me. I just – "

"Next time I get a call from someone saying "Sloan, that crazy girl of yours is into trouble over on yada yada yada...." He waved a hand airily. "I'll say 'Not my problem. Not my business.'"

"Okay."

"People calling in to report you're mixed up with mobsters, digging through Dumpsters, I'll just..." He trailed off and shrugged. "Okay. Send out a unit, pick her up."

"Okay," I said again. I really didn't know what else to say. "Will you give this to Detective Scott?"

"Nope." He popped the lid back on and slid it across his desk. "I'm gonna let you take care of that."

"Well, that's just fine." Viv snatched up the bowl and tucked it in her purse. "We will just leave! We will pursue this case ourselves! And we won't bother with keeping the police department informed!"

"Promise?" Bobby asked.

Viv stomped out the door and Ash and I followed her. Viv turned back and poked her head in the door. "And I left my recorder *on*, haha."

Detective Scott was way friendlier than Bobby had been. Not much more helpful, but at least she was polite.

"This can't be catalogued as evidence, I'm afraid, but we can certainly catalog it as a citizen tip and follow up on it."

"Good." Viv nodded. "Very good."

We all stood there. Detective Scott held the bowl and smiled. Nodded. Finally, she said, "Okay, then. Thank you very much."

"You're welcome," Viv said. "But you're going to follow up on it, right? You're not blowing this off. Because you don't want to blow this off."

She shook her head. "Definitely not blowing this off."

"I feel like you're blowing it off."

"Definitely not blowing it off. I'll catalog it as a tip, and I'll compare it to everything related to Gia."

"And to that girl they found outside of town," I said. "Because Helena told us about Gia's DNA being found at the site where the body was found."

"Did she?" Her head was nodding and her lips were still smiling, but her teeth clenched and her eyes said she wasn't thrilled with this news. "Great."

"We didn't tell the reporter about that, though," Ash said.

"She's not a reporter," Viv corrected. "Patrice Watson is the lead anchor."

Detective Scott's eyes bugged a bit more. "Who?"

"Nobody," I assured her. "We did talk to Patrice Watson at Channel 11 about the girl whose body was found, but we did not mention the possible connection to Gia."

At Detective Scott's silence, I repeated softly, "Did *not*."

Detective Scott drew a deep breath in through her nose.

I got this very distinct *she's-gonna-blow* feeling, and said, "Okay, well then, thanks very much, we'll get out of your hair." I took Viv's elbow and we hustled out of there.

Viv huffed as she got behind the wheel of the Caddy. "I don't know about you two, but I'm starting to feel unappreciated."

I leaned back in the seat and thought about everything that we'd just tried to explain to Bobby and Detective Scott. It was all so flimsy.

It was so flimsy that I was having major second thoughts about telling Helena. Why? Why do it at all? She didn't need to know. It would just upset her more. How was I helping?

But by that time, we were turning the corner onto her street. She was sweeping the front porch, and she'd seen us.

"Maybe we should keep driving," I said quickly.

Helena leaned the broom against the porch, though, and I knew if we kept going, she'd probably just come after us.

I sighed. "Pull over, Viv. It's okay. Let's just...get this over with."

"It's going to be fine," Ash said. "I get that she's a hothead, but she won't go off on you if we're there."

"Of course, she won't," Viv said. "Like I said, I'm not afraid of her."

Ash and I tactfully didn't mention that she'd seemed a *touch* afraid when we left the salon the day before.

Helena came down the steps to meet us on the sidewalk. "Did you find something?"

"Well, yes and no," Viv said. "Let's go inside have a seat."

"I'm not having any seats," Helena said. "What did you find?"

"Helena," Viv said. "Friend. Everything is okay. We just need to report some findings."

"So, you did find something. What? Tell me."

Viv sighed. I felt like running back to the car.

"Let's go inside and have a seat," Ash said.

"Is she dead?" Helena cried. "Did you find her dead?"

Since this clearly could not go any worse, I took Helena by the elbow and plunged straight into the deep end, forcing my voice to be low and controlled. "No, Helena. We haven't found her, dead or otherwise. What we need to tell you is that I knew your old boyfriend, Shawn, a long time ago."

"Shawn? What's -- what's he got to do with anything?"

"Probably nothing. But I wanted you to know that—that he was a friend of our family. He--he molested me when I was a kid."

She blinked, then looked from me to Viv. "What?"

"I recognized him from the pictures we looked through that first day we met you. Seeing him...well, it brought up old traumas and it freaked me out, to be honest. I panicked and left. I should have told you right away. I'm really sorry about that."

She shook her head. "What does this have to do with Gia? Shawn was a long time ago." She frowned and stomped up the steps. "I can't believe you almost gave me a heart attack over that. I mean, I'm sorry that happened to you, but..." Her voice trailed off as she stalked into the house, the three of us behind her.

"You could have just texted me about that, you know. Since it doesn't have anything to do with Gia."

"It may not have anything to do with Gia. But since I knew that the guy was a child molester, I started doing a little digging on him. I found out that he..."

I trailed off, because as I spoke, I saw the realization dawn on Helena's face. She stepped back, looked off as if she was processing, then snapped her gaze back at me. "I let a child molester into my home?"

I opened my mouth to answer, but no easy words presented themselves.

"*You* let me let a child molester into my home?" Her face tightened and already her hand was rising. Whether she meant to gesture or to slap me, I didn't know, but I steeled myself.

"Salem was a child herself," Viv said. "She was traumatized."

"It's been a long time since she's been a child," Helena spat. "And still you say nothing? How many girls has he hurt because you said nothing?"

"Listen, Helena, there's no sense in blaming Salem. She wasn't – "

"And you're defending her?" Helena stepped into Ash's face and shouted, pointing her finger. "Do you think I would have let that man into my home if I'd known?"

Ash closed her hand around Helena's and put her other hand on her shoulder. "Of course not. You're not to blame. Salem is not to blame. There's only one person to blame here."

"And you need to keep in mind, Shawn may not have even touched Gia. We have no proof that he did," Viv said.

Helena blinked and stepped back, her eyes wide and her face slack. "Oh. Gia. Poor Gia."

"Let's go inside and have a seat," Viv said.

Helena led us inside, still looking shocked. She fell into her chair and stared at the floor. "I let a child molester into my house."

"You didn't know," I said.

"Because you didn't tell."

I fought the urge to defend myself. "I know you would have avoided him if you'd known."

"If you'd told, he wouldn't have been *able* to be here. He would have been in jail. You..." She sneered at me, clearly trying to think of a word bad enough for me. "How old are you?"

I stifled a sigh. "I'm 29," I said.

"So even if you waited until you were an adult to tell, you could have reported it and he could have been in prison at the time I was meeting him. Not out at some bar looking for women with kids at home that he could have access to."

"That could be true," I said. There wasn't much point in mentioning how rare it was for a predator to be convicted years after the crime, based on nothing but a child's memories.

"Why didn't you? Why didn't you go to the police station the day you turned 18 and report it?"

My mind swam, wondering how much I was expected to reveal here. That I didn't report when I was 18 because I was already a walking train wreck by then, hiding bottles of cheap rum in my school locker and sneaking Tony into my house at night? Or should I tell her about how I was very busy getting pregnant, getting married to a man who didn't want to marry me, and losing the baby? Following that, my schedule was jam packed with drinking, running from the past, running from the memories, running from myself.

There had been no time to go down to the police station and take action on anything.

"I get why you'd be afraid to report when you were a kid. I mean, *I* would have." She looked at Viv and Ash. "I definitely wouldn't have put up with that."

"Careful about being judgmental," Ash said. "You don't really know how you would react if you weren't in the exact same position under the exact same circumstances."

"There are no circumstances where I would have tolerated being treated like that," she insisted. "I would have told."

Ash dropped on her haunches in front of Helena. "Look, lady. Maybe you would have, maybe you wouldn't. The point is, this didn't happen to you. It happened to Salem. She didn't ask for it to happen, it was forced on her. She dealt with it the best way she knew how at the time. You're comparing your non-traumatized brain to her traumatized one – "

"You think I've had life so easy? I lost my mom when I was fifteen! I had to become a mother myself! I had to become responsible for a toddler when I should have been out, having fun with my friends, thinking about what I wanted to do with my own life. Not taking responsibility for everyone else's lives! You think my life has been so perfect?"

She switched gears so fast she lost us all. But at the edges of my brain, a realization was dawning on me. Helena was, in fact, revealing her own trauma, and all the anger we saw was an outflow of that. She was, in essence, still that 15-year-old girl who felt the weight of responsibility she knew in her soul she couldn't handle, but somehow had to. Fear that she wasn't measuring up drove everything she did.

Speaking to the Helena in front of me was scary but speaking to that 15-year-old girl was much easier.

I put a hand on her knee. "You've done such a great job with Gia. Everyone we talked to has remarked on how hands-on you were with her, how you had high expectations for her and how you made sure she had everything she needed to do and be her best. How you protected her. And how fierce she was! Just like the sister she looked up to."

Helena's face contorted for just a second, as the battle to keep her fear at bay momentarily grew too much. Then she breathed hard through her nose and said, "Well..."

"I think you can take comfort from the fact that Gia probably would have told, too. Like I said, she was fierce like you. So, if she didn't say anything..." I shrugged. "Then there's every reason to think nothing happened."

Honestly, I didn't know if that was true or not. But I couldn't stop myself from giving the poor woman hope. "We didn't come here to tell you we think Shawn did anything to Gia. We came to tell you we have this information about someone who's had contact with Gia, and that we thought it was worth pursuing. So, we're doing that. And if you have any information about him, any recent information, it would be helpful."

"No, I haven't seen the piece of dirt since he stole my uncle's tools and I kicked him to the curb. But you'd better believe we're about to be reacquainted."

"Wait," Ash said. "What?"

"I'm telling everyone I know that he's a child molester." She picked up her phone. "This is about to go aaaaall over his social media."

"Wait!" Viv said. "You can't do that."

"Oh, you just hide and watch me. That dirtbag isn't going to –"

Ash closed her hand over Helena's. "Just wait. We have a plan. And calling him out in public could totally blow it."

"What plan?" Helena asked.

Yeah, what plan, I wanted to ask. Viv was also looking at Ash, the same question on her face.

Ash blinked quickly. "Well, okay. We weren't going to...well, yes. It's probably best that you know so you can help make sure it goes off okay."

"What?" Helena asked.

"Okay. Well. Here it is."

We all three waited.

Ash took a deep breath. "Okay. You know the girl they found outside of town."

Helena nodded.

"And remember how Gia's hairband was found there?"

"Of course, I remember that!"

"Well. We found out from another source that the girl had been in the Dallas area."

"Okay. So?"

"So. We also found out that Shawn – well, I'm afraid we can't reveal our source on this, but we have reason to believe that the Dallas area is part of his regular route. So, we're going to pursue that connection. And if he knows people are looking at him...well, he won't take his regular route, will he? He won't do anything to get himself caught. We need to be able to catch him in the act, right?"

Helena frowned. "We have to at least tell the police."

"We've told them. They won't share a lot, but I know they're looking closely at him, too." *At least, I hoped they were.*

"What does that mean, you're pursuing that connection in Dallas?"

Ash flattened her lips and thought a moment. "We can't reveal much. But we're going to retrace what we know of Charlotte Frank's steps there and see if there are any connections we find to Gia. Then we're going to go to the location we have for Shawn's route, and surveil that for a while. Whatever comes to the surface, we're going to pursue it."

I avoided looking at Viv. Man, Ash was *good.* Helena was calmed down, everything was transparent, everyone had all the pertinent details. It didn't really matter that much that we *weren't* going to go to Dallas, when it was all said and done. We had passed the information to the police, and they would follow up on it. I would make sure of it. I would call Detective Scott twice a day until she had something to report to me. And we could do online sleuthing – I had learned a few things from that.

Back at the car, I dropped into the back seat, my nerves frazzled from the last hour or so.

Suddenly, I wanted so much to be able to run to Tony's so he could sit with me on the sofa, my legs in his lap, my head tucked into the crook of his shoulder. I always felt so safe there.

"I have a pedicure appointment tomorrow morning, but I'm free any time after that," Viv said.

"Free for what?" I asked absently. I wondered if, when I got home, Stump would let me hold her or if she'd just stay in the princess bed and let me be lonesome.

"To go to Dallas," Viv said, as if this was obvious.

I gave a short laugh. "Viv, Ash was just saying that to get Helena to calm down. Keep her from torching Shawn on every platform she could find. We're not really going."

"Yeah, I made that up on the spot, but..." Ash said. "It's actually not a bad idea."

"But -- but –" I stammered. "It's not a good idea, either!"

"It *is* a good idea," Viv said. She pulled the tape recorder out of her pocket. "We have had the very good idea of going to Dallas to pursue leads."

"I can't just take off and go to Dallas!" I protested. "I have a job. And I've already missed too many days lately."

"It's okay," Viv said. "We don't all have to go. Ash and I can go, and report back. We'll probably just be interviewing people, taking pictures, that kind of thing."

She dropped me back at Flo's and I picked up my car. I called Frank. "How's Stump?"

"She tried to eat a bug, but I snatched her up too fast. Now she's pouting in her princess bed. Hang on."

I heard a ding and looked at my phone. He'd sent me a picture.

Stump lay in her princess bed with her back to him, her chin resting on the edge of the bed while she stared sullenly at the wall.

"I'll be home in a little while," I said. I started to add, *We have a few more interviews to do.* But lying was the first step back down the path to drinking. And I didn't want to go back down that road. It had already taken too much from me.

It had taken my ability to go to Tony for comfort. It had taken my freedom to go to Dallas with Ash and Viv.

Had it taken everything? What did I have left to lose?

The truth was, I felt restless and wasn't ready to go home yet. I drove around while I thought about what I *did* have to lose. I knew if I called Les, he would give me a list of all the things I still had, and he wouldn't have let me hang up without naming a few more ideas of my own.

I drove aimlessly for a while and tried to think. Stump was fine. I wasn't ready to go home yet. I knew I would have trouble sleeping and I wasn't ready to stare at the ceiling and feel awful for hours.

But who was I kidding? It wasn't aimless. I drove into Tony's neighborhood. I didn't turn down his street, but I drove really slow down the cross street. I stared at his house the best I could. No lights except the landscape lights. Man, his house was pretty. Not huge, but the yard was nice, there were big red oak trees, trimmed bushes, some colorful flowerpots on the front porch. He'd helped one of his cousins get started in a landscaping business, and pictures of Tony's yard were on the cousin's website.

I swerved to avoid the curb I'd almost hit. I needed to forget about Tony's nice house or about me ever living in it. I fit much better in my shabby trailer in Trailertopia. It wasn't impressive, but I was comfortable there. At Tony's, I always knew, in the back of my mind, that I was an outsider.

I glanced at my phone. It was almost nine o'clock. Sometimes Tony worked that late, but not very often. Only if something was going wrong—equipment broke down, or someone didn't show up for their shift. If he had paperwork to do, he did it from home.

I was pretty sure he wasn't home, but if he had his truck in the garage and was working in the back office, I wouldn't be able to tell from the street.

I made the block and circled back by his house, since he probably wasn't there anyway. I tried to think of a story to tell if he happened to come outside, look out the window, or drive up as I was passing. I couldn't think of anything, though, except something along the lines of, "none of your business why I'm driving here, you don't own this street." I hoped I wouldn't have to pull that gem out.

No lights on from the front of the house. No curtains twitched as I drove by. No Tony.

I circled the block again and asked myself why I was doing this. What did I think I was going to find? Tony keening on the front lawn, ripping his shirt and gnashing his teeth as he grieved the loss of me?

Or Tony cuddled up on the sofa with The Lovely Joanna? Joanna, who would be unproblematic. Joanna, who would be a great mother and would gladly have as many babies as Tony wanted. Joanna, who would pop out baby after baby and not one person in Tony's family would feel compelled to issue warnings.

I sighed and turned down the alley behind Tony's house. It was stupid and risky, but I needed to see...well, whatever I could see.

Tony's house was easy to spot from the back because those same landscape lights lit up the red oak trees in the back, and his fence was a bit different than the others. No ordinary wooden pickets for Tony. His fence had brick columns between the stained wooden panels. He had another cousin who was a bricklayer, and he helped that cousin's business as well.

I parked the Monster Carlo in the alley and killed the lights. I turned off the dome light and then opened the door carefully. A few houses down from Tony's, a dog barked. I left the door ajar to avoid making more noise than necessary.

I crept up to Tony's fence. The brickwork formed a low wall along the ground, with wooden panels inset between brick columns. I peered through the panels but couldn't see much. Finally, I grasped the top of the panels, put one foot on the lip of the wall, and hoisted myself up.

There. That was his office window, and it was dark. He wasn't working from home. The sliding glass doors to the patio led into the den, where he would be watching TV or reading if he was home. His bedroom window was dark as well, but he never went to bed this early.

Unless he was in there but not sleeping. In there with The Lovely Joanna.

I fought the urge to vault over the fence, run up to that bedroom and smash my face to the glass.

And here was the kicker. What if he *was* in there right now, in bed with Joanna—or any other woman, for that matter? What would I say? What *could* I say? I had no high ground to stand on. I'd been unfaithful to Tony for years. I'd thought we were divorced, but still. He'd been faithful to our vows, and I had not.

I sighed and dropped back to the ground. I was losing my marbles. I had to go home.

I *was* going to go home. It was a complete accident that I turned the wrong way when I got to the intersection. I was just distracted. And I kept driving in the wrong direction because I had my mind on other things. Like how I needed to get my act together and not obsess over Tony. Obsessing did no one any good, especially me. Obsessing made me anxious, and anxiety made me want to drink so I could release it.

I *could* drink. Viv and Ash were trusting me to do what I said I was going to do. They would never know. And even if they did know, so what? It wasn't as if the world was going to come to an end. I was definitely going to get sober again. For sure. I liked my life better sober. I was going to do the work to get myself back together.

It was just...a lot right now. Things were just too crazy to take on the stress of resisting alcohol along with everything else. I needed a break. I deserved a break. I had earned it. And I'd get back on the wagon tomorrow. Or the next day, for sure.

I thought about Todd's rants about celebrating milestones and how that became the goal—the adding up of days—instead of sobriety. I was starting to see his point now. If I had been facing this with over 700 days, I think I would probably be less tempted. But since I was facing this with less than five days...

So little to lose. Practically nothing.

Dang him.

I kept driving. I drove past two liquor stores and four convenience stores that sold beer and wine.

I thought a lot about turning into each one, but somehow my body kept the car headed straight to the east side of town. To the industrial side of town.

I was three blocks away before I admitted to myself that I was still looking for Tony. I needed to lay eyes on him, and I didn't even understand why. It wasn't going to change anything. It wouldn't do any good. I just needed to.

The offices for Solis Building Services were in a strip of warehouses. This part of town was dead at this time of day, but I could see from two blocks away that the light over his office door was on. He might have it on a timer.

But no. That was his pickup. He was working.

I turned off a block away and circled back. Should I talk to him? He was probably alone. His employees might be coming and going, but I could probably count on a few minutes alone with him.

I pulled into the lot at the end of the row, pulled forward just enough that I could see the office door.

What would I say? I'm sorry—again? I'll try harder—again? I'll get my act together—again?

Why would he believe me? Why would I even believe myself?

The past two years had been so good. Not perfect—I'd faced my share of challenges. But I'd honestly believed I was on solid ground. I'd honestly believed I could withstand any storm.

And here I was, once again fighting the urge to drink. Already knowing in my heart that as soon as I left here, I *was* going to stop at one of those convenience stores and pick up a cheap bottle of wine. Maybe two cheap bottles of wine. Inside, I'd already made the decision. I already felt the relief at knowing I was going to put off the struggle to be sober one more day. I already felt the easing of tension inside.

How could I go in there and try to sell him on any hope for us, when I already knew it was a lie?

You could go in there and tell him you're struggling. He likes to be the hero. He likes to be the savior.

The thought held a certain amount of appeal. Tony would definitely jump on the idea of helping me. If Tony had an addiction, it was helping people.

Co-dependency. We could have a happy little dysfunctional co-dependent relationship.

It would be better than nothing, though. Wouldn't it?

I would just go in there, tell him I needed his help, and he would be happy to help and I would be happy to let him.

I reached for my door handle.

I froze when someone walked around the back of Tony's pickup, coming from the other direction. She trotted up the concrete steps to Tony's office, long black hair swinging.

The Lovely Joanna.

Tony opened the office door for her. He was smiling. He held the door and stood back while she moved past him.

He closed the door behind them, talking as he did so. Talking and smiling. Laughing a little, even.

I sat there for a long time. Watching the door that did not open again. Seeing the happy, smiling, laughing face of my husband. Smiling at someone else.

Well, okay then. I had already decided I was going to drink, so there was no point in just sitting and putting off the inevitable. There were several steps between me and a glass of wine. First, I had to buy it. Then I had to stash it some place that Frank wouldn't see. I formed a vague plan in my head as I drove. I didn't want to put it in my trunk or anything, because Frank would be watching. I would have to buy the bottles, stash them somewhere on the Trailertopia grounds, and then take Stump for a walk. We did that sometimes, and I could legitimately tell Frank that I had nervous energy to burn off. He wouldn't offer to go with me because he never did. Stump and I could walk to wherever I'd hidden the bottles, then sneak back from the other side of the trailer and slip them into my bedroom window. I would have to remember to open my window before we went for our walk.

My mind focused on the details of my plan and I realized with a sense of dread that if I *wasn't* going to quit drinking again, I would have to move to somewhere with neighbors who did not care whether I drank or not. This was too much trouble.

But then, who would watch Stump for me while I was gone? Finding another Frank would be impossible.

I'd work that out later, I decided as I drove. Right now, I just needed to get the wine to quiet the screaming voices in my head and go home. I would be more creative once I'd had that first glass, and I could sit down and work out a plan.

There was a convenience store two blocks away. I just needed to get there...

Out of the corner of my eye, I saw the flying star logo of the Elite Moving Company, painted on the side of a truck parked on a side street.

I kept driving. I drove past the convenience store.

At the last second, I hung a right and made the block. That's the company Shawn drove for, that man had said.

Shawn, who was, to be perfectly honest, the reason I was going home to my trailer to drink while my husband smiled at The Lovely Joanna. Shawn who was behind every bad decision I'd made.

A voice in my head—the voice of Les, actually—told me that was an oversimplification and kept me locked in a box where I had no agency and no power.

"Screw you," I told that voice. "You shut up."

I drove past the house where the big truck was parked. In the yard, there was a For Sale sign with the Sold banner across the top. No other vehicles at the house.

He probably wasn't in there. There had to be many truck drivers who drove for that company. Even here in Lubbock.

If he drives across country, it wouldn't make any sense that he's moving a load here.

Of course, it would, I argued with myself. He could have taken a load to one location, then picked up another load on the way back. People moved to Lubbock. It happened. If he was already out on the road it stood to reason that he would be the person to bring loads here.

I kept driving, circling blocks.

What would I say to him? What would I do, if it was him?

Slap him, I thought. Punch him in the face. Ask him if he kidnapped Gia.

He would probably never let me get close enough to slap him. But I could spit on him. Spit right in his face and then run as fast as I could. Then buy two bottles of wine and drink.

I drove past the house again. The truck was parked along the curb, blocking the driveway and the alley. There was a light on inside.

I headed back out onto the main street. I'd had enough for one day, hadn't I? I knew where Shawn lived if I wanted to confront him. I could do it when I was in a better frame of mind. When I knew what I wanted.

So, I would just go home, cuddle with Stump, and drink and think too much about whatever Tony and The Lovely Joanna were doing at that very moment, and how it was really no more than I deserved. Think about how I was on track to lose my job. On track to lose my friends, my home. No, I wasn't close to any of those things yet, but I was on the path. I'd been here before enough times to recognize all the signposts.

I swung back to the right, making the corner too wide, and drove slowly past the Elite Moving truck.

I parked at the curb.

He'd done this to me. I had proven to myself over the past two years that I was capable of being a responsible person. I *could* hold down a job. I *could* pay my bills on time. I *could* maintain friendships with people and not end up using them, not beg from them and even steal from them when I got myself into scrapes I didn't know how to get out of. I could be a good person. I could be a decent person.

Until my mind got whacked out of control because *he* popped back into my life. Until the damage that he'd done to me reared its head and I couldn't handle it anymore. I understood I had free will and yada yada yada, the truth was if he had kept his filthy hands to himself, I wouldn't have to fight an overwhelming battle just to be *normal.* It was not my fault it got to be too much sometimes.

And Gia. What had he done to Gia?

Fury propelled me out of the car and up the sidewalk. I still didn't know what I was going to say to him, but I figured I would start with the spitting and then play it by ear. I pounded on the front door.

The door opened and I already had a good spit going before I realized it wasn't Shawn.

The man was large—not fat necessarily, but about six foot two, and solid. He was probably mid-fifties, with light brown hair fading to gray. His head was square and his face was full, bloated. His eyes were a very light blue—the lightest blue I think I'd ever seen. They were too small for his bloated face.

"Well, hello," he drawled, and gave me a knowing smile. "You're an eager one."

"I – umm –" I looked back toward the truck. "Is Shawn here?"

"Shawn?" He looked over his shoulder. I could see behind him to the empty entryway that led to an entry living room, and an empty kitchen beyond that. "Shawn who?"

My mind reeled, confused. I'd been prepared to confront Shawn, but instead I was talking to this man who seemed to know something I didn't. "I thought that was his truck," I said lamely.

He shook his head, that same knowing smile on his lips. "Nobody's truck but mine, darlin'." He waggled his eyebrows.

I shivered despite myself. Something about his face was so cruel. He was making me uncomfortable, and he knew it. Enjoyed it.

There was a noise behind him and we both looked that direction. A woman stood there, someone around my age or a few years younger. She wore jeans and a sweatshirt, her dark hair held back by a headband.

"You don't know anybody named Shawn, do you?" He turned his face back toward me, but his gaze stayed on the girl. "This nice woman is looking for a Shawn."

The girl didn't answer. She seemed to shrink into herself a bit.

"We don't know any Shawns," he said. "Of course, we're just the movers, we don't know anybody. I'd have to look at my paperwork to even know whose house we're standing in right now." He kept his gaze focused on the woman. "Isn't that right, honey."

The way he said it, it didn't sound like a question. And she didn't respond.

"My daughter and I don't know any Shawns. Maybe he's the one who moved out of this house? Or the one who's moving in?"

"I..." I didn't finish. There was such a weird energy in the air, I had no idea what to even think. It was like I'd walked into the middle of a play and didn't know the lines—didn't even know what kind of play it was.

I took a step back. Suddenly I wanted to get as far away from there as I possibly could.

"Yes, that's probably it," I said, not even sure what I meant. "Well, thanks anyway. Sorry to bother you." I was babbling a bit as I backed down the sidewalk.

"You sure you don't want to hang around a bit, see if he shows up?" He laughed.

It was a creepy laugh.

Then he said, in a low voice that managed somehow to carry all the way into my bones, "We could have us a little party."

I laughed too, awkwardly. Then I jumped in my car and locked the door.

As I drove away, I tried not to think about the woman, and how she'd refused to speak.

Back in the safety of my trailer, I paced for a few minutes. Stump and Frank watched me.

"You okay?" Frank asked.

"I'm..." I didn't know how to answer that. "I didn't drink," I said.

"Oh. Good." Then, "Do you want me to call Les?"

I shook my head. "No, I'll call him." I headed to my second bedroom.

"Salem," Les answered his phone.

"I almost drank," I said.

"Almost," he repeated.

"Almost."

"And where are you now?"

"Home. No booze. Frank is here."

"There's a meeting in half an hour, downtown."

"I went to the sunrise meeting at St. Matt's this morning."

"They don't limit you to one a day," he said. He liked saying that.

"I don't want to go to a meeting. I want to talk to you, about..." It was right on the tip of my tongue to tell him about Tony and Joanna. But I couldn't. They all knew Tony had broken up with me over my drinking. Saying the thing about Joanna out loud would be too...real.

"Yesterday I talked to Trisha, and she cried because her baby had to get shots," I blurted.

"Oh yeah. Those are awful. I remember those with my boys. Those baby shots can be bad."

"Yes, but...shots aren't *that* bad. But parents cry when babies get them anyway."

"Well, yeah. Because you know they're hurting, and you can't do anything about it."

"Why doesn't God cry when we're hurting?"

"He does, Salem. Of course, He does."

"But he doesn't do anything to keep it from happening."

"No. Just like Patrice didn't stop her baby from getting shots. Because she knows that ultimately, that pain is much less than the pain of getting a serious disease will be."

"Right!" I said. I was pacing in the bedroom now, and it was kind of pointless because the room was so small, but I couldn't be still. "That's right. Because you know with some kinds of pain, there is a benefit to be gained from it. But what about—what about stuff like what I went through? Like Gia's maybe going through? That doesn't *have* a purpose? Why would God just allow that to happen?"

"God can make something out of it, Salem."

"But – that's so—ugh!" I tried to put into words what had been rolling around in my head for the last week. I thought of all the pitiful analogies I'd ever heard, of arms broken that were stronger in the places where they'd healed. Of pottery that broke and the cracks were where the light got in. Right now, all those analogies just seemed like manipulative bull. "Sometimes a difficult experience makes you stronger. But sometimes it *doesn't*, Les. Sometimes it makes you less. Less stable. Weaker."

Through the phone, Les took a deep breath. "It can."

I felt myself getting irritated with him, thinking he was going to humor me, and I didn't want to do that. I wanted to make the point that I wanted to make.

I must have made a noise of frustration, because Les said, "Why don't you just tell me what you're worried about, Salem, and we'll talk about that."

"You know how..." I trailed off and thought about everything we'd been reading about the Psalms, and David, and crazy Saul. Les liked to focus on how God looked out for David, despite all the stuff he went through. First, he was the hero, so much so that Saul got jealous and tried to kill him. But God was looking out for him, and Jonathan was looking out for him, and David had refuge from...ugh, what was it? The Pharisees? That sounded suspiciously New Testament to me, so I wasn't sure.

I picked up the book we'd been studying and thumbed through it. I knew that David hid out in a cave and then with some people who were also enemies of Saul, so...in the end, David succeeded. God's plan was successful.

But...

"Okay, you know how you were saying that God's plan never fails, love never fails, David was a man after God's own heart, and he survived and succeeded, even though he had royally screwed up."

"Mmhhhm."

"So, he survived. And God's plan worked, and it all worked out. Except..."

"Except?"

"Except there were hundreds of people who were also caught up in that mess. They killed all those priests. They killed their wives and children. *They* didn't survive. It didn't all work out for *them*." I thought about David's daughter, who'd been assaulted by her half-brother. Girls especially were disposable in this world.

"No," Les said.

"And I get how that might seem kind of a silly consideration, being thousands of years ago and everything, but..."

"Go on."

"Okay, so...so here's the thing. You asked me what I'm worried about, and this is it. I believe that God cares about mankind. But I'm not so sure about... individual men. I mean, if David wasn't part of the plan and hadn't been identified as Jesus' ancestor, he could have been—been eaten by that lion early in the story, and we'd never know about him."

"True."

"So...I don't know. How is that supposed to make someone feel, if they're not a big cog in this master plan?"

"We're all cogs in the master plan, Salem."

I sighed. "I guess."

"I understand that it's frustrating, Salem."

I snorted. "Frustrating is not the word. It's...infuriating."

"You're wrestling with the same questions and doubts that men have wrestled with for centuries."

"Yeah, well...is that supposed to be a comfort? To know that for thousands of years, men have been asking why God is okay with innocent people's lives being ruined? People *themselves* being ruined? And nobody's found a satisfactory answer?"

"You aren't ruined, Salem. Your life is not ruined. You were never ruined."

"I sure feel ruined at the moment." I thought again about telling him about Tony's smile, about The Lovely Joanna.

"I know, sweetie," he said, and he shouldn't have said it so nicely, because that had the tears ramping back up.

"You're not ruined," he said again.

"I'm sorry, Les, but I have to say, when you say stuff like that, you probably mean it to be encouraging, or something. But it's not. It's -- it feels like you're minimizing what I've been through. Dismissing what I'm dealing with right now. It feels so—so *gaslighty*. What happened to me—what may have happened to Gia—it's not *nothing*, Les."

"Of course, it's not nothing."

"It's bad. It's...it's really, really devastating."

"I know."

"It can just...destroy you."

I was doing the same thing I'd yelled at Ash for doing, I realized. I was trying to find some purpose behind all the pain. Not a silver lining behind the cloud. Not beauty that God could make from ashes. I was looking for the reason that things *had to be* this way and couldn't be any other way.

That reason didn't exist. "And that's what's so devastating," I said out loud.

I waited for him to argue with that. But he didn't.

Instead, he said, "Salem, I want you to understand something. When I point out that you're not ruined, you're not destroyed, it's not because I think your pain is so small. It's not that I'm dismissing the enormity of what you've been through. It's that..." He took another breath, thinking, then said, "It's because I *know* that you're bigger. And God is bigger."

I considered that for a moment. I certainly didn't *feel* bigger than my pain. My pain had taken up every bit of me, obliterated everything else. It covered me like a tent, everywhere I went.

"I can talk with certainty, Salem, because I truly believe that. The question is, do you believe that?"

"No," I said. "I don't think I do."

Chapter Eleven

The next morning, I trudged, feeling unbalanced and uprooted, into my second bedroom. I'd slept blessedly well, and I was in a better place, emotionally, than I'd been the night before. But I still felt lost, unsure of myself and everything else.

In the two years since I'd become a Christian, I'd approached this morning Bible study and prayer time in every conceivable mood: frustrated, depressed, contented, overwhelmed, hopeful, seeking, cheerful, enthralled. Sleepy, of course, almost every single morning.

This wasn't the first day I'd approached the time feeling unsure of what I was doing. But I almost always emerged feeling more grounded, more focused. Today I had no hope of leaving this room feeling anything like that.

Honestly, I didn't even know what to say. I didn't know what to pray. I didn't know what to think. I sat, staring at the flames of my candle and lost in thought. Nothing made sense to me. Before, I'd assumed that, as I'd told Les, there was some big plan. Some reason for the world being the way it was, and if I had enough faith, if I studied enough of the Bible and the numerous Bible scholars, if I surrounded myself with enough faithful people like Les, if I prayed enough, eventually I'd figure it out.

I sat in a trance, wondering what the point was in...well, anything, really. I thought of the dozens of people at Gia's vigil, lighting their candles, handing out their posters, saying their prayers. A *year*. She'd been gone a year. A year ago, Trisha probably wasn't even pregnant, and now she had a fully-formed human being who was getting shots and running fevers and stuff.

What was Gia's life like, even—even five minutes out of the past year? Did she even have a life? It was possible she'd been dead since right after that "K" she texted to Sierra. It was possible she was alive, but Helena, Sid, Janet, Joe—all of them, would go to their own graves, not knowing what happened to her.

I didn't open my Bible or my study book. I just lay on the floor, staring at the flames, and whispered, "I'm just....so, so sad. It's so sad."

I know. It makes me sad, too.

There weren't many times that I'd been positive God was speaking to me, if I'm honest. Most times, I can't tell the difference between God speaking and my own conscience, or God and my own sense of humor. But this was so unexpected and so...so visceral inside me. Like a voice apart from me, but inside me at the same time. It's hard to explain, but I also knew it was real.

I know. It makes me sad, too.

Honestly, I couldn't explain why I found such comfort in those words. But I did. It wasn't the answer I was looking for. But somehow, it was enough to get me off the floor and moving forward.

Of course, I'm not sure how I made the leap from there to, "I need to go to Dallas with Viv and Ash." I did not hear God telling me to go. Then again, I didn't hear him telling me *not* to, either. Mostly, I just felt like...the world was a very hard, cold place, and we had to do everything we could to look out for each other, give grace to each other, give shelter. And the truth was, I couldn't sit back and let Viv and Ash do it by themselves. Because as the saying kind of goes, I myself am made entirely of flaws, stitched together with good intentions and stretched taut over a frame of FOMO – fear of missing out.

I made up my mind and approached Flo as soon as I came in the door, before Tammy got there. "Listen, I know this is short notice, but I wondered if I could take a few vacation days. I know I just had some sick days, but I need to—"

The bell dinged over the front door and I groaned. Tammy breezed in carrying her gigantic soda. She took one look at us and stopped. "What?"

"Nothing," I said.

"Salem is asking for vacation time." Flo said it like I had just announced I had weeks to live.

"Oh my god," Tammy said.

"It's not a big deal," I said. "People take vacations."

"I know, it's just that—" Flo started.

Tammy smacked her hand on the counter, stopping her. "It's just that we're going to be busy. We need time to plan for how to cover you while you're out." She shot a warning look toward Flo.

"Yes," Flo echoed. "Time. We need time to plan."

I gave them both a flat smile. "What about Barbara? Do you think she'd be willing to pitch in a couple more days?"

Flo and Tammy just stared at me. Then, Tammy nodded, her lips a flat line as if she'd just made up her mind. "Excellent idea."

"It is?"

Tammy nodded and gave her a look that was so clearly trying to silently convey something that Flo just as clearly wasn't getting.

We stood silently looking at each other until I finally decided to leave them to it. "I'm just going to Dallas with Viv for a few days. Nothing dangerous."

"Oh, okay. Sure." Tammy looked at Flo, still with the bug eyes. "Are you...telling anyone else where you're going?"

"Who else would I tell?" I swallowed. Maybe I should tell Tony. He was still my emergency contact. I guess that was something else I would need to change. Welcome back to the hotseat, G-Ma.

"You know, you could let me sit up front for a change," I told Ash after we'd piled our bags into the trunk of Viv's Cadillac before we left town.

Ash bent slightly at the waist. "These legs don't fit in the back seat."

I looked at my own stubby legs. "Fine." I flounced into the back seat. "But I'm going to complain about it the whole time."

I was joking, but I needed to joke because I was still kind of sad about leaving Stump. Kind of *really* sad. I figured she would be okay—I mean, she had her new love, the princess bed—and I knew this was the responsible decision. I couldn't very well lug her around bus stations and back alleys looking for Gia. Even an irresponsible parent like me could see that. But I missed her already and kind of wanted to cry.

Viv was stressed because we were getting a later start than she wanted, but I'd insisted I finish up the day at Flo's first. As many times as she reassured me it was fine if I took another three days off, I couldn't help but think they were just waiting for me to leave so they could change the locks.

Viv climbed behind the driver's seat wearing black cargo pants, a black t-shirt, and her combat boots. She made up for the late departure by holding that boot against the gas pedal all the way to Abilene. I kept my seatbelt on and mentally counted all the airbags in this car. The sun went down, and it became harder to tell how fast we were going in the dark, so that was nice.

Ash kept looking in the side mirror. "Okay, don't look, but I think we're being followed."

Viv and I both looked. When Viv looked, her arms followed her eyes, so the Caddy swung into the right lane. Horns blared.

"I said—holy smokes, get back—"

Ash cut off as we hit the rumble strips on the side of the road and Viv returned her attention to the task at hand.

Ash glared at her. "You're going to get us killed before we even get to the Metroplex," she said.

"Oh, hush. Everyone changes lanes from time to time."

"And that's what you call that? Changing lanes?"

Viv held out a hand, like, *See*? "We're in a different lane, aren't we?"

Ash looked over the seat at me.

I shrugged. "You wanted the gig. One of the responsibilities of the front seat passenger is to keep one hand ready to grab the wheel at all times."

Ash nodded. "Okay then."

I turned sideways in my seat and fit my back into the corner. "How can you tell we're being followed?" All I saw were headlights. Different heights to differentiate cars from SUVs from trucks, but that was all I could tell.

"There's one car that's sticking with us pretty close."

"That doesn't mean anything," Viv said. "People get on the interstate and then fight to keep pace with each other. It's like the Indy 500 here. Completely ridiculous how—hey! Nuh-uh. You're not passing me!" She punched the gas and darted into the middle lane. The car that had been about to edge past us fell back.

"Well, I need to hit the bathroom," Ash announced. "Take the next exit and we'll see if that draws them out."

"Wait," I said, looking back at the indistinguishable crowd of headlights. "Do we want to draw them out? We don't want to draw them out, do we?" *I* certainly didn't.

"Salem, if we're going to find Gia, you have to stop being a fraidy cat," Viv said.

"I'm not a fraidy cat," I protested. "But, well...what good reason would there be for people to follow us?"

When neither Ash nor Viv could think of a good reason, I said, "See? I think it is best to use caution." I checked the lock on the door.

"And we will," Ash said. "We'll park in a well-lit area. You two can watch the car while I go to the bathroom, and then I'll watch the car while you go. That way we can keep an eye on each other, and also make sure no one is putting a tracker on the car or anything."

"Who's going to watch your back while you're in the bathroom?" Viv asked.

Ash gave her an indulgent smile. "I can take care of myself."

"*I* can take care of *myself*," Viv insisted. "I am carrying."

"I know you can. But someone has to watch out for Salem, and I can't protect the car and her at the same time. I'm counting on you."

Viv grew taller in the driver seat. "Yes, of course. That makes sense."

We exited a ramp that led up the side of a hill. At the top was a bridge to the other side of the freeway and a brightly lit truck stop and convenience store. Viv pulled into the parking lot, then turned to Ash. "Maybe I should park out there. If they're watching us." She pointed to the dark area behind the store.

Ash shook her head. "No, if we're being followed, they already know where we are. We just need to lose them at some point. Park right up front. But we won't let on like we know they're there, okay? We'll just act normal, then we'll lose them when they're not expecting it."

Viv nodded. "Lull them into a false sense of security. Clever."

"There," Ash pointed to a slot between two other cars. "So, they can't park next to us."

Viv slid into the spot and Ash hopped out. "Okay, remember, eyes peeled. Don't let anyone get near the car. But don't let on that we're watching them."

Viv nodded quickly. "Right. You can count on me." She raised her hand, but then let it drop.

"You were about to salute, weren't you?" I said after Ash had closed the door.

"No, I wasn't," Viv said with a sneer. "You're such a pain sometimes, Salem."

I just grinned and sat back, scanning the parking lot while trying to look like I wasn't scanning the parking lot.

A noisy group of girls got out of a car at the end of the row and made their way up the sidewalk. They were the teenage version of that table I'd been watching at the Loose Caboose.

As they neared the Caddy, one of the girls squealed and pushed another one. That one stumbled toward us, laughing, and put her hand out to catch herself.

"Hey!" the girl cried. "You idiot!" She was laughing, though. She fell against the hood of the Caddy but righted herself immediately.

Viv laid on the horn, then sprang from the car.

"What do you think you're doing!" she barked. "Back it up! Back! It! Up!"

The girls squealed and jumped back, shocked by the loud horn and the vehemence in Viv's voice. Then, as if on cue, they all burst into fresh gales of laughter.

"Holy smokes, old lady," one of them said. "Chill out."

"It was obviously an accident, and I didn't hurt your fancy car."

"Yeah," another one laughed. "Did you forget to take your hormones this morning?"

Viv put a hand on her hip. "What did you just say to me?" Her voice was deadly calm.

Jeez-o-Pete. Was she reaching for her *gun*?

I leapt out of the back seat. "Viv! Come on."

She gestured toward the girls. "Did you hear what they just said to me?"

I hurried around to where she stood. I stepped close. "They're just goofy teenagers," I said through my teeth. "Don't lose your mind." I turned to them. "No harm done, sorry for the...reaction."

They giggled and muttered some more but turned to go into the store. One of them looked over her shoulder, rolled her eyes and said, "So bizarre!"

"They touched the car," Viv insisted. "They could have planted something."

"She touched the car for half a second."

"They're quick, these trained agents."

"Viv, get a grip." The girls were giggling and pointing through the windows at us. "They're just silly teenagers."

"Yes, and who are we tracking? Silly teenagers! Maybe Gia has joined a gang, Salem. And maybe that's a *rival* gang. Did you think about that?"

"Viv, please, this is—"

I cut off as I looked back at the store and saw that one of the girls had her phone out and was holding it up to us.

They were recording the old lady in the ninja suit and her chunky sidekick. Who had not put on makeup in a week.

I dove into the back seat. If I was going viral, it would be after I'd had my hair fixed and lost another twenty pounds.

Ash emerged from the bathroom and then grabbed a few things from the shelves—good, I thought. I was too embarrassed to bring up food, but no good road trip was complete without prepackaged junk food loaded with preservatives and various poison that have managed to escape the FDA's net. She watched the giggly drama at the window with her mouth quirked.

Ash came out carrying two plastic bags of junk and Viv hopped onto the sidewalk to report to her commanding officer.

"Those girls were acting like they were horsing around and one of the *fell*—" She made air quotes at *fell*, "against the car. I assessed the situation. I reacted swiftly and with authority, and she retreated, so I don't think she had time to plant anything, but..." She trailed off and swallowed. I wondered if she was going to cry at the notion of having failed her mission.

"Good work!" Ash said. "Very well done. I know what to look for, as far as any kind of tracking devices are concerned. I'll take care of that while you two are inside. Make sure you have each other's backs in there."

Viv shot ramrod straight and nodded once, quick. "Yes. Yes, we will." She snapped around to me. "Let's roll, Salem!"

I prayed the girls would leave us alone in the store, but it was a prayer completely devoid of faith. They laughed louder when we walked in.

"Are you famous?" one of them asked. I realized she was looking at me. "Is that your security detail?" They collapsed into fresh giggles.

Viv marched toward the ladies' room, then remembered she was supposed to have my back. She turned around and barked at me. "Get a move on! You said you had to go!"

I had not said I had to go, but in fact, I did. So, I got a move on. Surely, they wouldn't follow us into...

Yep. They were following us into the restroom.

Viv marched through, shoving open each of the stall doors with a bang. She came to one that was locked, then crouched.

"Umm," said the woman inside. "Hello?"

I stepped close to Viv and hissed through my teeth, "Would. You. *Please*. Just. Stop."

Viv lifted her chin. "I have a job to do, and I intend to do it. Semper fi!"

"Stop it!" I hissed. "It's probably illegal for you to say that if you're not a real Marine."

"Just go pee," Viv said. She nodded toward the next stall, then said, "No, not there. One between two empty ones."

I found a stall that was empty on either side. Maybe I could just stay in there until the girls left. I tore the paper liner from the dispenser on the wall, placed it, and sat.

Just outside my stall, I could see Viv's combat boots, planted in a defensive stance, as she faced down our aggressors. A couple snickered. Then the room grew deathly silent.

So silent. So horribly, horribly silent. You could hear a pee drop.

There was no way I could perform under that kind of pressure. I really did need to go, but my bladder got shy.

Finally, I sighed and stood.

Back in the car, my bladder really started to wonder what was going on. I watched out the passenger window as Viv steered the Caddy back onto the frontage road. It wound down the hill, and a long onramp back to the interstate snaked out to the left. I checked the miles to Fort Worth—147. Oh well. I had a bladder of steel.

Lights in the mirror caught my eye. I checked behind us and noticed that Ash was doing the same in the side mirror. "They're definitely following us," she said. "And they're not managing to hide it very well."

"Maybe they're stupid," Viv suggested.

"Or maybe they're trying to intimidate us. Letting us know they're there."

My bladder did not like the sound of that.

"This baby has aggressive acceleration," Viv said as she entered the onramp." I can outrun them."

"No," I said. "You already have too many speeding tickets."

"I could outrun the highway patrol –"

"No," I said again. "We'll find a way to—"

Viv yanked the wheel to the right. The car veered off the road, into the grassy verge between the on-ramp and the frontage road. We bounced hard into the ditch.

I screamed bad words. Ash screamed bad words. Viv cackled. "Look at them!" she crowed as we bumped and lurched across the ground. "Got 'em!"

The nose of the Caddy rose and fell as we bounced across the grass, back toward the frontage road. My head hit the roof. Ash screamed, hand braced against the roof. "What are you doing?"

"I'm losing them!" Viv howled. "Ha ha ha! Look at them! I waited until they entered the on ramp behind us, and then I took off! I knew—ugh!" She stopped as a hard bump clomped her mouth shut. Something banged against the undercarriage.

We slid back onto the frontage road with another lurch. After she'd righted the car, Viv punched the gas.

"Viv, slow down!" I shouted.

"No, I have to get us off this road or else they'll just find us again."

"If a highway patrol car doesn't find us after all *that*, it will be a miracle."

"You have to play the odds, Salem. Yes, there are highway patrol somewhere on this interstate right now, but the odds there are any who can lay eyes on us are very slim. But the odds that someone was following us are much higher." She leaned over the steering wheel and searched the road ahead of us. "*Was* following us," she emphasized. "Now they're stuck on the highway because they don't have the guts to get off."

"That was a bold move," Ash confirmed. "Now that we're out of immediate danger, let's play it a little more conservative, okay? Save our big moments like that for when we need them most."

"Roger that," Viv said. "I'm looking for a conservative—oh!" She swung the car hard to the right, and we shot onto a narrow dark road. She shouted, "We'll keep to the back roads until we get to Fort Worth."

I took in the unlit asphalt and the scrubby trees that flashed past as we sped into the darkness and asked, "Is this—is this even a road? There are no markers, and no center striping. This might be someone's private driveway." We'd taken the corner so fast, I hadn't seen any signs marking it.

"Of course, it's a road," Viv said. "Get out your map and find out what road it is."

I pulled out my phone and pulled up Google maps. My heart was still thudding from the shock of leaving the highway, and I realized that my head kind of hurt where I hit the roof of the car. I felt my scalp, but I decided I was okay when I didn't feel blood.

The indicator on the map spun and spun. "I'm not getting service out here," I finally said.

Viv dug around in her handbag between the seats. "Use mine. I got all the upgrades they had to offer."

Viv didn't have service either.

In the passenger seat, Ash checked her phone. "If I'm looking at this right, we're going to be approaching I-20 in a few miles."

"But we just left I-20," I said.

"Oh." She tilted her head. "Maybe I'm looking at it upside down. Oh, okay. Yeah. So, this little road goes on for...gosh, a long time. But eventually it ends at a smaller highway that will take us back toward Fort Worth."

"Good," Viv said. She turned to me. "See? I know what I'm doing. That was a good tactical move."

Personally, I wasn't thrilled with the pitch-dark night out here in the middle of nowhere. I also remembered with a worried knot in my stomach that the Caddy had been through some stuff back there. I imagined right now that oil or gas or...something *important* was quietly dripping away, until any moment a warning light would come on and then the car would overheat or just die in the middle of the road.

If that happened on the interstate, help would be just minutes away. I had no idea how we would get help out here. I kind of felt like we were the last three people on earth. Plus, I had to go to the bathroom really bad.

I leaned forward. "Viv, you have to pull over. I still need to use the bathroom."

"But you just went!" they both snapped at me.

"No, I didn't. Viv made a big production about protecting me, and there were all those girls in there listening, and I couldn't do it."

"You'd never make it in the Marine's," Ash said.

"Yeah," Viv echoed. "I kind of have to go, too."

416

From there, we entered a very fraught period of trying to find a place where we could pull off the road that was secluded and would protect us from any passersby but was also not scary. Every time Viv got near the edge of the road, she freaked out that we were near a steep, dark ravine and we were all about to plunge to our deaths. Finally, she just parked in the middle of the road, and we took turns going to the back and relieving ourselves on the asphalt.

"Wow, Salem," Viv called when it was her turn. "You really did have to go!"

"That woman is a trip," Ash said. "I think we're about five miles from the next intersection, so we'll find a place near there to stop and regroup."

Viv got back in and we drove until we reached a four-lane highway that was actually fifteen miles away, not five. I breathed a sigh of relief when I saw headlights far off in the distance. There was someone else left on the planet! Then Ash pointed to a structure across the road and down a little way.

"Hey, look at that. How cool!"

It was an old 1950s era roadside rest area, with concrete picnic tables covered by slanted metal roofs.

"Let's pull over there and take a quick snack break. Look at the stars for a while."

That sounded good to me. I was exhausted.

The night was cool and crisp, and the air filled with the sounds of crickets and the occasional coo of a dove. I walked around, the gravel crunching softly under my feet, while Ash stretched her back and laid her convenience store bags on the picnic table. Viv studied her phone and muttered under her breath.

I let the breeze float over me and tried not to miss Stump too much. It was good she wasn't here, I thought, because places like this always made me nervous when I had her. I was afraid she would take off after some smell, or find a snake, or dart out onto the highway into the path of a car.

There were no cars now, though—the night was still and peaceful. Crickets chirped, cicadas buzzed, doves cooed, and Viv ranted about her cell phone coverage.

I texted Frank. How's Stump?

Three dots danced. Good. Sleeping. She snores.

I smiled at this and my heart squeezed hard.

"Look at this! *Your connection is unstable!* What the actual freak?"

"Here, have some mini-Oreos," Ash said. "That will cheer you up."

"Not getting ripped off by my cell phone plan would cheer me up more," she said, but she took a mini-Oreo.

I hopped onto the table, my feet on the bench, and took in the dark, undulating hills that stretched out from the blacktop. The moon was full and getting brighter. In the distance I could see the dark shapes of buildings, someone's farmhouse or barn. To the east was the cluster of lights of a small town.

Gia could be there, I thought, focusing on one of the lights. Or there, I thought as my gazed moved to another in the small cluster. Or another girl, held against her will. Right now, maybe not Gia and maybe not in *those* houses, but definitely somewhere, someone was being forced against her will, praying for help.

It makes me sad, too.

"Dig in, Salem," Ash said. She'd opened all the packages. "It's a smorgasbord of sugar, salt, and preservatives."

She was right. There were chips, pretzels, beef jerky, M&Ms, Twinkies, and Reece's Pieces.

"Check this out. This is the best." Ash poured a few chips into her hand, followed by a couple of M&Ms, a couple of pretzels, and three Reece's Pieces. She crunched them all together, then threw her head back and slammed the whole mess into her mouth.

"That's disgusting," Viv said.

"Disgusting," I echoed.

"Try it with the barbecue chips," Ash said. At least, that's what I thought she said. It was a little hard to understand with her mouth full.

She was right, though. I tried it with the barbecue, then with regular potato chips and pinches off a chocolate brownie, then with mustard pretzels, pieces of a Snickers, and a couple of Reece's Pieces. We all eventually agreed that the beef jerky was better off alone. My favorite combination, though, was barbecue chips and mini-Oreos.

Simple, but with a flavor combination unequalled by anything experienced by my palate.

I chugged a lemonade to wash everything down. The carbs and the night air had brightened my mood considerably. Stump was safe at home, I was sober and among friends, and we were on our way to help someone. Yes, the world was full of evil people doing evil deeds. But there was more good than bad, and we were refueled and ready to fight.

"What is that?" Viv said, jerking her head up.

Ash and I turned to see what she was looking at.

In the dark of the bushes around the rest area, I saw the glow of eyes, about a foot off the ground.

I jumped up. "Is it a possum?"

The bushes shifted a bit. If it was, it was an awfully big possum.

Ash bent and peered. "I think it's a—yeah, it's a raccoon."

As if waiting to be announced, the raccoon stepped out of the bushes.

"Awww, he's cute!" Viv said. "Look at him!"

He *was* pretty cute. My homesickness for Stump had me wanting to pet him.

"Hey, little guy." I stepped off the concrete pad and crouched a bit, my hand out. "You come to join our picnic?"

The raccoon was immediately flanked by two—no, by *three* others.

"Oh," I said. I stepped back, stumbling on the concrete.

Ash waved a hand at them. "Shoo! Get out of here!"

The one in the lead advanced.

I took a step back. They looked menacing to me. A raccoon gang.

"Shoo!" Ash said again.

Three more raccoons stepped out of the bushes. They made this chattering noise.

"I think I'll wait in the car," I said. But I didn't move.

Ash waved a hand again and stomped to show the raccoon she meant business. She clapped her hands hard. "Get out of here."

Two dozen more raccoons stepped out of the bushes. Or maybe it was just a few. It was hard to tell because at first there was just one and then suddenly it was like we'd found a raccoon factory.

Ash grabbed a couple of the chip bags and clapped them together. I think she was trying to make a rattling sound that would scare them off, but these raccoons were clearly familiar with the sound of a Frito Lay bag.

The one in the lead walked up to her, stood on his back legs, and took the bag from her. Not rushing or aggressive, just kind of like, "Thanks, I'll take that."

Good, I thought. He'll take the bag and go back into the dark.

But that bag was clearly just the first thing they meant to take. As a group, they advanced toward us, not rushing, but inexorable.

"Umm," Ash said. She stepped back again. "Back!" she shouted. "Get back!" She darted toward one, then another, waving her arms at them.

They all ignored her.

The group had been one loose, cohesive unit. Suddenly, they split, creating multiple paths, worming their way toward us. I realized there were fewer than I'd thought at first, probably no more than ten or twelve, and they managed to be everywhere.

I had been steadily backing up, I realized, with my eyes on them. I heard something crunch under my feet and realized that I had backed right up to the concrete bench and then onto the table. I'd crunched into the box of Reece's Pieces. Viv sat, frozen, watching the little grey and black bandits swarm the table. We both heard another crunch. Viv looked to her right.

A fat raccoon sat there, calmly putting mini-Oreos into its mouth.

Viv screamed.

The raccoon opened its mouth and gave a guttural growl.

I don't know who broke first. I just know that one second, we were on the concrete pad, and the next we were all three pounding for the car.

We jumped in and slammed the doors behind us, the air filled with the sound of our heavy breathing, like we'd all just crossed the finish line of a 100-meter dash.

"Holy moly!" Viv said. "There must have been a hundred of them!"

It was hard to tell how many, exactly, because they kept moving and the moonlight could only show so much. But I figured, from the safety of the car, that I counted eight or nine.

"I didn't know they growled like that," I said.

"He was definitely about to eat my face off," Viv said. "No doubt in my mind."

They weren't the least bit bothered by us. They lumbered, fat and happy, on the table and around it, casually devouring everything that we'd left.

I sighed. "Oh well. We were pretty much done anyway, right?"

"I wasn't," Ash said. "But I guess we can find another convenience store when we get to Fort Worth."

"Yeah. Or a Waffle House," Viv said. "I could handle some peanut butter waffles."

Peanut butter waffles sounded amazing, actually. Let the stupid raccoons have the chips and M&Ms. "Let's go," I said.

Viv reached for the ignition. "Oh," she said. She looked back over her shoulder, at the picnic table.

"Your keys are back there, aren't they?" Ash asked.

Viv nodded. "And my useless phone."

We all stared at the table. Raccoons everywhere.

"One of us could dash back there, grab the keys and phone, and dash back," Ash suggested.

The car was silent for a second, then Viv said, "Yes, you could do that."

Ash nodded. "Or, we could just wait. Raccoons are nocturnal. They'll head back for shelter as soon as the moon starts going down."

Nobody spoke for a long time.

"Waiting seems like a good idea. I mean, what if Ash trips while she's running back to the car and they swarm her?"

"Then we'd never get the keys back," Viv said.

"They can open car doors," Ash said.

Viv hit the button and the locks clicked. She hit it three more times, for good measure.

We watched in silence as the foraging at the table slowed. Good, I thought. When they run out of food, they'll leave and we can get the keys.

Except they didn't leave. Maybe a few did, but a big one—I think the one that growled at Viv—laid down flat on his back like a fat old man and slept.

"I didn't know they sounded like that," Viv whispered.

"It was like a mountain lion." Ash nodded.

"I don't think I'll ever forget that sound," Viv agreed.

Two more curled up on the bench closest to us and fell asleep.

I heard a soft snore and realized Viv had dozed off.

Ash looked at me and shrugged. Then she leaned her seat back and closed her eyes.

I didn't think I would go to sleep, I was too keyed up from our multiple brushes with death. But I was wrong.

I woke later to honking and screaming. Ash had gotten out to go to the bathroom and set off the car alarm. The screaming was me. It was scary.

The sun was barely up, but the raccoons were gone, so we figured we could get back on the road. Unfortunately, Viv's keys were also gone. We hunted around in the grass and bushes.

"Maybe we should call Triple A," I suggested. "Have them bring new keys."

We all three checked our phones.

"My battery is dead," Ash said.

"I'm on five percent," I said. "But I have no reception."

"Me either," Viv said. She slumped on the concrete bench and crossed her arms over her chest. "Doesn't this beat all."

I looked down one end of the lonely highway, then the other. I was pretty sure not a single car had passed all night. I looked back down the hill in the direction I'd seen last night. "Are we going to have to go down there and ask for help?"

I really did not want to do that. Probably it was because of where my mind had gone last night, but this felt ominously like an early scene of a horror movie.

I stood on the picnic table and tried to get a good look at the buildings. I leaned to look past a tree, when a glint in the tree caught my eye.

"Do racoons hide things in trees?" I asked, peering at it.

"I would do a Google search on my phone, but I have no service!" Viv stood and stomped off the concrete pad.

Ash and I climbed over the barbed wire fence and stomped through the tall grass to the tree. "Hey, snakes, don't mind us!" I said loudly. "We'll be out of here in just a minute."

We stood under the tree and peered up. "I think that's them," Ash said. "Stupid racoon stole them."

"Hoist me up," I said. "I'll get them."

She squatted and held her fingers laced together. I stepped into her foot and jumped with the other foot, managing to land on the branch with a grunt. I used to love climbing trees when I was a kid. I edged out onto the branch. Yep, those were definitely Viv's keys, I could see as I edged closer. Also, I didn't remember the ground seeming so far away when I was climbing trees as a kid. My heart began to pound and I had to look straight ahead to keep from freaking out.

I stretched out on the branch and fumbled in the leaves for the keys, untangling them and almost losing my balance in the process. I dropped the keys and Ash caught them, then said, "You want to just drop from there?"

I did not want to drop from there, that felt like a very bad idea. However, I also didn't want to look like a chicken in front of Ash. Surely, I couldn't hurt myself from this height.

I clung to the branch and willed me legs to swing free. For a long time, I just lay there, frozen.

"Ummm..." Ash said.

"Yeah, I'm doing it. Just making sure I have a good grip."

Okay, you big chicken, you can do this. Just do it.

My body wouldn't move. I was lying prone on the branch, and all I had to do was slide my legs so they were hanging, and I could drop from there. But for some reason, I pictured my legs swinging wildly down, flipping me so that I fell from the branch onto my back on the ground.

"Just...slide your legs off. I'll catch you."

"I got it," I said. "Juuuuust a second."

Finally, I edged my legs off. They swung wildly. My belly scraped against the branch. I gasped. Then I crashed to the ground.

"I thought you were going to catch me," I groused.

"Sorry," Ash said. She knelt over me, cringing. "Are you okay?"

I stood and dusted myself off, then lifted my shirt. Streaks of red, scraped skin ran from my belly to my side.

"Ouch," Ash said. "Sorry about that."

I sighed. "I'm fine. But somebody owes me peanut butter waffles."

We planned to visit Wally's World of Exotic Pets first, but somewhere between the peanut butter waffles, a fitful night's sleep, and getting lost finding our hotel in Dallas, even Viv hit a wall.

"I have to take a shower before we go back out," Ash said. She came out extolling the virtues of good water pressure and hot water, and Viv walked into the cloud of steam Ash had left behind and said, "I left behind my days of cheap motels with tepid showers when I left my third husband."

Ash dressed and stretched out on the bed opposite where I sat, texting Frank to get Stump updates (she peed and pooped, ate, drank, went back to the princess bed, no that's really all to report, I swear, no bugs) and then flipped through all my Stump pictures that were really just a thousand variations of Stump's adorable snaggletooth underbite.

Viv came out and laughed at Ash, who'd dozed off. "Lightweight," she whispered. "Hurry and take your shower, Salem, so we can get back out there."

As I stood under the hot spray, I did my best to rally my own energy. I could do this. I just needed to get a cup of coffee and then I'd be good to continue for a few hours.

I came out of the bathroom to find Viv and Ash back-to-back on one bed, both snoring.

"Thank you," I whispered. I crawled under the covers of the other bed and fell asleep.

By the time we woke from our nap and got back out, Wally's World of Exotic Pets was closed for the day. We staked it out for a while, but there didn't seem to be anything going on.

I pulled out my phone and looked at the address Patrice had given me. "We could go to this address where Charlotte was arrested. Try to find someone who knew her."

Viv and Ash looked at each other.

"Might as well," Viv said. "There's nothing going on here."

I only got us a little bit lost this time. I expected a downtown, busy place, but it looked more like an industrial park, adjacent to a neighborhood. There were some fenced off parking lots, closed now so they must be for whoever worked in those warehouses. Down the street, I spotted three liquor stores, a smoke shop, a convenience store. And more people walking around than I might have expected, if I didn't know this was a common place to come buy drugs or sex.

Honestly, I didn't know what I expected. Slinky clothes, high heels, movie-prostitute kind of stuff. And there were a few women dressed like that. But there were more wearing jeans and t-shirts, or shorts, and they didn't have any particular hairstyle or fancy jewelry. They just looked...*normal.*

"I'm really nervous," I admitted.

"What do you think they're going to do to you?" Viv asked with a laugh.

"I don't think they're going to do anything to me," I said. "But I'm still nervous. What if I say something stupid or—or rude?"

"Just let me do the talking," Viv said.

Viv would definitely say something stupid or rude—probably both—but she wouldn't feel foolish about it, so her plan sounded good to me.

We parked on a side street and walked toward a woman standing near the corner. Viv held up the picture of Charlotte. "Do you know this girl?

The woman ignored us and turned back to watching the street.

"What about this one?" Viv switched to Gia's picture.

"Get out of here," the woman said. "I ain't talking to you."

We moved on and got basically the same response from four more women—one of whom looked so tragically young, it broke my heart.

We approached another cluster of women. "Oh look, it's the do-gooders," one of them said.

Another one waved at us. "Hi, do-gooders."

"You comin' to tell us how to turn our life around?" one laughed. "Give us *hope*?"

They all laughed at that. My face burned. I felt like such a fool.

Ash took from Viv the flyers with Charlotte's and Gia's pictures. "We're looking for anyone who might have seen either of these two girls."

"I'm a girl," said the youngest one. She leaned at Ash and giggled.

Ash showed her the paper. "Do you recognize her?"

One of the older women drew the younger girl back to her side. "If she wants to be found, she'll be found."

We looked at each other. "I'm afraid she won't," Ash said. "We're looking for people who might know her, because she's been killed."

That changed the mood instantly. Death on the streets was not a laughing matter. They approached us then, studying Charlotte's picture.

"The reason we're asking around here is, she was arrested at this spot a while back—about a year and a half ago."

Several of the women shrugged. "I was staying in Houston a year and a half ago, I think," one of them said.

"Yeah, I haven't been in the area that long," said another.

The young one giggled. "I was a cheerleader a year and a half ago."

Ash frowned. "Is there anybody you know who might have known her?"

They shook their heads, then one of the women said, "Wait. Maybe." She pulled out her phone. "Hold that up." She took a picture of the flyer, then tapped into her phone.

"That's Charlie," she said, a few minutes later.

"Charlotte," Viv corrected.

"No, Charlie." The woman turned her phone around so Viv could see. I peeked over Viv's shoulder.

Thats Charlie.

"Show her this one, too," Ash said. She held up Gia's picture.

The woman did so.

"She says hang on. She doesn't recognize her, but she's asking her girls."

Her girls. I wondered if this was some madam somewhere, and my heart sank.

What was happening to Gia right this moment? Was she being hurt as we stood there? Was she being tortured right now?

"She doesn't know her, but one of her girls says she think she recognizes her. Pretty young girl."

"That's right," I said. "Only sixteen. Does she know where she is? Her family is looking for her."

The woman typed in the question. I tried not to get too anxious.

"It's been a while," she read. "Last I saw her, she was at that truck stop in Garland."

"Oh," one of the women said. "If she's out there, there's no telling where she is now."

I looked around, struck suddenly by the enormity of what we were hoping to do. Find one girl, on a planet.

God, I prayed instinctively. You know where she is. Please.

Immediately, though, I was swamped with a feeling of helplessness and defeat. Apparently, part of me still believed in a God who could help us. But did I still believe in a God who *would* help us?

Viv had been asking the woman questions that I hadn't been paying attention to. I started to, though, when the woman stepped back, put a hand on her hip, and cocked her head. "You mean a ho like me? You coming in here with your purple hair and calling me a ho?"

"I did not call you a ho," Viv clarified. "I'm just trying to determine who we're going to see. I would never call you a ho."

"Why not? I am one."

"Well, I just..." For once, Viv appeared to be at a loss for words.

"We don't like labels," Ash clarified. "Very limiting. You're a person caught in the *ho lifestyle*."

I don't know if that was her purpose, but that sent the whole group into gales of laughter. The one who'd been searching her phone grabbed Ash's elbow. "I like that. That's a good one." She laughed some more. "Marge runs a place to get women *un*caught from the ho lifestyle."

"Oh," we three said in unison. I hoped our relief wasn't noticeable.

"She will meet you in an hour at the McDonald's on Pearl Street, downtown, if you want to talk."

We found a parking lot a block from the McDonald's. "Did we get a description of who we're meeting?" I asked. "What was her name? Marge?"

"I don't think we're going to need a description of her," Ash said. "I'll bet she has a description of us."

Sure enough, as soon as we opened the door and walked inside, a woman sitting at a table along the side of the restaurant, the path to every restroom in every McDonald's in the world, probably, stood and waved toward us. I supposed three women together, one over six feet tall with a mohawk, one in her eighties with white and purple hair, and one chubby girl fighting to blend into the background were easy to spot.

Marge was a woman in her forties who conveyed no-nonsense right off the bat. She wore her hair short, too, and had on jeans and a t-shirt.

"Thanks for meeting with us," Ash said. She introduced us and Viv sat beside her, while Ash and I took the two chairs opposite.

"We have a podcast dedicated to true crime solving," Viv said as she pulled her recorder out of her handbag. "Do you mind if I record this?"

"I do mind," Marge said. "No recording, no pictures." She shifted in her seat, prepared to leave if this was going to be an issue.

Viv blinked, but put the recorder away without turning it on.

"Thank you for looking out for Charlie," Marge said.

"I'm afraid we did nothing for her," I said. "We didn't even know who she was until she was identified by the coroner."

"I know," Marge said. "But you're here, following up. Her story doesn't just get forgotten now that she's dead. That counts for something." She looked up as a girl passed behind us. "Hi, Nic," she said.

I turned to see the woman about my age, strolling past, holding a soft drink. The woman nodded curtly and kept walking.

Ash laid out the picture of Gia. "We're also looking for this girl. A runaway."

"Maybe a runaway," Viv said. "We're not sure."

"When Charlotte's body was found, something with this girl's DNA was found nearby. So, we have reason to believe that at some point, their paths crossed."

Marge nodded and studied the picture. "I'll be honest with you—she doesn't look familiar to me. You said she ran away. Do you know what she was running from?"

We all looked at each other.

"Not completely," I admitted. "Her mother died when she was just a toddler, and her older sister helped raise her. Her dad's...well, he's sweet, but the sister kind of rules the place, and she admits, she's very strict."

Marge nodded. "Yeah, a lot of times these kids think they have it bad at home, and then they get on the streets and realize an early curfew and household chores are the least of their worries. Sometimes, though, they really are going out of the frying pan and into the fire. That frying pan isn't a place you want to go back to."

"Gia had run away in the past, but it's not clear that's what happened this time. That was the assumption at first, because of her history, but..." I took out my phone and found the Channel 11 news story of the vigil earlier in the week. I handed the phone to Marge. "This is her aunt, her sister, her cousin, talking about her. They don't know if she's alive or dead."

Marge watched the video silently, then handed it back to me. She opened her mouth to say something, then stopped as something from the front of the restaurant caught her eye.

Viv, Ash and I looked, too. A man had just walked in and he stood staring at Marge.

The look in his eye made my blood run cold.

I looked at Marge. She sat, calm, unflappable, and met the man's gaze. It was obvious they knew each other, and it was equally obvious that there was no love lost there.

The man smiled, a mocking derisive smile, then boomed, "Well, if it isn't my old friend Marge! Hi, Marge! *Marge Simpson.* Why'd you color your hair, Marge? Where's the blue?"

His voice filled the space. He strolled down the aisle behind me, his shoes scuffing against the tile floor.

Marge didn't respond, she just met his gaze, unflinching.

"I think you looked better with the blue hair, Marge. Why'd you need to change it, huh? Homer getting bored? That's understandable, a woman your age. *Maa-aarge,*" he singsonged.

"Who is this bozo and why—" Viv started

Ash kicked her under the table. Viv stopped, but she narrowed her eyes at the man.

The man kept his one-sided banter going as he made his way toward the restrooms. I expected him to turn to the left where the men's room was, but he stepped to the women's room and rapped loudly on the door. His eyes still locked on Marge's, he pushed the door open and shouted over his shoulder, "Nicki! Get a move on!"

"Hang on," said Nicki from inside the restroom. She pulled the door fully open and tried to step past him.

He looped a possessive arm over the girl's shoulder and held her as he strolled once again, past us. The hair on the back of my neck rose as he passed. He stared at Marge all the way back. Nicki looked the other way, her pale face reflected in the windows of the bright restaurant. Her chin was set, but her eyes looked fearful.

"Is that her pimp?" Viv stage-whispered as they walked out the door.

Marge nodded. Now that the loudmouth was gone, she looked worried. "Yep. Hang on a second." She texted something into her phone, then slipped it into her pocket and turned back to us. "Okay, where were we?"

"When we talked to those other women," Ash said, "They said you might have seen Gia at a truck stop."

Marge shook her head. "I have not. One of the women I work with said she might have." She nodded back in the direction the man had just left, and as we watched, another girl came in. She seemed to be around the same age as Nicki, with dyed black hair, a baggie hoodie, and scuffed Chuck Taylor's. She slid into the table beside ours. "They just went toward Ross. Do you want me to follow them?"

Marge thought a moment, then shook her head. "She's in enough trouble, just being seen in the same place as me. She knows where to find me if she wants to. I've told her enough times."

She turned back to us. "We've been trying to get Nicki out for about four months. She's almost ready—I'm pretty sure that's why she came in here tonight. She knew I'd be here."

"Did we mess it up?" Ash asked, her brow drawn. "Oh, no. I'm sorry."

Marge shook her head. "No, it's not you. He's watching too closely. But maybe she'll get another chance. That's how it is with these girls. They're so scared to leave, and they have every reason to be. It usually takes five or six tries before they ever get fully out."

The girl beside us laughed. "Made it in four!" she said, with a raised fist.

"You always were exceptional, Marie."

"Surely leaving can't be any more frightening than staying with someone like that," Viv said.

"Surely it can," Marie corrected. "I got whipped across the face with an electric cord the first time I tried to leave." She pointed to a small scar on her lower lip. "Tore my lip open, gashed open my cheek. Makes you a bit hesitant to try it again."

"The traffickers know that fear is their most effective weapon, and they make sure that their bite is much, much worse than their bark. It works." Marge handed Marie the flyer. "This is the girl. Do you recognize her?"

Marie studied the picture. "I'm *pretty* sure? Like, it was just a second, but I think I saw her out at the big truck stop in Garland. You know that one we went to a couple weeks ago?"

"You saw her a couple of weeks ago?" Viv asked.

"No, I saw her, maybe..." She twisted in her seat and looked at the ceiling, thinking. "Let's see. I do remember it was cold, because I thought she wasn't dressed warm enough. That's why I thought she was being worked. So, maybe six months ago?"

"That truck stop is a known hub for trafficking. We go out there periodically to see if there's someone we can help. I have to warn you that if she was there, though, she could be anywhere by now. These girls can get passed around, moved away from their support system so they have no way to contact a possible ally. Then they can be moved a little more openly, without the fear they'd be recognized."

"I think that was the same time we saw those Black Mamba guys," Marie said. "Maybe?" She scratched her head. "I don't remember."

"Black Mamba guys?" Viv asked. "Who are they?"

Marge sighed. "I'm still not entirely convinced they're real."

"Oh, they're real," Marie said. "Ainsley told me she heard – "

"That's the thing. Everyone has heard *about* them. To my knowledge, no one's actually seen them. Seen this deadly snake."

"They keep highly venomous snakes to threaten the girls with – like, snakes you have to get imported illegally from Africa or someplace. And they all drive black SUVs."

"What kind of SUVs?" Ash asked.

Marie shrugged. "All kinds, I guess. I don't know. But every time I see a black SUV, I get the heck out of there, just in case."

I considered that. This was Texas. There were SUVs of all colors, everywhere. If I ran from every black SUV I saw, I figured I'd be running for a long time.

"Anyway, like I said, I've been hearing rumors about this Black Mamba ring for a few years, but I've never met anyone who's actually seen them. So, they may be real, or they may be urban legend."

"Marge, once you've actually seen the black mamba, you're dead. You get that, right?" Marie rolled her eyes, then handed the flyer with Gia's face on it back to Ash.

Ash waved it away. "Keep that, please. Our numbers are all on it. Contact us if you see her, or if you hear anything?"

The other women nodded, and we prepared to leave. I had to ask one more question, though. I pulled up Shawn's Facebook profile picture on my phone. "What about this guy? He's a truck driver, and he was a friend of Gia's family."

They both looked at the picture but shook their heads. "I'm sorry, he's not familiar. Most of them are not as bold as..." She nodded in the direction the loudmouth guy had gone. "As that bozo was." She managed a smile, but her eyes still looked worried.

Chapter Twelve

Because of the two-hour nap that afternoon, I had a hard time sleeping when we got back to the hotel. I kept thinking about that girl, Nicki, and the "bozo" who held her like she was his possession. The arrogant way he taunted Marge.

I sneered in the dark and rolled over, punching up my pillow. Pig. Arrogant, vile pig. I had no problem imagining Shawn take that same smug attitude, flexing his power, talking loudly, taking up all the space in a room so he could intimidate.

On the other side of the room, Viv snored, and Ash grumbled occasionally in her sleep.

I lay in the dark and burned with fury at the helplessness of it all. How dare that pig just waltz out of there with a human being on his arm, flaunting his power, knowing we couldn't -- or wouldn't -- do anything about it.

God, I prayed silently. *These arrogant, disgusting men. They get away with it. They **always** get away with it.*

I rolled over again and pulled my phone off the nightstand. I checked the time—after midnight.

What if Gia was in this hotel, right now?

What if she'd been in the area around the McDonald's we'd been to earlier?

What if I'd passed by her and been too preoccupied to notice?

I sighed and wished I could rub Stump's ears and hear her sleepy snorts. I was much more homesick than I expected to be for a short trip. I thought, briefly, of texting Tony. What would I say?

I had no idea, of course, plus anything I thought of would come out angry right now. I was so furious about the state of—well, of everything.

I thought again about the Psalms and stories we'd been studying. David got furious sometimes. I knew he did.

I had a Bible app on my phone, and I thumbed through some of the Psalms, but none of them were doing it for me. I went back to Google and searched "Psalms David Angry"

The first one to come up was Psalm 109.

> *Be not silent, O God of my praise!*
> *For wicked and deceitful mouths are opened against me,*
> *speaking against me with lying tongues.*
> *They encircle me with words of hate,*
> *and attack me without cause.*
> *In return for my love they accuse me,*
> *but I give myself to prayer.*

So they reward me evil for good,

and hatred for my love.

That one was good, I supposed, but didn't really relate to my situation. My anger was at abuse of power, not at someone telling lies about me. I supposed I cared about my reputation at some point, but not now.

The next one, though, hit pay dirt. Psalm 52.

Why do you boast of evil, you mighty hero?

Why do you boast all day long,

you who are a disgrace in the eyes of God?

You who practice deceit,

your tongue plots destruction;

it is like a sharpened razor.

You love evil rather than good,

falsehood rather than speaking the truth

You love every harmful word,

you deceitful tongue!

Surely God will bring you down to everlasting ruin:

He will snatch you up and pluck you from your tent;

he will uproot you from the land of the living.

The righteous will see and fear;

they will laugh at you, saying,

"Here now is the man

who did not make God his stronghold

but trusted in his great wealth

and grew strong by destroying others!"

Oooh, that was good. I thought of that arrogant face this afternoon, of Shawn's wide grin. "Surely God will bring you down to everlasting *ruin*," I hissed with great relish. "You men who grew strong by destroying others."

I did not understand why it was comforting to know that our time wasn't unique in having evil men who did evil things. But it was. It was also depressing.

I wondered briefly if David wrote any psalms about men being pigs. I yawned and made a mental note to check that in the morning. I was finally growing sleepy.

Just before I drifted off, I thought again of Tony. I checked my messages, just in case he'd texted me.

Nothing. Had he blocked me?

In my sleepy and vulnerable state, I needed to check—to at least know if he was still getting messages from me. I typed and deleted several things.

How are you?

Are you okay?

I'm out of town with Viv, in case you're wondering.... I deleted because I didn't want to hear about how he had *not* been wondering what I was up to.

Finally, I just typed, *I'm sorry. I know I said it already, and I know I'm a lot to deal with, and I know you've been a saint.*

I hit send and started a follow-up. *And I want you to know...*

Zhwoop. His reply came quickly. *Stop calling me a saint, okay?*

Zhwoop, came another one on its heels. *I'm not a saint.*

I stared at that for a while.

I'm not a saint.

I could take that a couple of ways. One was that he was humble. Another was that he was guilty.

Okay, I finally texted back. *I won't say that anymore.*

I wanted to talk more, to ask more questions. But every question I could think of brought fear of the answer. I found myself dozing off. I waited, wondering if he would respond again, would be more specific. I fell asleep waiting.

The day got off to a less than stellar start because there were three of us in the room and only two coffee sachets for the little coffee maker. After we got ready, we went downstairs to the continental breakfast, but there was only about half a cup of coffee left in the urn and Viv was in too much of a hurry to get started to wait around for the hotel staff to make more.

Viv spoke into her recorder as we crossed the hotel parking lot. "Tired, with little sleep and not enough caffeine, we prepared for another day of chasing leads that might, just *might*, take us to Gia."

"We could have more caffeine," I said loudly. "You're the only one holding us back from more caffeine."

She continued to speak into the recorder as she opened her car door and tossed her handbag inside. "Delete that. Tired, with broken sleep due to Salem's incessant snoring, and with not enough caffeine, we prepared for another day of chasing leads that might, just *might*, take us to Gia."

She clicked off the recorder, then pointed at me. "Be a good girl at the pet store, and I'll take you for coffee and donuts after."

I smiled and fastened my seat belt. "I'll be the very model of an investigative podcast co-host."

Wally's World of Exotic Pets was a low cinderblock building at the end of a low cinderblock strip mall. The asphalt parking lot crumbled to dirt and gravel at the edge, leading to an empty dirt lot. It wasn't the best part of town, and I realized we were only a few blocks from where we'd interviewed the prostitutes. I wasn't sure if that meant anything or not. A lot of people passed through these few blocks every day. It could be coincidence.

But we were here, and we could find out whatever there was to find. Someone had done a very ambitious mural on the front and side of Wally's. A giant tropical fish tank was painted over the plate glass window to the right of the door, and another tank with an iguana roughly the size of a t-rex was painted over the one to the left. On the side of the building was a mural of kids awestruck with wonder as they petted a hairy tarantula, with the backdrop of a rainforest full of colorful snakes, birds, and other critters I couldn't immediately identify. Presiding over it all in a blue-with-white-fluffy-cloud sky with a radiant sun backdrop, like God looking very pleased over his creation, was the bearded and tattooed Wally.

"I might get a tarantula," Ash said. "That would be sick, right?"

Viv, not understanding the context of the word, agreed wholeheartedly. "The sickest."

"Exactly. Okay, here's what I'm thinking our tactic should be. We split up. Talk to as many people as we can. Viv, you and Salem talk to management if you can. Go in a little hot – a little aggressive. Not *too* aggressive, but if you be nice, they'll think you're about to give them a sales pitch."

Viv pointed at her. "Yes. Genius."

"I'll be talking to lower-level employees. I'll be nice and chatty. They'll be looking for an excuse to milk the clock. I can probably get some information that way. Keep an eye out for each other, and whichever of us leaves first, the other will leave within about ten minutes. Got it?"

Viv saluted. "Sir yes sir!"

Ash laughed and patted Viv's arm.

Inside the store was huge – much bigger than I'd expected. Long aisles of dog, cat and hamster supplies gave way to long aisles of tanks housing small animals like hamsters, rats, and guinea pigs, then to the less creepy reptiles (the ones with legs) and then to the creepiest of reptiles (No legs. Snakes. Snakes is what I'm talking about here.)

"Oooh, look!" Ash said. "The birds are in the back. I'm going to go check them out."

"Your bird might eat your tarantula," I said. "You never know."

Viv and I strolled around for a while, but for the life of me, I couldn't find anything that would indicate any nefarious reason Shawn would be here. He was getting food for his snake. And food for his snake food. The creep.

"Let's find the manager and see if we can rattle his cage a little bit."

"So to speak," I said as I followed her past literal cages of society finches.

The manager was Wally himself. I recognized his bearded face from the store logo. He and a teenage employee stood in the wide entryway to the dark fish tank section of the store.

"Get the ones on that row cleaned first, then we'll talk about the next row," Wally directed the kid, who walked off carrying a five-gallon bucket of cleaning supplies.

Viv introduced us to Wally and handed him a card. I waited for the inevitable look of confusion, but he just studied it a second, nodded, and then slipped it into his pocket.

"We're a true crime podcast and we're investigating the link between exotic pets and illegal activity."

Wally wasn't going for that. "There is none." He pulled the card from his pocket and handed it back to Viv.

"Oh, that's not what we hear," Viv said, ignoring his hand. "We hear there's a direct correlation between criminal activity and the ownership of creepy exotic pets."

"Ummm, Viv," I said.

"Who sent you?" Wally glared at both of us. "Did Ferguson send you?"

"We sent ourselves!" Viv snapped. "We are capable of that, you know!"

I put a hand on her arm to stop her. This felt like a door opening and Viv was about to slam it shut again out of spite. "Ferguson is onto you, isn't he?" I said.

"That man is on to nothing but slander and liable and lies! He'll do anything to shut me down because he can't handle a little competition. Have you looked at his credentials? Huh? Have you looked at his paperwork?"

He stood there with his arms crossed over his chest, waiting for a response.

"Of course," Viv said with a sniff. I had to hand it to her. She'd made the course correction with style.

"Of course," Wally sneered. "Of course, you did. And every jot and tittle were in order, I'm sure."

"Would we be here if they weren't?" I asked. Honestly, I had no idea.

"Who knows? You money-grubbing ghouls. Who knows what you'd do?" He leaned close and stuck a finger in my face. "I have nothing to hide, but I'm not going to waste my time with the two of you. True crime podcasters my fat hairy behind! You're nothing but click-baity sensationalists looking for your fifteen minutes of fame.

449

There's nothing to see here, and you can get your old butt out of my store." He pointed to the door.

Viv drew her head back in outrage. "Have you never heard that the customer is always right?"

"Out!" he shouted. A macaw screeched.

Viv and I turned on our heels and headed for the door. Once we were out of his sight, I dropped back to the shelves full of dog supplies and Viv fell in with me. We hid behind the shelves and regrouped.

"We've been in the store less than ten minutes," I said. "Ash probably hasn't had time to get any information."

"Yes, she's not as quick as we are," Viv said. "But she's coming along."

"What? What did we get except tossed out on our ears?"

"We got the name Ferguson, who apparently has a beef with this guy. It could be something." She rose on tiptoe. "Ash is still back there talking to the bird guy." She gasped and dropped back down, grabbing my hands.

"What?" I gasped, too. What had she seen? I rose on tiptoe to look.

"What if she really buys a tarantula! Salem, I don't want a tarantula in my car."

I sighed, annoyed that she'd made my blood pressure spike for no reason. "Then tell her you don't want a tarantula in your car."

"She'll think I'm a sissy."

"No, she won't. And so what if she does?"

"I don't want her to think I'm a sissy old lady. She thinks I'm hard core like she is. I don't want her to be...disappointed."

"Well, I'm sure whatever they put the tarantulas in will be secure and will be fine in the car."

"You tell her you're afraid of it."

I cocked my head. "Come again?"

She tapped my chest. "You do it. She doesn't respect you like—"

"Excuse me?"

"You know what I mean. She respects you, of course, she just doesn't think you're, like, an honorary Marine the way she does with me. If I say it, she'll become disoriented. Disillusioned. We need to keep our heads in this game."

"You are unbelievable," I said, shaking my head. Then something caught my attention from the corner of my eye. "Ooooh, look." I bent to pick up a silver food bowl with "Daisy" engraved on the side. "Do you think they have one with "Stump" on it?"

The door dinged and I looked up. A man in a plaid shirt and a trucker cap walked in.

I froze. "That's him!" I tried to say. My voice caught in my throat, and I just made a squeaky sound.

"What?" Viv looked around. "What happened?"

I crouched and duck walked to the end of the row. The man had headed toward the reptiles. Was it really him? The disturbing guy with the Elite Moving truck I'd seen when I thought I was confronting Shawn?

I shuddered and gripped Viv's hand.

"Who is it?" she whispered.

"A guy I saw the other night. I didn't tell you about him, but..." But what? What did this mean?

And was it even really him? He was wearing the standard middle-aged Texas male uniform. It probably wasn't –

He spoke, his voice carrying throughout the building.

I dropped the bowl. It clattered to the floor, drawing the attention of the entire store.

It was definitely him.

I dropped to a squat, my heart thudding.

"Who is it?" Viv hissed again. "What's going on?"

I looked at her. "I don't know. Let's—I have to get out of here."

I didn't wait for her to answer. I just rose to a crouch and headed for the door.

Viv joined me on the sidewalk, and I rushed to the Caddy. I was terrified, and I wasn't sure why. It didn't make sense, and that was the most terrifying thing of all.

I got into the car and locked my door as soon as Viv got in. I checked the vacant lot behind us. If I'd had any doubts that he was the same man from the vacant house, they were erased by the green and black truck that sat there.

I explained to Viv where I'd seen him before.

"Well, they do both contract for the same moving company, and maybe they both have some kind of exotic pet, like Shawn's snake,"

She said. "It would make sense that they share information on where to get supplies. Maybe it's just that."

"Yeah," I said. I didn't feel any better, though. "Ash is in there."

"Ash can take care of herself. Plus, there's a store full of witnesses."

"Yeah," I said again. I sank down in my seat, one eye on the door.

"This guy really has you rattled, doesn't he?"

I nodded. "I can't even explain what it was. You know how guys look at you with that smirk like they're looking at a juicy steak or something? Except—except not like they *love* steak. Like, they hate *nothing more* than steak, and their greatest pleasure in life is annihilating steak with as much violence as possible? And you just feel..."

"Oh yeah," she said. "I know that look."

"It was like that, but it was more than just sexual. It was more like...cruelty. And that woman standing in the house – she looked frozen with terror."

"Maybe we should go back in and get Ash," Viv said. "No man gets left behind."

Just then, though, Ash came out the front door. She saw us and got a huge grin on her face. She held up a white bag with triumph.

"Oh no," Viv said. She leaned out the window. "Is that a tarantula? Salem's afraid of tarantulas. She told me to tell you, because she's so afraid she can't even say the word."

Ash trotted to the car. "No, it's just some treats I got for Stump," she said as she climbed in. "Is that okay?"

"Sure," I said, leaning to look past her. Was he following her? "Let's just get out of here, okay?"

Viv started the car and had it rolling before Ash was buckled up. "Hey, hang on," she said with a laugh. "Good work on triggering the owner, Viv. I ended up getting some good information from his son because of it."

She turned and began to speak again but stopped when she saw me watching out the back window. "What's going on? What are you looking for?"

"Just making sure no one is following us."

"Who would be following us?"

I watched for a few more seconds, but of course *no one* was following us. I faced front with a suppressed groan. "I don't know." What was wrong with me?

I remembered the day we'd told Helena about Shawn, and how I'd realized she was operating out of the trauma of losing her mother at such a young age and being thrust into a position she wasn't ready for. Even though she was an adult when we spoke, she still viewed the world from that scared kid mentality. She saw everything as a threat that she was responsible for fighting off.

Was that me?

From the moment I'd seen Shawn's picture, I'd become that same scared, confused kid. Trying to make sense of things that didn't make sense. Trying to protect myself. Trying to feel okay in a world where everything was *not* okay.

And every single thing terrified me. Every. Single. Thing.

And now here we were, hundreds of miles from home, and my heart was pounding out of my chest because some *other* guy who'd never actually done anything to me showed up in a place where he had every right to be.

I scrubbed my face with my hands. "Okay. We have to stop. I have to...my brain is not making any sense, even to me. I need to talk this out. Get some perspective."

Viv kept her word, and we found an open donut shop. Over coffee and apple fritters, I told Viv and Ash about the man at the empty house, the one I'd stopped at when I saw the Elite Moving truck.

Over coffee, I tried to explain just how terrifying it had been, but the best I could manage was, "He was just so..." I shuddered. "I don't know. But...it was like, I could feel the evil in him, and I couldn't get out of there fast enough."

"That could be intuition," Viv said.

"Or the Holy Spirit giving you a warning, speaking to *your* spirit," Ash said.

Did I believe that the Holy Spirit might speak to me that way? A couple of weeks ago, probably. Now... I wasn't so sure. "But what if that had just been my freaked-out mind?" After all, I had just come from seeing Tony with Joanna. I was upset, desperate almost. I'd been prepared to confront Shawn. Maybe my traumatized brain was seeing evil in him and fear in the girl, when really it was just a guy who was trying to manage the bugged-out woman who'd showed up looking like she was ready to throw some punches? Maybe the girl had been afraid of *me*.

My mind spun as I fought to figure out a way this might be connected to Gia. But...nothing. I had nothing.

"I don't even know what we're doing here," I admitted as I tore off a chunk of apple fritter. "What if I've dragged us out here on nothing? What if Shawn has nothing at all to do with Gia's disappearance? And I've got us out here and—and *bullied by racoons* for no good reason."

"It's not just Shawn, though," Ash pointed out. "There's Charlotte Franks. And the ponytail holder. And that girl last night recognized Gia at that truck stop."

"*Might* have recognized her," I said. But Ash was right, and considering the other factors made me feel better about us being here. We weren't just here because we went through Shawn's trash and found the connection to Wally's. "Are we going to go out to that truck stop?"

"That's next on the list," Viv said. "This morning while you two were still snoozing, I identified six major truck stops on the east side of the metroplex. I think we should hit all of them. Show Gia's picture. Rattle a few more cages."

"Oh, speaking of cages," Ash said. "While you two were bolting out the door, I was chatting up the owner's son. I found out that it's possible, for the right price, to get animals that might be a little bit restricted."

"Restricted?"

"Like, illegal," Ash clarified. "I honestly think you could get anything from that place, if you were willing to spend enough money. The kid actually said, 'Have you ever seen a Bengal tiger? Because I have.'"

I shuddered. "Did you ask him about getting black mambas?"

Ash slapped her thigh. "Dang it! No. I should have thought of that."

"Well, it's no wonder Wally got all bent out of shape when I started talking about exotic animals and criminal activity," Viv said. She took out her recorder. "Note to self: next podcast is on the illegal exotic animal trade."

"You are not going to become the next Tiger King, are you?" I asked.

Viv raised her eyebrows and shrugged. "Anything is possible."

I sighed and drained my coffee. "Okay. I feel better." I patted the table. "Do we need to make more flyers of Gia before we hit the truck stops?"

"Hang on," Ash said. She pulled up her phone. "I checked the Elite Moving website, and their warehouse is about a mile and a half from here. Let's just stop by there and scope it out, since we're in the neighborhood."

I wrinkled my nose. "There's probably nothing there," I said. "They wouldn't bring any illegal activity to their workplace."

"Maybe not," Ash said, tucking her phone into her back pocket as she stood. "But I'm still open to the possibility that the Holy Spirit was giving you direction. I mean, back at Wally's, you panicked when you saw him, right?"

"And you weren't alone then," Viv pointed out. "You weren't upset before that, looking for a fight. You were looking at dog bowls and thinking about Stump. Your traumatized brain wasn't in control. Your dog-mommy brain was. And you still freaked out." She stood and hoisted her handbag to her shoulder.

I joined them and on the way to the car said, "Okay, but I think it behooves us all to keep in mind that I might have overreacted in both instances because I am, in fact, just a dazzling dumpster fire."

As we approached the Elite Moving warehouse, I was struck by a new thought. "If Scary Truck Driver was at Wally's, he might have been on his way here." My heart thudded again at the thought.

I shivered in the back seat as we drove slowly past the long warehouse with its numerous overhead bays. Some had trucks parked there, but the distinctive black and green rig wasn't one of them.

"Maybe he'd just left here," Viv said.

"Yeah, I'll bet that's it," Ash said.

"That's a relief," I said. Then again, maybe we'd missed our chance to check his truck. For the thousandth time, I thought about Gia and wondered if she was in his truck, right now. Handcuffed to a bed in the sleeper cabin. Drugged to the point where she couldn't resist.

There was no reason to think she was, of course. But every time I thought of her, I looked at the world around me and almost obsessively wondered, "What if she's in there? In that trunk? Locked in a closet in that store? In that house?"

God, I prayed silently. I wanted to pray, *Please help us*. I wanted to pray, *Give us wisdom, give us strength*. But I couldn't believe enough to even form the ask. But I couldn't stop myself anyway, just a one-word plea. "*God.*"

"Okay, I have an idea," Ash said. "I'll tell them I'm looking for a job. Tell them I have my CDL and need work. I'll snoop around a bit."

"I like my podcasting idea better," Viv said. "Because I have a tape recorder."

"I get that," Ash said. "But maybe it would be better to just let one person go in. If they see two people, their suspicions are going up. Three, and everyone is going to start paying attention."

I did not like this, because in either scenario, I was left out. And could end up alone. Alone in a place where Scary Truck Driver could pop up again.

"Ladies, you're overlooking an obvious compromise here. Viv and I go in one entrance as podcasters, Ash goes in the other end as a job seeker. They don't have to know we're together. We'll distract from each other, in fact."

Ash pointed at me. "That's a good idea. That's probably a divine idea."

For a second, I forgot I was annoyed by that theory and nodded. "Yeah! I mean...maybe. Probably not. But anyway. Let's do that."

We all agreed we needed to park far from the warehouse, but there was some disagreement about how far was too far. Viv was definitely playing it on the safe side. She didn't want to risk anybody spotting her car and following us when we left.

"You know what," Ash offered. "Let me off here, then you two can park somewhere and come around the other way."

We dropped her at the side of the road around the corner, then drove down past the Frito-Lay plant and parked behind it. The smell of potato chips made my stomach growl. I looked at it. "Seriously? I just fed you apple fritter."

Again, I wished Stump was with me, but was also glad she wasn't. It was hard enough to distract my own stomach; I wouldn't have a prayer of keeping us both from looking for a free sample.

I had to book it to keep up with Viv's long, skinny legs. She had her tape recorder out.

"We are approaching the Elite Moving Company warehouse, where thousands of families all across this great country have entrusted others to store their most treasured belongings and bring them back home safely. Some might argue that is the most sacred trust one can bestow on another: keep great grandad's cuckoo clock safe from harm. Bring it home. But we're here today to determine if they're keeping more than family heirlooms stored in these metal buildings. Are they storing..." She paused for dramatic effect. "*Your loved ones?*"

She clicked the recorder and raised an eyebrow at me.

"I don't think you're laying it on one bit thick," I said.

"Of course, I'm not. Okay, here's what we're going to do. I'm going to switch the recorder back on and walk in holding it. Let them see it. I'll ask if we can record, and if they say yes, I'll act like I'm switching it on. If they say no, I'll just slip it into my pocket, like this." She let it drop into her jacket pocket. "Just follow my lead."

"I always do," I said. Because really, I almost always did.

The big open bay doors led us from the bright afternoon sun into the dark warehouse. I could only see shadowy shapes near us, but all the way across the wide warehouse, I saw that there were open doors on the other side as well—we hadn't seen that on our drive past. Ash stood talking to someone on that side of the warehouse--not Scary Truck Driver, thankfully. They walked slowly around a different rig, and she appeared to be asking and answering questions, pointing to various features on the truck. Either she knew something of what she was talking about, or she was a very confident BS-er.

As my eyes adjusted to the darkness, I saw that there was a row of offices along the wall to our right, with pane glass windows overlooking the warehouse floor.

I heard beeping to my left and looked down the long row of floor-to-ceiling shelves. They were stacked all the way up with uniform wooden boxes, banded with metal sides. A tall lift was pulling one of the boxes from a middle shelf to bring to the floor.

"Can I help you?" It was one of the women from the front office.

I had not even considered speaking, but Viv immediately put her hand up to me as if to ward off my torrent of words. "Yes, I certainly hope so!" She thrust one of the awful podcast business cards at the woman, then the tape recorder. "We are with Discreet Podcasting, and we are doing a series called Our American Life. Have you heard of it?" She tilted the recorder at the woman.

The woman looked at the card and her eyes went wide. "Our...what?"

"Our American Life. All about the average American experience. What makes us unique, what ties us together. Shared experiences that are truly..." she paused for dramatic effect. "*American.*"

The woman was still processing the image, I could tell. Only a few of Viv's words were registering.

"...what ties us together?" She held the card out to Viv and took a step backward.

"Well, like this!" Viv swept her hand toward the huge warehouse. "What could be more American than picking up and moving across the country? Packing everything you own to chase a dream? Starting over somewhere new and foreign, and yet still here, in the good ol' US of A?"

The woman blinked. I could practically see the first impression of the card slowly draining away, but it wasn't completely gone yet. It left a whole 'this is weird' vibe on the conversation.

"Oh," she finally said. "Well..."

"So, with that in mind, we would love to interview you. Right here, right now." Viv shoved the recorder closer to the woman's face. "Would that be okay? We'd love an in-depth look at this whole operation."

"Well, I don't know if I – "

"Let's say I'm a woman living in Dallas, and I just got my dream job offer in, oh, I don't know...Seattle. Let's say Seattle. I need to pack up a lifetime of living and loving and start over somewhere new. Find a new house, the whole nine yards. What would you advise me to do?"

"Well, I would imagine you'd be more likely to move somewhere like Arizona or Florida, you know, like most women your..." She trailed off as she noticed Viv's narrowed eyes and my look of horror. Behind Viv, I gave her the tiniest headshake I could manage. "Seattle is lovely," she said. "First, we would want to get an estimate of the square footage needed to pack up your things and whether you'll need storage in between places. If you sell your home here and you haven't bought a new one there yet."

"I see. Yes."

"So, all these boxes are for people who are storing their things between the moves?" I asked. I had to admit, the uniform boxes had

had me a little confused. We'd moved a lot when I was a kid, but only to the next town or a different house around Idalou. We usually moved everything in trash bags and whatever free boxes we could find thrown out behind the grocery store.

"Yes, these are all being stored while the family drives to where they're going, finds their house or apartment. That's part of the service we offer."

I looked over at Ash. She had a clipboard now and was filling out a form. She was going all in on this job application thing. I suddenly remembered our foray into lawn care and stifled a laugh. What if she ended up doing a test drive? Wouldn't that be hilarious?

She looked at the man and laughed, but something in her laugh made me wonder if she was in so far she didn't know how to get out, now.

As the woman talked, I strolled in that direction, leading our little group closer to Ash. Viv and the woman were so busy chatting, they moved along with me, no problem.

As we drew closer to Ash, she also began to slowly back toward the other end of the warehouse. That whole side of the building was lined with tall bay doors, and four or five of them had trailers inside. Boxes were being loaded into the trailers by forklift. Ash bent her head and scribbled on the form, but she lifted her gaze and her eyes met mine. She gestured with her head door behind her, where the back door to a trailer was being lowered. As I watched, one of the men with Elite

Moving shirts on slammed the swiveled hooks that held the door down and then locked them.

I looked to see what Ash was so concerned about. The trailer was the standard Elite moving one, with the flying star logo. Then I stepped to the side so I could see the cab.

Shiny black with emerald green diamonds.

I snapped my head up. Where was he? Had he seen me?

I heard his voice then, from out in the driveway. I could see just the top part of his head and his cap. He was talking to someone out of sight.

I stepped closer to the bay doors, but not so close that he could see me.

Then he walked into the open where I could see him. He was followed by Shawn.

I gasped. I couldn't help myself.

The woman stopped talking about whatever she was talking about and looked at me.

"Sorry," I said. "I just..." I looked at Viv desperately. I just what? I latched onto the first thing that came to mind. "I think I know that woman."

"What woman?" the woman asked, looking around. Then she saw Ash. "Oh. Okay."

"I'll bet you don't know her," Viv said, then bugged her eyes at me. "I'll bet she's a complete stranger."

I had forgotten that we were supposed to be distracting from each other, but still, my answer was a whole lot less awkward than Viv's efforts to refute it. Still, I went with it. "You're probably right," I said. "She just looks like someone I know."

"Really?" the woman said doubtfully.

"Maybe I should go talk to her and find out," I decided. I walked over to where Ash was handing the clipboard to the guy.

"I'll just turn this in and grab the keys," he said cheerfully as he headed toward the office on that end of the building.

"I'm sorry to bother you," I said loudly to Ash. "But you look familiar. I wondered if you..." Then I turned my back to Viv and the woman and hissed, "They're both here! Both of them!"

"Both of them?" She looked around and gasped when she saw Shawn, who was now walking toward the other guy's truck with his keys out. "Oh my gosh!"

"I know!" I said. "I knew they were connected somehow!"

I edged behind Ash and positioned ourselves so that we could see what he was doing out of our peripheral vision. He climbed the steps on the passenger side of the truck, unlocked the door, and climbed inside.

"Is that his truck?" she whispered.

"I didn't think so. I thought he drove a white one." There had been a white one parked beside his house the night we stole his trash. Something else nagged at the edges of my mind and I said, "Why is that guy going to get keys?"

She cringed. "I think I'm going to have to do a driving test!"

"Do you even know how to drive a truck?"

"Yes. Well, a little. I did train in the Marines, but it's been forever, and I wasn't very good at it then."

As we watched, the passenger door opened again and Shawn hopped out, slamming the door behind him. I kept my faced turned away. It took everything in me not to run back toward Viv and her gun. He strolled off, whistling. He called a cheerful greeting to someone else out on the driveway.

I looked back at the truck. In the tiny window in the back of the cab, I saw a head move. The window was dark, and it was just a glimpse, but I could have sworn I saw a woman's head with long dark hair.

Of course, I was so focused on Gia, I could have conjured her up with my imagination.

But, a little voice in my head said. But it could be a divine appointment. God could be letting you know she's in there so you can save her. You're his hands and feet, Salem.

"There's a girl in that truck," I said to Ash.

"Oh my gosh!" She flipped around and stared at it. She looked at me with wide eyes. "We have to get her out."

It was so weird. One moment I'd been terrified and doubtful, and the moment Ash said that, it was as if a switch inside me flipped. *We had to get her out.* No more following, no more wondering. Who knew what would happen if we let that truck drive away with her in it? We might never get another chance like this. And no matter what, I wasn't going to go back to Sid and Helena and wonder if I'd done enough to save Gia.

I strolled back over to Viv and interrupted her conversation. "Well, it turns out I didn't know her, but she's applying for a job here and I think her story would be great for the podcast. Do you mind if we interview her right quick? She has to go do a test drive soon, so she doesn't have much time." I looked at the woman. "Do you mind very much if we do that? We can come back to you in a little while."

The woman put up her hands. "I don't mind. In fact, I really need to go in and contact corporate to make sure even this much is okay. I've just been giving you the same sales pitch I would give a potential client, but I'm not sure they would allow that to be broadcast on a...what is it again?"

Viv tried to reassure the woman we would get releases before we published anything, but I took her elbow and dragged her away in mid-sentence. I didn't want Scary Truck Driver to come back, and I didn't want Shawn to come back before I had a chance to talk to whoever was in that cab.

I gave Viv a frantically whispered update as we made our way outside onto the driveway and around the truck. I needed to make sure no one was around to stop us from going in. Down the row, I saw Shawn getting into his own truck--the one I'd seen parked beside his house.

Scary Guy was nowhere around, though. With every second that passed, I grew more convinced that Gia was inside that truck and we could save her. I craned my neck to see if I could see anything inside, but the windows were dark and it was so high off the ground, I couldn't see much at all.

Finally, I sighed and said, "I'm going in there."

With one more quick look around, I hopped up on the passenger step and yanked open the door.

I climbed over the passenger seat and my heart thundered again as I immediately spied a long-haired girl sitting at the table, her back to me. "Finally," the woman said. "Shortstop came by and I thought I was going to have to kick him out."

Behind me, Ash and Viv were scrambling through the passenger door.

That got the woman's attention, and she turned – revealing what I'd already discerned from her voice: this wasn't Gia.

This woman was probably around Gia's same height and weight, but she was at least twenty years older. It was hard to tell, though. Her hair and clothing style was young, but her face was wrinkled and had a caved in appearance. When she turned and saw us, she looked confused for a moment, then smiled wide. Her teeth were awful.

"Good God," she cackled with a smoker's laugh. "What did he promise the three of *you*? Medicare supplement insurance?"

I turned back to Ash and Viv and frowned at them. I was so disappointed. Viv was mad, though. That Medicare line had drawn some blood.

"Who are you?" Viv demanded. "And where is Gia?"

"You old cow, I don't answer to you," the woman said. "What are you doing in Buck's truck?"

Buck. What a name, I thought.

Ash tried to step forward and be the diplomat, but Viv was blocking the way. "Sorry about the intrusion," she said over Viv's shoulder. "We thought our friend was in here. Maybe you've seen her?" She reached to take Gia's picture out of her pocket.

Behind her, I saw the guy who'd taken Ash's application, wandering on the driveway, looking confused.

"Uh-oh," I said.

Ash turned and saw him. "Uh-oh."

He looked into the cab at that moment and saw her. His head drew back in shock, then darted a frantic look around. He hurried to the driver's side door.

Ash dropped into the seat and rolled the window down. "I'm ready," she said cheerfully. "Let's roll."

"Not – oh man, not that truck. That truck's – " He stopped and grimaced. "You need to get out of that truck. Now."

"Oh, I thought you said this was the truck we were going to do the test on."

"No! No, not at all. Please. Come out of that truck before..." He darted a look toward the direction Buck had gone.

"Oh, okay, my bad," Ash said with a laugh. She rolled the window back up and then joined us in the sleeper cabin again. "Look, we really need to find this girl, and someone said they saw her near here." She slid the picture back out of her pocket.

The woman with the bad teeth didn't look at the picture. "Look. I haven't seen any girl, and Brownie is right – you need to get out of this truck before Buck comes back. Unless you want to go on the adventure of a lifetime." She cackled again.

I did not like this woman.

The guy outside knocked on the door. "Ummm, ma'am? You coming out?"

"We'll be out of your hair in just a second," Ash ignored him and said to the woman. "We just need – "

She stopped when the woman gasped and looked past Ash's shoulder. "Is that a black SUV?"

My blood ran cold.

"Who's in that black SUV?" I asked her. "Do you know them? Have you seen them?"

She whistled. "It ain't nobody good, I'll tell you that."

"We'd better get out of here," Ash said.

"But Gia," I said.

The guy knocked again.

"Do you see any Gia in here?" the woman yelled. "Get out!"

I could see the truth in what she was saying, but it was bitterly disappointing.

"We can't get out," Viv said. "The Black Mambas are watching."

The woman crossed her arms over her chest. "Well, that's just your bad luck. You're not bringing your bad luck into my cabin. Get out."

I checked the window over the sink. That black SUV was definitely there, idling at the other side of the wide driveway. Waiting.

Waiting for us, no doubt.

The interview guy crossed the front of the truck and moved toward the offices. As he walked, his shoulders hunched and he grew visibly shorter. I saw why a second later, when Buck entered the frame of the window.

"Well, you've done it now," the woman said, sitting hard back at the table. "When he catches you, you ain't getting away."

Viv, Ash and I looked at each other. The black SUV was still there. "What do we do?" I whispered in despair. How had I gotten us into this mess?

I could hear Brownie through the window. "Is there...is there supposed to be a girl in there?"

Buck laughed. "That's Jackie, son. You know Jackie."

"Yeah, yeah, but...well, if that's all that's supposed to be in there, that's fine. But if there's someone else who's not on your insurance list, of course..." He trailed off. "Not back there," he said when he saw that Buck was looking intently at the back of the trailer and underneath. "In the cab."

He looked at the cab. Viv, Ash and I were gawping from the inside. We dropped instantly, but he'd seen us.

"Oh, them. I didn't realize they were going to be here today. Don't worry, they're not hanging around."

"What do we do?" I hissed at Viv and Ash.

"We have to hide!" Viv said.

As you might have already surmised, there weren't a lot of hiding places in even the biggest, fanciest sleeper big rig. We bolted for the shower.

It was an impressively big shower, but still. We packed in there with desperation. I hissed at the woman —Jackie, "Don't tell him we're here!" I slammed the door.

The driver door opened and Buck groaned as he climbed in. The door slammed behind him, and less than two seconds later, the woman said, "There are three crazy women in the shower."

"What are they doing here?" he asked. He didn't seem mad. He didn't seem surprised. Just like he wanted some more information.

"Looking for a girl," she said, in a tone that conveyed they'd encountered people who were looking for a girl many times before.

"Like, looking for a girl, or looking for a *particular* girl?"

"A particular girl," she said. "I think one of those that Shortstop brought in last year."

In the dark of the shower, Viv, Ash and I were standing frozen, trying not to breathe too hard. Suddenly it hit me. Why? He knew we were there. We'd lost the element of surprise already. What else did we have going for us?

The sheer ridiculousness of it struck me, and suddenly I let out a bark of laughter. I clapped my hand over my mouth.

"What are you doing?" Viv hissed at me.

"He knows we're here," I whispered back.

I heard a thin snick sound.

I reached out and tried the door.

"We're locked in!" I whisper-screeched.

"Not for long," Ash said. She edged out of the shower, leaned against the wall and kicked the door.

The engine revved. He was getting ready to drive away.

With us locked in.

Ash kicked again. There was a loud crack as the wood started to give.

"These idiots are kicking the danged door in!" Jackie shouted.

The engine sound rose again.

Ash kicked again. A crack of light appeared briefly between the door and the frame.

"Stop that!" The woman slapped at the door.

Ash kicked again. The door broke loose.

"Buck! Buck, they're getting' out!"

Ash kept kicking until the door broke completely loose and hung from the frame. She stepped out, over the broken pieces of door.

Viv and I both lunged for the open door and collided into each other. I grabbed for something to steady myself. Whatever I grabbed hold of wasn't bolted down, though. The truck lurched and I pulled it off of what I assumed was a shelf. It crashed to the floor and shattered.

"Buck! They're tearing everything up back here."

"I know it!" Buck roared. "I hear 'em. They're not gonna like how they have to repay me for that!"

I looked out the window. We'd moved from the bay to the driveway, but we were still moving very slowly. Definitely slowly enough for us to jump out. I worried about Viv's bones, but bailing out was obviously our best option, even if the black SUV was right behind us. The black SUV was a maybe. What we were in right now was definite horror.

I looked at Ash and could tell she was thinking the same thing. She reached for the side door, then let out a shout of pain.

"You sick freak!" she shouted at Buck. "You hotwired the door!"

He laughed, his big shoulders hunched as he turned the steering wheel and maneuvered the truck down the driveway. "Touch it again, darlin. I got all shivery inside when you yelped like that."

Ash pulled out a gun and shot him in the neck.

I screamed. Viv screamed. Jackie screamed.

Buck made the funniest, "Kaaaaghk," sound, then flopped in his seat.

It was a stun gun. It popped loudly as Ash held it pointed at the man like a death ray.

Ash ripped out the cartridge, reached into her pocket and slammed another one into the gun.

The truck lurched hard, then slammed to a stop as he pulled the brake.

Buck roared as he lunged up from his seat and reached for her.

"Round two!" Ash screamed. Then she shot him again.

That did him in. He thudded to the cabin floor like a felled 100-year-old oak.

Ash shoved the stun gun at me. "Put another cartridge in!" Then she turned to Viv. "Help me find something to tie him up with. We have to disable him."

I ripped out the cartridge like I'd seen Ash do and shoved in another one.

Viv stared at Ash with wide eyes. "I – uh – I – what – "

"There are some wire ties in that drawer," Jackie said.

We all turned to stare at her.

"You don't know Buck. When he comes 'round he's going to take down everything in sight. I need a head start." She yanked open the drawer open. "Here. It'll probably take two, he has big arms."

He *did* have big arms. We yanked his arms behind his back, and Viv and I held them together while Ash yanked the plastic strips tight.

"Let's do his ankles, too," I said. I knew those strips were much stronger than they looked, but still. They were just plastic. And he was a monster.

"Too bad you kicked in the bathroom door," Jackie said. "We coulda locked him in there."

"Well, we can still try to get him in there. Wedge something up against it," Viv said.

"Here." Jackie opened a drawer and pulled out some hand towels. "Gag him with this or else he'll be yelling the place down.

The truck door opened again. "What in the world is going on in here? We have to get on the – "

We all froze. It was Shawn. He took in the scene with his jaw hanging open.

My mouth went dry. My heart pounded so hard it hurt. I froze, terrified.

"Salem, let me handle this," Viv said.

"Handle what, old lady? What are you crazy women up to?"

"We are apprehending a human trafficker, *Shortstop*," she sneered. "You're all going down. Right now."

"Is that right?" He grinned a slimy, crooked grin. "Apprehending a human trafficker. Whoop-di-doo!" Then he stopped, seeming to remember something. He looked at me. "Wait. Did she just call you – did she call you *Salem*?"

I swallowed. I felt half an inch tall. I wanted to hate him, but all I could do was feel terrified and small.

"Surely not!" He kicked Buck's feet out of the way and took a step toward me. "I used to know a sweet little girl by that name. There can't be that many girls by the name of *Salem*." He cocked his head like he was remembering. "Wait a minute. *You're* the reason that cop showed up at my doorstep, asking all those questions about way back when." He leaned close. So close. I could feel his breath on my face. "Aren't you?"

I stumbled back a step and trod on Buck's arm. He grunted through the gag.

Shawn chuckled and gave me an up-and-down look. "I bet that hurt, Buck. Because this little girl sure filled out."

I shot Shawn in the face with the taser. I hadn't planned to. And it, honestly, wasn't because of the thinly veiled crack about my weight. I just...I had to make it stop.

He shouted and fell in a twitching heap onto Buck's legs.

Viv and Ash jumped into high gear while I stood and shook. They zip-tied Shawn's hands and feet and gagged him with one of Buck's flannel shirts. Jackie perched on top of the table and looked down at them, grinning. "Get a load of all these tables turning, huh, boys? Tittin' for tattin' and all that?" She cackled her maniacal smoker's laugh.

Surely everyone in this whole place would be on us within seconds. We had to be making a huge racket. Then again, those diesel engines were loud, and with the beeping of forklifts and everything else, maybe...

"I have to admit, this has been a lot more fun than I would have anticipated," Jackie remarked. "I never could stand that little weasel. I like the idea of me bein' outta here, though."

"No, you're not," Ash said. Once she got Shawn tied up and both of them gagged, she jumped into the driver's seat and slipped it into gear.

"Wait," I said. "What?"

"Where are we going?" Viv said.

"I don't know," Ash said as she maneuvered the truck out of the parking lot.

"But...what are we going to do with them?" Viv asked.

"I don't know that, either. I have to think."

"Well, I mean...we could think *here*," I said.

The truck lurched forward.

"No, we can't. Those two were in on it. How do we know the whole company isn't in on it? How do we know who we can trust? I need to get these guys somewhere....else. Somewhere else."

Viv and I looked at each other.

We looked at the bodies of Buck and Shawn, lying together on the floor. Buck had rolled partway onto his side and was giving me the most murderous look I'd ever seen.

Shawn wriggled and twisted, jerking on his arms to pull his wrists from the ties. He grunted with the effort, and to my horror, one of his hands began to slip from the tie.

"Oh no, you don't!" Viv screamed. She put a foot on his shoulder and drove him down against the floor, steadying herself against the table.

I stepped close to help, but the look in his eyes chilled me to the bone.

He stilled, but not in an I-give-up way. More like an I'm-biding-my-time way.

He still had the gag in his mouth, but he worked it so he could mumble around it. The words weren't clear, but I still managed to make out, "I *will* kill you," just fine.

He was so close. I wanted out of that truck so, so bad. My mind spun, searching for some response that would give me back some of my power. I hated that even with him tied up and powerless on the floor, I was terrified of him.

I blinked, then bent over his prone frame and said the only words I could think of in that moment.

"Surely God will bring you down to everlasting ruin. You pig."

"Yes," Viv echoed, shoving a bit with her foot to make sure he knew he wasn't getting up.

"Yeah," said Jackie. Then she hopped over the dinette seat and began opening cabinets, pulling things out. "Y'all drop me off at the next intersection. I need a running start."

Ash was silent, though, concentrating on grinding gears and keeping the truck on the road. I was dismayed to see we were gaining speed, and a freeway onramp loomed ahead. Surely, we weren't going to get on the freeway?

"How about if we just...pull over and jump out," I said. I was trying to stay calm, but I wasn't sure how Ash running off with us in the truck was much better than Buck doing the same thing.

"We'll pull over. But first we have to get away from that place."

I remembered the black SUV then. I couldn't see behind us from the cab, so I hoisted myself between the table and the counter and moved to the passenger seat. I checked the side mirror.

"Black Mambas still back there," I said.

Ash frowned, then hit the gas. "We'll lose them on the highway."

"That's true," Jackie said. "You can outrun everyone on the highway, if you have the nerve for it. You gotta barrel through, but people'll pretty much get out of your way."

I didn't care for the sound of that. I turned and looked at Viv. She seemed to think this was an excellent idea.

I tugged to check my seatbelt.

There was a lot of gear grinding and liberal application of cuss words, but we made it to the freeway without flattening anybody. I kept looking back at Viv, but she'd switched out Ash's stun gun for her real gun, and that did make me feel a bit more secure. Of course, Viv and guns was a risky proposition on its own, but we were most definitely in a 'beggars can't be choosers' situation.

We took the on-ramp a little too wide for my liking, but Ash handily tuned out my gasps of terror and merged into traffic. Jackie was right. Most cars would get out of the way of a semi barreling toward them, like it or not.

"So..." I said as I fought to keep my voice steady. "Do you have, like, an exit plan for all this?"

Ash nodded toward the side mirror. "Outrun that black SUV, then call for police backup. Unless the police find us first. In which case we pull over and us them as protection from the people in the black SUV."

"Ha!" Jackie cackled. "You really think anyone can protect you from them?"

Ash frowned and shifted again, and we picked up some speed.

Buck lifted his head and mumbled something through the gag in his mouth. Jackie planted one of her tiny feet on his forehead and pushed him back down. "You hush now," she said.

I don't like this, I thought. I would like a do-over, please.

I mulled Ash's plan. Here were the facts.

1. We had entered the truck and hid in the bathroom.

2. We had broken the door down and tased two people. We had then tied them up and held them at gun point.

3. We had stolen the truck.

4. We had not rescued Gia.

I knew we probably needed the police. I couldn't see any way this was going to end well without them. We couldn't just...keep driving until we reached the middle of nowhere, dump Buck, Shawn, and Jackie out, and leave.

...could we?

My mind raced as Ash wound her way through traffic. She honked at one slow moving hatchback and I screamed.

She looked over at me and laughed. "You're a bit tightly wound."

I nodded quickly. "Yep. How much do you think this thing is worth? This is huge, what we're doing. I don't want to be back in trouble with the law."

"Neither do I. So we have to make sure we get our stories straight." She cursed and swung the truck into the passing lane.

"Okay," she shouted once the road opened up a bit. "Here's our story. We were looking for Gia. The guy gets into the truck, locks us in the bathroom, and takes off with us. We manage to break free while the truck was on the road, and we fought back. We disarmed the aggressors, and then we took over the truck and brought it to a stop so we could get help."

"That is what happened. Kind of," Viv said.

"Yes, except for the part where we took the truck out on the road. The part where this all could have been over back at the Elite warehouse parking lot," I pointed out. "Except for that one small part."

"Well, it's working out because – " She hoisted herself up in the seat using the steering wheel and checked her mirror. "Yep, we're losing them." She shifted gears again and pushed on the gas. "This is pretty fun, to be honest. Maybe I should look into getting my CDL."

I caught something moving out of the corner of my eye and looked at the dashboard. Something slithered along the dash.

I stared at it. Then I screamed.

I tried to get out of my seat without unbuckling my seatbelt. Then I tried to just shove myself through the seat, into the back of the truck. "Snake!" I shrieked. "Black mamba!"

Jackie screamed, too, jumping up on the table and clinging to an overhead cabinet. She saw the snake and said, "That's not a black mamba, that's Diablo!" She looked at the bathroom door we'd broken. "You idiots broke his aquarium!"

I finally managed to get out of the seat and into the cabin, crouched and ready to fling myself from the window of the moving truck to get away from that thing. I looked down and saw Shawn on his back, glaring up at me with impotent hatred, and for a second wished I had the courage to grab that snake by the tail and fling it at him.

"You're such a lunatic, Salem," Ash said. "This is just another ball python. He's fine. He won't bite."

"He'll bite," Jackie called.

"Well, he's not poisonous," Ash said. "He's just scared." She tugged on the steering wheel and lifted herself to reach for the snake. Gingerly, she picked him up and cradled him loosely in her hand. "See? He's fine. He just – "

He bit her.

Viv, Jackie, and I gasped. Ash just went quiet. Then she said, "Okay, guy, I get it. You're scared. It's fine."

"You're nuts," I said. I was aware, in theory, that not all snakes were poisonous. But I come from the land of the rattlesnake and the water moccasin. When I see a snake, and I scream and run first, and check out markings later.

"*You're* nuts," Ash said back. "It barely even stings. Get me something to put him in, okay?"

Jackie groused, but she rummaged around in the cabinets until she found a plastic bowl with a lid. She took a knife from a drawer and stabbed air holes in the lid. "This'll have to do until we can get another tank."

Ash was struggling to drive and still maintain a hold on Diablo, who wound around her hand and arm and stretched his head toward the dashboard. Jackie held the bowl under her hand and Ash dropped the snake. Jackie popped the lid on.

"See, if you just keep your head, you can maintain focus amidst any distraction," Ash said, settling back into her seat. "That's what I learned in the Marines. The mission is critical. So, you push on, no matter what." She clapped her hand on the steering wheel. "No matter..."

Her hand on the steering wheel showed two neat drops of red, and thin rivulets of blood trickled down her arm.

Ash slumped over in her seat.

The truck went silent, just the dull roar of the asphalt moving under us. We began to drift slowly to the left.

Chapter Thirteen

"Ash!" I screamed.

She jerked and sat up. "See." She looked around, dazed. "No big..." She looked again at the blood running down her arm. She slumped again in her seat.

"Salem, get up there and get this thing pulled over!" Viv shouted.

"I can't drive a truck!"

"We're going to get us and everyone else on this highway killed if you don't!"

"Do you know how to drive it?" I asked Jackie. At least, that's what I meant to ask. I was basically just shouting incomprehensible noises, though, because the truck was drifting and soon we would hit the median.

I leapt back into the cab and grabbed the wheel. It was so *much* harder to steer than my Monte Carlo. But I managed to get us back between the lines, anyway.

Ash's head bobbed against my thigh. "I'm okay," she mumbled and straightened.

"Then get this thing off the road. "I'll call the cops." I welcomed the cops. I welcomed jail now, if that's how it went.

She reached for the wheel. She saw her hand again. She fainted again.

They say fear gives you superhuman strength. I prayed that was true as I reached under Ash's armpits and dragged her out of the seat. I got her mostly into the passenger seat and hopped behind the wheel.

"You better downshift!" Jackie shouted.

"How?" I shouted back. I grabbed the shifter. Then I saw the red triangle, the universal symbol for hazard lights. I punched that. I figured that no matter what else happened after that, I could at least say I'd tried to warn people.

I looked at the floorboard, relieved to see that there were only three pedals. I tapped on the brakes.

"Downshift!" Jackie screamed again.

I shoved in the clutch and grabbed the gear shift, but I hadn't the faintest idea what to do with it. I moved it, and it moved much easier than I expected. Were we in neutral? That seemed like a good place to be. I checked the mirrors to see if it was clear for me to pull over to the right.

And there were cops. Sooo many cops, lights flashing, filling up the entire highway behind us.

"Uh-oh," I said. I know just a few minutes ago I'd thought I would be happy to see cops, but man.

That was a *lot* of cops.

Ash checked the mirror. "Dang," she said. "We'd better get this thing pulled over."

"Just don't look at your arm again," I said.

"Yeah, I sometimes faint when I see blood. It's a hassle."

"*Sometimes,*" Viv said. She tossed Ash another kitchen towel. "Cover it up with this."

Ash did as instructed while I hit the turn signal and began moving us to the right.

There were too many numbers, and I only had a passing knowledge of how to drive even a five speed. How many did this thing have?

"Just let it stay in neutral and coast to a stop," Ash said. She checked the side mirror. "Whoa. Yeah. Just tap the brakes a little, and let it coast to a stop. We don't want them to think we're going to try and make another run for it."

Once we'd come to a complete stop, I looked at Ash and Viv. "Are we ready for this?"

"I don't think it matters," Ash said.

Viv tucked her purse on her shoulder and said, "I'm ready. Let them do their worst."

It was easy for Viv to say. They were naturally going to go easier on the 80-year-old woman than they were Ash and me.

I opened the door and there was a cop already coming up the side of the truck, his gun drawn. "Hands up!" he shouted.

I put my hands up and slid onto the running board. He handcuffed me, and from the other side I could hear Viv and Ash being apprehended as they came out of the truck, too.

Jackie chattered the whole time. "Thank you, officer! You saved us. They were going to do who knows what with us!"

I was getting really irritated with her until I realized she was counting 'us' as *us* – me, Ash, and Viv. 'They' were Buck and Shawn, who were led out a few minutes later, hands still zip tied.

I don't know how to describe what happened next except to say it was complete chaos. We were walked over to the shoulder where the cop cars were parked—there were actually only five at first, and a couple more joined a few minutes later. They had looked like a lot more when they filled three lanes behind me.

Traffic started flowing beside the truck again, and I saw a news helicopter overhead. Lovely.

"We were looking for a runaway girl, and then this monster locked us in his bathroom and took off with us!" Viv was explaining indignantly. I noticed that *she* didn't have handcuffs on. One of the cops had his hand on her elbow and wasn't letting her go anywhere, but still. Sometimes I think I can't wait to be eighty.

We were all talking at once, trying to explain what happened. "These women are heroes, officer," Jackie announced. "They were about to be sold off to a trafficker, and they used their wits, strength and cunning to get free!"

"And a taser," Ash said. "We used a taser."

I had to hand it to the cops. They only showed a little bit of disbelief that the three of us were in danger of being sold to traffickers. Then Jackie said, "You want proof? Open up the back of that truck and you'll see proof."

They separated us after that, but I could still see what was going on. I sat in the back of one car while Viv and Ash were led to others. The back of the truck was opened and some of the cops climbed inside while Jackie stood at the bumper and chattered. "Look for one with a piece of black tape on the side. No, not that one.

I heard a shout and looked up, but it was coming from the front of the cab of the truck. Jackie, still handcuffed, leaned around to see the front of the truck and said, "Sounds like they found Diablo."

"See! See, I told you! No, stop it! I'm going to talk to her!"

I leaned back to see out the back window of the squad car I was in. I blinked. Shook my head. It couldn't be.

But it was. Tammy was hurrying toward me. *Tammy*.

Behind her was Bobby Sloan.

Behind *him* came Flo, carrying her purse in the crook of her elbow, picking her way through the grass toward the car I sat in.

"Oh my gosh! I can't believe it! I just knew you were a goner for sure!" She bent and hugged me, her big blonde hair all in my face. "I can't believe it!"

" *You* can't believe it?" I stuttered. "What is going on?"

"We saved you! We saved you from the mob!" She burst into tears.

She turned to Flo, who stood, breathing hard from the exertion, at the bumper of the squad car. "We did it, Flo. We rescued her."

Flo nodded, but honestly, she looked as confused as I was.

Tammy turned to Bobby and jabbed a finger at him. "I told you! You didn't believe me, but look!" She pointed at me. "And look! And look!" She pointed at the truck and at Buck and Shawn, who were busy vehemently shaking their heads at the two cops who were questioning them.

Bobby opened his mouth to say something. He closed it again. Then another cop came up to him and they started talking.

"I can't believe you're here," I said to Tammy and Flo. "How did you know how to find us?"

"We followed you, of course," Tammy said. "We've been following you since you left town. I knew it was going to be the only way to really get you away from the mafia. I tried to tell that clueless cop friend of yours, but he wouldn't listen. So, I had to follow you to the source." She looked triumphantly around at the spread of squad cars, trucks, and general mayhem. "I feel like...I feel like Erin Brockovich."

I nodded. That made as much sense as anything else did. I looked back in the direction they'd come. "Well, thanks," I said. "Did you bring anyone else with – "

I stopped when a shout – several shouts, actually – erupted from inside the trailer.

"Don't open that!" Jackie shrieked, bouncing on the balls of her feet. She backpedaled, almost falling over in the gravel. "That's a black mamba! You'll die instantly!"

Ash stood, and the cop watching her put a hand on her shoulder.

One of the patrolmen stuck his head out of the trailer and said, "Get animal control out here. Tell them we've got –" He looked over his shoulder, jerked a little, then said, "Tell them we have venomous snakes out here."

Flo heard that and said, "Well, we'll get out of your hair now. Glad you're okay." She was already picking her way back across the grass. "Call me when you can, and we'll talk about when you're coming back to work."

Tammy bent and gave me one more hug. "I can't believe it," she said again. "I knew it! I knew that Polk guy was bad news." Then she ran after Flo.

Bobby came back from talking to the other cop, frowning hard at me.

"Tammy got you into this?" I asked.

"Oh yeah," he nodded, his eyes bugged. "She hasn't stopped bugging me for a solid week. I thought she was crazy."

"Oh, she's crazy," I said. "And she's wrong. This isn't mob stuff, and it has nothing to do with Charles Polk. It just..."

I stopped as a small commotion started at the rear of the trailer. One of the cops hopped down from the trailer, while another one held his hand out to usher a young girl out the back. The girl blinked as she walked into the light. She refused both the officers' offers of physical assistance. She sat on the bed of the trailer and slid to the

493

ground. Behind her came another girl, a few years older but still younger than I was. Behind her came another one.

Three altogether.

The last one was Gia.

My heart stopped. And then I burst into tears.

We still had to go to the police department and answer a lot of questions. I don't think they believed that we were completely blameless in the whole situation, but since we had flyers with Gia's picture on them, Bobby was a cop and vouched for the fact that we'd been looking for her, and we had a busted down bathroom door in the truck to confirm that we'd been looking for her when we'd been held against our will, we had evidence to back up our story and they didn't press for very long.

Added to the fact that they had two human traffickers, three rescued trafficking victims, and a venomous snake from the rumored Black Mamba gang, the police had enough on their hands at the moment.

They finished with me, and they let me wait in a small empty hallway while Viv and Ash were being questioned. I sat at a row of hard plastic chairs, thinking about Gia, walking into the light.

I didn't know what was going to happen to Jackie, but since she seemed to be more than willing to help, I figured she was going to be okay, at least from a legal standpoint. I wasn't sure how I felt about that. I remembered how she'd laughed at the thought of us going on 'the adventure of a lifetime,' and I had no problem imagining she had a hand in entrapping any of those three girls who'd been stored in one of those big wooden moving boxes.

"The one with the black tape," she'd said. She knew how it worked.

I blew out a gust of air and looked down the empty hallway. I kept waiting for another surprise. But it didn't come. I rubbed my wrists where the handcuffs had been.

Bobby came up behind me.

"Do you want me to call your husband?"

I had to swallow hard not to cry. I shook my head. "Nah. I'll just..." I didn't know what I would *just*, but I couldn't call Tony.

"Salem, I know you two are split up or taking a break or whatever, but...he would want to know."

"No, he wouldn't. He's had all he can handle of my drama."

"*Drama?* What drama?" He grinned a crooked grin at me.

I tried to smile back, but it didn't get any lift at all.

"Look." He sat beside me, his elbows on his knees, and looked at me. "I don't know what's going on with you two, but Tony is a good guy. He cares about you. I know he has a lot on his mind now, with this thing with his nephew. But he would want to know about this. He would want to take care of you."

My heart was so tender at the notion of Tony taking care of me just then that I almost missed what Bobby had said. "What thing with nephew?"

"The..." He started to answer, then stopped, an 'uh-oh' look on his face. "He didn't tell you."

I shook my head. "Apparently not." Tony had been so distant the last few months. I tried to remember if he'd said anything about one of his nephews. He had so many family members, and he was always helping one or another out with something.

"I know he gave his nephew Jordan some kind of supervisory position at his cleaning company a few months ago. But he hasn't mentioned him since."

Bobby frowned and nodded. "Well, then I shouldn't have either. I'm sorry I did. I just assumed..."

"He told you, but he didn't tell me?"

Bobby sighed. "Just because he needed my help."

"What kind of help? Is he in trouble? Is Jordan in trouble?"

He screwed up his mouth tight, shook his head, then stood and cursed. He paced a few steps. "I really thought he would have told you."

"Bobby, if you don't tell me *right now* what's going on, I'm going to – "

"Tony is fine," he said. "I'm not going to tell you what's going on because it's not my place. I can't. But I can tell you that Tony is fine. It's just a personnel matter."

"A personnel matter," I said flatly. "That required the help of the police department."

"Not the police department. Just me."

"And what did *just you* do for him?"

"Actually, I didn't do anything. I listened to his concerns, I recommended a course of action, and I put him in contact with someone who could help him. Salem, it's not a big deal, I swear. He was concerned about one of his employees, and he was afraid he wasn't getting a straight report on this guy's behavior. So, I hooked him up with someone who could do a little undercover work for him and report back. He needs to know what's going on when he can't be there to oversee, right? He just needed some help –"

"Oh my gosh!" I asked. "Is this The Lovely Joanna? Is she doing some kind of undercover work for Tony?"

He just looked at me with a flat mouth, then shrugged. After a few seconds, he braced his hand on the wall and muttered, "The lovely Joanna. I have to be sure and tell her about that."

I dropped my head and stared at the ground. "So, she's...she's spying on Tony's employees?"

"I don't know that I would call it spying..."

"And *that's* why they're meeting in secret? Not because they're having an affair?"

"What?" Bobby stepped in front of me. "Salem? No. Holy cow. No." He dropped to the chair beside me again. "Is *that* why you broke up? You thought he was having an affair with Joanna?"

"No, we broke up because I drank."

"Really? I mean...relapses are pretty common."

"Yeah, well...the expectation is still perfection."

We sat in silence for a while.

"So. He's not having an affair with The Lovely Joanna." I thought I was probably too numb to be relieved by this news. But then I was suddenly crying again, so I guess I wasn't that numb after all.

"Definitely not," Bobby said. He put a hand on the back of my neck and rubbed it.

"I mean, you don't really know that, though," I sniffed. "They might be meeting for business purposes but have also developed an... attraction. Tony is pretty hard to resist."

"Definitely not," Bobby repeated. "Joanna is married to a very lovely woman named Kirstin."

"Oh," I said. There didn't seem to be much else to say. So, I just kept crying and thinking that it didn't really matter, because we hadn't broken up over that, after all. We really had broken up because I drank. And there was no misunderstanding about that.

I'd really done that. So, in effect, Bobby's revelations about The Lovely Joanna had changed nothing.

Viv and Ash were released not long after that. Bobby stood with a groan. "I suppose you need a ride back to your car," he said.

I expected Viv to have something smart to say about that, but she just said, "If it's not too much trouble."

We headed toward the door, then all froze at once as another door on the other side of the lobby opened. A woman in a suit walked out. It was Detective Scott.

"How did she get here so fast?" I asked. "Did Tammy get her roped into this mafia story, too?"

"No, she flew," Bobby said. "I called her as soon as I saw it was Gia on that truck. She called Charles Polk, and he got his private plane to fly her out here. They're flying Gia back this afternoon." He squeezed my shoulder. "She's going home."

Gia came out, behind Detective Scott. Oh, she seemed so small. She wore jeans and a thin striped t-shirt, ratty looking tennis shoes. Her hair hung long down her back. I couldn't breathe, knowing it was her. Knowing we'd done it.

Bobby helped Viv into the cab of his pickup, and Ash and I climbed into the second row. We rode in silence back to the Elite Moving company. I was exhausted from all the adrenaline, and it looked like Viv was, too. I was so numb to it all that it took me a while to realize that Ash seemed more than just...tired.

I studied her as she stared out the window. She looked pale.

"You okay?" I asked in a low voice.

She was silent for a moment, then nodded. "We did a good thing."

I nodded and grinned despite my exhaustion. "Yeah. We did a good thing."

She sighed and settled back against the seat, stretching her legs out. "I wish it was enough."

"It's enough for Gia. For the Perez family."

Ash nodded, and I remembered that drunken night in her Uber. "I mean, I have to make it right. Right? I have to. It's not going away. But..." Spreading her hands. "How?"

I reached out and squeezed her hand. "It *is* enough for now. We'll figure the rest of it out later."

She cocked her head at me. "Did you remember? What I told you, about..."

"No. Just that you have to make it right, but you don't know how."

"And that's all?"

"That's all," I confirmed. I studied her for a second. "Ash, whatever it is, Viv and I will be here for you."

She swallowed and nodded. "Okay. Yeah. That's good. That's good."

"For now, let's just enjoy that we did a very good thing."

She smiled and nodded. "Okay. Yeah. Because we did."

We got into Viv's car and drove back to the hotel. "I need lunch and a nap," Ash said. "In that order."

We ordered room service, and I made it through half my burger before I lay down on the bed and pulled the bedspread over my eyes. Viv closed the blackout curtains and said, "I'm not going to sleep, but I do want to rest my eyes a little." She was snoring within minutes. I listened for how long Ash would last, but I think I feel asleep before she did.

I woke up not knowing where we were or what was going on. Ash was laughing.

I sat up in the bed. She and Viv were watching the hotel television. "Oh my gosh! Look at that!"

It was footage from the helicopter that had been flying over us at the side of that highway.

"Three women are being hailed as heroes today," Viv crowed, apparently echoing the news anchor's words. "We're being hailed as heroes."

Now that I had rested, I really felt like celebrating. I watched as the scene replayed and laughed as the cops bailed out of the cab of the truck, fleeing at the sight of Diablo.

"I wonder what happened to Diablo?" I said.

"No telling," Ash said. "Hopefully when animal control came, they got him."

She glanced down at her arm and I reached out to cover it. "Don't," I said. "Don't look at it."

My phone dinged and I checked the text messages.

It was Tony. "Are you okay?"

I blinked back tears. I answered. "Yes, we're all good. Been an exciting day."

"So I heard. Take care of yourself, Salem."

That was all, so after a few minutes I quit staring at the screen and put the phone down. That sounded too much like a farewell message, and I wanted to focus right now on all the good things.

Viv and Ash were flipping through channels to look for more footage of us, and when they couldn't, Ash went on her phone and found some videos on YouTube. We clustered around her phone and laughed about the chaos of that scene, then grew silent as first one girl, then another, then Gia slid out of the back of that truck.

I sighed. "We did a good thing," I said again.

Ash put up a hand to high five me, then Viv. "We sure did."

My phone dinged again, and I snatched it back up. It was Les this time.

"Are you okay?"

I sat on the bed. "I'm great," I typed. "I guess you heard?"

Three dots floated for much too long for the answer that eventually came -- "Yes, I heard." So, he must have typed and deleted something. Probably along the lines of, "Why can you never stay out of trouble?" But he had deleted it, so...who knew?

I didn't care. I decided to take the advice I'd given to Ash, and just enjoy everything that was going right at the moment.

I typed:

You remember when you asked me if I believed I was bigger than my trauma, and God was bigger than that?

"*Sure.*

I remember.

Do you believe it now?"

I thought about it for a long time, then finally typed:

"*I'm not sure.*

But I'm beginning to suspect..."

We were too tired to make the drive back to Lubbock, so we decided to spend another night, which left us with some free evening hours. We drove around and looked at the pretty city lights and talked about going to a restaurant or a movie or something. But nothing sounded just right, and really, we just wanted to drive around and be together.

We ended up at an AA meeting, not far from where we'd met Margie the night before. It felt like home. Plus, someone recognized us from the news that day and we were minor celebrities for a few minutes. That was fun.

We stopped at a convenience store and sent Ash inside to buy junk food. She came out, talking on her phone, and climbed into the car next to us.

"Should we tell her?" I asked. The driver of the other car was just staring at Ash, wide-eyed, while Ash nodded and talked into the phone, one foot still on the pavement and the door open.

"Nah, we'll just see what happens," Viv said. "That's what friends do, right? Tease each other? Play jokes on each other?"

"Sure," I laughed. The driver of the other car was reaching for the door handle, but clearly didn't want to leave Ash there in her car.

Ash finished her call, slid the phone into her back pocket, and swung her foot inside and closed the door. She looked up to see a stranger staring back at her, and she hopped out of the car.

"Sorry, sorry," Ash kept saying as she backed away from the stranger's car.

Viv and I were laughing too hard to speak when she slunk to the Caddy and dropped into the passenger seat.

"You two are a couple of jerks," she said, but she was laughing, too. "Oh my gosh. *That lady let me finish my conversation!*"

"She didn't want to be rude," I said.

"Unlike you two," Ash said, buckling herself in.

"It was funny," Viv declared. "That's what friends do. Laugh at each other. Like you two do with me, pretending you think I'm a tough Marine like you."

Ash's and my laughter tapered off.

"Right?" Viv said. "It's funny! I mean, I get it. I'm an old lady with skinny legs, and I'm afraid of spiders, and I'm always wanting to be younger and tougher than I am. That kind of stuff is hilarious. Entire sitcoms are made about stuff like that."

"Viv," I said.

"But it's okay, because we're friends, and I know you love me, and we have fun together."

Silence filled the car. Then I said, "Exactly," and Ash clicked off her seatbelt and lunged across the console to hug Viv, and I did the same from the back seat.

"Oh, get off me," Viv groused, batting us away. But she was smiling.

"Oh, and you just reminded me," Ash said, bending to dig under the seat. "I completely forgot about..." She drew out the white bag she'd bought earlier that day at Wally's. She pulled a clear plastic box from the bag. "Look at this."

She took out a hairy tarantula the size of my hand.

Viv screamed so loud the windows shook and the car alarm went off.

The lady in the car beside us had had enough. She threw her car into reverse and careened out of the parking lot.

"It's a molt," Ash laughed. "The tarantula's exoskeleton." She held it out so Viv could get a closer look.

Viv screamed again and slapped at it. The thing bounced off the dashboard and shattered into several hairy pieces.

Then Viv laughed and said, "See? It's funny. Now pick that up. I don't want any tarantula legs in my car."

Frank and Stump were waiting for me the next afternoon when I got home. Stump started to whine as soon as I got out of Ash's Uber. It was like one of those videos when a military person returns home after a two-year deployment, except I'd only been gone three days.

I picked her up and hugged her the best I could, but I finally had to sit on the steps because she was wiggling so hard, I couldn't hang onto her.

"She only ate one bug the whole time you were gone," Frank reported. "That I saw."

"I guess that's not too bad," I said as I rubbed her stomach. "Did she do okay otherwise?"

"Yeah, okay. I mean, she got lonesome and kept looking for you. She did okay the first night, but by morning she was walking around the trailer looking for you. She snorted at me when I tried to pick her up, so I think she thought I'd done something to you."

"I figured the princess bed would be enough to keep her satisfied."

"That worked for the first day. Then she got antsy and just stayed by the door. Wouldn't even sit in my lap very much."

I rubbed her ears. "I'm sorry I was gone too long," I said. "But mommy did a very good thing." *And Mommy's happy that I can't be replaced by a dog bed – even a $400 one.*

Tony pulled up within ten minutes of me getting home – I hadn't even taken my suitcase inside yet.

He got out of his pickup and my heart thudded. I hadn't seen him since the night he'd told me he couldn't handle my craziness anymore.

Oooh, he was so handsome. *Why, God? Why'd you have to make him so handsome my heart seizes in my chest when I look at him?*

He gestured toward my hair. "I like it," he said. "It looks nice."

I touched my hair. Viv's fancy-schmancy hotel had had fancy-schmancy expensive shampoo and conditioner, and I had taken full advantage that morning. "Do you find it dazzling?" I wanted to say. Lightly. As if him saying anything except "yes, of course" wouldn't completely break my heart.

I was afraid to open my mouth, though, so I just smiled my thanks.

I was afraid to stand, too, so I scooted over so he could sit beside me on the deck steps.

He didn't sit. He stared intensely at me.

"Hey," Frank said into the silence. "How's it going?"

"I need to talk to my wife," Tony said, not looking at him.

"Sure," Frank said. Then, a full ten seconds later, he said, "Oh. You mean alone."

Neither of us spoke as Frank left. I'm pretty sure he went next door to his trailer and then watched us through the windows, though.

Tony sat on the step beside me. Stump snuggled down between us, and it hurt my heart a little to think how much it felt like a little family. She probably missed him, too.

"So," Tony finally said. "I spoke to Bobby Sloan. Sounds like you guys had quite the adventure."

"Mmmmhmmm." Really, what was there to say? We'd tased two people, stole a truck, and crashed it a little bit. This was exactly the kind of drama he could no longer deal with.

Well, that and my drinking.

"You exposed a human trafficking *and* an illegal exotic animal smuggling ring. That's pretty impressive."

I shrugged. "Well, you know...we got lucky."

"You rescued those girls," he said.

"The *police* rescued those girls," I said, "When they rescued us." But I couldn't help but smile. I didn't feel any particular sense of accomplishment about it, just...dang. That *was* a very good thing.

And I was grateful to have been a part of it.

"They were really using empty houses to traffic people?" Tony shook his head. "That is diabolical."

I nodded, thinking about that first girl, who wouldn't let the police officer help her down from the bed of that truck. Diabolical about summed it up.

We fell into a tense silence. Finally, Tony said, "Sloan told me he might have let it slip about what Joanna was doing for the company."

I shrugged. "Just that she was working undercover. He assumed you'd told me, and he said you had a lot on your mind with the situation with Jordan. He didn't want to say anything else, but I guessed that Joanna was part of it."

"Yeah, I know I should have told you, but I just...I was really preoccupied with the whole thing and worried about what I needed to do. I didn't know who I could trust or what I needed to share until I got it worked out in my head."

"Mmmm," I said, remembering what Les had told me about the 'I know, but' defense.

He studied me for a minute. "I should have talked to you about it."

I nodded. "Yeah. You should have."

"I put Jordan in a position of authority over a group of workers. Mostly women workers. Then all of a sudden I had reason to wonder if I could trust him around them." He rubbed his hands against his jaw and leaned his head back. "I wasn't sure what to do."

"What about just asking the women who work with him? Can you not believe them?"

He waved his hand helplessly. "I mean...no. Not really. Not that I think they'd lie to cover for him, but...you probably know the statistics of victims of sexual assault and sexual harassment. People are afraid to talk about it. Ashamed to talk about it."

"Why do you think that is?" I asked softly.

He shrugged. "It's trauma. I read an article a while back that explains it pretty well. When you're traumatized by something, everything related to that event sends you back to that moment. So even if you're a grown person, if in that moment you feel helpless and terrified, the moment you remember that event, you're thrown back to feeling helpless and terrified. Even if you're completely safe when the memory comes up. You're not the strong, clear-minded adult-- you're whoever you were at the moment of the trauma. Except now you know you shouldn't be, so there's shame in not being able to respond how you logically think you should."

I nodded. That's what Ash had said, too. And what I'd noticed when we were talking to Helena. I could completely understand. Every time I'd seen Shawn, I felt exactly like that seven-year-old kid – even when I was standing over him while he was trussed up like a goat that had been roped. Believing I *shouldn't* feel that way did add another layer to the burden.

"So, when I brought it up, part of me wondered if I was—was sending someone into a traumatic memory or something. I don't have any idea how to handle that. Plus, he's my nephew. They might feel some pressure to cover up for him or they'd lose their jobs. And no matter how much I tried to assure them they could be honest...well, you know." He sighed. "I didn't feel like I could put them in that position. What if, in the moment they panicked and said he was clean, but then had to come back and change their story? It's just too much pressure on them. Especially since I didn't have anything to go on except a hunch."

"What was the hunch?"

He sighed. "Honestly, I don't even know if you could call it a hunch. He was in the breakroom with Rollie and Josh, and they were joking around, laughing, cutting up. He didn't know I could hear. And then he made this joke, and it was..." He groaned. "I mean, there are dirty jokes, and then there are filthy, disgusting jokes."

I nodded. Tony was a bit of a prude. His idea of a filthy joke was probably not quite the same as mine.

"But Salem, this was neither. This was a *rape* joke. It was sadistic. It was...." He shuddered. "It was really disturbing."

"Oh," I said. "How did the other guys react?"

"My sense is, they were as stunned as I was. They laughed, but it was more like an awkward reaction, not like they agreed with him."

"What did you do?"

"I got on him immediately. I shut it down. I got on all of them, actually." He gave a short humorless laugh. "Slammed some stuff around. Yelled a bit. I think I shocked all of us."

It was pretty shocking. I had assumed I was the only one who could manage to get Tony to lose his mind like that.

"Then I called them all in the office one by one, and we had a discussion about the expectations. Rollie and Josh were both very apologetic that they'd laughed at something they knew had crossed the line. They were shocked that he'd said it. I said I understood how they felt in that moment, but they were on notice that they had one shot. They were expected to take a strong stand immediately on anything that could be perceived as inappropriate – and they sure as *hell* were expected to take a strong stand against a remark like that. I really think they got it. But when I got Jordan in there, he was just..." He shrugged and frowned. "Defiant. Insolent. Shocked that his uncle wasn't letting him get away with 'joking around.' He kept saying it was just a joke, that he hadn't hurt anyone. He said the words he thought I was looking for, but at the same time, he clearly thought I was overreacting."

"Can you not just fire him?" I asked.

"I could. And I came very, very close to doing just that. But, well..." He frowned. "For one thing, I reviewed the employee handbook and his violation fell into the category that warranted a write-up, not a firing."

"But...aren't *you* the employee handbook? It's your company."

"Yes, and I'm the one who's legally liable if I make the wrong decision. That's why I developed the handbook, and that's why I consult it when I have an issue. But the main thing is..." He shook his head again, and his face became pained. "I couldn't just shove him off

511

onto someone else. Someone who doesn't know this about him. I could fire him, and I could include a warning to anyone who called to check his references, but you know as well as I do, he would just play it all down or not even include the job in his reference list – he's only worked for me for a couple of months. And two..." He shifted on the steps and rubbed the back of his neck. "He is young. He is stupid. His brain is still growing. Maybe he *does* just need somebody to jerk him into line and he'll straighten up."

"Maybe." I brought my knees up to my chest and tried not to think too much about Tony's capacity to accept another person's ability to change.

"Anyway," he said. He rose and stretched. "I didn't know what to do about it, so I called Bobby Sloan and he recommended this. Joanna had worked undercover before and they were getting ready to move her to a different department, so he suggested I ask her to go to work, see what came of it."

"That's great. She seems perfect for the job."

"Yeah." He nodded. He glanced over at Frank's trailer, then down at Stump. Everywhere but at me.

"Great," I said again. "So. I can certainly understand why you were stressed about that. That's a heavy situation."

He nodded.

"And I can understand why you would be attracted to Joanna."

He sighed and his shoulders dropped. "Salem – "

"You're either attracted to her and feeling guilty about it, or you

512

knew I was jealous of her and pretended you didn't know." I shrugged. "Or both."

"You had no reason to be jealous," he protested.

"Which is not the point. The point is, you knew how it looked when I came over and there was a strange woman in your house. A beautiful woman young woman, in your house, in the middle of the day. And you could have immediately put my mind at ease. You chose not to."

"I told you we were working on a work situation. And I've already told you why I wasn't ready to talk about Jordan yet."

"I know what you've told me. And for what it's worth, I don't believe you and Joanna have done anything except work. I wouldn't be surprised to find out you are attracted to her. She's an attractive woman, and she seems to have some admirable qualities. But I'm not particularly bothered by that – we're all human. Even you. I trust you to make good choices."

He opened his mouth, then closed it again. There wasn't a lot he could say to that.

"More than you trust me to make good choices. More than I trust myself to make good choices, in fact. But I think it highlights an underlying issue that we *both* thought was resolved. You let me be jealous because you wanted to get revenge for all the things I've done to make you jealous."

"That's not –"

"Yes, it is." I nodded. "That's exactly how it is. Think about it."

He sighed and looked out at the yard. He was silent for a long time.

"I don't blame you," I said. "You have a lot to forgive me for."

"Salem, it's not that I don't forgive you. It's just..." He swallowed. "You were all excited about your two-year chip, and talking about moving in together, and... I don't know. It just seemed like..." He shrugged. "Like the last ten years didn't happen."

Ten years of me thinking we were divorced, living like a single woman, while he waited for God to help me get my act together and be the wife he deserved. Ten very long years.

"They happened," I said. "Believe me. I never for one day forget that they happened." I swallowed, too, because the burden of that was just a *lot* sometimes.

"I don't want you to feel guilty, Salem," Tony said.

"Don't you?"

"No."

He seemed so sure. I reached out and stroked the hair over his brow.

"Maybe not," I allowed. "But you're not okay with me being free of it, either. Not yet."

He opened his mouth to disagree, but closed it again.

"It's okay," I whispered. "I don't blame you."

He took my hand and held it between both of us. He bent his head to mine. "I don't know, Salem. It's a lot sometimes."

"I know." It *was* a lot, and a lot more was becoming clear to me, now that I'd had some time to think about it. "I'm sorry I pushed too fast for you. I could tell you weren't on board with me moving in just yet, but I thought, somehow, that I could make it okay. I should have backed off. And I'm sorry I call you a saint. I never really thought until...well, until you asked me not to, that it was putting additional pressure on you."

He leaned his head against mine, then kissed my forehead. I drank in the contact. Then I stood. I dusted my hands against my pants. I took a deep breath. I said:

"But I can't do this anymore, either. I can't always be the one who screws things up, forever. I can't be the one who's trying to make up for the past, forever. I can't be the walking hand grenade, forever." I stopped. "I *was* moving too fast. I see that now. And I was probably minimizing everything, acting like everything was fine when there's obviously a lot of work left to do. I'm willing to do the work, Tony. But I'm not willing to be the bad guy forever. I need – I need the hope that someday, things *are going* to be okay. Good, even. I need to know I'm working toward *something*. Toward freedom."

He nodded. "Bonnie keeps telling me I need to go to Al Anon with her. So I'll do that." His mouth twisted. "I thought I had everything figured out. I mean, I read books. I don't drink around you. I kind of thought that was the extent of my responsibility in the matter." He sighed. "And, I think we need to go to marriage counseling."

I blinked. I was, frankly, dumbstruck.

Marriage counseling?

Like, real, actual, *what responsible-grownups-do* marriage counseling?

Like...as if we had a *real* marriage?

...how had we not thought of this before?

"What kind of marriage counselor is going to be willing to take on *us*?" I blurted.

Tony just looked at me for a second. Then he burst out laughing. "Someone who's up for a challenge?"

Sid and Helena invited Ash, Viv, and me to a celebratory cookout the next evening with the entire Perez family.

I called Les before I left my trailer. "I am going to the Perez family celebration," I said. "I'm scared. What do I say to Gia?"

"What do you want to say to her?"

"That I'm sorry I didn't speak up sooner."

"Then tell her that," he said.

"What if she's mad at me? What if she blames me, the way Helena does?"

"What if?" he asked. "*Are* you to blame?"

"I'm not to blame, but...if I'd done things differently, this might not have happened to her."

"Maybe not. You don't really know that, but that's a possibility." He took a breath. "How are you going to feel if she *is* mad at you?"

"I'll understand," I admitted. "I might feel that way, too."

"How are you going to feel if you don't tell her what's in your heart?"

"Like a chicken," I said. "Like I should have said something and didn't. Again."

"Would you rather feel understanding from Gia, even if you disagree with her?"

"How do you always make hard stuff so clear, Les?"

He sighed. "Well, sweetheart, it's a whole lot easier when it's not your own hard stuff. Pray for discernment, Salem. This girl has been through a lot, and you want to be careful with her. But I'm still betting she'd receive what you say in the spirit it's intended."

I showed up before Ash and Viv did, but the place was already crowded with family, delicious barbecue smoke scents and loud music filling the air. I saw Sierra and waved. I saw Charlie Polk and would have waved, if he hadn't been so busy regaling the small crowd around him with stories that made it sound suspiciously like Gia's return was all down to his benevolence. I supposed he had some credit, since he'd started this ball rolling in our direction, but I made a mental note to have a serious talk with Sid and Helena about how inflexible they needed to be with their selling price, if they now planned to sell this place.

Helena and Sid both hugged me. Janet hugged me three times. Joe shook my hand – as did a great many Perezes I had not met yet. Gia sat at a picnic table at the far end of the yard. She looked small and...I wasn't sure. Distant, maybe? Like she was watching everything, and she was there, physically. But she was closed off from it. Amused by everything going on, appreciating that she was at a celebration, but not a part of it.

I made my way over to her. I'm not sure if I've ever been more terrified. Maybe that moment when Shawn smiled at me in the cab of that truck. But maybe not.

"Do you mind if I sit down?"

She shrugged. She was watching the groups of aunts, uncles, cousins as they laughed and celebrated.

I picked at my brisket. I tried to keep what Les said in the front of my mind, but I also didn't want to come off as defensive. I prayed for the right words to say.

She giggled, and I jerked my head up. She laughed with her mouth open, white teeth flashing. The wind blew and long strands of cinnamon brown hair blew into her face. She brushed them away carelessly, focused on the scene before her.

What a miracle she was, I thought. What a miracle we all were. We could walk through the absolute worst experience imaginable. We could look into the most vile and evil that humanity had to offer. And then we could sit and eat brisket and laugh at our cousins. From the outside, one would never know what those eyes had seen. What that mind still processed.

Things were different for Gia on the inside. I knew that as well as anyone. She was smiling now, but the nightmares, both waking and sleeping ones, were still there and would always be. The last 12 months would have changed her. But she was here, sitting, head up, laughing, eating. Living.

"You're a miracle," I said. It was cheesy, and I was immediately embarrassed that I'd said it, but it was true.

"That's what my dad said."

I swallowed. "Your sister told you about me?"

She met my gaze. She nodded once.

I searched for the right words, but they weren't there. I'd have to settle for the wrong ones. "Look. I'm not looking for forgiveness. I just want you –"

"There's nothing to forgive. Not for you."

I shrugged. "Well, your sister is of a different opinion. She thinks —"

I broke off because Gia smiled then. It was such a shocking sight— a bright, honest, sincere smile. It stopped me in my tracks.

"Yeah, she told me what she thinks. And I have to say, I'm..." She shook her head and looked off, as if searching for the right words. "I'm really happy about that, you know?"

"Uh..."

"Because she's so *sure*. She's so *definite*. I mean, Helena's always definite, but...about this, she's so positive how things *should* have gone if everyone just did what she thinks they *should* do. And that tells me one thing." Gia leaned forward, her brown eyes intent on mine. "She doesn't know what she's talking about."

I blinked, lost.

"Right? She doesn't know." She straightened. "You and I... we know. For her, it's all just what you *think* you would do in that situation. Theoretical right and wrong. On paper."

"Right," I said. I understood exactly what she meant, because Ash had already described it. *It's different when it's your own stuff.* "Yes, well..." I cleared my throat to say more, but stopped when Gia giggled at something over my shoulder. "Is that the one Helena told me about? The old woman with the purple hair?"

I turned to see Viv there with her recorder, talking to a group of Perezes. "That's her."

"She's amazing," Gia said. "I want to be like that when I'm her age."

As we watched, Viv said something into the recorder, then held it quickly out to the man nearest her and said something that had the entire group howling with laughter. She'd brought Ken with her, I saw. He looked completely besotted.

"Me, too," I said.

"She's a badass."

I nodded. "You're a badass, Gia."

She gave a soft snort and rolled her eyes. "All I did was hang on long enough to not get killed."

I nodded. "Yeah. You did. That's badass. Buck in particular struck me as someone hard pressed to choose a preference between torture or killing."

She shuddered. "You got that right. He had told me I might get a little more freedom, if I behaved myself and didn't cause any trouble. Then he took me where they left Charlie and told me what they do with girls who cause trouble. He said, 'Please cause trouble, Gia. Pretty please.'" She shuddered. "Freak."

"But you still had the courage to leave your ponytail holder."

She shrugged. "It was the only thing I could think of. I knew what came with more freedom. More freedom meant more responsibility." She gave me a look. "Bringing other girls in. Or at least not warning them away."

She gave me a miserable look, and I knew she'd struggled internally with how she would have handled that 'responsibility.' A year ago, she might have been like Helena, might have been confident in how she would respond to a situation like that. This girl was infinitely more knowledgeable now in the effects of fear and pain, and that broke my heart.

"Look," I said. "I'm glad that you don't blame me. I don't blame myself, but...at the same time..." I swallowed. "I'd give anything to go back in time, speak up sooner. Do everything in my power to guarantee he couldn't get anywhere near you." I shrugged. "I just – I wish I'd spoken up sooner."

She nodded, smiling again, a bit sad this time. She leaned forward and wrapped her thin arms around me. "I wish you had, too."

Want more of Salem and the gang? Sign up for my newsletter and get free short stories, excerpts from upcoming books, and publishing news. Go to www.KimHuntHarris.com.

Other Titles in the Trailer Park Princess Series
FULL LENGTH NOVELS
The Middle Finger of Fate (Book One)
Unsightly Bulges (Book Two)
Caught in the Crotchfire (Book Three)
Knickers in a Twist (Book Four)

BOX SETS
The Trailer Park Princess Books 1-3, with Exclusive Content
Holidazed and Confused: Four Trailer Park Princess Holiday-Themed Novellas

SHORT WORKS
Gold, Frankincense, and Murder (Short Story)
The Power of Bacon (Short Story)
Mud, Sweat, and Tears (Short Story)

ABOUT THE AUTHOR

This is me. I bought this outfit and got my roots done for this picture. You can't tell, but I also got a pedicure. It was a big day for me, let me tell you. My hands are curled up because I didn't want to spring for the mani.

The award-winning author of the Trailer Park Princess comic mystery series. Kim Hunt Harris knew she wanted to be a writer before she even knew how to write. When her parents read bedtime stories to her, she knew she wanted to be a part of the story world. She started out writing children's stories, and her stories grew as she did. She discovered a gift for humor and a love for making people laugh with her tales, and the Trailer Park Princess series was born.

Kim loves to not only make her readers laugh and entertain them with a good mystery, but also to examine the issues the everyday people face...well, every day. Issues like faith and forgiveness, perseverance, and tolerance. Set in Lubbock, Texas, the fun books feature a cast of quirky characters, outrageous situations, a drama queen of a dog, and from time to time, a tear or two.

Kim lives with her husband of more than thirty years and two kids in West Texas.

www.ingramcontent.com/pod-product-compliance
Lightning Source LLC
Chambersburg PA
CBHW072010020726
47501CB00006B/1753